NEW YORK REVIEW BOOKS
CLASSICS

BLOOD DARK

LOUIS GUILLOUX (1899–1980) was born in Brittany, where he would spend most of his life. His father was a shoemaker and a socialist. At the local high school, he was taught by the controversial philosopher Georges Palante, who would serve as inspiration for the character of Cripure in *Blood Dark*. Guilloux worked briefly as a journalist in Paris, but soon began writing short stories for newspapers and magazines, and then published his debut novel, *La Maison du peuple*, in 1927. During World War II, his house was a meeting place for the French Resistance; on one occasion it was searched by the Vichy police and Guilloux was taken in for questioning. Following the war, he was an interpreter at American military tribunals in Brittany, and the incidents of racial injustice that he witnessed in the American army would form the basis of his 1976 book *OK, Joe*. In addition to his many novels—including *Le Pain des rêves* (1942) and *Jeu de patience* (1949)—Guilloux also translated the work of Claude McKay, John Steinbeck, and several of C. S. Forester's Horatio Hornblower stories.

LAURA MARRIS's recent translations include Christophe Boltanski's *The Safe House* and, with Rosmarie Waldrop, Paol Keineg's *Triste Tristan and Other Poems*. Her work has appeared in *The Cortland Review*, *Asymptote*, *The Brooklyn Rail*, and elsewhere.

ALICE KAPLAN is the John M. Musser Professor of French at Yale University. She is the author of *Looking for "The Stranger": Albert Camus and the Life of a Literary Classic*, *The Collaborator*, *Dreaming in French*, and *French Lessons: A Memoir*. Kaplan's book *The Interpreter* explores Guilloux's experience as an interpreter for the U.S. Army courts-martial in Brittany in the summer of 1944. She is also the translator of Guilloux's novella *OK, Joe*, which inspired her research for *The Interpreter*.

BLOOD DARK

LOUIS GUILLOUX

Translated from the French by
LAURA MARRIS

Introduction by
ALICE KAPLAN

NEW YORK REVIEW BOOKS

New York

THIS IS A NEW YORK REVIEW BOOK
PUBLISHED BY THE NEW YORK REVIEW OF BOOKS
435 Hudson Street, New York, NY 10014
www.nyrb.com

Cet ouvrage a bénéficié du soutien des Programmes d'aide à la publication de l'Institut Français.
This work, published as part of a program of aid for publication, received support from the
Institut Français.

This work received support from the French Ministry of Foreign Affairs and the Cultural
Services of the French Embassy in the United States through their publishing assistance
program.

Library of Congress Cataloging-in-Publication Data
Names: Guilloux, Louis, 1899–1980, author. | Marris, Laura, 1987– translator.
Title: Blood dark / by Louis Guilloux ; translated by Laura Marris.
Other titles: Sang noir. English
Description: New York : New York Review Books, 2017. | Series: New York Review Books
  Classics
Identifiers: LCCN 2017008649 (print) | LCCN 2017026714 (ebook) | ISBN 9781681371467
  (epub) | ISBN 9781681371450 (paperback)
Subjects: LCSH: World War, 1914–1918—Fiction. | France—History—
  1914–1940—Fiction. | Psychological fiction. | BISAC: FICTION / Psychological. |
  FICTION / War & Military. | GSAFD: Historical fiction.
Classification: LCC PQ2613.U495 (ebook) | LCC PQ2613.U495 S313 2017 (print) | DDC
  843/.912—dc23
LC record available at https://lccn.loc.gov/2017008649

ISBN 978-1-68137-145-0
Available as an electronic book; ISBN 978-1-68137-146-7

Printed in the United States of America on acid-free paper.
10 9 8 7 6 5 4 3 2 1

CONTENTS

INTRODUCTION

THERE are no trenches, no German submarines, no gas attacks in *Blood Dark*, yet Louis Guilloux's epic novel ranks among the most powerful French depictions of the First World War. By 1935, when it was published, suffering on the front line had already produced a series of classics: Henri Barbusse's *Under Fire* and Maurice Genevoix's *'Neath Verdun* (1916); Blaise Cendrars's *I've Killed* (1918); Roland Dorgelès's *Wooden Crosses* (1919). Guilloux's contribution was different. As an adolescent in provincial Brittany, he had seen war reach behind the front and penetrate civilian populations and institutions; in *Blood Dark* he set out to create a war literature of the home front, a toxic zone where rumors do battle with the truth and witch hunts are carried out in the name of patriotism.

Blood Dark takes place on a single day in 1917, in a town recognizable as Guilloux's native Saint-Brieuc, population twenty-four thousand, perched on the north coast of Brittany. The war has reached a low point after the debacle at the Chemin des Dames, and the American doughboys are still nowhere in sight. Patriotism has grown hollow; for some young people, revolutionary Russia is becoming a source of hope. Into a classical frame—unity of time and of place—Guilloux sets a riotous cast of some twenty main characters whose destinies combine and reverberate in a series of short episodes. He finds a way, through this form, to explore the effects of the war on an entire community and to delve deeply into the consciousness of one flawed individual who is both a spiritual guide and a living symptom of the society in disarray.

This guiding light or rather guiding shadow of the novel is an unhinged teacher of high-school philosophy named Charles Merlin, nicknamed "Cripure" by his students—a play on Kant's *CRItique of PURE Reason*. He is in charge of teaching ethics to the draft-aged boys, young men condemned to spin the wheel of fortune on the front. Guilloux's portrait of Cripure was inspired by a teacher and mentor of his own, the eccentric philosopher Georges Palante (1862–1925), though Guilloux once said that Cripure was "derived from Palante"—a starting point for his fiction, rather than a model. Like Palante, Cripure is a renegade from the Sorbonne, a man of broken friendships and a failed marriage, sharing his bed with an uneducated housekeeper, the affectionate, saintly Maïa, who dispenses level-headed wisdom inflected with Gallo, the local dialect of eastern Brittany. And like Palante, Cripure is disabled in the cruelest way, with huge, deformed feet that make it difficult for him to walk. At one point, the town boot-maker shows off Cripure's shoes to a visiting circus director, who wants to hire him: "But when the circus manager had learned that the owner of those astonishing boots was a professor, and of philosophy! He'd simply shrugged and changed the subject."

The action of the novel revolves around a few signal events: a schoolboys' plot to unbolt the front wheel of Cripure's bicycle; a Legion of Honor ceremony at the local school, now partly transformed into a military hospital; rioting soldiers at the train station who don't want to return to the front; Cripure's aborted duel with his colleague Nabucet; and the adventures of an even larger cast of characters that includes draftees, antiwar students, amorous spinsters, hypocritical school officials, and pedophiles; slick politicians and young men on the make; a revolutionary leaving for Russia, an amputee, and a couple learning of their son's execution for mutiny at the front.

Guilloux's fiction touches on issues that are still matters of great contention among French historians of the Great War: To what extent was there a consensus about the fighting? What was the nature of the mutinies that broke out as the war dragged on? Did they occur at random or were they part of a deep current of antiwar sentiment? Soldiers in transit demonstrating at train stations, individual deserters, fomenters of revolt on the front were all in some sense "mutineers," and their numbers add up to a few thousand or to tens of thousands—depending on your definition of "mutiny." What is clear is that antiwar sentiment, moral exhaustion, and episodes of disobedience flourished in the summer of 1917, the summer of *Blood Dark*.

The best-known scene in the novel is certainly the riot at the Saint-Brieuc train station. Guilloux has a genius for portraying chaos and for letting us see the drama of the individuals inside a crowd. He doesn't spare his readers a close-up of one of the men disfigured by trench warfare—a *gueule cassée*, or "broken face." For his novel to begin in a carnival of cruelty and end in tenderness is one of its great achievements. Cripure, impossible to categorize by any of our literary labels—hero, victim, genius, idiot, madman, muse—is another.

Albert Camus considered *Blood Dark* one of the few French novels to rival the great Russian epics. "I know of *no one* today who can make characters come alive the way you do," he wrote to Guilloux in 1946. Guilloux, Camus said later, was uniquely attuned to the sorrow of others, but he was never a novelist of despair.

Camus was only one of many French writers at the forefront of literary life in the 1930s and '40s who considered *Blood Dark* a masterpiece. Louis Aragon said that Cripure was the Don Quixote of bourgeois ruin; André Gide said that the novel had made him lose his footing. On the left, Guilloux's contemporaries understood *Blood Dark* as an important political response to Louis-Ferdinand Céline's nihilistic *Journey to the End of the Night*, published three years earlier. "The truth of this life is death," Céline wrote in *Journey*, and Guilloux responded: "It's not that we die, it's that we die cheated." The publisher used that line on a paper band around the book cover. For French intellectuals in the 1930s, there was a crucial difference between Céline and Guilloux: Both writers denounced the patriotic lies that lead men to their deaths, but for Céline the violence of man to man was inevitable, biological. Guilloux, by contrast, held out hope for fraternity and for collective struggle. In his world, and in his fiction, there were always causes worth fighting for, always zones of tenderness.

When *Blood Dark* missed winning France's biggest literary prize, the Goncourt (just as *Journey to the End of the Night* had missed it in 1932), Guilloux's fellow writers, among them Gide, Dorgelès, and Aragon, as well as Paul Nizan and André Malraux, protested by organizing a public meeting to laud his vision and underline his blazing critique of war and human hypocrisy.

Literary historians of existentialism have argued that *Blood Dark* launched the notion of the absurd well in advance of Jean-Paul Sartre's *Nausea*, Samuel Beckett's *Molloy*, and Camus's *The Stranger*. Yet Guilloux is often dismissed as a regionalist. In fact he was a transnational writer at a time when many of his contemporaries were taken up with ingrown literary rivalries. Just before beginning to work in earnest on *Blood Dark*, he translated Claude McKay's *Home to Harlem*, rendering black American English in vibrant Caribbean slang—a Creole of his own making, adapted for French readers. Guilloux's notebooks make clear that more than a realist, he was a voice writer, testing dialogues and send-ups of bourgeois language, recording conversations, and compiling lists of idioms and ridiculous expressions. The black English in *Home to Harlem* surely inspired Maïa's Gallo-speak. Guilloux read well beyond the French canon, translating Steinbeck and McKay, on the one hand, and drawing inspiration from Dostoyevsky and Tolstoy on the other.

Blood Dark is still considered a masterpiece in France, but in English the book remains little known. Part of the problem is its first translation. Samuel Putnam's version, titled *Bitter Victory*, appeared in simultaneous American and British editions shortly after the original French publication. A former expatriate, a columnist for *The Daily Worker*, and a translator of Rabelais and Cervantes, Putnam saw in Guilloux's novel a condemnation of "the bourgeois culture that had made the war." Was it he or his editors who chose *Bitter Victory*, a misleading title for a book set a good year before the war's end, when no victory was in sight? Putnam translated in the "mid-Atlantic style" then in vogue, neither American nor English, supposedly pleasing to readers in both countries but actually quite lost at sea. As a result of this linguistic compromise, Guilloux's most remarkable quality as a writer, his sense of each character's unique voice, is muffled.

Part of what makes this new translation so riveting is the attention that Laura Marris has given to the novel's distinct voices and places. As a poet, and the translator of the contemporary Breton poet Paol Keineg, Marris has immersed herself in local Saint-Brieuc culture and has studied Guilloux's papers, attending to the voices and sense of place he captured. From its new haunting title on, she has brought *Blood Dark* to life for the American reader. In this centenary of the darkest year of the Great War, what truer novel to read? In one respect, Guilloux's story could not be more contemporary: as violence and terror seep into every aspect of his characters' lives, they try to hold the chaos of the world at bay.

—ALICE KAPLAN

A NOTE ON THE TRANSLATION

EVEN BEFORE I began to translate *Le Sang noir*, I thought of Louis Guilloux as a master listener—someone with an ear for dialogue, but also for the voice of thoughts. With linguistic ability and empathy, Guilloux was capable of capturing each character's private language of symbols and associations.

As is so often the case, what makes a book great is also what raises questions for a translator. I have done my best to preserve the contrasts between characters—Maïa's matter-of-fact speech and Cripure's introspective madness, Simone's teenage wisdom and her father's complacency, Kaminsky's sick wonder and Madame de Villaplane's desperation. Since so much of this novel takes place in the minds of its characters, my challenge was to render the wild mania of Guilloux's close third-person perspective in English syntax. The beauty of certain passages creates a romantic lyricism that becomes absurd in context and generates a cyclical pattern of rising emotion undercut by reality. In the sentences themselves, the characters try to climb out of their lives and fall back against the (sometimes self-created) limitations of their situations. The more their society enforces self-consciousness and militant patriotism, the louder these thought voices become.

Because the specific place and time are so important to Guilloux's feelings of disgusted claustrophobia—in a society Cripure calls a "menagerie," while a horrific war is going on outside—the language of the translation can't lose too much of its sense of place by sounding like it belongs in any particular English-speaking culture. The previous translation by Samuel Putnam, published in 1936, uses quite a few British English expressions ("old boy" and "old chap" or "By Jove!") that now seem odd in a French setting.

This realization left me with a difficult task—creating a voice for Maïa without removing her character from its local context. In the original, she sometimes uses phrasing from Gallo, a dialect primarily from Brittany and neighboring parts of France. Unlike Breton, it is Latinate, so French speakers can understand it. Though there are very few Gallo speakers today, the dialect is older than French and mixes medieval words with more modern usage. Guilloux studied Gallo with respect, but he also knew that the average French reader would interpret this nonstandard speech as provincialism and lack of education. Perhaps this disjunction is why the author made Maïa's character—sharp-witted, sensible, and sane—a bastion of reason in contrast to literary, tortured Cripure. Class takes place in language, but Guilloux does not privilege one voice over another. I've chosen to use small grammatical changes and colloquialisms to demonstrate Maïa's background, rather than relying on any particular British or American dialect. In a few places this strategy required me to tweak a spoken idiom ("keep the pig and eat the bacon," for example) when a literal translation would have been too distracting and an English equivalent too culturally marked.

These conditions also posed a problem in translating the book's title. *Le Sang noir* literally means black or dark blood, an English phrase with a history of race and racism that is not intended in the French original. At first, I thought "le sang noir" might be an idiom related to "se faire du sang noir" or "se faire du sang de l'encre," both meaning something like "to get upset," and derived from the medieval idea of bile, one of the humors that determined angst in human character. But when I visited Saint-Brieuc and asked about the title, scholars of Guilloux's work told me that "le sang noir" was an un-idiomatic phrase and that "sang noir" was the blood of dead and wounded soldiers. *Bitter Victory*, the title of Putnam's translation, was probably good marketing in 1936, but it now seems tacked on to the book, since in 1917 the characters have experienced neither the victory nor the full brunt of its bitterness. And the phrase *le sang noir* appears nowhere in the body of the novel.

Searching through Guilloux's papers in the archives of the Saint-Brieuc library uncovered a slew of earlier titles Guilloux (or his publisher Gallimard) had rejected—and a literary mystery. He had considered *L'indesirable* (the unwanted) as a working title. Then *L'education révolutionaire* (a revolutionary education)—to which Louis Chevasson at Gallimard had replied, "I don't think *A Revolutionary Education* is a good title, but it would be a great cartoon." Other choices were *Cripure*, *Les chevaliers de la lune* (knights of the moon), *La mort dans l'âme* (death in the soul), *La clé des songes* (the key to dreams), *Le cloporte-roi* (the clopper king), *La vie perdue* (life lost), *Ame morte* (dead soul), *Le secret de polichinelle* (Punchinello's secret), and *Les feuilles sèches* (dry leaves). But the genesis of *Le Sang noir* is nowhere to be found in Guilloux's correspondence, except in a very last-minute note stating the date of the novel's completion. This gap left me to assume that the title had come from a conversation with someone, most likely his friend Pascal Pia, a well-known editor and man of letters who had connections to Gallimard. But it didn't get me closer to an English version.

Like *Le Sang noir*, *Blood Dark* came from a conversation with a friend—Breton poet and playwright Paol Keineg. I liked both its weirdness and the way it makes "dark" less adjectival and more symbolic, representing both the middle of the war and the ignorance of the town's inhabitants who are blind when it comes to the consequences of their patriotism. Last, for a novel with a wine-soaked protagonist who embarks on many asides and long journeys through the labyrinthine town of Saint-Brieuc, I liked the echo of *wine-dark*. This title hints at an Odyssean allusion that is not in the original. But it is consistent with Guilloux's ambitions, which are more modern than they first appear. It would be like him to subvert the old myth of homecoming while placing his masterpiece among the classics—a context this book deserves.

—LAURA MARRIS

BLOOD DARK

To Renée

MAÏA ENTERED with a racket of clogs. Not the slightest care for the sleeper stretched out, fully clothed on the couch, his little dogs around him—she knew that he wasn't asleep.

What did she come in here for? Stopping in the middle of the room, she reached to open the shutters, then hesitated.

On a little side table, near an open book and a pile of grading scribbled with red ink: her workbasket. She bent down, rummaging. *What was she missing? A needle? A spool of blue thread?*

She didn't know how to read, but it still bothered him to think she could see his papers. Pimply dunces! They'd found yet another way to mock him. One of them had traced across the page, in big letters: CRIPURE! *My name is Merlin!* Hadn't he shouted *My name is Merlin!* countless times, banging his fist on the lectern? Yes. And so what? It had only made them snicker. If anything, they'd become even more determined to call him Creep ... Creep ... Cripure behind his back, to write his nickname on the blackboard. Filthy rabble. And it had gone on for so many years—

Maïa was still rummaging.

It was taking a while.

He didn't want her right then, of course. But even so his hand clutched at the slut's hip, slipped down, reached the threshold of the skirt, disappeared. He chased off the little dogs, pulled Maïa closer. The workbasket tipped, buttons rolling. Maïa put down the newspaper—which she folded into a policeman's hat and wore for doing the housework—and climbed onto the couch without a word.

He threw himself at her as though scaling a high wall, with a hoarse but affected shout, his eyes still closed, thinking, *Why? Why? Why?*

Mireille, the pretty spaniel, tugged on a panel of upholstery, growling. Turlupin, with plaintive howls, bounced around the room. Petit-Crû yapped, in his shrill, panicked voice; fat Judas wandered, a blind black ball.

"That do it?" said Maïa.

He sat up. She slid to the floor. Cripure kneeled on the couch, thighs naked, fists pressed into a cushion, and began to insult her, scarlet-faced. He couldn't stop himself.

"You've tumbled in every haystack in the country..."

Why bring it up? Case closed, finished. That had only lasted for a little while anyway—she'd gotten married, been widowed. Since then she had only been with him and Basquin. But Basquin—she'd met him first. And so what, hadn't he told her a hundred times that it was precisely because she'd done it for money—not worth busting your skull to figure that out!

"Want some more, kitty cat?"

"You're disgusting."

She didn't insist.

It was strange that he hadn't yet told her to go find forty sous in his waistcoat pocket, since that was usually his first insult—her price, forty sous—

She helped him readjust his clothes. Passive as a child, he let her do it.

"Filth—"

She didn't flinch.

Hadn't she heard all about that night, at the brothel, when he insulted a girl who was coming back from her room, client in tow? He'd rushed at her. He wanted her right then and there. It excited him, he said, to think she'd just done it. They had a hell of a time calming him down, but in the end, he hadn't wanted the girl anymore, and he'd left. *There are men like that*, thought Maïa. It meant little to her that in leaving the brothel, Cripure had muttered strange threats about the officers, leading those who witnessed the scene to think he was drunk or maybe crazy.

He finally quieted, stretched out. Maïa picked up her hat, righted the workbasket. One by one, the little beasts jumped on the couch and settled around him again. He reached out a hand to pet them.

Maïa returned to her housework. Cripure could hear her coming and going, pushing the broom, clomping in front of the sink. Upstairs, Amédée was getting dressed. He kept walking back and forth across the attic where they had made him a bedroom. The loud steps right over his head exasperated Cripure.

He consoled himself that this was the last day. Tomorrow this penance would be over. But right away he was guilty of an inhuman thought: Wasn't it actually today that Amédée was returning to the front? If he had coped for five long days, he could certainly put up with him for another few hours . . .

Of course, in that house (which, with a bourgeois affectation, he called "rustic," though in this case, the word was apt) it was pretty hard to put a guest anywhere but the attic. This little house, which Maïa had inherited when her husband died, consisted of only two rooms—the "study" where Cripure was sprawled at that moment and, beside it, the kitchen, which also served as a bedroom. And above, the attic (half storage, half garret) where Amédée continued to make so much noise with his foot soldier's boots. But he would go out soon, probably to meet up with some barmaid.

Thank God Cripure could go late to school this morning. An hour of class—ethics, for third years (those urchins!). And then this afternoon, that party . . . What a bore.

He sighed, opened his eyes, confirmed with pleasure that the shutters were closed. Somewhere in the neighborhood a military unit was training, endlessly repeating the same formation. Fine! Fine! All that was their business. Love for one and all! They needed a God to come and teach them to love, but they learned to hate all by themselves . . . Fine!

Cripure sat himself back down on his couch and the little beasts stirred, wagging their tails, but as he stopped moving and closed his eyes, they became still again.

Not much would change the day he stretched out, just like this, in his coffin. What difference would it make? Nothing missing but the little voice in his head, so vain, so obsessive, that he pompously called his thoughts, nothing missing but the coward's angst that clutched his heart—

He had undoubtedly drunk and eaten a little more than was sensible on the way home from his cottage last night. He had gone straight to bed, but sleep had been slow in coming. Recently, the nights he'd once loved for their silence and their peace had nothing to offer him except lingering anxiety. When he couldn't sleep, he was afraid. The slightest creak of a floorboard—he would jump out of bed, his heart pounding. Maïa lay next to him sleeping, alas dreamless, leaden.

Last night, he had barely closed his eyes, hearing, until late, the chorus of Russian soldiers billeted close by.[1] Then, as so often happened, he heard the Clopper.[2]

At night, the Clopper, who hid by day—nobody knew what he did with his time—would make the incredible effort to don his frock coat, to climb down his stairs or rise out of his cave. He would appear in the streets, sidling along the edges of the walls like a marauder. Clop! Clop! Clop! The Clopper announced himself, dragging his paw, and with every step the iron tip of his cane slammed the stones of the sidewalk, echoing like a cracked bell. He paused, sometimes for a while, leaning on his cane, chin in hand, for such a long time that Cripure thought he was gone. But—clop! clop! clop! And once again the night resounded with the solemn beat of his steps.

Why did he come back so often? *Why to my street?* That night, Cripure had gotten up cautiously, had opened the window a crack: gaslights in the silence. It wasn't easy to spot that silhouette in the shadows, and it was even harder to stop searching for it. He'd waited a long time to see that morsel of night sliding along the walls—he'd sometimes watched until dawn. Clop! Clop! Clop! Still nothing but steps, nothing but a ubiquitous presence ready to spring from the walls. The iron tip of the cane had rung out against the stones, triumphal, like the halberds of Swiss Guards on holy days. Then nothing.

Cripure had stuck his head out: standing under the lamp, the Clopper was still as a saint in his niche. Around his bowler hat, the gaslight blazed like a stained-glass halo. Chin in the palm of his left hand, the other hand resting on his cane—what a perfect target. The day—the night—would come when Cripure would fire his revolver and—tac! tac! would settle his score. It would make so little noise, maybe just a little clicking of the hammer or the trigger. It would be more like crunching a flea under his fingernail. Just like that, the earth would be cleansed of the Clopper forever.

After the Clopper left, Cripure had gone back to bed, then slept—how?—but his sleep was laced with nightmares. Then came a furtive presence—a woman murmured in his ear: *What is there to cry about?* Who? Who was she? An instant after waking, he'd understood that his nocturnal visitor was Toinette, whose arrival he continued to hope for, even in the abyss of dreams, as he had hoped these twenty years. Toinette whom he had never heard from again, what had become of her, out there? Maybe she was a female clopper, like the woman who had wandered the streets of the town for years, humming airs from operettas, a horrible hunchback always leading a little dog, yellow and haggard, on a leash.

He had been tempted to pick up the book at his bedside, but thought better of it—the *Memoirs of Benvenuto Cellini*, no less!

He stretched out a hand to stroke the head of one of the little dogs, Mireille, his favorite.

Sweet little creatures!

But it wasn't wise to trust them too much, either, even the little dogs. They could also betray! Stories for kids often had those faithful dogs who followed the fortunes of their masters to the point of starvation. Yes. But he had read in the police log about a man who killed himself and was immediately gobbled up by his faithful companion.

The attic door slammed and Amédée's huge treads battered the staircase, heavy, like those of a man who finishes getting dressed while walking, buttoning his belt or his jacket. What farm-boy steps! The whole house shook.

His son went into the kitchen; Cripure peeked through the glass door. Amédée was joyfully giving orders to Maïa, who got to work serving his breakfast. Good. No danger Amédée would come to greet him. That would be after, on his way out. Amédée would open the door a crack after knocking softly. "I'm going out . . . see you later . . ." They would shake hands without looking at each other.

Cripure closed his eyes, feigning sleep. He was sure that no one would disturb him. Maïa would send any visitors away. But who would visit him? In the kitchen, Amédée was chatting with Maïa while he ate breakfast. He heard their laughter and the fanfare of Maïa's wooden clogs on the cement. Here, no one. He murmured, "No one!"

Surprised, irritated by his own voice, he raised his eyelids. And as though he had sought a desired, maybe dreaded presence, he cast a long uneasy glance over the room.

"No one . . ."

Unless some half-crazy person appeared, like the other day . . .

He'd been nice, that young lieutenant, but naive. Ultimately, that would do him in. If he wanted to believe that humanity could be . . . bettered, well, that was his business. He'd get his comeuppance, one of these days, and break his neck. Poor kid! A waste! He was gifted, of course. His best student back then. What's more, he had a noble character. A born victim. But this victim was no lamb to the slaughter. The lieutenant had revolted; that deserved some admiration, no matter what else you might think. Cripure could understand why officials and the elderly might be conventional—but the young! The more he thought about it, the more it seemed that one young person in a thousand was incredibly blind, and the rest were consciously abetting. This one had spoken of sweeping it all away. Sweeping! Well sure . . . Cripure would love to see that. If it were only about cleansing the earth of the whole mess of swindlers and imbeciles, to empty the world of its riffraff, he would lend a helping hand. But if they would only stop coming to him, like that lieutenant, to talk about man's triumphs over himself. *Humphgarumph* as Father Ubu says, that's too ridiculous! Outrageous lies. My argument is negative. I destroy all idols, and I have no God to put over the altar. It takes a pretty substandard experience of life to believe in such nonsense. Humanitarian paradise, sociological Edens, humpf! Just wait till he's forty and his beloved wife has cheated on him. Then we'll talk. Tsk, tsk. In this world, it was every man for himself, to save his own skin. And triumphs? Those of one's own making. Yes: to be the wolf.[3]

He stayed motionless, applied himself to performing sleep. But that mouth, tightened as though in anger, the chest which rose in spite of itself, the hands upturned on the goatskin like those of a corpse—this was less the posture of a sleeper than of a conscious man suffocated by sorrow. It had returned all of a sudden, as always, like an incurable disease you're tired of monitoring, which comes back to seize you when, almost at the peak of happiness, you hoped the truce would stretch out a while longer. So it would always go! He had counted on wisdom to come with age, like a benefit or recompense, like the spiritual equivalent of the pension that the state, in the name of retirement, would furnish him for good and steadfast service. Would the sorrow that had desolated his life never take a day's rest? Would there be time, before death, for him to take a clear look at himself and the world? This hope, once realized, would enable him to accept a death that otherwise would be no more than a theft, a shameful fraud. But the older he got, the more he told himself that he would have to renounce this hope as well, since sorrow would not relent and since, in this moment, he was gritting his teeth against the pain, which, despite all these years, was as strong as the day after the catastrophe.

It was Toinette he had loved—he could say loved!—But he'd gotten this son of his, this Amédée, from a horrible rag of a woman, a hotel slattern who wouldn't have been worth shaking a stick at. It happened in the same year as the catastrophe, a few months after the break with Toinette, in Paris where, under the pretext of finishing his thesis on Turnier, he had taken refuge. A memorable year in every way. He had partied endlessly: drinking like a fish, spending without counting, keeping women, losing a large part of his savings at poker, and crying under the covers in sorrow and rage when he was alone at night and thinking of Toinette. And it had to be precisely that year, when he'd had his fill of so many lovely women (by paying them of course), that he'd gotten that faded little blond pregnant.

She had come in and out of his room, dusting the furniture, re-making the bed, not speaking, just barely smiling. No one knew where she came from, if she had a life, and he had been absolutely fine with knowing nothing: a slattern. Why did that day have to be so hot, why did she come to clean the room barely clothed, a thin shirt over her camisole? And the shirt itself half unbuttoned. *She did it on purpose, the slut.* In any case, she hadn't resisted. She let herself be quietly taken and pushed away.

After that, he would fuck her and reject her on a whim, a cruel game in which he was, for once, doing business with a weaker party. But he had always treated her kindly, even the day she had come to announce that she was pregnant. He had given her some money, to at least get herself a decent place to sleep, and later, he had acknowledged the child. Amédée bore his last name.

She hadn't asked for anything. Afterwards, as before, she was always unresisting and resigned to her fate, as if nothing that happened to her, not even motherhood, could rip her from a languid dream. And spontaneously, just as he was leaving Paris, he had promised to send her a monthly check.

He had kept it up for the first four years, not otherwise caring for news of his son. But towards the end of that period, he got it in his head that maybe the boy wasn't his, that he'd been fooled again, taken like an imbecile, and that this slattern he thought was so stupid had at least had the sense to choose, from the mob of her lovers, the most idiotic—meaning him. *Me!* Having acquired the "moral conviction" that during the last four years he'd been the victim of a swindle (a point of view that also satisfied his greed), he'd stopped sending money. No complaints. The slattern didn't even seem to perceive that the money had stopped, though she could have easily made a fuss since he had already committed the unpardonable idiocy of legitimizing this child with thirty-six fathers. With that in mind, a long silence stretched. But not forgetting.

Once the war broke out, Cripure had calculated that the slattern's child must be old enough to get himself killed. And he had wanted to find him.

Letters sent to the old addresses had come back to him. He wrote to the mayor of the little village where the child had grown up: Amédée had already been deployed to the front for a year. A correspondence started, and it was arranged that Amédée would come see his father during his next leave. They would say he was a nephew.

Maïa had agreed.

What a ridiculous scene at his arrival! That anxious sob which had gripped his throat at the sight of the young man, and that extravagant way he'd opened his arms, shouting, "Embrace me, I am your father!" Would the parting scene be equally grotesque? He feared so, all the more because Amédée's stay with him, all things considered, had been a mistake, a bitter pill. He didn't feel so much responsibility for Amédée and the slattern. This situation was probably due in some part to indifference, and because he had not let himself forget that Amédée might not be his son.

Whether he was or not, Amédée remained a stranger. There was a reason for his rough manners, his loud feet every morning, that pipe Cripure didn't dare forbid, even though it gave him exasperating migraines, his evident lack of education which Cripure never would have wished to criticize in someone else and which was his own fault. In Cripure's eyes, this boy, nice but ordinary, was the living illustration of a ridiculous fate. Amédée's presence reminded him more cruelly than ever of a time when everything had broken once and for all, when he had needed to tie himself to Toinette forever. He had lost Toinette, and today, after all these years, this unfamiliar and vulgar son sprang from another corner of the world, fell from a star, like a fragment of someone else's destiny mixed with his own by mistake.

Someone tapped softly: Cripure barely moved, bristling nonetheless, like an animal in a trap. He raised one eyelid, an imperceptible movement, but just enough to allow him to glimpse Amédée looking like an extra who might be fired from the farce.

"Are you asleep, Father?"

No response. Things would go more quickly that way. The door closed as softly as it had opened.

An instant later, Amédée was outside and passing, like a shadow puppet, in front of Cripure's blinds. So much the better. An hour of peace on the couch. Wasn't this where he suffered best?

He'd thought he would get over it—that this was only an attack like all the others. But no, on the contrary, the farther along he got, the more he struggled with this sorrow he thought he had exhausted, a pain which still had so many revelations for him.

Words people said, or songs, came like arrows to target places he'd thought were forgotten in the vastness of memory. That time had stayed in him like an era all its own. Memory had its own, proliferating life. There had been many Toinettes, all passionately loved across unpredictable cascades of memories, and memories of memories. All with the same silent smile. Love was the fatal consequence of that smile, which he hoped would accompany him till the end, even though he wasn't exempt from the anguished thought that one day everything would become not only indifferent but empty to him, that there would be nothing left of his love but the shame of no longer loving.

He foresaw it as he had always foreseen everything. Because he had predicted everything that happened to him from the moment he'd started to think seriously about marriage, which is to say he had determined it, not of course, intentionally—could someone premeditate his own ruin? But, he thought, in the sense that destinies require our stubborn collaboration to accomplish themselves, that characters play out their fates, he had determined it from the first moment Toinette deceived him; and he had set it all in motion, though he pretended otherwise. At least, he had done everything to make it believable.

But about Toinette—silence! Not a word about Toinette to anyone! Even to the point of trying to make Maïa believe that the large portrait of Toinette hanging in his study was of an aunt, and he had taken the trouble to invent a whole story about her—a total waste of course—Maïa knew perfectly well what he was doing.

That sole image on the walls of the house (except for a colored portrait of President Fallières that Maïa had cut out of the *Petit Journal illustré* and hung in the kitchen) was an enlargement Cripure had commissioned *after*, from an amateur photo he had found in his briefcase, the only one of Toinette he possessed. The others, the ones from the wedding, all the many photos from the first year, he had abandoned with the papers, the books, the memories, and the rest. Following a habit he had taken up since the engagement (like a schoolboy) of never being without a photo of her, he couldn't help but save at least this little image of a smile from disaster. Toinette was represented from the shoulders up, hatless, her hair a little bit messy. He had taken the photo himself, just a few days before the marriage, in the course of a walk in the woods. He could tell the day, even the hour, the photo itself took hold. Hanging from the lace of her neckline was a little gold watch he had given her that very morning.

Maybe this watch was the reason he so rarely dared to raise his eyes to the portrait. The presence of the watch had eventually become intolerable to him—heavy symbol, extravagant rhetorical flourish, as if man's destiny never expressed itself but through heavy symbolism and clumsy rhetorical flourishes! Whatever it was, he had no way to say or to will the contrary, the watch was there, black and white, nestled against the fabric with its face fixed, sealed like a tomb, the face like one of those famous watches that stop forever at the moment of accident or death.

Three twenty. At that moment, that day, he had been busy taking pictures like a lucky hairdresser's boy with his shopgirl, like the lowest of the petty bourgeois he was, low in every sense of the word. Idiot! He had lost the prey by grabbing the shadow. And that watch face, with the two unseeing features of its hands, reminded him of what was without a doubt the most banal hour, instant of his life— the one where a man busies himself around a Kodak and gravely pronounces the order to keep still.

Toinette's smile seemed oblivious to the presence of that watch, the way a person is blind to the presence of death once it's upon him, alone and ignorant, in front of all the others who stand by, who see and can do nothing. Everything's been played out. And what name do you give Chance *after* your chance?

Maïa reappeared. Did he want her to prepare his "dressy clothes"?

"You're going out to their party later?"

He replied with a large, irritated frown, but his voice was astonishingly soft after the insults of a moment ago.

"Their party?"

She thought he was asking her. He was the one who should know…

"That ceremony for Deputy Faurel's wife. You still going?"

She waited, standing in the doorway.

"I know!"

He added, in a murmur to himself, "Buffoonery!" The general, the bishop, the prefect, the mayor, so what, the whole menagerie would be there.

"You going?"

He made a face, rubbed his temples with the tips of his fingers, and pushed his spectacles back in place: a tic.

"What does it look like, Maïa? Of course I have to."

"Then you should've said so. If you're going to be all fancy, don't it make sense to get dressed this morning? So it'll be out the way?"

"Whatever you say."

"And then you'll make sure to not be late for taking Amédée to the train?"

"Fine."

"Fine what? Fine no or fine yes?"

"Fine yes."

"So now you're telling me—"

"There's no rush Maïa—what time is it?"

"Nine."

"No rush—meaning I have class at eleven."

"So, what'd you say? Do I fix up your dressy clothes?"

"Well yes, Maïa."

He would go out on the early side anyway. He would stop by the bank. Maybe see Monsieur Point, his notary. But that was none of her business. He didn't mention it.

She opened her chest (where his scholar's gown and hood, which she called his "jack-in-the-pulpit outfit," were sealed in a hatbox) and pulled out her man's "dressy clothes": his jacket, his pants, and his waistcoat. All were carefully folded, preserved in mothballs. The smell rose, a smell he hated, which reminded him of all things familial and sad.

"What a bore!"

"Nobody's making you."

Poor Maïa! She didn't understand! Of course, no one was going to come take him to this party by force. They weren't going to send the police. But those scumbags! He knew them by heart. Dangerous rabble! Always ready to get even. And not just getting even, always ready to do harm, for the pleasure of it. She would catch on the day those asses—all Freemasons, naturally—made him leave his job, marched him out, sent him to the other side of France with a kick in the pants . . . Weren't his assets here? The houses, the little cottage . . .

"You don't know anything about them!"

"Oh, I'm not scared of them. Cause if it was me instead of you, they'd be under my thumb . . ."

What was the point of arguing? She didn't know anything about anything.

She was brushing his dressy clothes. An iron was warming on the fire. Soon, she would go over the shirt, the tie. But as for the creases in the pants, there was no point in trying. With those shanks . . .

THERE were days like this when he lost his taste for vengeance. A scattering of notes in his books, material to serve his life's work: *The Chrestomathy of Despair*—such was the pedantic title he thought of giving it, unless he called it *Sad-Sackery* or even *Death to the Rats*— he put it out of his mind. All of this belonged to someone else, a stranger, and the ambition to justify himself through a book? Absurd. And yet, if I had enough talent! Another question entirely. But why wouldn't I? Talent, that means having courage, courage enough to kill yourself. By that reckoning, I'd write it—my *Chrestomathy*, my *Apocalypse*, yes, my *Stuck Pig*…

He got up, and crossed over to his desk. A note? He wrote:

"If I so often cite Hoffmann, Edgar Allen Poe, Gogol, it's not that I think the petty bourgeois life of provincials—and why not Parisians?—recalls in any way the environment of these great geniuses, unless you think about it after the fact. The thought that a thousand quotidian examples could grasp absolute reality. From that perspective, I could call my book: *The Sufferings of a Petty Bourgeois, or Hoffmann Resurrected*."

He thought for a moment then wrote again:

"They express, in this world, the fantastical within the non-fantastic. The inverse, the reverse, the soul in turmoil. If I also often cite Flaubert with these others, it's because that dear Gustave, who was one of them—a bourgeois—was also the first to attempt and even to achieve this portrait of the NO."

He threw down his pen. Enough work for the morning. Enough ruminating. "Literature makes me shudder…"

The doorbell: who, who could it be? At that hour of the morning, Basquin, the old couple's only visitor, had guard duty at the camp for civilian prisoners.[4] And if it wasn't Basquin, who could it be? A mistake maybe.

Maïa's clogs clattered down the hallway.

Cripure came forward. "I'm not home—"

A sigh. He waggled his finger twice in front of his nose. Then— since he certainly couldn't tiptoe, but with a bizarre mincing that was its equivalent—he returned to the couch and sat down, ears pricked.

Maïa was speaking. But again, with whom?

"He's sleeping, sir."

"I can wait," the visitor replied.

"But that's a bother . . . and plus, he'll maybe sleep like that till noon . . ."

"Too bad. I'll wait anyway."

"Where?" Maïa was insolent.

"Outside."

Cripure got up and took a step toward the hall, his hand cupped behind his ear. There was something familiar about that voice . . .

"And who are you anyway?" Maïa wanted to know.

"One of his former students."

"Oh you think he cares about chasing after his old students! Old or new, it's the same difference to him, you know . . . what are you called?"

"Étienne Couturier."

"Oh yeah? So your papa works with Master Point, the notary?"

"Yes," the young man quickly replied, "but that's neither here nor there. I have a note to give him . . ."

"For my man?"

"Yes."

"Ok . . . give it here."

"No, Madame—excuse me—I need to deliver it with my own hands."

"It's from the notary?"

"No Madame."

"Well, that's not unheard of, you know. So who's it from?"

"A friend of mine—a monitor at the school."

"Give it here."

"I cannot, Madame."

"Putting on airs!" Maïa was angry. What did he take her for, this little sniveller? Did he think she was nobody? Good for nothing? "You've got some nerve," she said. "If that's the way it is, you'd better clear out and come back later. And that's that."

"I promise you, Madame, this is quite necessary..."

"Quite necessary!" Maïa simpered. "You can't talk like everybody else? What a little fancy-pants, 'quite necessary!'"

She moved to slam the door in his face, it served him right, that idiot, to teach him she wasn't just some cleaning lady, but Cripure's sudden voice in her ear made her whirl, furious.

"Well, look who's here!"

"Come now, Maïa, my little chickadee, come come..." He had dragged his hampered steps to the door and smiled vaguely, standing on the threshold, deformed giant with his too-small head, with his too-long limbs. An old hunting jacket in maroon velvet, spattered with ink and grease stains, missing more than half its buttons. Wrapped around his neck, a red muffler with one end tossed over his shoulder, like the ermine ends of the scholar's robe he wore for prize days, or for the funeral of a colleague. Dangling on his chest by a thread, a little penny whistle, which he used to call his dog Mireille, who so loved to run out of sight, to jump, to leap—at the risk of getting bitten by a rabid dog or humped by a mongrel. His gray slacks, much-mended, barely held up by a leather belt, sagged over his slippers. And beneath the jacket, a little vest, black and old-fashioned, opened to reveal a shirt that was abundantly stained by flea bites.

"Come now, Maïa, come now..."

Maïa crossed her arms gravely. "What's this—you want to keep the pig and eat the bacon? I'd sure like to know how you manage that!"

"That's enough Maïa, come! Let him in, why don't you let him in," and turning to the young man, "Please come in, sir."

"You really don't have a clue, do you!"

"Enough, enough!"

"Double-dealing, all right. There's no point in me telling him you're sleeping if you drag yourself out here and bring him in. Go on you old waffler—" she said, withdrawing into the hall.

She gave an exaggerated shrug and flicked her thumb at the young man: "Well come on in now. I guess he's his own boss, eh." Grumbling under her breath that she couldn't make head or tail or whiskers or feet of any of this, she went into the study, opened the blinds, and got back to her cooking.

Étienne still stood by the hall door, hat in hand, his face marked with pale nervousness. This was not how he had expected to find things!

How many times in the last year had he circled this house, never daring to approach and ring the bell, how many times had he lain in wait in some town doorway, wondering if Cripure would pass by, renewing for the hundredth time his resolution to approach and speak to him! Cripure, the only man capable of answering his questions, the only one who could be like a brother, the only pure one, amidst the sellouts and the butchers! He hadn't found the courage to execute his plan, he kept pulling back, retreating further and further into solitude, debating with himself in a shadowy world, more and more at a loss. For a year, he had lived only for this huge, sickly phantom, dejected, disdained, whose presence had provoked (and still provoked) an embarrassed silence. All the paths were blocked. His relationship to his father, and to pretty much everybody, was a miserable game of hide-and-seek where each side found a way to cheat. They feared the truth more than death. Cripure, at least—

Cripure asked, in a quiet, polite voice, "You have a note for me? I thought I heard—but please—won't you—please come in. It's from the school?" he continued, walking into the study.

"Yes, sir."

"The principal?"

"No."

Well then. It wasn't serious. He'd have been surprised in any case that the principal would disturb him.

"No," continued Étienne, holding out the letter, "It's a note from my classmate Francis; I just ran into him. A dorm monitor, sir—"

"Lovely..." Cripure took the letter and set it on the table without opening it. It must be something about a detention, some kind of community service project. It could wait.

He eased himself down behind the desk piled with books and paper in total disorder, a real pigsty, Maïa called it. He pressed his temples with his fingertips, adjusted his spectacles, wiggled his false teeth around in his mouth.

Étienne still stood.

This "study"—they weren't kidding! It was a cave all right, and even a dank one, since he could see, under the hanging tapestry, the yellowed plaster, crumbling, the large green stains on the ceiling, the low light. He was suffocated by whiffs of cooking mixed with the smells of ink, dust, old books, and above it all, the reek of dogs.

"Please don't pay any mind to that little tiff earlier," said Cripure with an embarrassed air. "In this dog's life, you know," he forced a laugh, "you've got to know how to stick up for yourself—pity you got caught in the crossfire. My woman, you understand, following orders—for me—one must—"

Étienne responded by babbling too. His visit, he said, wasn't just random. He would not have allowed himself—without a serious reason, to disturb the solitude of—he had enough respect for his teacher—

"Oh, respect." Cripure showed his disdain. It wasn't respect he looked for in youth. He would have wanted camaraderie—if he had wanted anything. But it was the same as with everything else—hopeless! Popular with his students? Ha.

"Please have a seat, sir."

Étienne sat down heavily. No, he definitely hadn't imagined the meeting this way. On his way over, he had a thousand things turning in his head. How easy it had seemed! He had even entertained the idea that Cripure would be equally happy to see him. His loneliness must have been so overwhelming! But the words he had prepared would not come.

"This is a farewell visit, sir."

Cripure slowly raised his big, lazy eyes to the young man. Practically a child's face. Seeing his bowed skull, Cripure understood the goodbye in question.

"So soon!"

"This evening, sir. But before leaving, I was determined to come see you, to ask you ..."

His ear bent, Cripure gave a kind smile, but how remote it seemed! "It's very nice of you," he said, "I'm very—touched, you know, by this—thoughtful gesture on your part. So—you didn't have such a bad memory of your old teacher after all?"

They so rarely remembered him except in mockery! So unusual that a good kid, like this one evidently was, would seek him out.

"Quite the opposite."

"Oh?"

"I owe so much to you, you were, for me, something else—more than just a teacher. May I say so?"

"Why of course, my friend!"

"I wouldn't have allowed myself," Étienne went on, fidgeting on his chair, "without the circumstances that will ... send me away. But everything has changed. I had to come see you. I had to tell you—"

"I'm listening," said Cripure, becoming more and more immobile behind his rampart of cluttered papers.

"Pardon me. If ever I caused you any trouble, please—"

"In class?"

"Yes, sir."

"But you're joking. Not at all! Not the littlest bit. On the contrary, you were a very gifted student and—thoughtful. What an idea!"

"I want to be—pure, to cleanse myself."

How melodramatic the pathos of youth, and in a way, how comical. Particularly these young provincials. They took everything so seriously. What a look this one had! He was fretting like a goody-two-shoes with such a fate before him—he'd come for absolution—

"Leave your childhood be," said Cripure. "The moment has passed, don't you see, to burden yourself with daydreams and worries. We've entered an era—hm!"

Hands between his knees, he bowed his head.

"What era? Sir—"

Cripure was silent. He looked pained. "A clean man," he continued, "what's that? A man who decides for himself, who doesn't submit. Not a part of the herd. Basically, a man like—"

Once again he trailed off. Modesty, maybe. A least he hadn't ended with: *the man I wanted to be*. It was clear he hadn't made it.

"But the others?"

"What others?" Cripure protested, ironic. "Our fellow men? Bah!" He batted the air in front of him. Then he laughed softly, almost without making a sound, shrinking into his chair. When this boy had suffered as much as he had at the hands of his beloved fellow men, then they could talk ...

"But the war?"

"That's the way it is!"

Étienne fell silent.

So this was the man he had searched for! He looked again at the small, reddened face leaning towards him, a face almost without wrinkles. His hair was short and came down over a narrow forehead, but what a look of sorrow! How different it was from how he used to look, in the street, at the door of his class, when he waited for the janitor to ring the bell! His look turning morose, Cripure opened his mouth, wiggled his dentures. With a quick gesture, revealing long practice, he trapped a flea on his neck and crushed it. He rubbed his temples with his fingertips, adjusted his pince-nez. Then nothing else moved in the face except the eyes, when he noticed a little book that, from the start of the conversation, Étienne had been holding on his lap.

"Where did you find that?" His thesis on Turnier!

Since its publication, this was the first time he'd seen it in someone else's hands. His expression changed.

"May I?"

Étienne passed him the book.

It was a little worm-eaten volume that must have moldered for years in some stock room. It must have taken a great love, a great determination, to rescue it.

"How did you…"

"I wrote to the used book dealers, sir."

Étienne didn't say at what cost or how many times. He admitted only that he'd been lucky to finally get his hands on it. The edition was out of print. They had all told him that.

That volume on Turnier wasn't the most important of Cripure's works, but it was the only one he held dear. As for the others, he had simply renounced them. For a while, when his study of *The Wisdom of the Medes* was first published, Cripure had enjoyed a certain cult following. There wasn't much left of that celebrity these days, except people around town knew that he'd had his moment of fame in Paris, and that he read Sanskrit. A few, like Deputy Faurel, who, without being truly cultured, were neither ignorant nor stupid, knew that for Cripure, all this Eastern mysticism was only understandable as a way into a psychic state that was an end in itself—not as a system of concepts. Interpreting Zoroastrian texts through this lens, Cripure understood Greek tragedy as the result of Persian influences. There followed a few short volumes and articles, written in a literary more than technical style. But he had stopped thinking about that nonsense a long time ago, renounced and forgotten, and once, when a student brought it up in front of him, he had scoffed, "The Medes! You can't be serious!"

Cripure flipped through the book. Should he tell this young man the truth? That his dissertation was never out of print—in fact, it hadn't been picked up. After the Sorbonne had refused to accept his "fantastical" work, Cripure had put it out for the public's consideration (at his own expense of course). But he hadn't found a single reader, and to avoid seeing his book trotted out on the sidewalk, he had brought all the copies back home. The entire printing was piled in the attic in boxes. No need to reveal that.

"A Paris used-book dealer?"

"No sir—from Angers."

"A moment—"

He buried his face in his handkerchief, like a man who feels the onset of a coughing fit, and stayed like that for a minute, his eyes shut. Angers!

It must have been that huge bandy-legged fellow, hidden in the back of his den like a snail in his shell, a filthy penny-pincher. How many times had he visited with Toinette! It had amused them to pay for their books with gold Louis, for the joy of seeing the miser's hand tremble.

"Do you know his name?"

"Why yes sir."

Cripure wiped his face with his handkerchief, and removed his spectacles, rubbing the lenses. "Branchereau, I'd guess?"

"No sir, it was a certain Ménard—"

"Hold on—" Had he really thought Branchereau was immortal? He must have died ages ago, covered in gold and filth. "It's true that since then—but, if you don't mind?" he asked, bending over the book again.

"By all means."

Cripure adjusted his spectacles, and carefully examined the title page, where once upon a time he'd written a dedication. He had once given this book to someone whom he had doubtless seen fit to call "my friend," but the friend had promptly seen fit to scrap it, not without first taking the precaution of erasing his vile name. But the rest of the dedication was there: "To my friend . . . this story of a man who was lofty and pure, written by his unworthy brother. François Merlin."

"Ah, ah," Cripure groaned, looking for a magnifier in his drawer. And he bowed over the page. "Who? Who was it? Who was enough of an ingrate—"

Cripure hadn't handed out his book carelessly. Nor had he carelessly chosen Turnier for its hero. In the development of his argument, he had combined a challenge and a hope. The challenge had been to declare himself a rebel, and in a certain sense, a martyr; the hope was that Toinette would read his pages, and the broken ties would be renewed. He had sent the book to their mutual friends, hoping that one day it would fall into her hands, that she would take it home. Whole pages were written just for her—she alone would have been able to understand their sense, their bitterness, their misery, she alone could answer. But she hadn't answered. This supreme letter had been lost, a cruelty unequalled in the rest of Cripure's life. But it's true that certain long-held hopes become reflexes, since at that moment, Cripure, forgetting Étienne, put down his useless magnifying glass and flipped through the volume with the unreasonable expectation of finding some notes, the draft of a forgotten letter...

To see her handwriting!

Alas, page after page of virgin white space. It looked like the pages hadn't been cut until recently—he couldn't bear to ask. If he had, he would have learned, to his great sorrow, that Étienne received these pages in the same state they came off the press. He slowed down to reread some fragments, which he'd never done since its publication. He never climbed to the attic. And then—to have to face himself? Sighs mixed with groans escaped him. With his magnifying glass by his side, he looked like an old antiquarian or a specialist, a Doctor Faust in need, thought Étienne, casting an anguished look around him. What hours of darkness! *"Das ist deine Welt! das heisst eine Welt!"*

It must be said that following *The Wisdom of the Medes*, which dated back to before his marriage to Toinette, Cripure had done nothing but repeat himself. The little following he'd earned from that text quickly grew bored. And Cripure with his public. After a while, everything was back to normal. What Cripure called "being sent back out to pasture."

Out of self-respect, out of admiration and love for Cripure, Étienne had always refrained from asking questions about his affairs. But the stories had come to him anyway.

People said—people whose *unwavering* good sense, mind you, went unquestioned—that Cripure wasn't quite what you'd call certifiably crazy, but still a little touched in the head, a little cuckoo, as sometimes happens with great minds. Or they said he was an original, not like the others, a man apart. A useful method of explaining away the teacher's subversive ideas and scandalous behavior. In fact, he was a man apart through his obvious, cartoonish deformity, by his pedantic way of speaking, his senile schoolboy jargon; by his habit, picked up as he got older, of talking to himself when he was alone; by his extraordinary gait, impossible to copy. The funniest moments were when, with that Maïa of his, he went biking. Étienne had often seen them, on Thursdays or Sundays, leaving together for their little cottage at the seaside. Cripure rolled along, nose in the air, peeking from underneath his pince-nez, having to sit up straight, since at each turn of the pedals, his thighs sprang up so high they risked banging the handlebars. He cycled carefully, with a serious expression, his little cloth hat held in place by an elastic, or if the elastic was broken, a handkerchief. His alpaca jacket rippled. A rifle slung over his shoulder, bundles piled on the racks, he would go "blow off some steam," shoot a rabbit, maybe a curlew or a sea swallow, "poor little beasts so good to eat..." Maïa and the four dogs would follow. In summer, she generally wore white from head to toe, including her stockings. Swollen as a wineskin, amply buttocked, her nose buried in net bags of provisions, she wheezed along, yelling after the dogs that capered ahead.

For more than twenty years, he had been the laughingstock of the whole town. One day Étienne had fought with a stranger who too openly mocked Cripure.

How did they know that he had been married once before and that he had divorced? He had never breathed a word about his past to anyone. But in spite of his embarrassed silence, he was nothing if not a drinker. As for his secrets, everybody knew them as intimately as he did. If it had been someone else, he might have admired the largesse by which a town of twenty thousand souls was informed about the most hidden parts of his life. Not only did they know he had been married, but where (at Angers) and that his wife Antoinette (they knew her name!) had left him for a handsome captain. But how, but why, by what stretch of the imagination had a woman become enamored of such a being and married him? No one would have dreamed of denying Cripure's genius, and on occasion they were even proud of it. They well knew he had published a book about the Medes, a dissertation on Turnier, that he had taken courses at the highest level. But marry someone for his research? That Antoinette, all things considered, had done well to leave him. Was this turn of events really so shocking when you considered that this genius was also a gambler, a womanizer, and by all accounts jealous to boot? Once again, that Antoinette had done the right thing. She must have been a delicate woman, accomplished. The daughter of a magistrate! Not at all the type for Cripure, you could tell by the next one he took up with, that Maïa, an old sailors' lass, pulled out of the muck. Still they recognized, in all fairness, that Maïa, however ugly, fat, and uneducated, gave him the attentions of a mother, not a servant-mistress. It was she who bathed him in the morning, who scrubbed him like you scrub a child, who helped him get dressed, tied his tie, fastened the laces of his monstrous shoes. A faithful servant—like a certain Hélène, much discussed in his thesis, who had been a faithful servant to Turnier.

They had at least this much in common, Cripure and Turnier: both had shared most of their lives with a servant, the big difference being that Turnier's servant wasn't his mistress. Another connection: they were both sons of ruined bourgeoisie. Turnier's father had possessed a considerable fortune, frittered away by unknown means. In Cripure's father's case, everyone knew perfectly well that it was the war of 1870 that had destroyed his industry, depriving him of his job as a factory manager, and making him an office drudge. From grade school on, Turnier had been a brilliant mind, as Cripure argued, marked. Marked, evidently, for ruin. At the town library, even though they didn't have Cripure's thesis, they still had a few articles on a so-called bizarre and intriguing local character. Étienne had asked for them to be brought out—and Babinot, though he was astonished by such a request, nonetheless did it, all the while talking to Étienne of other things— his "dear students," his son who was at the front, the bad faith of "Lady Germania." He had pulled a few clippings and a portrait out of a dusty folder. The clippings were run-of-the-mill articles about Turnier's death. As for the portrait, picture a small face, perfectly round, a splendid forehead, a long beard, and two eyes that pierced with their sadness. It was said—by the same people, mind you, who considered Cripure a little crazy—that Turnier's drama all started when he ran out of money. Turnier had, it seemed, managed to bankrupt himself without noticing. Head in the clouds. He'd turned his back on teaching, which Cripure had never dared to do, and he'd come back to live with his old cleaning woman, in a house that used to belong to the Turnier family, staying from then on, and dedicating himself to a life of the mind. He must have been just a little over thirty. The old servant, Hélène, welcomed Turnier like a son. For his part, he went straight up to his childhood bedroom and started clearing out everything besides a bed, a desk, a chair. He even removed the portraits and paintings from the walls, and the room became something like a monk's cell. He cut out a large red paper cross and glued it to the wall, and afterward that cross was the sole ornament. It was huge, so big that if Turnier had propped his back against the wall and stuck out his arms, he could have played at being the Christ. No one knew, wrote Cripure in his book, if he had ever enacted that blasphemous parody, but a similar impulse must have occurred to Turnier's religious and lunatic spirit, since he inhabited the house for ten years without any occupation besides meditations on the mysteries of predestination and evil. Not once, in the course of those ten years he had left, did he inquire where the food old Hélène served him came from. Yet he never wanted for anything. Around town, they thought he had gone crazy when they learned how he lived, not talking to anyone except drifters he met, when they heard he'd glued that big red cross to the wall. A few friends from grade school, most of whom were businessmen, potters, hatters, innkeepers, and others who were magistrates, came together in secret and agreed to aid this "poet" without Turnier ever suspecting a thing. When Hélène went to buy food in town, someone would have already paid her bill. At the house, the firewood replenished itself as if by magic, new outfits replaced the old, and so on. Turnier passed whole days in his room where he paced incessantly, praying out loud and writing. Sometimes he went out, went to the sea and swam for a half hour. He was a remarkable swimmer. Things went on that way for several years, until Mercédès arrived on the scene.

It was likely that Turnier had never loved anyone before he met Mercédès. She wasn't quite twenty, and he was already pushing forty. As Cripure described her, she was spirited and kind, a good heart. Étienne imagined her in a long, white dress, wearing a lace cap with ringlets peeking out at the sides, a parasol on her shoulder. She lived with her family in a chateau. That family, thought Étienne, must have been pretty upper-crust—men with riding crops and monocles, their stiff, matronly wives. They took very badly what they called the glances of that good-for-nothing, that vagabond dressed like a beggar who let his beard and hair get as long as a prophet's, who walked around town with the slack jaw of a monk at prayer. They never thought for a second that Mercédès could do them the bad turn of falling in love with Turnier. Étienne could easily imagine Turnier stopping sharply in the middle of the road to watch Mercédès with his clear visionary stare, and Mercédès passing by on the arm of some chaperone, not acknowledging the crazy man's eyes. Did he even dream of greeting her? Probably not. And so it went on for a while.

Finally they spoke. Nocturnal meetings. Love letters. The whole story was full of romantic clichés and sentimentality. The love letters were left in the hollow trunk of an oak. They must have held hands, but as for kisses? No. Turnier offered to marry Mercédès. He would change his life, go back to teaching. He arrogantly refused a dowry, making this one of the conditions of their marriage. Everyone expected a big fight. They expected to see Turnier getting his hair and beard trimmed, perfumed and pomaded, running to the town hall to "extract" the certificate of good moral conduct and character, and arriving at the chateau in a new suit, boots polished, hat in hand, to make the official offer. But things didn't turn out that way. He went to the chateau all right, but he presented himself in his ordinary clothes, and Monsieur Baron or Marquis didn't even bother to receive him. They simply left him on the doorstep. That evening a letter appeared in the oak trunk, in which Turnier reminded Mercédès of what was agreed between them, asking if she would run away with him if they refused him her hand. She should be ready to leave the next day. She didn't appear. Her father had discovered the hiding place, stolen the letter, whisked Mercédès off to Paris. Turnier waited for two days. When he had understood that she was lost to him forever, he went down to the ocean, plunged into the water as was his habit, and swam toward the deep, to his death.

Cripure pushed the book away, raising his chin with a sad, bored pout. "Turnier was a misfit," he said, "a dissenter, of course, but..." His hand made a vague gesture, at once scolding and calming, then, with a new frown (again the dentures), he added with lowered eyes "but he was pretending."

Étienne startled.

"Pretending?"

"Oh it's a fact! Proven. What did you expect," he said, in a wavering little voice, "I don't want, you see, to set myself up as a judge, but all the same...all the same, I'll allow myself to entertain certain doubts, you understand. He had sides to him that were, let's say, less than noble."

He lifted his gaze. Étienne caught his look, astonished to find in it something like hate.

"What interests you about Turnier?"

"His unwillingness to compromise, sir."

"Not so fast!" replied Cripure's simpering little voice. "He was a man of faith, you understand—I find all belief suspicious. You see, I'm with Stirner, whose real name was Kaspar Schmidt—" he became pedantic, warming to the subject, "therefore I think that 'everything sacred is a fetter' when it is not pretense. What follows, I'm not borrowing from Stirner," he said, raising his pointer finger. "One can develop that crack through nobility, but also through...its opposite, as a kind of wickedness," he said with a disgusted frown, as if hurrying to unburden himself of the thought.

There was a little pause, then Cripure added, "The way of living, that's the distinction."

Étienne heard himself reply, "And of dying?"

"He loved Mercédès, you see," parried Cripure, with a sigh. "His suicide had no bearing on anyone but himself, since, after all...each of us is the sole judge of whether or not to make the verdict final. That had nothing to do with his faith. All the truth in that man was his love. The rest..."

Once again, his hand batted the air in front of him.

"What are you trying to say?" murmured Étienne. "Just now you said something about pretending."

Cripure looked like a man who is grieved to curtly disabuse another, but who is resolved, because he has no choice. His fat hands fell heavily on the books in front of him. Then, returning to his childlike pose, bowing his head and letting his joined hands fall between his knees: "Pretending... It's better to say it frankly: tricking. I'm thinking of his relationships with his friends."

"It's one of the most moving parts—"

"Not at all! Now see here, it isn't at all," said Cripure, shaking his head. "You're thinking of his friends' secret intervention after he was ruined?"

"Yes, sir."

"A tale! A fairy story. But you see, firstly: Turnier's ruin was his own fault and not his father's. He had only himself to blame for pissing away his little fortune, and afterward he lived on subsidies from his friends, it's true, but the kindness of the latter only went so far as to never ask him to repay the sums he borrowed. Because in the end, dear sir, this will hurt you, but it wouldn't be fair to let you ignore it any longer—Turnier was a damned leech!"

And to underscore his point, he knocked twice on the edge of the table with his index finger.

Étienne froze. Why was he so determined to discredit him? What for?

Cripure looked him over.

"Am I destroying your illusions?"

"I want the truth."

Again the comedy of adolescence! With a face like that, he would believe in absolutes. "You are brave," said Cripure.

"Yes."

"You have to be very brave," he continued, his voice altered. Evidently, it wasn't Turnier he was thinking about. "I mean that in general," he added, with a round gesture of his hand.

"I want to be sure... that you're not belittling him on purpose."

Cripure rubbed his temples—his tic—and frowned his frown.

"What does it matter?" he replied, with a laugh that barely concealed its sarcasm. "To each his own aesthetic. I steer mine by a certain sense of... honor." He stopped and turned away, as if ashamed.

"Honor?"

"A faith in the self, an absolute unwillingness to compromise," he continued, shooting Étienne a defiant look. "Your Turnier" (that *your* made Étienne jump) "didn't hold that opinion at all. But how could he! He ran for public office!"

"Him?"

"You didn't expect that?"

Étienne didn't have to respond—his disconsolate face spoke for him.

"It's totally verifiable," Cripure replied. "Of course, when I wrote that . . . thing—" he picked up his book with disgust and threw it in with the others, at the other end of the desk—"when I wrote that . . . novel, I ignored it all. I didn't have the necessary documents at hand, you see. Besides, I was . . . rushed. I didn't see Turnier as anything but a romantic, a man of passion and ideas, who walked by the sea at night in meditation. A very interesting figure, taken that way, you understand, a brilliant hermit. He had his years of meditation, in any case, before . . ."

"Mercédès?"

"Not so fast," said Cripure, with a curious little smile. In a little nasal voice, he added, raising his pointer finger—"madness."

Then he laughed.

What a strange man! And how hard it was to breathe in that murky room! Maïa lit the furnace and he could hear it snoring. She'd propped open the glass door so that the heat would spread. But with the heat, the smells of dogs and mold became unbearable. If only he could have opened a window.

"Do you know the story of the axe?"

"The axe?"

"One day, he picked up an axe, in order to chop off his arm. He succeeded only in getting himself committed to an asylum. Once he got out, do you know what he did? He sold his last plot of land and he left. He became—you'll never guess."

Cripure's eyes glittered. He was watching Étienne with the malice of an underhanded haggler.

"You can't guess?"

"No, sir."

"An accountant!" he cried with a shout of laughter, that was forced, repellent even to himself, and he stopped short. "Naturally, that didn't work out. His accounting wasn't the kind that pleased *them*. He was mired in lawsuits. Then, back to the asylum. Then, finally, here . . ."

"Mercédès?"

"She too . . . you no doubt believe like everyone else—no point," he interrupted, seeing Étienne was about to speak, "I know what you think. But no, Mercédès was nothing like that, dear child, she didn't grow up in a castle as everyone wrongly reports, and I was the first. She was the child of some bourgeois, a childhood friend, and by no means a person he met by chance. Another thing: she wasn't the first woman Turnier had loved. Not by any means. He had affairs with many women before her. And at the time we speak of, he was closely tied to another woman, a Madame . . . her name escapes me. And it's true that he offered to marry Mercédès, and it's also true that she refused him. Yes! Oh come now . . ."

This time, it wasn't one hand that batted the air in front of him, but two at once.

"In the end," he finished, with a bitter twist of the lips, "you see, this Turnier was a poor fool, an unhappy fellow torturing himself, a victim! What good was a love that gave him nothing but the courage to die? It's not about giving up. In this world where everything's a conquest, you have to know, if need be, how to take by force!"

He calmed down, stopped waving his arms, his hands falling between his knees as if by their own volition, his shoulders slumping, and said in a small voice that was not without tenderness, "A bankrupt in life, in thought, in love . . ."

Silence.

Cripure lowered his head. He seemed to have forgotten Étienne's presence. Slouched, his big hands joined between his pointy knees, what was he thinking? Of Turnier's suffering, the day after Mercédès had fled, or of his own, when Toinette . . . It would have been so much better to end the day courageously, as Turnier had. And since that blond officer's sword had scared him, why hadn't he taken his pistol and—he shrugged a little, a gesture of self-pity no doubt, but still without a word, drifting further and further, oblivious of Étienne.

The little dogs dozed, now and then letting out innocent little sighs like the sighs of children. Étienne, perched on his chair, was motionless, fascinated by the paralyzing feeling that within these walls, the slightest noise would reverberate like the loudest echo—huge and irreverent.

From the kitchen came the splash of dishes in a basin.

Strange to find himself alone with this man, within these walls blackened by humidity, the dimness deepening since the rain had started to fall around the house with a little rodent sound, as if an army of rats were laying siege. Strange and suffocating. He wished he were already far away, leaving behind this conversation that was so painful, so dishonest. How complicated everything was, how tangled and fake! They had lied to themselves and told him only falsehoods. And Cripure kept on. Would he ever snap out of it? Would he find, beneath so many lies, a truth? Would he have the time? *Guess or I devour you.* The sphinx's maw was already opening—tonight, the barracks, in three months—

He passed a hand over his skull, sheared as of the day before.

In the street, the black silhouette of the mayor, with his black umbrella in his black-gloved hand, his frock coat like crows' wings, his galoshes: clip, clop, slosh. He began his rounds so early this morning! How many mothers and fathers today would receive from his hand—here, my friend, this one's for you!—the little paper marked in red with the death of a beloved child? There had been too many, and Étienne had heard people saying that the mayor wasn't keeping up. He had to hire secretaries! Étienne noticed that his belly hadn't shrunk, that legislative belly, so perfect for the tricolored sash or a poster, a glorious belly, a real signpost, fastened like the umbrella and not less voluminous. Was he keeping track of the doors where he hadn't yet knocked? Or where he'd knocked only once? It was like

St. Bartholomew's Day—he might as well build crosses for them all. *I will no longer exist and that's it*, thought Étienne.

What would that be like? He would want nothing, he would love nothing. Impossible to picture. Others spoke of the blank, the cruel loss played out in the person of the mother, getting out her mourning veil, saying that all the same she hadn't expected to wear it again so soon. And the father hiding away somewhere, not at the café in those hours of pain, but in the attic, like the other time he cried there for hours, sitting on an empty box, his hair full of spiderwebs. There. That's all there would be to say. All? No. If he had enough "luck" to not be entirely pulverized, they would be certain to collect his corpse. Ceremony at the station, the church, the cemetery. And on All Saints' Day they would do it again—some graybeard, a Babinot, a Nabucet, would make a speech under an umbrella. Then, Chopin's funeral march. And in the afternoon, the clergymen would process through the graves in habits, their hands joined, their backs hunched, pouring, on the pain of the world, the opium of their prayers...

Étienne stood up. Cripure came out of his reverie, shaking himself like a big dog.

"What is it?" He was dead to the world. What? The young man was leaving? Already? But why? "You're leaving?"

Étienne wanted to say that there was nothing else left to do. But he didn't say anything, and Cripure gave his shadowy figure an astonished glance. What did it mean, that tense, drawn face, those hard eyes, that bristling pose? Étienne's hands made two pale stains in the gloom. Cripure could no longer see his features—only the silhouette of an adolescent with a shaved head. "I have to tell you that you are the only man I wished to speak to. I ... I don't know why I live, sir." Then, in an even lower voice, "I'm not sure why I'm telling you this either."

Cripure wriggled deeper into his armchair. Dear God it was dark in this study, but he wished it were darker still. A sharp feeling of shame overwhelmed him, against which all considerations of youth and comedy were powerless. He was quiet. The rain had stopped. Maïa had closed the door, and they could no longer hear the furnace snoring. In the deep silence, he perceived only the young man's quick breath.

"Live!" he murmured, as if talking to himself. He raised his head, "You are still young—"

Étienne didn't budge. Was that all Cripure had to say? Really?

Cripure turned his eyes away. The cruel silence stretched out again. Then he said, "Living is difficult." An instant later he added, "for everyone—" How hard it was to force the reply!

Étienne slowly lifted a hand without speaking. Then he let it fall; his two pale fists closed, hardening like two pebbles beside his thighs, his chin trembling.

"Your question," said Cripure, still not looking at him, "your question—" He wanted to say *your question catches me off guard*. Before that formidable confession, he balked. "Your question," he was slow to continue. "Bah! ah! It's the question, precisely—"

"I don't know why I must die either." It seemed to Cripure that Étienne had shouted.

"You're looking for an idol," Cripure muttered. "You'd like to put . . . an idol between yourself and your fate. Eh . . . an idol . . . hard to get around them, isn't it? See how you can or can't get along with idols. No, believe me, there is a point in our being where love meets the love, by which I mean the love of a thing or a person. That point is the center of the world, the world of . . . psychologists, geographers, imbeciles, geniuses. The world gravitates around that center, that gravity has laws, and now we find ourselves at the heart of an order . . . No, that's not what I wanted to say. Not at all. Life is an affirmation," he continued, swelling his voice, "an affirmation!" And he slapped his hand on the table.

"Of what?"

"Why . . . of the self!" He thought he heard Étienne say "absurd"— but he couldn't be sure. "Absurd? Of course. Why of course it's absurd. The world is absurd, young man, and all of man's greatness lies in understanding that absurdity, and all of his justice, too. But," he said again, waving his hand, "that's enough philosophy. No, see here, life is something you seize."

"But let me ask again—and as for others?"

"Don't be stupid!"

"But then..."

"Seize your happiness, that's my advice, without thinking about anything or anyone. Don't be a Turnier. These Renaissance men were different types anyway, gentlemen of another scope. Real men. Our questions would have made someone like Benvenuto roar with laughter. He would have felt nothing but scorn. Bah! The world is fallen. Men like that are no longer possible. We barely see the rise, from time to time, of a Mangin—what an admirable war hawk, my boy—or a Clemenceau—"

He stood, and from the table he picked up the letter Étienne had given him. He slit it open, still talking. "I have no end of admiration, you see, for this Clemenceau who, arriving at the end of his career, seems to be independent enough, detached enough to want everything, to risk everything, to swat down a Chamber made up of idiots and goofballs." He pulled the letter out of the envelope, waved it without reading, and continued, "When it comes down to us, my boy, ah! We're debased, you see, screwed... but all things considered, it's better to be beaten that way. There's a certain feeling of dignity..." he began to read his letter, "or honor. As for the rest... man doesn't deserve our attention."

He stopped, the letter under his nose. Suddenly everything changed.

Like someone choking, Cripure raised a hand to his throat. He stayed like that for a few seconds, then, letting loose a loud cry, he fled his table, knocking over, in his clumsy haste, a pile of books which collapsed onto the floor. He rushed toward the kitchen door, shouting at the top of his lungs:

"Maïa! Come here. Maïa!" She didn't respond fast enough for his liking. And so he yelled again, even louder, "Maïa, for the love of God!"

From the back of the kitchen Maïa replied, "What is it, babe?"

"Get over here!"

"Coming…" The way the man shouted! What a pain he was! "Quit screaming yer head off," Maïa said, opening the door. She planted herself on the threshold, arms dangling. Drops of water fell from her fingers onto the floor. "OK, what's this?"

Cripure's voice had taken on a curious crybaby tone. "They've unscrewed the bolts on the bikes again, Maïa!"

"They what?"

"The bolts on the bikes."

"Oh!"

"Pimply dunces! Scum … filth! They're out for my blood, but …" Crazed with anger, he brandished the letter.

At his cries, the little dogs chimed in with whimpers, growls, then, as if in agreement, they howled all together, running in circles around the room. Fat Judas, with his black and tan fur, gave the impression of a giant, dirty mole. Petit-Crû trembled from head to toe. Turlupin, his big ears batting the floor, readied himself to flee the first blow from Maïa's clog. Only Mireille, the lovely Mireille, his noble companion on shooting expeditions by the sea, his favorite little beast, dared to approach him. She snuggled up to his leg, and, sitting on her haunches, raised her wet nose to him, lifted a paw, and with her most reasonable little barks, started scratching his thigh.

"God almighty," yelled Maïa, "nothing but Barnum's circus! You can't hear nothing. Hush! And you first of all," she said, turning to Cripure. "Nothing but a yeller! Get along!" She waved a hand, "Out!" She took up the dogs by the armful, with the exception of Mireille, and threw them in the kitchen.

Cripure was still yelling about complaining to the police, to put them on trial. It was a repeat offense. "A repeat offense!"

He shouted too loudly; he squealed too much. All this felt both unnatural and unjust. An anger in bad faith, thought Étienne, and in any case, pretty unflattering.

Cripure was threatening: "I'll, I'll …"

"Quit howling like that!" Maïa was sharp. "How's this? Like the other time?"

"Identical." He pointed his finger, gesture of the victorious orator.

"Talk so I get it. The bolts on the forks?"

"Yes."

"On both bikes?"

"Yes. Both of them."

"How do you know?"

Cripure jerked his chin at Étienne.

"Oh and how'd *you* know about it?" She seemed furious, as if she thought he was responsible for what had happened.

"But...I didn't know," said Étienne.

"It was a letter," said Cripure.

"What's that you're stuttering?"

"Me, stutter? I stuttered, you see, that—" if she only knew how to read! He waved the note under Maïa's nose. "It was a monitor, a friend of this gentleman's who let me know...Right here, Maïa, there's a warning: *Check the bolts on your bicycle.*" Cripure's two long arms fell heavily along his body, and he let out a sigh. "*And Madame Merlin's as well.*"

"And just now he told you that?" said Maïa, puffing up her whole torso. "And it's been more than an hour he's been in there?"

"I didn't know, ma'am. I hadn't read the note, you understand. It wasn't addressed to me."

"He didn't say anything to you?" Cripure asked.

"Who?"

"Your friend, the monitor. In giving you this letter, he didn't give any indication of its...object?"

"No."

"Ah!"

Maïa was listening. "And him, how'd he find out?"

Étienne shrugged. "I don't know."

"What! He don't know? Oh I'll get this cleared up, just you wait. Let's go see 'em," she said, walking out.

They kept the bikes under the staircase that climbed to Amédée's room, in a corner dark as a coal bin. That's what had been stored there, during Maïa's first marriage. But Cripure wanted the coal moved elsewhere, because of the noise Maïa made when she went to get some, the scraping of the shovel on cement, the avalanche of coal in the bottom of the bucket, the doors she slammed as if for pleasure as she came and went. All things that drove him crazy, kept him from thinking or dreaming. Maïa got out the bikes and brought them one at a time toward the door, under the light from the window. All three of them bent down, Cripure, calm, almost curious, holding his pince-nez between his thumb and index finger. But still, he held his breath.

Under Maïa's big finger, a bolt wiggled like a loose tooth. With a little poke of the thumb, it fell to the ground.

"The others, check the others…"

She repeated the procedure four times. They watched in deepest silence as one after another, the bolts fell to the ground at the slightest touch.

"There…you see?" As if he'd ever doubted it was true! "You see? Nothing but a touch with the tip of a finger, the slightest tap, almost nothing—"

Fists on her haunches, she stared at the bikes, then gave them a sudden kick with her clog. "Darned machines from h—" Polite, despite her anger, she didn't say the word and addressed herself to Cripure, who had his back turned, scratching his chin. "What're you planning now?"

He didn't answer.

"Hey you, I'm talking to you—what's yer plan?" The words tumbled out of her mouth; with each one her fat shoulders rose, seeming to absorb her too-short neck almost completely.

"Done for…" murmured Cripure without turning.

"You can't just sit on yer nest…"

"Done for." He stared at nothing and continued to scratch his chin. All of a sudden, he turned to Étienne, and in his polite, simpering voice, he explained, "The…vibration, you see, is particularly bad when coasting down a slope and would surely make the bolts pop off… In those conditions, the front wheel gives out, literally mowed down, and the fall is unquestionably fatal. Fatal. Because of the way we would have been thrown to the ground, head first, you see. Oh…

those bastards. And this is the second time we've escaped from such an attempt. The first time, it was only because our ride was delayed. The second, thanks to you—and to your friend."

He spoke with a dull, flat voice that was toneless—nothing like his usual speech. "It was yesterday they did their wicked deed," he said, turning to Maïa. "You remember? While we were having a drink. We left the bikes outside on the sidewalk..."

"Sure," she said.

"They must have had a monkey wrench. They would have followed us for a while, planning their trick. Fourteen-year-old brats!"

"But are you going to complain?"

Cripure closed his eyes, a bitter wrinkle, a disillusioned mouth. With his fingers he brushed her off. "Bah! A complaint? To whom?"

"Eh? To the police."

"The police! And against whom?"

Maïa looked at Étienne. "You have no idea?"

"No."

"He knows nothing, eh?"

"But Madame..."

"Bah, Maïa, let it go, let it drop. Poor Cripure," he groaned, with a slow gesture of his arms, and he shrugged his shoulders, half closed his eyes. "Oh, oh, oh! They wanted to kill me!" he cried, lurching into his study.

It sounded like he was having a seizure. The door slammed shut, and in the returning silence they could once again hear him cry, "Me! Me! Me!"

Étienne bit his lips. At each of Cripure's howls, he replied between clenched teeth, "Crook! Crook! Crook!"

Yesterday, the hazards of war brought to Nabucet's doorstep one Captain Plaire, a childhood friend he hadn't seen for thirty years, whom he certainly wouldn't have recognized on the street. They'd grown up next door to each other, but life had ... separated them. While Nabucet was becoming a teacher—building, in his little town, a reputation for elegant intellect—Plaire, seduced by adventure, re-enlisted, went to the colonies, rose through the ranks, and was named a captain. In the meantime, like Nabucet, he'd become a widower, and when the war loomed, he'd returned to service. They'd just changed his garrison. Then, remembering his old friend Nabucet, he'd written to him.

He'd been here since the day before—for pleasure and economy. All things considered, it was nice to stay with Nabucet. The house was large, comfortable, well heated, very well furnished. What good taste Nabucet had! Nothing crass in his house. You could see right away he loved beautiful things. Rugs, tapestries, paintings everywhere. And what a comfy bed had been made up for the captain! Real feathers your head sank into, so pleasant, so soft, you could smile just thinking about it. Yes, he certainly would've done well to establish his quarters here. Unfortunately, it wasn't to be. Anna, the elderly maid, didn't seem at all receptive to the idea, and Plaire had noticed, on Nabucet's part, allusions to certain hotels that were "completely dependable." The captain wouldn't press it. This evening, he would go to a hotel; it would be less nice, it was true, but he would have more freedom. They both had comforts and advantages.

Captain Plaire made these reflections in front of a cup of hot chocolate that was beyond anything but the wildest dreams. The cream! He savored it, and, his cup empty, he took a stroll around the room, sucking on his mustache ends, which he wore long, drooping, and gray. What would life be like here? He wondered, lifting up a curtain.

He frowned. Wasn't life the same everywhere? Wasn't it sad everywhere? The sky was gray, the garden naked and drowned. He thought of Indochina. And then, of the concubines. As for this place . . . Letting fall the curtain, he repeated the story he had been telling himself every day, for years.

It was a simple story, almost naive. The war would end, he would retire to a little town and live off his pension in peace, without getting involved in anything. He would rent a little house, rather out of the way so as not to be bothered, and—and here the tale really began—he would become friends with an inspector of public welfare. Real friends, close. And then voilà—he'd be free to take into his service, in that little out of the way house, some pretty girl of sixteen or eighteen. Just like that. He'd go to his old friend, say a couple words in his ear, and the inspector would trot out the prettiest wards in his care. The captain would have his pick. That little blond didn't speak to him? Well then there was that brunette, who, once she was bathed— a dream. And Captain Plaire's heart raced. He would bring the little brunette home. They'd be all alone together in the house. *I'll be like a father to you.* And, truly, he would be kind, indulgent, reserved. Then he'd start giving the little one advice, he'd buy her a dress; one day, he'd do her makeup. *If I put a little rouge on you! Wouldn't that be fun!* And the pretty thing would let him do it, delighted, happy, overcome with appreciation. And then from there to . . . Everything would be charming. No one would suspect a thing—a real pasha's dream.

It was a story he fell into as soon as he was alone—he walked with it in the street, took it to the café, the barracks, wherever he went. He had tried a hundred times to link himself to an inspector of public welfare. Without success. It was becoming odd—his inability to make friends with someone in that role. Almost as if there were a hostile will against his plan. "Bah! Bah!" he murmured, rubbing his eyes.

He approached a mirror. Of course, he was aging, but he wasn't so decrepit yet. His cheeks were soft, his eyes were starting to cloud, his hair and mustache were gray. But he wasn't bald, his color was rosy, his teeth were good, and his energy was intact. Fifty-eight. It could certainly be said that old men of sixty still found ways to make girls of eighteen adore them.

He arranged his tie, brushed his hair, combed his mustache, slapped a little lavender water on his cheeks, and went out.

The previous day, Nabucet had shown him the house from cellar to roof. When they parted, he pointed to a door on the landing, saying, "Tomorrow, when you're ready, knock at that door and you'll find me in my room. Very simple." The captain went to the door, knocked, and bent an ear.

"Come in, come in, my friend," replied Nabucet's smooth voice, "come, turn the knob." Like every morning, Nabucet was engaged in his "physical culture." In pajamas, bare-chested, his hair and beard soaking wet, he stood in the middle of a rug. Respiratory exercises. He came over, shook Plaire's hand with a smile.

"You don't mind if I continue?"

"Why—I'm curious," Captain Plaire replied, looking around for a seat. He found a footstool. "Go on, have at it."

"Just a minute—open that little cupboard in front of you. Yes. You'll find a bottle of port in there and some glasses. Help yourself."

"With pleasure." Port after chocolate? Why not?

"Sleep well?"

"Like a baby."

"Excellent."

And Nabucet continued his exercises.

He was small but solid, muscled, hairy. He seemed, with the point of his little goatee, to be conducting the universe through his exertions. He looked not a day over fifty, but he was fifty-five. Three years younger. And he's even more tanned than I am! Nabucet's chest slowly swelled, the muscles in his arms flexed and relaxed with well-oiled ease. What health!

The captain looked at him for a moment, then took a sip of port, dried his mustache, and got up to set his glass on a side table. "My dear Adrien, would you like a little tip, eh? Would you permit me to make a suggestion?"

Nabucet crossed his arms behind him, put his shoulders back, crossed his legs. A resting gymnast. "Of course, dear Paul."

The captain tapped Nabucet's chest with his index finger. "You're not doing that at all like you're supposed to, my friend."

"Oh?"

"No . . . your rhythm's wrong, my dear Adrien—either you go too fast or you go too slow. Permit me to say that it's working against you. The rhythm, you understand? Otherwise the heart suffers, the lungs, the liver, the whole body. I go blue in the face telling them that," he finished, planting himself in front of Nabucet, legs apart.

"Telling whom?"

"Why, the instructors. Would you allow me to . . ."

"By all means."

"On guard!" the captain commanded, snapping to attention, hands on hips. They did the movement together. "Hands on your hips! Leg lifts—begin! One!" Slowly they raised their right legs, eyes locked. When his leg was about to be horizontal, the captain made a sort of grunt "Huh!" and let his leg down. Nabucet's came down too.

"At ease!"

Nabucet crossed his arms.

"You see what I mean now?" The captain asked. "With the rhythm. You want to do another set?"

"Certainly."

"On guard! Good. Hands to the chest. There! Keep the head up, the shoulders loose. Tuck the tummy. Good. Deep breaths. Good, very good. Sideways extension of the arms—begin! One! Slowly, slowly! With the rhythm. Empty out your lungs. There! Halt! That's perfect. You see, you get the subtlety, the method? Between us, my friend, you're an extraordinarily well-preserved specimen. I've seldom seen arms like that at your age—not an ounce of fat, all muscle. Do you exercise a lot?"

"Every day."

"No equipment, eh?"

"Never."

"Don't trust equipment. I go blue in the face telling them that too. We're not trying to become acrobats, eh? Just calisthenics done with the rhythm, that's all. Then there's no need to fear old age." He drained his glass.

"That's enough for this morning," said Nabucet. "I've got a very busy day ahead. Do you mind if I dress?"

"Shall I step out?"

"Not at all. We can chat in the meantime." Nabucet went behind a screen, the captain poured himself a second glass, took his place on the footstool, and the conversation continued.

"Between us," said the captain, "life is short. And what's the point of this life, besides happiness?"

"*Carpe diem*," Nabucet replied from behind his screen.

"What's that?"

"You've got to seize the days as they come."

"Hm!" Another sip of port. "How big is this town?"

"Twenty thousand people."

"Is it a lively town?"

"It's not exactly lively. But it's a town . . . you get attached to. Attractive. You'll see if you stay among us for a while—you'll succumb to its charm."

"A theater?"

"Yes. And cinemas."

"Cafés?"

"Goodness! Where do you think you are, my dear Paul? You're not in the colonies anymore, you know. This is a town like any other, neither livelier nor more run-down than any other. You're afraid you'll get bored?"

"Where does one not get bored?"

"But here you'll have the Officers' Club, receptions at the prefecture, what have you. Do you shoot? Are you a swordsman?"

At the mention of swords, Captain Plaire's ears pricked up. "That," said the captain, "is right up my alley."

I wonder if he's ever fought a duel, thought Nabucet.

"I've been involved in thirteen duels," Plaire said, "which, it must be said, were all settled on the field. Two for my own honor."

Nabucet whistled. "Fancy that! You're quite the swashbuckler."

"I've never compromised on a question of honor," the captain solemnly agreed.

"Oh! You'll have to tell them that. The Fencing Club will be thrilled to have a recruit like you..."

Captain Plaire didn't say anything else and neither did Nabucet. Secretly, Nabucet hoped that this brilliant recruit he was about to introduce to the Fencing Club wouldn't stick around too long. If need be, he'd say a few words to the general. These childhood friends were charming, but they talked rather a lot. They knew too much about... origins. Yesterday, this one had a way of speaking about Nabucet's father the carpenter, his mother who ran a small grocery store—hm! He would have to keep an eye on him. Nabucet had replied that, for personal reasons, he didn't like to hear about his family. But this heavy-handed fellow was still capable of alluding to certain things which would reveal how Nabucet had lied when he pretended that his father had a "big business," in the same way he had lied about his mother's "receptions," when all she'd really received were tirades from him and his father.

On his part, Captain Plaire was also having second thoughts. The theater, the cinema, all that was well and good. These connections, receptions, the bridge parties at the Officers' Club, sword bouts at the Fencing Club—he wouldn't say no. But what about the secluded little house, the pretty girl...

"I'll be ready in a second. We'll walk a little ways together, no? Where are you headed? The Square? I have to go by there as well, to hear news of the general. I heard yesterday that he was feeling better. We'll see soon enough," Nabucet said as he emerged.

The captain widened his eyes and whistled. "Goodness! Dressed to the nines!"

He certainly was. A fitted frock coat that was molded to his chest, a beautiful shirt, in perfect taste, the creases in his pants absolutely straight, his shoes polished so you could see your face in them. The outfit was elegant in a discreet and intellectual way. The tie alone was a marvel.

"We're decorating Madame Faurel this afternoon," said Nabucet. "I think you know who she is, even though you're not from here?"

"The deputy's wife?"

"Exactly. They gave me the honor of organizing a little party, you see. I've even accepted the task of saying a few words," he continued in a nonchalant tone. "I couldn't refuse of course—I don't know who else could have done it."

What would they do without me, said Nabucet's face. And it was true. Without him, they wouldn't have done anything. He was the one who always took the initiative. Who had founded the Lecture Group? Nabucet. Who directed the Theater Company? Nabucet. If they got Madeleine Roch to sing "La Marseillaise" from in between the folds of the flag, well that too would be one of his feats. He was involved with everything, he directed everything. It was impossible to avoid him.

"And you say the general will be there?"

"Not only the general, but also the duke, the prefect, the mayor— really the whole circle."

"You must be quite somebody," said Plaire.

"Oh it's such a bother. But it's necessary if you want to amount to anything. It's a pity you can't join us, dear Paul."

It was out of the question. The captain was booked all day. "Another time."

"It would have been such a pleasure to introduce you to my friends. You seem melancholy, my dear fellow—"

"It's true," the captain admitted. But he'd always been a bit melancholy, even in the colonies. And after he was widowed . . .

"Listen," said Nabucet, putting a hand on his shoulder, "why don't you remarry?"

The captain started. "Me?"

"You're a widower, you're not old, you're not short on cash—so?"

"I've thought of it sometimes," said the captain, hanging his head.

"So, why not?"

"I don't know. The opportunity hasn't appeared. What can you do..."

Nabucet shook his head, took his hands from Plaire's shoulders and clicked his tongue. "Nonsense! You're not being reasonable. But therein lies the only solution, my friend." He grabbed his hat, took a last glance at himself in the mirror. "Let's go."

They went down the stairs, side by side. It was a huge staircase, which could easily fit two abreast. The rug muffled their steps. Paintings, engravings, signed photographs covered the walls. Statues on pedestals rested on the landings. Everything about it was cozy, comfortable, creating an agreeable feeling of security and bourgeois happiness.

Nabucet pranced along, his hand barely touching the banister. He was proud of himself, of his house, of the part he was about to play in the decoration of Madame Faurel, of his supple gait.

"Your house is splendid."

"Oh yes," said Nabucet, "It's not too shabby, my little spot."

On a small table at the bottom of the stairs, the mail was waiting—newspapers, brochures, letters. "Do you mind?"

"Of course not!"

Nabucet slid the wrappers off the papers and scanned them with a serious face. He flipped through the brochures, then turned to the letters.

A huge guard dog appeared and stalked towards the captain with a menacing air.

"Here, Pluto!" The dog came forward, his ears back. Nabucet put his letters down on the table, took the dog by the collar, and made him sniff the captain's legs. "Don't forget, the captain is a friend." And he let the dog go.

"I hope he doesn't forget," said Plaire with an uneasy laugh.

"From now on you have nothing to fear, my dear Paul. Not only will Pluto never attack you, but he'll also come to your defense. Isn't that right, Pluto?" The dog lay at his master's feet. "Good boy," said Nabucet, taking up his letters. But he looked through them distractedly, and quickly put them in his pocket: "I'll show you right now. Some sugar, please Anna!"

The old servant came out of the kitchen carrying sugar, barely greeting Captain Plaire, the intruder. She left as quickly as she came.

"This is to show you just how intelligent these dogs are, my dear Paul, and how well you can train them. He's a prize specimen. But what can I do? I live here in a sort of hermitage, and you must wonder why. I'm far from the heart of town. But it's because of the light, my friend. The light is amazing here. There are landscapes of light, just as there are of greenery or water. Here, sometimes, it's magical. But of course, when you live in such an out-of-the-way place, it's prudent to give a trusty guardian the task of watching over my sleep—and my valuables. I own a few pieces of art, as you might have noticed, and people know that. Oh, it's not Mr. Pierpont Morgan's collection, but as modest as mine is, it's known, and I wouldn't be surprised to receive a visit from certain specialists one of these days—" While he talked, he broke the sugar cube into little pieces in the palm of his hand.

"With a beast like that," said the captain, "I don't know what you could possibly be afraid of."

"I let him loose in the garden every night. Any fool who risked breaking in to my house would have the dog at his throat before he took three steps. Pluto!"

The dog pricked up his ears.

"You'll see," said Nabucet. "Sit nicely, Pluto."

Pluto sat up. Nabucet placed a tiny piece of sugar on his nose. "It's Captain Plaire who's giving you this piece of sugar," said Nabucet.

A quick movement of his head—the little piece of sugar flew through the air like a fly and was gulped with a dry snap of canines. And then the dog froze.

"You see that Pluto is your friend, my dear Paul."

Second bit of sugar.

"This time it's from—the kaiser." The dog didn't move. "You won't accept a little bit of sugar from the kaiser? Good boy! So it's not from the kaiser it's from his son, the klownprince."

Again, the dog didn't budge.

"Fine, it's from—Monsieur Poincaré."

Snap! The bit of sugar went flying and was snatched from the air as before.

"What do you say to that?" asked Nabucet.

"Amazing."

"Places, Pluto, places! Sit up, my friend."

The session continued. Third bit of sugar. "This one's from General Joffre—"

Snap!

Fourth bit of sugar:

"Monsignor the bishop."

Snap!

Fifth bit of sugar:

"Cripure."

The dog didn't move.

"You don't like Monsieur Cripure?" mocked Nabucet, grimacing. "Why don't you like him, you naughty dog? Go on, go on, Mister Pluto, make up your mind!"

Nothing.

"Good dog! Monsieur Cripure is no friend of yours, that's plain to see. OK, that sugar isn't from him, it's from—Madame Faurel."

Snap!

"And that will be all for this morning," Nabucet finished.

"Who is this Cripure?" asked the captain.

"It's a nickname, given to this self-important person, a colleague, a so-called philosopher, but really, a disappointment. The nickname comes from the fact that he's always talking about the *Critique of Pure Reason*, which the students call the *Cripure of Tic Reason*, hence: Cripure. Personally, I have nothing against him, the poor fellow! But Pluto can't stand the smell of him, probably because of an ancient goatskin cape he's always wearing, which makes him look like a giant ape."

All the same, Cripure! If he hadn't been there, with his so-called Sanskrit and his convoluted books on Medic wisdom—then Nabucet would have been, without fail, the foremost "intellectual" in town.

This fallen Cripure seemed to have pulled a few pieces of fame down with him—or rather, notoriety, as Nabucet corrected people when he heard them speak of Cripure's work—and there was nothing Nabucet could do about that.

Nabucet sat down to put on his galoshes. The dog, having received his daily ration of sugar, went off. Nabucet asked permission to take another glance at his letters, and this time he read them more carefully. They seemed to bring him bad news, since he clacked his tongue several times with an annoyed air and eventually put the letters in his pocket, saying, "They'll end up making me a Minister of State. Because I'm a friend of the general—and of a few other dignitaries—not a day goes by but I'm asked to intervene on the behalf of someone or other, whose case is explained at great length. Two more mothers wrote to me this morning, and for what? But I won't set myself the task of telling you those miserable stories. Anna!" he said, standing up, "my umbrella! We're ready, we're leaving." And, thinking of the letters, "What do they want me to do anyway? They should know I'm not God in Heaven!"

Anna brought the umbrella.

"I'll come back at noon for a quick lunch. What are your plans?" he asked the captain.

The captain was very busy. They would undoubtedly ask him to eat at the mess hall. His time wasn't his own. It would be best if they didn't expect him, pretended he wasn't around. He didn't want to be any trouble. He had packed his things and would call for them.

He explained all this, babbling.

"Fine," said Nabucet. "As you like. As long as you don't forget one thing, my friend: that my house is at your disposal. You understand?"

It was confirmed.

"Good, then—let's go. See you at noon, Anna."

The rain had momentarily stopped, and Nabucet could let his handsome umbrella dangle from his arm without trepidation for his dashing formal wear. They kept up their conversation, walking sometimes on the sidewalks when they were passable, and sometimes on the verge when there weren't too many puddles. This gave their walk a prancing and runaway air, which Nabucet managed to use for a million elegant little effects, but which annoyed the captain no end—he feared for his nice boots. What a poorly maintained town! He had to admit the one he'd come from was no better, but he'd had high hopes for this one, like a green young man who travels for the first time and expects to find palaces from the *Thousand and One Nights* twenty miles from his door. Speaking of palaces, they were walking beside an endless high wall, green with moss, which threatened to collapse in places. An abundance of leafy branches poked up behind it. Nabucet explained that they were the walls of a convent, that behind those walls some few hundred nuns prayed and fasted, those of course, whose vows prevented them from bending over the cots of the wounded. It took all kinds to make a world. The captain agreed. He wasn't particularly anticlerical. Of course, he always thought it was a shame when some lovely girl entered a convent rather than making some man—himself—happy. But after all, there had to be some girls like that. And anyway, you never knew, prayers might do good. But he also thought: *Did they really do nothing but pray?*

"There must be some pretty little unripe ones behind those walls," he said, batting an eye.

"Oh, I've never been inside to check!" replied Nabucet in a tone that made the captain's ears prick up. Well, well! You'd have thought it touched a nerve, that sort of comment.

"Is it a big place?"

"It's a real palace. But there are others. We have a few convents here. I'll give you a detailed tour of the town one of these days—you'll be astonished, my friend. The clergy is very rich here. To give you an idea of just how rich, think about this: by my calculations, and including the bishop's residence and its grounds—which are splendid—properties owned by the clergy make up about a quarter of the total area of the town. And I'm not even counting the seminary—as big as a barracks—nor, you understand, our thirteen churches."

"Thirteen?"

"There are also a few chapels."

"Goodness!"

A puddle separated them for a moment. Nabucet gracefully leapt over it. The captain jumped clumsily, and dirty water squirted on his boots. He groaned.

Nabucet continued: "You see my friend, I won't naysay religion. Without being a believer, neither am I an atheist. Whatever you choose, we have the chance to create our own philosophy, a stoic one, if need be. The world of ideas is open to us. But the people! They have no ideals but in prayer. The other day I saw a poor mother, overcome, you see, at the death of her son. She was praying all alone in a little chapel where I had gone with a visiting friend to show him a magnificent work from the thirteenth century, a ducal tomb. Well, at the sight of that poor woman—some laundress if what they told me is correct—I'm not ashamed to admit that tears came to my eyes. You want to be able to do something for downtrodden people like that."

"It's hard."

"Alas! But all the same there are charities—specifically, Christian ones."

"That's true."

"His grace the bishop told me the other day that between the running of his charities and his domains, he has work enough for the staff of a cabinet minister."

"You know the bishop?"

"A truly remarkable man."

"And the inspector of public welfare?"

"I don't mean to say," Nabucet continued, "that the laity isn't doing enough. We're of the laity, and we've done everything in our power, and we'll continue with perseverance. But it's certain that the war has revealed the astonishing charitable capacity of the Church. Yes, my friend, these people are doing admirable things. And I, in a spirit of justice and holy union, I say that the chaplain and the socialist laborer are perfectly worthy of each other's brotherhood, and they should forget their old and futile quarrels."

The captain agreed. He replied dully that Nabucet was right and thought that they should have been talking about something else. He was finding Nabucet tiresome, with a dangerous tendency to take a moralizing tone. Who the devil did he think he was? Between two old friends, friends from childhood, that tone was all wrong.

At the end of the street, the humid sky seemed to detach in one piece, pushed gently towards the west by a wind they could not feel. They moved forward, still jumping over puddles and potholes, and finally the wall ended, and they were passing houses with smooth façades and bristling grilles on the windows. A murmur reached them, a kind of creeping, buzzing litany, a sad moan. The nuns, no doubt, at prayer?

"That's the chapel?"

No. It wasn't the chapel. The chapel wasn't in view; it was inside the convent.

"This is attached to the convent—an asylum, a house of correction."

The grilles were now perfectly clear.

"Have you heard of Saint-Blème?"

"No."

There were branches of Saint-Blème everywhere. "But here," said Nabucet, "is the founding chapter. Saint-Blème is a house of correction for recovering...you know...bad girls," he rapidly finished.

"Well, well, well!"

"The prayers you hear come from them, my friend. They pray while they're at work. Poor girls!"

The murmur of prayers increased. In unison, the whole workshop took up the rosary—"Hail Mary full of grace..."

"You'd almost say it was bees buzzing," said Nabucet.

The clouded, stuffy sky held no birds. The smoke from chimneys climbed slowly, spread, disappeared into the lowering fog. The murmur of prayers diminished, becoming more and more feeble as they walked. Soon it was gone.

"How old are they?"

"All ages. Some aren't yet thirteen."

"And what work do they do?"

"They make clothing. They also do ornaments for the church. I believe they even work for some of the big Paris fashion houses."

Silence.

"They're very strange creatures," Nabucet continued. His voice trembled a little. "Very curious creatures..."

"Oh! Ah, yes?" The captain searched out Nabucet's eyes, but he was looking straight ahead, so that it was impossible to see anything of his face but his bearded cheek, the point of his ear, his neck, chafed by his too-starched, too-white collar. "In what way?"

"In what way are they curious? In this, my dear Paul, that they are quite cunning. It takes great patience to care for them. I assure you the nuns deserve credit! I've heard several tales of their ways from a few of my friends. I was interested in the question from a... psychological, moral point of view, naturally, as well as a humanitarian one. To spend one's youth imprisoned? That's harsh. Not everyone believes in it. But what can you do? It's anyone's guess. As soon as you let them out, they go back to their sins."

"Then what's the point of locking them up?"

"You have to try everything. Society owes it to these poor wayward souls to do everything it can on their behalf, and it has to... ahem... protect itself. They pass love notes to one another, you know—I've seen it with my own eyes."

"What?"

"You must remember, my friend, that even though the society is a religious one, those in power still have the right to oversee it. The prefecture even allocates a certain amount of money to the house, doubtless for the care of those children the Board of Public Welfare trusts to them. Meaning the inspector of public welfare is constantly working with Saint-Blème. So he showed me—"

The captain turned purple. "You know him?"

"He's an excellent fellow," said Nabucet.

"Oh? Oh! Yes? Who—how so?"

"A real fatherly type."

The captain didn't press it. But there was definitely something there.

"So he showed me the notes these... young ladies passed among themselves. You'd be dumbfounded—they call each other dearest, darling...very revealing!"

"You think it goes further than that?"

Nabucet laughed, a snide little giggle, the laugh of a wicked old man. "Here, there was, but you must promise not to repeat this, there was a nun who had been...deviant when she was a girl. They thought she was totally cured. She had taken vows, donned the veil. She was thirty-three. One day, a peasant came to deliver wine to the convent. And then the old girl somehow got a baby inside her." The story ended as it had begun—with the same elderly laugh. "What do you make of that?"

"They're all the same, aren't they!"

But Nabucet objected: "Not at all! Certainly not! Since we're on the topic, I'm going to tell you another story. A story that happened to me personally. I took an interest in one of the girls placed in (or better to say recommended for) residency there by his grace. One of his little unhappy ones, you know, an innocent victim. Yes, I thought she was innocent," he said in a vaguely wounded tone. "I heard the whole story from the bishop himself. The girl was fourteen, a timid little peasant who'd never known anything but rough farm ways, and she had the misfortune of losing her mother, who had remarried. The stepfather started beating her. She ran away for the first time. They brought her back, she ran away again, and they brought her back once more. But the devil was on her shoulder—she left again and, according to some, stole." Nabucet made an evasive gesture. "So she got picked up by the police, brought to court, sentenced. His grace let me know, and I attended her hearing. The girl behaved very badly— cried, stomped, made threats. They decided to put her in Saint-Blème. I was struck by the intelligent air of that young thing. When I saw his grace again, I confided my impressions. He agreed with me in thinking that the story was based on a real injustice. It was also true that the girl couldn't get used to Saint-Blème, that she..."

"But what does this have to do with the bad girls?" the captain interrupted, disappointed. He had been expecting something a little racier.

"What do you mean, what does it have to do with them? She stole."

"That's it?"

"My dear Paul, stealing is also a vice."

"Sure. But it wasn't proven."

"So I said. But anyway, that's not the issue. The real problem was, you see, that they had thrust her into a situation where she might have been contaminated."

"They shouldn't have put her in there!"

"That's exactly what I said to his grace, not in so many words, of course, but I made it understood that we had perhaps made a mistake, and that mistake might be taken back if he would only let me intervene. A delicate affair. You can see our laws are not perfect. She had already been sentenced. It became, after the fact, very difficult, not to say impossible, to spring the girl from her jail. It's not too much to say it would have taken the banner and the cross for my plan to succeed. But finally, thanks to the concerted effort of his grace, of my friend the public defender, of the prefect, of the inspector of public welfare..." ("Hm!" went the captain) "I was able to bring into my service, as a maid, this poor, unfortunate girl."

"But I never saw her at your house!" Plaire cried, getting red in the face.

"Wait! Wait for the rest. No, you didn't see anyone but my old Anna. A heart of gold, that one."

The captain didn't say anything.

"A simple heart, as Flaubert would say. Such a dear, a jewel of a woman. She doesn't trust anyone but me. She even came to me for advice about where to invest her little savings... Anyway, to get back to the story, when she saw the child arrive, my brave Anna threw up her hands. 'What can we possibly do with that poor little girl? She doesn't look strong enough to hold a broom.' I made it clear to Anna that it wasn't about that. This little one was unhappy. We needed to take care of her, to give her some trust in the world. For, after all, my dear Paul, what is real kindness anyway? The kindness that changes things, or the kindness that doesn't? 'The pretty one! The pretty one!' Anna kept saying. As it happens, the girl was quite pretty, but prickly, you know. It seemed like she was afraid of me. She didn't speak, lowered her eyes as soon as I looked at her, ran away if I so much as brushed her cheek with a caress...oh! Of course you understand, in a fatherly way!"

"Yes, yes. Go on."

"I was always afraid she would run away. I even wondered, seeing the way she lurked by the door, if she had a real mania for flight. She was really quite feral."

"And then?"

"We tried for fifteen days to civilize her. All in vain. She wouldn't eat. She was wasting away right before our eyes, despite our best efforts. She would only say one thing—that she wanted to leave, return to her home."

"But she had run away three times!"

"That's what we told her. She would reply that she wanted to go back anyway, and that this time, she'd be good, she wouldn't budge. But that was impossible. Anyway, she became ill, and we had to take her to the hospital."

"You didn't care for her at home?"

"See here, my dear Paul, and what if she had died there?"

Plaire hadn't considered that. He made a face. "Fair enough!"

"What would people think?" said Nabucet. "Wasn't I progressive enough, taking a girleen into my home, under those circumstances? It's true that Anna was there and who cares about gossip anyway, but all the same!"

"But did she really die?"

"Alas, my friend!"

"At the hospital?"

"It was a horrible affair. The doctors didn't know what was wrong. Medicine is a poor science, and doctors poor scientists! They couldn't understand her wasting sickness. I told them to warn me if her condition worsened. Just think—she had no one but us! But me! And one night—it's hard to think about, my dear Paul—one night, the doorbell rang and they brought me a note to say the girl was dying and had called for me."

"Oh! Really?"

"In my...sorrow, it was a comfort, I'll admit. She had finally felt a moment of understanding. I got up, dressed, and—" Nabucet didn't say anything else. Plaire glanced at him and was surprised to see him wipe something off his cheek. A tear?

"You came too late?"

"It wasn't that...it was something completely unexpected. Once I was ready to leave, I found I couldn't."

"Huh?"

"I couldn't make up my mind. I...I was..."

"Afraid?"

"No, not afraid. But I couldn't leave the house."

"That's strange."

"I was completely bewildered. But I couldn't even take a step. I couldn't make myself open the door."

"Never heard anything like it."

"Indeed. I still can't make sense of it."

"And so what did you do?"

"Nothing. For a long time, I did nothing. I dawdled..."

"But in the end, you went?"

"Yes, I went eventually. I don't know how."

"Was she dead?"

"No, that's exactly it, she wasn't dead yet. When I went in, I wondered if she really had called for me. She made a little movement to refuse...poor girl! But then yes, it must have been true, because she let me come closer." He paused for a long moment. "She died in my arms."

They didn't say anything more. That was the end of the story. Why had he told it?

"Some kids are dealt a miserable hand," said the captain.

"Oh that one could have been helped, if she'd only let me. I wonder what she died of," Nabucet said through his teeth, as if talking to himself.

The captain was thinking.

If picking up little maids from public welfare brought on stories like that one, he might need to reconsider. "You don't always know what you're getting yourself into," he said.

And Nabucet replied: "Life is a matter of…tact. You see, my problem is that I'm too kind-hearted. Just because I wanted to save that girl from tragedy, God knows what they could say about me. And no doubt, they've not missed their opportunity."

That was true, but it had no practical importance. Everyone in town knew that Nabucet was a bit weird, a bit creepy, but that didn't at all prevent bourgeois mothers from sending their daughters to his theater company, which periodically put on big productions like Edmond Rostand's *Pierrots*. It was Nabucet himself who did stage makeup for the young ladies. From time to time, he got slapped. "You know what I want?" he said. "I want everyone to be happy."

This declaration met with no response.

"You don't agree?"

"It's impossible."

"Well, I have my own opinion on the matter. Yes, my friend, it's possible. All over the world, we've got to undertake a great crusade to show people the light, the pure, simple light of the sun that no one knows to look for. The light! Sometimes I spend whole hours just looking at the light."

"Didn't you write verses when you were a kid? You're a bit of a poet, you know, when you're lost in thought."

"I've stuck with it. You see, my dear Paul, I have my fun. When I'm retired, I'll amuse myself by composing an epic poem. And do you know what the title will be? *The Sun*. I want to encourage mankind to rediscover the light. Humans have sunny dispositions or they have nothing at all—I'm sure of it. That's what will bring on a revolution! They make me laugh, those others with their so-called demands. All that's just for profiteers. Let's go back to the old myths."

"How much further to the square?"

"Not far at all. We'll be there in a moment. I have to take you through a neighborhood where you'll need to…hold your nose. Then we'll be at the Square."

As they went on, the streets became dirtier and less well kept. Some had no sidewalks, and the rain shower, instead of pooling there, had flowed into whole streams in the center of the streets. Here and there, the houses were old, run-down, dark. But Nabucet said they weren't lacking charm. A few of these houses were big tourist attractions, and as a member of the Public Improvement Society, he had done all he could to make sure some of them were classified as historic sites. The loveliest ones, from the twelfth and thirteenth centuries.

"If you're not afraid of the stench, let's stop a moment," he said, pointing a finger at a ruined structure. The ground floor was occupied by a baker, and colorful tatters hung from his windows. The captain stopped and looked.

The street smelled of sewage, fish, and smoke, but there were other scents mixed in—fresh bread, laundry someone was ironing, a smell of resin. There must be a carpenter close by. They could hear him manning his saw, as Nabucet's own father would once have done. And from the cobbler's shop came the pounding of a hammer on a stone—the whole street echoed with it. The captain raised his nose, looked at the house, and found nothing to say, except that it was dirty and even unsanitary, and that everything inside, humans and objects alike, must be rotting as if it were a cave. The sounds of working mixed with the shrieks of a gang of urchins, the calls of women who ran errands, fetching water from the public taps, or bread from the baker. It was strange, this noise of life, after the prayers of a moment ago.

"Isn't it beautiful?" said Nabucet.

"That house?"

"Yes."

"You know...it's not really for me."

"It's quite remarkable to a connoisseur." And with the same teary tone he'd used for the girl: "I hope to save it." He would use all of his *devotion*.

"That one maybe," said the captain, "I wouldn't know. But the rest..."

"Oh, you're absolutely right, this neighborhood will be demolished. The town's going to buy all of this, and these houses will be razed. It's part of the town's improvement plan."

"You're on the town council?"

"Oh! No, no. I leave politics to others . . ."

He expanded on this theme—these lower streets were an eyesore, a breeding ground of infection, of epidemics. All the diseases came from there. Besides, "these people" lived in a repulsive, shameful state of filth. You knew it just by looking at them.

"Take a passing glance at the state of one of these . . . interiors."

"Slums."

"That's the word."

"But where are all of these people going to live, once they've torn down their houses?"

"They'll find other houses, my friend. Like everyone else. What are we supposed to do about it?"

Good sense told the captain that it would have been fair to build somewhere else for them to live.

"It would be just as dirty as this after a month," Nabucet replied.

They kept on walking.

"Not that way," said Nabucet, lightly touching the captain's arm. "That street has a bad reputation."

"Oh? Yes?"

"We're in a sort of . . . ghetto, even though there isn't a single Jew here. We're walking this way because it's the fastest. But that way would lead us God knows where . . ."

"How many are there here?" asked the captain, who had seen only a single red lantern.

"Three."

And the silence continued.

No use asking Nabucet *how* they were. And what good would that be anyway, when the captain couldn't set foot there. One of the annoying things about these provincial towns was that you really couldn't make the rounds when you were a captain or a teacher. And there were no refined brothels, as there were in bigger cities. Toulouse, for example, or Lyon. As for the cafés, there was nothing to hope for. They were all devoid of women. So how was he to enjoy himself?

The captain asked the question in the abstract, with the air of wondering about people other than himself.

"That, my friend," replied Nabucet, "touches on a subject that is completely unfamiliar to me. I'm not up to speed on those matters."

"But if one wanted to spend an evening there...?"

In the past minute, Nabucet's air had totally changed. His steps became more rapid, as if to distance himself as quickly as possible from that disreputable street, and instead of looking around, his eyes were lowered. He'd kept this position, like a crick in his neck, since he'd violently turned his head away at the sight of the lanterns, and his voice had shifted. "There aren't all that many who like to 'spend an evening,' as you say."

This astonished the captain. Nabucet expanded upon his thought. Most people settled down very quickly. It was a mistake to think they really wanted sex that much, after a certain age, which was sometimes very young—around thirty. For the most part, they became indifferent. A drink and a night of cards sufficed. Others, in large numbers, were simply gourmets.

"They don't sleep with other men's wives?"

"Not as much as you'd think." That too, was a myth. Naturally, there were affairs here and there, but very rarely. Once again, people were more indifferent to these matters than one would think.

Nabucet turned red, sashaying and skipping as he walked. "You'll laugh at me, my dear Paul—" he giggled shiftily, the fake laugh of a confused little boy—"you'll laugh, but I've never set foot in that country."

The captain, who was no longer wondering about the red lanterns, had the naiveté to ask where.

"But...you know. You know what I'm trying to say."

"Never?"

"Never. It's the truth."

"You mean to say, here."

Nabucet shook his head. The captain asked, "You mean to say you've never been to one? Anywhere?"

"Never."

A moment passed.

"But what about—what about when you were younger?"

"Never."

"That's unheard of. Why didn't you?"

"Because that's not what I'm looking for."

"What, then?"

"Tenderness."

The captain burst out laughing. If it was tenderness he wanted…

"But the women in Paris? No mistresses?"

"Not those either."

"You're a saint, old friend."

Nabucet didn't seem to hear. He was still talking, "You were speaking of happiness…Well then, true happiness is what one gives." And he continued, talking to himself as if he were alone, not bothering or perhaps not able to form complete sentences, "Little child you rock…not a grown woman…to make her die of love…simpler than that, love…to take her whole self, even make her cry…"

The captain was beginning to understand that, in the ten years he'd been widowed, Nabucet hadn't slept with a woman, and he hadn't become a gourmet either. And as he reflected on that he found himself among the shops in the Square.

AT SCHOOL, in the large but poorly lit lodge, near a window with dirty glass panes looking out on an alley, a girl who was clearly the older sister walked back and forth, rocking a baby in her arms. The mother was ironing. Below the window, a young man stretched out in a wheelchair and Madame Marchandeau, the principal's wife, stayed beside him, sitting in an armchair.

She was the only visitor who still came to sit with the crippled boy. At first, they would stop by to visit him, bring him sweets, books, newspapers. But people had gotten tired of it. He had so little to say to them!

The baby quieted—he was about to fall asleep. Nearby, in the cloakroom, two teachers were talking.

"Have you read the papers, Moka?"

"Oh, I glanced at them."

"You're not so curious, my friend. Even the war doesn't interest you? And the revolution in Russia, that's nothing too? If you had read the paper this morning, you would have seen proof that Lenin has sold himself to Germany. What do you make of that?"

Apparently Moka had nothing to say about it, since there wasn't a response.

The crippled boy turned to Madame Marchandeau. "It seems like they make very good mechanical legs now. I saw it in the *Excelsior*. Is it true?"

"Of course it's true."

"Legs you can walk with?"

"No doubt . . . have faith, my dear Georges, get totally healed, and don't worry about anything else for now. Isn't that right?"

"It'll never be like before."

"Come, come . . . if it's nice out later, they'll take you out into the courtyard, and you can visit with the other wounded men. You know Roques the shepherd?"

"Yes."

"Well I'm teaching him to read. He's happy as a clam."

The mother walked up to the girl and bent over the baby. He wasn't yet asleep. She smiled at him, tickled him under the chin with the tip of her finger, kissed his little hand. In the next room, the conversation continued:

"In the first place, the name isn't Lenin, it's Oulianoff. He's a fugitive from justice like the rest of his crew. Smugglers and forgers. But they've been unmasked—just think—they've seized the account books with all the names and amounts!"

"How do you know that?"

"You think I'm lying?"

"I didn't say that, Glâtre . . ."

"You'd be better off thinking about your plan."

"I'm thinking about it, Glâtre, I'm thinking about it."

"And telling Monsieur Babinot about it. Then he'll talk to the general, you see, and the affair will be prioritized. That at least, that'll be useful . . . more so than saying stupid things about the Bolsheviks. I've given it some thought—they should put your museum in the parlor, eh? Don't you think?"

"That's a wonderful idea."

The concierge came into the lodge, a thin, nervous man who wore his mustache like a peasant. "Nabucet hasn't come?"

"No," said his wife.

"As soon as I ring the bell, I'll go back upstairs to finish arranging things. Remember to tell him."

Madame Marchandeau turned. Goodness, it's true, she thought, they're going to honor Madame Faurel soon! She'd completely forgotten. And her husband too, must have forgotten, since at any rate he hadn't mentioned it. In other news, it had been fifteen days and Pierre, who was at the front, had stopped writing. On purpose.

"Has the mailman come, Noël?"

"Yes, Madame."

She didn't ask anything more.

"Nothing yet?"

"Nothing. We'll have to wait."

Madame Marchandeau turned back to the wounded man and concentrated on talking to him. She wanted to be especially nice to him this morning, she thought, since she wouldn't be able to take him to the courtyard herself.

Noël took his keys, tucked the attendance sheets under his arm, and ran out. It was time to ring the bell.

Students, teachers hurried passed the lodge in little groups. Hall monitors entered, glancing at their mailboxes: "nothing for me?" then ducking out. The cloakroom was silent. Messieurs Glâtre and Moka, their cigarettes finished, left to pursue their engrossing conversation while strolling beneath a gallery in the Honor Court. The bell rang, letting loose the hullabaloo of recess, and almost immediately the lodge was flooded with students buying candy, erasers, and pencils. The concierge's wife left her ironing to wait on them, in the middle of the mêlée, defending herself as best she could. The young girl fled to a corner, protecting the baby from all that noise. It didn't last though. The bell rang a second time, the students fled—in a few seconds, all was silent again.

"Why are they decorating her?" Georges asked.

"For taking care of the wounded."

"Oh?"

She had taken care of typhoid patients, it was said, in another hospital, close to the front. Here—where most of the school had been converted into a hospital—she had been head nurse for a while. And then she had been sick herself.

"Do you know her?"

"By sight."

"Oh Madame Stuck-Up," said the concierge's wife, who had gone back to her work. "Is it true what they say, that she had herself—oddly enough—enameled?"

"It's possible."

"But what does that really mean, enameled?" she pursued.

"Beauty treatments," Madame Marchandeau explained, without showing the slightest interest in continuing the topic.

"What a funny world. They say too that she bathes in milk. Is that even possible?"

"Not unheard of."

"It must be true," said Georges. He laughed thinking that hers wouldn't be watered down, unlike the milk his baby brother drank.

"It's a harsh world," said the girl. "Did she really take care of contagious patients? A woman like that?"

"Let us hope so," said Madame Marchandeau.

The girl didn't say anything else. She continued across the room. The students, with their racket, had upset the baby. His naptime had passed. She started to hum, her mouth right next to the baby's ear, rocking him with a smile, a tender, almost childlike expression.

They had been right, his mother and father, in saying that even though this baby had been a surprise, it was even more surprising that he'd chosen to come into the world at such a moment, and it would have been better for him to stay where he was. She knew they didn't mean what they said, and besides, she loved him. She would have brought him up all alone, if she'd had to, she would have sacrificed everything. They had cut the legs off her older brother, but they'd leave this one alone, or else—

"Sleep, my little one, sleep..."

Madame Marchandeau and Georges were whispering in the back of the room, which filled with the good smell of warm laundry. The mother bent over her iron, her cheeks red, her hair messy.

"What is it?" she said suddenly, turning around.

The girl raised her eyes and the song vanished from her lips—Monsieur Nabucet was standing in the door, his hat in his hand. "I ... I'm not intruding?"

"Noël is in the hall, Monsieur," said the wife with bad grace.

But Nabucet, seeing Madame Marchandeau, rushed over to her. "What a surprise! What a lovely surprise ... my regards Madame, my regards ..." and he bowed low.

Of all the teachers, Nabucet was certainly the most considerate and the most refined, the most cultured—after Cripure anyway—the politest, the most "Old France," as he said himself, about himself. It was to the point that, if they had decided to teach etiquette and deportment at the school, as they supposedly did at religious institutions, the whole town would have spontaneously agreed to give Nabucet the job. And if he'd only taught his students the right way to greet people, already that would have been a great step forward! The way he greeted people was so flattering, all the more because he always appeared not to see you at first, to be absorbed in some profound thought, or, in other instances, to be contemplating the light. But how the first moment of greeting compensated for that distractedness! How remorseful he looked, how quickly he put a hand to his hat, with what slow, unctuous grace he lifted it and inclined his head. Could such a thing be taught? Or was it more like an inborn talent?

"What a surprise," he murmured again, clasping the hand Madame Marchandeau held out to him. She didn't mistake for an instant what he meant by the word "surprised." He was saying, loud and clear, that he was shocked to find her in a concierge's lodge. Come, come, was that really her place?

"I hope you're well, my dear Madame?"

"I thank you."

"Monsieur the principal is well?"

"Very well, thanks."

"I'll see him soon. And by the way, I have a piece of good news to announce—the general is well again. He'll be attending this afternoon, I just received official confirmation. The gods are with us," he said, his voice smooth. And he bowed again.

"The general has been ill?"

"A congestion, Madame, a terrible congestion, which sometimes leaves him bedridden. It's too cruel."

"Poor general," said Madame Marchandeau.

"Oh we were all on edge! It would have been such a letdown for Madame Faurel, you see. She was so hoping to be decorated by the general's own hands. But now we're out of danger." He gave a little laugh that was silken, elegant, and rubbed his hands.

The concierge's wife watched this scene, her two hands folded on the iron, her back hunched. She exchanged a look with her daughter, who had stopped in a corner, and was holding the baby against her as if someone were threatening to steal it. She wasn't smiling anymore.

"And how are you holding up, my brave little friend?" said Nabucet, as if he'd only just noticed Georges's presence. He'd been standing right in front of the wheelchair the whole time.

"Bad," said Georges.

Nabucet looked uncomfortable.

"Is that so?" he said, turning first to Madame Marchandeau and then to the boy's mother. He didn't dare look at the girl.

"Did you expect him to sing," said the mother, "the way he is?" The words had come out before she could stop herself. But even so, when it came down to it . . . "Poor boy." That Nabucet, he should have just left him alone, not mocked him right under his nose with his talk of decorations and generals!

"But Madame, I understand, I understand! We're not asking anyone for the impossible—" It was clear in his eyes that the concierge's wife would pay dearly for her violent remark one of these days. "It's not a question of singing, it's a question of beating the blues, there," he said making an elegant gesture like a light benediction, "You've got a touch of the blues, haven't you, dear boy?" He put a hand on his shoulder.

"More than a touch."

"Listen—why are you so down in the dumps?"

"Leave him be, Monsieur Nabucet," said Madame Marchandeau. This horrible scene was beyond her. She made a movement to take his hand from the boy's shoulder. Nabucet saw and removed it himself. "This boy has no reason to rejoice, but he's a very good kid, isn't that right, Georges? He's doing everything he can, I promise you. And so are we," she added, almost under her breath.

"If I may?"

Oh! Why did he insist?

"A famous philosopher—Monsieur Merlin must know him—a great philosopher once said that all sadness is a diminishment of the self.[5] And so, my dear young man, you mustn't..."

"Two legs gone, that's also a diminishment."

"He's reasoning!" cried Nabucet, "A headstrong lad, you see. What a rascal," he said, bursting into a flabby, spineless laugh, as if all of it had been nothing but a joke. "It's reasonable to...reason," he replied, turning serious. "It's fine, it's even very fine. But remember one thing: life is internal. In-ter-nal..." Making a quick pivot, almost a pirouette, he turned on the girl and cried, "What a magnificent baby!"

She had no time to recoil. What a horrible face he had—watery eyes, colorless, dull skin, covered in frizzy hairs, gray teeth, a big, quivering nose veined with blue. He tilted his head towards his shoulder, like a virtuoso with his violin, and smiled. But his eyes were defiant.

"What a lovely child."

"He's sleeping, sir."

"Oh, have no fear..." with a trembling, almost involuntary gesture, he slipped his hand between the little baby's body and the girl's breast. She went pale, blushed, her eyes widened—he was still smiling.

"Leave me alone!" she said, jumping back.

"Little wildcat..." The word had escaped him. He was definitely going to have to get a handle on himself—wasn't it just last week he'd been slapped by a brat of fifteen?

"I love babies," he said (Nabucet never lost his composure for long). He bowed to Madame Marchandeau—"My respects, Madame."

She couldn't avoid extending her hand.

He nodded right and left, pirouetting as he imagined the marquises of old would have done, and hurried out.

"Just because we're only concierges!" the girl murmured with angry tears in her eyes. Madame Marchandeau was thinking it was a blessing he hadn't asked about Pierre...

The mother went back to her work with a sigh.

Nabucet left the lodge, scarlet-faced. A young man running across the corridor almost bumped into him and didn't apologize. He was one of his old students too, who had become a monitor, a scholarship case—a boy who should at least provide a model of decorum! In his haste, the young man had dropped a book and hadn't even noticed. Nabucet picked it up, smiling. "Monsieur Montfort!"

He whirled around.

"Your book, my dear Francis," said Nabucet, tipping his hat.

Montfort hadn't yet taken off his own. He came forward, clearly quite frustrated, a sign which Nabucet deliberately misinterpreted, for instead of giving him back his book, he took his outstretched hand and shook it vigorously. "All's well with you?"

"Yes, thank you, sir." With visible effort, he added, "And you?"

Nabucet smiled. "Oh very well," he said. "It's very kind of you, my dear boy..."

He didn't let go of Montfort's hand, and smiling all the while, his head tilted, he examined the strange monitor's outfit with invisible irony. It was so silly to dress this way! Why those boots? He wasn't going riding. Why that bowler hat? It was grotesque to see that hat on the head of an adolescent. It was an old one, worn out along the edges, clearly too big, and Montfort wore it on an angle, so that it didn't fall into his eyes. But big as it was, it still left an abundance of curly black hair showing. As for the pockets of his jacket, they were full of books, and he had yet more under his arms. A real bohemian!

"You seem quite rushed, my dear Francis?"

"It's true, sir."

"Don't you have a minute," said Nabucet, looking into his eyes, "couldn't you *grant* me a minute? Yes? I need to tell you..."

He lead him out into the Honor Court, a vast square that for the moment was gray and empty, surrounded by columns supporting the semicircular arches of the galleries. There, he finally dropped his hand. "You're aware, of course, of all the affection we have for you, aren't you? Well then, I was with the principal yesterday and ... your name was mentioned. You understand?"

"Perfectly, sir."

"The principal is an exceptionally tolerant person. He's a good man. I'm not saying he's too good, you hear, I'm not saying he's weak. Far from it! But in these times, I believe, and he does too, that ... energy is vital. Isn't that so?"

"Of course."

Nabucet steepled his fingers as he spoke.

"I believe—and this is an unofficial notice I'm giving you, my dear Francis—I believe he intends to call you into his office today."

"Fine."

"Don't say *fine* in that insolent tone. The principal and I myself, and everyone here, we only have your best interests in mind, whatever you might think. For whatever reason Monsieur Marchandeau might want to call you into his office—and I don't know, you understand— but I'm certain, you take my meaning, absolutely certain, that he has a great affection for you. Really so much. He takes you for a star, an ace, as they say these days." He put a hand on Montfort's shoulder and paused: "Promise me that whatever happens, you'll strive to be worthy of that affection?"

"But Monsieur Nabucet, I have no idea what it could be about."

"Is that so?"

"Surely not a fault with my work, in any case. I'm very exacting with my work." Montfort was proud.

"A certain flippancy of dress ..."

"I make sixty francs a month, Monsieur." Could he not, finally, leave him the fuck alone, this ... parson?

Nabucet exclaimed, "You see that! You're a bit headstrong! Hmm, my dear Francis, allow me, permit your old teacher—yes, old, I'll have a head of white hair soon—I'm saying, permit your old schoolmaster who, once again, cares for you very much, allow him to give you a piece of good advice: don't go up against authority. You'll be broken.

Oh, oh!" he said, throwing his head back, "I know what you're think-ing. I've been your age, I understand your rebellions, they're so natu-ral! But they're only paper tigers, my boy, flimsy paper. Come, you'll come round like I did, and so, if I can revise your memory a little, you'll say to yourself, 'That Nabucet wasn't all wrong. He knows how the world works.' And then, see here, just see here, at a time like this, mustn't each man think only of his duty? Go on, don't be late. We'll see each other again and return to this debate. It's my mission to follow my students long after they've left my class. Go on! Learn how to live in the real world. Don't be too much of a . . . poet." He shook his hand.

"My book?"

"Oh, excuse me . . ."

The whole time they'd been talking, Nabucet had kept the book under his armpit. Perhaps he hoped Francis would forget to reclaim it? He handed it back, glancing at the title. "Excuse my meddling, my dear boy. Frankly, it wasn't on purpose . . . That's a very controver-sial book, isn't it?"

"Thank you, sir." said Francis, taking back the book.

"*Above the Battle*,"[6] said Nabucet, shaking his head, "I wonder what he means by that—really!" And he watched Francis who hurried away, settling his bowler hat on his overabundant hair as best he could—an operation which never succeeded on the first try. "Ideal-ist!" he muttered with contempt.

If he'd been in the principal's place, he wouldn't have tiptoed around. He would have made this long-haired romantic dress more appropriately, in a way that better suited his position; he would have forbidden him to spread his absurd ideas, to bring books into the school that were as subversive as that outrageous, poorly conceived, and poorly written volume by the despicable Romain Rolland. And if he'd had to, he would have tossed out this . . . poet, if that had been the simplest solution. This was the case he'd made to the principal the day before, remarking that if the principal wasn't careful, he might get into a scrape with this undesirable. But the principal was such a weak man, so hard to persuade, and lately so sad! It was difficult to watch. He wasn't up to his job, he had to admit it. A man who allowed his wife to spend whole hours a day at the bedside of a wounded man, that was permissible, but in a concierge's lodge, that was doubtful, it was really unacceptable—it lacked dignity. He should have had the tact to make his wife understand it wasn't her place. If she had so much charity to dispense, there were organizations, weren't there! She could certainly work with one of them. But she didn't visit anyone else. As for that loose cannon, the poet, clearly the principal's duty should have been to protect himself against juvenile follies that would lead where? Nowhere. To starvation. One of Nabucet's students had become a poet, a writer—no need to ask where that ambition led! And what happened to him? Nabucet had run into him one day in Paris on the boulevard Saint-Michel. *In rags*, wearing shoes *run down at the heels*. He told that story as often as possible to his current students, to warn them, to give them a taste of "real life," to press them into graduating with honors. Because the diploma opened doors, while poetry closed them. That was his view. But the principal seemed uninterested in everything. Oh sure, he hadn't heard from his son in a while, that was a pain, but really, he wasn't the only one.

SINCE the ballroom had been turned into a hospital ward, they planned to decorate Madame Faurel in the library. Everything was ready for the ceremony. Monsieur Bourcier, the dean, who had the apartment adjoining the library, had given the organizers the use of one of his rooms for the buffet. The room was generally unoccupied, and they had hastily decorated it with flags and brought up chairs and tables. The bursar had supplied the tablecloths, the cups for hot chocolate, the champagne glasses.

At that moment, Noël and a young Alsatian cook named Werner were setting out the pastries that had just arrived from the best shop in town.

Werner was a good-looking boy of twenty-five, a sleepy blond with sentimental blue eyes. Detained in an internment camp at the start of the war, he had just been assigned, on account of his good conduct and talents, to the makeshift hospital at the school, and this made him wild with happiness.

"That's it, I'm fed up with the adjutant. When he was drunk, he was yelling at everybody. Yes. He broke up all the groups of people who were just strolling in the courtyard, quiet as you please."

Noël dried the glasses.

Werner was telling him that once, there was a huge party at the camp, for New Year's. "Oh, that party makes this one for Madame Faurel look tiny. Just think, Monsieur Noël, they put on a little one-act operetta for the party, yes, which people loved. And a concert afterwards. Yes. And I made seven hundred and fifty little doughnuts with jam that sold right away, by arrangement with Monsieur Basquin and the canteen manager. At eleven forty-five, someone made a speech that ended on the stroke of midnight with cries of 'Vive la liberté!' And, Monsieur Noël, I myself got to sound the twelve blasts for midnight on the officer's bugle while at the same time a candlelit procession entered the room, lead by an old woman with a lantern for 1914, so the candle wasn't lit, and a second woman whose candle was lit, for 1915. A beautiful party, Monsieur Noël. I wrote every detail down in my journal. But then came a miserable time."

"You're one of the lucky ones," said Noël, thinking of his own unhappy invalid. "You've been spared. Better to be stuck in the camp and alive. You still have your parents?"

"Yes."

Noël sighed. He was kind, honest, this young cook. He didn't have to do anything but stay calm, do what he was told, wait like that until the war ended. His parents would get him back in one piece. Not so with his own poor son . . .

And to be unable to talk about it, do anything about it, to have to always accept it. He was still supposed to be happy, since they'd only cut off both legs. Oh! Those Nabucets had played their cards too well. They did whatever they wanted with him, and he said nothing, happy to have a crumb of bread to share with his poor invalid boy! *If only I hadn't left the farm to become a concierge!*

It was Faurel who had gotten him this job. Noël had thought he was right to take it. Working the land was running him down, and his wife had encouraged him to accept, looking at it only in terms of profit. But what a swindle! They could barely make ends meet, not to mention the humiliation. Before Georges had been wounded, Noël had dreamed of returning to farming one day. He wasn't too old to go back to working in the fields, and with the help of his wife, his daughter, his son, he could have brought up his youngest child properly, made a man of him. Too late now. He'd be a servant till the end of his days.

Nabucet entered unannounced. His galoshes gave him the great advantage of muffling the sound of his footsteps. *If he overheard us,* thought Noël, *we'll each pay dearly for those comments.* It was possible

Nabucet had been listening from behind the door. Noël knew that Nabucet had a habit of doing that, and once or twice he'd surprised him at it.

"Good day, sir," he said. He had to say it first.

"Good day, sir," said Werner.

"Hello, hello," Nabucet replied—he started taking off his gloves—"all goes well?"

"Yes, sir."

"I see that the pastries have arrived. Good."

Werner blushed to the tips of his ears. This Monsieur Nabucet, did he know the exact number of cakes...was he going to count them? He bent over the plates, sniffing the merchandise, moving slowly from one table to the other, letting the silence and the uneasiness grow like an examiner in the middle of a class.

"Very good," he said, "everything is in order. We need napkins?"

"Fine, sir."

"Ask for napkins from the steward. You may leave us, Werner. I think we won't need you again until this afternoon, and you'll be more useful assisting in the hospital kitchens. Go on."

"Yes, sir."

"You, Noël, follow me. We'll go into the other room." He went out, slapping his gloves against his palm. Noël followed. Two steps in the hall, a double door, and they were in the library.

"Nothing amiss here either?"

"I don't think so, sir."

"We'll see about that." Nabucet gave the room a circular glance, wrinkling his forehead and murmuring "fine...fine...that's all right... Say, Noël?"

"Yes, sir."

"For starters, you can open those windows."

Noël opened the windows.

"Very good. Now go fetch me some flowers and bring them to the sideboard, that's all. I told you I'd arrange them on the tables myself. Then, once you've brought me the flowers, chat with the steward about finding me some firewood. I need a nice basket of logs here. You'll make a big wood fire in this fireplace. We won't light it till the afternoon. Understood?"

"Yes, sir."

"And now go. I need to be alone. When you've brought the flowers, just knock on that door; I'll know it's you."

"Fine, sir." Noël went out. Flowers! Where would he find any? And firewood? If there wasn't any cut, he'd have to busy himself with splitting some. The boys had better things to do than get ready for this party.

He rushed downstairs.

Nabucet strolled around the room, taking little steps and smiling. Once again, he congratulated himself that the usual ballroom hadn't been available. The library was much better, and the combination presented many advantages that gave him great pleasure. First of all, this library, though it was spacious, wasn't big enough to make it "logistically possible" to invite the wounded themselves to see their benefactress decorated. And so he had easily eliminated a group that, all things considered, would be happier elsewhere, in the cafeteria, obviously, where they would throw something together (*they'll be in their element and so will we*). Another advantage: the ceremony, in such a setting, naturally took on the air of an exclusive reception and, since it was Nabucet who played the host's role, he could, with little expense, give the impression that he was personally receiving the best of society. What he would have wished for in his dreams was of course something more sumptuous, a cascade of parlors, their parquet floors polished like mirrors, and footmen everywhere, like Swiss guards in white stockings and brass buttons, offering refreshments—luxury cigarettes, cigars fit for princes, etc. There would have been a profusion of flowers, and invisible musicians playing enchantress melodies, and everything would have stretched out until the evening, which would take place in a garden. This would have been his greatest triumph, definitively cementing his reputation as an organizer of charming parties. But that would come, perhaps. There was no need to give up hope. All things come to those who wait. Help yourself, and heaven helps you. And as everyone knows, you don't need hope to get started, or success to persevere. All the same, Nabucet had succeeded brilliantly. He had known how to make the absolute most of this library. This tall, empty room, so exceptionally pathetic with its white marble fireplace and hundreds of books with identical black bindings—he had known how to make it into what he called a "candy box." All he'd needed was free rein. It had taken a huge amount of work. Noël had sweat blood and water to get rid of the dust that had coated everything in this solemn and solemnly respected place—no one ever set foot in here—and he had scoured the fireplace and made sure that it functioned well. Yes, of course Nabucet offered his guests the luxury of a wood fire in the back of the hearth, that crackling wood fire, so poetic and cheerful to look at, so nice to be near, made for dreaming and finding yourself among friends. It seemed like nothing, really, this little idea of a fire, and so it was a delicacy of detail! He was sure the general would appreciate his effort, and the deputy, and the deputy's wife, everyone would. So he had set up a wood fire, as you would for travelers coming a long way by coach. Nabucet waved his hands gently and kept smiling as he walked around the room. He was delighted with his undertaking. The flowers were the perfect thing to decorate the space. He had the hanging chandelier covered with them, and it now resembled a huge bouquet, held upside-down by an invisible hand; he'd stuck them in the curtains too, the nice way believers did on Corpus-Christi Day, when they spread their conjugal bedding in the street for the procession to bless. He had garlands made and thrown about the library, draped every which way over the Greek busts he'd had brought from the art room. Even the art teacher, that fat, sullen Monsieur Pullier—who for more than twenty years had been telling everyone at the Café Machin about his hundreds of successes when he was in art school, when he thought he was a rising star—this big cockroach had given him a hand and drawn a magnificent life-sized pastel, showing a young blue, white, and red Republic bent over the cradle of a newborn. The caption—a quatrain—was his own invention:

Sleep, great dead, in your long-trenched rows
Bless the stalks that grow anew
A golden crop that's never mowed
France shall always cradle you.

This decorative panel, a good source of encouragement, took up most of the wall above the fireplace. To the right, a Victory of Samothrace. To the left, a Minerva. Because one mustn't forget that this gathering was taking place not only in an atmosphere of refined patriotism (that was obvious) but also of culture. Ah! How well things had come together and how the whims of chance—others, less philosophically minded, would have said the will of the Lord—were full of precious teachings and thought-provoking encounters! Wasn't it just amazing, if you thought about it even a little, that this presentation of the Legion of Honor, which couldn't be held in the ballroom, was instead taking place in the library—in a place of culture and civilization, as a church was a place of God? You had to be quite sensitive to understand that, but if you did, if the chain of reasoning was even a little bit accessible to you, in short, if you knew how to follow a thought, what could you but conclude? There, where unsophisticated people would only see coincidence, Nabucet found a sign. And in truth, the heroic Madame Faurel had risked her life to care for contagious patients, but why had she done it? What was the point? He would say in his speech this afternoon that the triumph of culture was the point.

If Madame Faurel had agreed to care for typhoid patients, and the poilus themselves had accepted disease and death, it was because there was something to preserve and hand down to future generations living in the era of prosperity which would follow the war—in sum, so that our children and grandchildren could continue in material abundance, which was necessary, as Saint Thomas said, for the practice of virtue—so they could continue to read Boileau as their grandfathers had, and to learn by heart Racine's epistle on Phèdre's failure. He would know how to make all that felt in his speech. And all he said on the subject would be even clearer in such a well-chosen place.

He walked around the Venus de Milo and made a scholarly allusion to Paul de Saint-Victor's famous page that he'd assigned his students to memorize all these years. "Blessed is the Greek peasant..." Since the others—with the exception of Cripure—wouldn't know who Paul de Saint-Victor was, they'd be impressed by Nabucet's erudition, an advantage not to be overlooked. He would refer to the *Prayer on the Acropolis* as well, and everyone would be struck by his elegant way of expressing the role Madame Faurel had played in the epic battle between "our luminous culture" and the dark intelligence of the Germans. Everything would be in perfect harmony. Synchronized. It was to demonstrate, in his role as apostle, this luminous genius, that he'd had all the plaster statues brought down from the art room and placed in the four corners of the library. Those perfect torsos— he would discretely allude to them too, he would mention the Greek "sense of proportion"; he would speak on Apollo, the dancers... He'd even mention their philosophers. Since it was unavoidable, for Christ's sake, that Cripure would be at the ceremony, he'd had a blackened, leprous bust of Socrates brought down from the attic so Cripure could see the resemblance. The ripples of a flag brushed Socrates's shoulders. Who could doubt, standing before this little scene, the happy effect flags produced in a library. Nabucet had worried for a moment about the success of that important part of his décor. In a room that was so closed and gloomy, there was a chance the flags would have made an undesirable impression. But quite the opposite was true. Everything depended, he thought again, on the taste with which you arranged things, and the experience had proved that the allied colors blended in a most harmonious fashion with the books and the Greek plaster casts. The four walls covered with books also had flags, but they had taken care not to tangle the poles with the banners. Instead, the flagstaffs were invisibly anchored behind the books, and the flags themselves were pinned together all around the walls like a vast garland which was also stuck with flowers.

Finally, in huge letters on a calico band over the door, was a phrase taken from a recent speech by Poincaré, affirming yet again that this war was the Just War. For one last examination of the room before letting go, Nabucet sat in the armchair the general would soon occupy, casting his eyes all around, stroking his beard, always smiling.

Someone at the door: "knock, knock, knock..."

Without moving from his perch, Nabucet asked, "Is that you, Noël? Did you find some flowers?"

"Yes, sir. Roses, sir. The steward had to cut them from the greenhouse, sir. They were the last ones."

The steward! Another one who didn't dare refuse him anything.

"You've put them on the sideboard?"

"Yes, sir."

"Good." He didn't say anything else. He knew that Noël was behind the door, waiting for permission to leave. It wasn't the first time he'd played this game with the concierge. And Noël knew better than to open the door instead of waiting.

"May I go, sir?"

"One moment." He smiled to himself, pretending to reflect and consider. "The firewood?"

"Yes, sir. I'd thought of that. I'll have to chop some logs, sir, then split them."

"Well then, Noël, hurry up! You'd best be a good logger! But hurry, hurry. We don't have any time to lose."

"Very well, sir..."

Nabucet heard the heavy, tired steps of the concierge fading as he headed down the stairs.

> "...go see if the rose
> which just this morning disclosed
> her purple robe to the sun..."

Nabucet murmured these lines to himself as he walked over to the sideboard, where he found a magnificent bouquet of roses. The steward had bled for these. He would make a special visit to thank him.

But wait! He froze, a rose between his fingers. There was an argument underway in the dean's rooms.

He could hear violent shouts coming through the partition. He put the roses on the table, ran on tiptoe to the door, which he locked, and then he returned to the partition as quietly as he could, pressed his ear to it, and didn't move.

THE WHOLE disagreement seemed to be about whether Lucien, Monsieur Bourcier's son, an ex-infantry lieutenant, would consent to don his uniform for that afternoon's party in honor of Madame Faurel. The uniform question, which no one had thought of, had popped up like a jack-in-the-box, and they were all caught off guard by the sudden importance it had assumed. In a few moments, the quarrel had taken a harsh, almost violent turn, revealing to all of them just how deeply they were divided. It had been brewing for a long time, and the occasion had finally presented itself. Anger is an accident.

Several of them, the two men especially, would have preferred to avoid that accident. They didn't necessarily need to say what they thought about each other. But the women—the mother and sister— were less careful.

On the topic of the uniform, the women deployed great passion, full of pacing away and turning back, of wild gestures, of pleading, convincing, and prayers. They hadn't yet resorted to tears, but those were clearly on the way.

Lucien was unmoved. The question of putting on his uniform—for one last time, they incessantly shouted in his ear—was less important to him since, as they had neglected to learn, he'd never had any intention of going to this party, in civilian clothes or otherwise. He hadn't thought to say so in the first moments of the argument—he'd let himself be taken over by surprise and rising anger—but now he was calmer, he regained his stoic attitude, seeing the comedy in all of it. But he would have liked to avoid hurting them.

The scene was taking place in Lucien's own room, which Madame Bourcier had just entered, delicately carrying the infamous uniform in her arms, fresh from the ironing board—a handsome dress uniform destined to make an impression and attract the eyes of everyone, especially the ladies. But he hadn't seemed to react with joy at the sight. More like disgust. Madame Bourcier found her son ready to go out, wearing rough traveling clothes—a gray suit, warm and comfortable but inelegant, that he'd ordered a few days ago in preparation for his travels. Of course, since he had been demobilized and was going to England, she understood that he'd stopped wearing his uniform, but he very well could today of all days, considering that it was the Legion of Honor ceremony for Madame Faurel and that he was leaving for England in the morning, he certainly could have done something so simple to please his mother. He wasn't thinking of coming to the party in those clothes, was he? It would be indecent. It would seem like an insult to everyone. Why wouldn't he put on his uniform? She couldn't accept or understand it.

So the scene had started, with Lucien's astonished face at seeing his mother appear with the uniform, and with his question "why are you bringing me that?" She had carefully laid it out on the bed. The maid followed, bringing the cap and gloves. He expected to see his father appear with the sword and his sister with the boots. But no. Not yet. The maid relieved herself of the gloves and hat, not by placing them on the bed, but by handing them to Madame Bourcier who didn't want to leave the preparations to anyone else's care. She savored getting ready almost as much as the gatherings themselves. Nothing pleased her more than a handsome tailcoat or evening jacket hung on the back of a chair, polished shoes at its foot, a white, placket-front shirt on the seat, and on the shirt, a beautiful cravat, and a top hat if possible. She found a particular beauty in these things, like a well-set table, or a pastry made in the best tradition. All the more reason she should have been sensitive to the uniform laid out on Lucien's bed—it hadn't even crossed her mind that this was the way officers' uniforms were laid out on their coffins.

When they had coffins.

Once the maid left, Lucien, who had finished arranging some papers on his table, got up and came over to his mother limping, a limp from a bullet in the knee that would never go away. But this injury wasn't the one that had changed him. The hit to the lung had been much more serious—it was a miracle he'd escaped. After months in the hospital, he was stronger again, strong enough anyway to carry out the plan he had slowly developed while he was bedridden. The limp aside, he had the air of a totally sound and healthy man. On the short side, with broad shoulders, his whole person radiated the mastery and gentleness particular to men who inhabit a worldview of their own, whether it is given or permanently won. His face was still very youthful—Lucien wasn't yet twenty-five—and though there was no question of finding a wrinkle, there was still something around his eyes that didn't belong to youth or age: subtle traces guessed at rather than perceived, accumulations of sorrow and wisdom.

Right then, he knew exactly what he wasn't going to do, and he would say so. "Look, Maman," he said, laying an affectionate hand on her shoulder, "what does it really matter to you, in the end?" He gave a sweet smile.

His father, Monsieur Bourcier, a heavy, sullen man, and his younger sister Marthe, a dry, thirsty, ungrateful character, had been standing behind the door from the beginning of the scene, not really sure what it was about. They were a bit too late to get a sense of the heated exchange between mother and son, but as soon as they learned Lucien wouldn't wear his uniform, they had protested, vigorously taking up Madame Bourcier's cause. Marthe accused Lucien of not knowing "how to please," and the father scolded his son for being too independent, which was to say, uncharitable. Lucien hadn't responded to that, except to shake his head a little, which seemed to indicate that he didn't put much stock in that kind of comment. The father paced the room, his hands at his back, thinking up new arguments, which was his usual strategy in household spats. But why bang his head against the wall! Wasn't he a living example? Had he gone through such antics this morning to put on his nice starched shirt, his tailcoat, to knot his white cravat around his apoplectic neck? Of course not, he had done it with pleasure. Marthe stayed by her mother, who didn't give an inch when Lucien repeated, "in the end, Maman?"

And he looked for her glance, ready to laugh it off if she'd only let him.

She was bitter: "Don't make fun of me."

He walked away, still limping. But he didn't smile. Once again he'd proved how capable his mother was of crushing all good will and smiles. "Too bad," he muttered.

"Come now," his father said, "surely you have a reason?" Planted in front of his son, his hands still at his back, he braced his legs, pressing his weight to the floor, becoming one with it like a piece of furniture.

What could he say?

"No answer?" said his father.

"He's pigheaded," said the girl.

A silence.

"Come now, what does this mean, not speaking?"

Lucien thought and finally admitted, "In any case, I'm not going to this ceremony."

"What did you say?"

Lucien didn't repeat it.

"Are you serious?" his mother asked.

"Oh, let him go!" said Marthe. "He's already about to. All this, it's against us."

Lucien gave Marthe a look that was devoid of tenderness. *Here's another one who knows exactly what she's doing*, he thought. But it would be better if she kept her mouth shut sometimes. He might be willing to make an effort to spare his mother and father, but he wasn't at all sure he'd do the same for Marthe. If she pushed him, he'd tell her exactly what he thought.

"Don't you think," said Lucien, "that it's horrible to fight the day before I have to leave for a long time?" He was thinking *probably forever*, but he didn't say that.

Monsieur and Madame Bourcier looked at each other in astonishment. What was this new tone in their son's voice?

"Faker!" said Marthe.

He pretended he hadn't heard and repeated, "Listen . . . don't you think it's horrible?"

His father had taken on the heavy, imposing look he used for lecturing his students. There was something primitive, animal in him, something curiously unintelligent, that made even the simplest words seem as if they came with difficulty. The man couldn't even write a letter without drafting it ten times.

"Horrible . . . you dare use that word!"

"But you don't have an answer?"

The mother interfered. "This isn't the point, Lucien. It's not about fighting. Why can't you do me the favor of . . ."

"Surrendering," Marthe interrupted.

"Quiet!" said the mother. "I beg you to be quiet. That wasn't at all what I was going to say."

"Oh I've had enough of this!" Marthe cried. She was ready to stomp her feet and claw at him if need be. Clawing might have done her some good.

"Have you thought of the scandal this will create?" said his mother. "Everyone's counting on you. And you refuse to show up! Is that it, is that really what you said? You refuse? Did he really say that, Papa?"

His father shrugged. "Evidently!"

"Listen," said Lucien, "there's not the slightest chance you'll convince me to change my mind. Since that's the case, wouldn't it be better to forget it . . . and talk about something else?"

This time the girl really did stamp her foot. "Oh, oh, oh!"

"Is that your final word?" said his mother.

"You're sticking to it, eh?" said Monsieur Bourcier.

Lucien was leaning on the table, hands in his pockets, his shoulders a little slumped, and he looked at them one after the other. Impossible.

They had arrived at a lag in the scene, not the breaking point, but a time of rest and recuperation after the first skirmishes, when all parties involved in the conflict still thought they could turn it their way. But it was already too late. What had started the fight was forgotten. No one gave any more thought to the uniform stretched out on the bed like a piece of evidence, but for another trial. Since Lucien had so firmly expressed his determination, there was nothing left to say. There was nothing to do but look elsewhere for things to feed the fire that was burning, and there was fuel for each of them, stored up in abundant reserve over the years. Enough to ignite a whole furnace. The trouble was that a phoenix always rose from the ashes—in bourgeois families, these bonfires never cleared the air. He knew this from long experience. When they'd said everything, they still never got to the bottom of it. Once they hurt in such subtle ways, these arguments never lost their venom. They could be reused again and again, equally painful the hundredth time as the first, and finally, as he'd seen so many times, they could kill with a slow poisoning. And that was what they called family life, the sweetness of the hearth and all that garbage! When you realized what a load of hypocrisy and wickedness their world rested on ... Because of course a scene like this one, so trivial, would be fought in the name of the noble things they pretended could justify it—in the name of Love, as the war was in the name of Justice. In less than a minute, Lucien knew, his mother would try to con him with sentiment, demand that he obey her, calling on his filial love, and if Lucien didn't give in, she'd simply say he was a bad son. His sister, once again, would pretend to be shocked that a brother she'd loved so much and done so much for (what? he wondered) could treat her with such "contempt." As for his father, he'd resort to his role as head of the family, but fortunately without being at all compelling, unless he called Lucien a guttersnipe, as he'd done not too long ago. But he'd get over that. He could only hope they'd stick to arguments of nobility, to which Lucien could turn a deaf ear. But if they spoke of family interests—it wasn't impossible—he felt he'd lose all patience.

Deputy Faurel would pull strings for the dean.

"You've really changed, Lucien," said Madame Bourcier, letting herself fall into a chair as if overcome.

Yes he had changed. What did they want him to do about it?

"You've become hard."

He nodded, without saying anything. She took it as agreement and said, "At least you'll admit it?"

"It's not that simple, Maman." He regretted answering. If he went along with her, all would be lost.

"You have no more respect."

He wanted to say that her point was invalid because how could he respect his mother for what he hated in other people?

His father and Marthe stood behind the chair where Madame Bourcier had collapsed, hands on her knees, wounded, and the way she pressed her neck into the back of the chair gave her horsey, chalky face, really her whole pose, the air of high-and-mighty victimhood. Tall and dressed in black from her neck to the tip of her toes, the rest of her was completely white—her hair, her cheeks, her lips, what you could see of her ears, and even her eyes, which were usually blue, but such a pale shade! Her hands, too, were white against the black silk of her dress. His father had put a hand on the back of her chair, looking very embarrassed. He gave every sign of wishing to be somewhere else, not having to intervene in this argument. But he couldn't abandon his wife.

The three of them made a perfect group for a portrait. But no one dreamed of laughing, not even Lucien, the only one who could have been capable of humor. If his father wished to be out of there, Marthe on the other hand was desperate to say her piece, and she took advantage of the silence that descended to assert that there was one true thing at the bottom of all this—Lucien didn't love them anymore.

"Once again, Marthe, I'm begging you to be quiet!" cried Madame Bourcier.

"Oh," said Lucien, "if that's what she wants ..." He was beginning to hit his limit.

"It's not your place to speak about these things," Madame Bourcier continued, without moving, to address Marthe, who was biting her lip. "If someone has the right to speak here, I imagine it's me. Your father and I. Yes, it's true, Lucien doesn't love us anymore. He's succumbed to influences that have pulled him away from us, he's ... against us," she said. And Lucien understood that she was about to go into one of her fits. He'd seen this phenomenon a hundred times, not just in his mother's case, but from many women who made scenes. Not only watched, but felt. Though Madame Bourcier hadn't made the slightest movement, not even a wiggle of her pinky finger, and even if her appearance was unchanged from a moment ago, he suddenly sensed emanating from her a subtle electricity which filled the room, rolling in waves, creating a very different state from the atmosphere of annoyance and anger they had already reached—a state of angst.

Was she aware of this disorienting power she had over people? If she sensed anything, it was only the signs of an impending breakdown, the long-awaited end to the scene. Madame Bourcier plunged into a new phase, a sleepwalker's reverie, saying the kinds of things people only dare to say in dreams, asserting with a total lack of pity or embarrassment everything she secretly thought about her son. He was a bad son, of course, and that accusation summed up all the others. But she described her grievances in detail, proving to have an exceptional memory, which became even sharper when she slipped into this emotional state. Her problems weren't just from that day, and the question of the uniform was just one bitterness thrown in with the others. She took up again what she called, in a calm voice, the cross of Lucien's early childhood. Even as a young boy there had been a thousand signs of his black heart. He hadn't been affectionate or obedient, wrapped up in himself, sullen, you would have thought she was treating him like a child martyr, but the exact opposite was true. And as he grew up his evil tendencies had only grown larger and more complicated. Heaven knew why she had loved him, coddled him, pampered him as if he were a prince's child. Everything he'd asked for, he'd been given, never refused him a pleasure, never denied money when he was a student. He had gone to the front, that was understood, he'd been wounded and taken for dead, but that was just doing his duty, and he wasn't the only one. He didn't need to take such pride in it, such a desire to bend other people to his will, which wasn't anything in the end but arrogance. And then she turned to the real grievance of the moment, which had nothing to do with the question of his uniform—that of his departure for England, which he said he wanted to visit, but he hadn't explained why. What was he going to do in London? They'd never thought there was anything for him in that city. He'd never studied English. He'd chosen philosophy, gotten his degree, a path he'd been led down by Monsieur Merlin, who he'd been to see again yesterday, she knew, and who had a despicable influence on him. She wished Lucien had never met him, that no one had ever met that teacher of disorder, that enemy of family and society who didn't believe in God or the devil and who spit evil around him like a tubercular man spits germs. A danger to the public. She forbade Lucien to see him again. But forbidden! What did forbidden mean to Lucien! She'd lost all power over him. He was leaving for England, which was to say—did he think she was so stupid?—that he was giving up his studies after all the sacrifices they'd made for him. Well then, he could go, he could get out!

All of this was issued in a mechanical tone, without the shadow of a gesture, the words coming out of her mouth one after the other like coins from a minting machine. The anxiety had reached its peak. Lucien hadn't lost his self-control, but he was unsettled, like his father and like Marthe, by a silent anxiety that was at once a violent desire to flee and a powerlessness to stop the flood of words in which so many lies slithered, that she could never bear to say, Lucien knew, except that she'd forget them entirely and immediately, as if they were dreams or hypnosis. It wasn't true that he'd been a bad child, it wasn't true that he ever wanted to make anyone think his mother was torturing him. She had to know that. The truth was that he'd been crushed like all the children, then again as a young man and a grownup, one of those whose life had been stolen in bits before they tried to take it wholesale. That's what he would have said if he'd thought for a second that he needed to justify himself or that his mother could have understood. But she couldn't, she never would. It was bad luck they were parting on bad terms, since with a different set of circumstances they could have parted amicably, sweetly led up to the moment of separation by the hand of hypocrisy. After all, that would have been better for her. She would have suffered less. He pitied her, believed she was truly unhappy. But what could he do for her? Nothing. The reasons she suffered were detestable, which didn't prevent Lucien's compassion or love for her. But he couldn't sacrifice anything to her, and certainly not the fate he had chosen. She had actually guessed! There was something clairvoyant about her, since, even though he'd said nothing, had spoken of his trip as a vacation, she knew he was leaving with another idea in mind, and in any case, he was giving up the illustrious career they'd prepared for him since childhood. No, in fact, he was not going to be a professor. He would leave the official philosophies there with that dress uniform that became him so well! And as for Cripure, who his mother thought was a teacher of disorder, she would have been totally surprised to learn that Lucien thought Cripure was one of them, and that the influences she lamented so bitterly came not from him but from a few comrades in arms whose names would have meant nothing to her—men who'd shown him his calling and his true self. During these reflections he'd been sorting the papers scattered over the table, the ones he'd been organizing when his mother entered. She took the gesture as a provocation, which didn't stop Lucien from continuing, with an appearance of total calm, torn as he was by stress and sadness. It was a terrifying spectacle—this old woman abandoned in her chair talking nonstop as though she were insane. Since the start of her speech, the two others had become shadows, dancing, grimacing, futile, wanting to cover their ears since they couldn't stop the harpy from screeching, circling her like two people possessed. There was nothing to do but wait and hope that this nervous breakdown would, in a great epileptic shout, bring an end to this general torture. But it was slow in coming.

When Lucien had finished sorting his papers, learning many new things about himself, most notably that he was a miser—seeing as he was taking several thousand francs with him—he took his suitcase, shoved everything in there, and pulled on his overcoat.

"Farewell," he said.

No one tried to stop him. His mother kept speaking. He went out, carrying his little suitcase. He didn't need much where he was going. *What a shame*, he thought, his steps limping down the corridor, *what a terrible shame.*

But he could either stay and die with them or refuse, get out, and work toward what would change everything, including this.

NABUCET leapt toward the door and opened it silently, slipping into the corridor like a shadow. He disappeared into the library. An instant later, he emerged, innocently finding himself nose to nose with the dean, red-faced and still feverish from the scene that had just taken place. But Nabucet didn't appear to notice. His hand outstretched, his head coquettishly tilted to one side, a wide smile behind his beard, he approached this large man, weighty and respectable, who smelled of tobacco, cheap cologne, shoe polish, and whose hand—what an admirable tool for slaps—was hairy as a monkey's paw.

"You're just the man I'm looking for," Nabucet chirped, who, though he was still holding the dean's hand, found a way to avoid his blank stare, the sad, resentful look in his protruding eyes, where the light lay like a reflection on stagnant water.

"Do you have a question for me?" His anger hadn't yet passed.

"No," said Nabucet, "Nothing in particular my friend, just your opinion on the set-up for the party."

"Oh?"

"Is this a bad moment?" said Nabucet, letting go of the dean's hand. He certainly was a brute. It would never have crossed Nabucet's mind to behave like that. Family quarrels were no excuse, by God. It was no fault of Nabucet's.

A feeble smile—the dean was making an admirable effort. "A bad moment? Not at all ... I was ... I myself was just going to ask you if I could see the arrangements."

So much the better. Since he had decided to save face, there was nothing more to say.

"Excuse me," said Nabucet, opening the library door. They went in, and Nabucet said, "Please, I want to know exactly what you think. I'm counting on it." He'd say that over and over this evening, to everyone. "Oh but before we start," he said, "I have good news for you—the gods are with us! The general has recovered."

The dean seemed impatient. "What general?" He was miles away. Fortunately, he remembered. "I didn't know the general was ill."

"Goodness!" cried Nabucet, "I did a good job of keeping it from you. *Cui bono*? You would have panicked, my friend, you would have worried that the party, without the general, would be totally ruined. I wanted to spare you that torment. And I was right, since the danger has passed. Having the general here is a huge, huge coup!"

The dean agreed, letting himself fall heavily into an armchair. He sighed.

"Are you … unwell?"

"No, no, not at all," the dean replied, tapping on both arms of the chair at once.

"Everyone in your family's all right, I hope? Madame Bourcier is well?"

"Why, yes, very well," said the dean, still tapping.

"And your charming … your exquisite young lady?"

"Very well, thanks."

"Lucien?"

The dean stopped tapping. His face twisted into a sort of quick groan. "Lucien's fine."

Nabucet easily hid a venomous look, and said in an innocent voice, "Lucien will be among us, won't he? We're counting on him."

The dean's answer made Nabucet gape with shock: "Yes."

This way, thought the dean, *he'll leave me alone.*

"Bravo," said Nabucet. "He'll be our best addition. A real wounded soldier. I thought he would be the one to pin the cross on Madame Faurel … if the general hadn't been able to come …"

But the dean had gotten up. He pulled his pince-nez, which he used like a handheld magnifier, from their holder. "Perfect... these flowers mixed in with the flags, that's perfect. These statues, perfect." And turning back to Nabucet, "all this is perfect, my friend."

"You think so?"

"Without a doubt. It's perfect."

"This... this pastel?"

"Ah, the pastel," said the dean, moving toward the fireplace. He looked for a long time at the art teacher's masterpiece.

"Perfect."

"You know who made it?"

"Who?" He let the hand holding the pince-nez drop.

"Monsieur Pullier."

"Ah? Monsieur Pullier? Oh, I didn't know. It's very good, it's perfect," he said, bringing his pince-nez back to eye level...

"And the statues?"

"Excellent idea."

"In conclusion, Monsieur Dean, you're in agreement with everything?"

"Well... everything is perfect, my friend."

"But didn't you read the banner?"

"Where?"

"Above the door."

He raised his nose, adjusted the pince-nez, and spelled out "... *The Just War*... It's perfect."

"A quote from Monsieur Poincaré."

"Oh! Perfect."

He walked around taking little steps, still looking through the pince-nez. "Say, my friend," he hesitated, "what about the Russian flags?"

Nabucet jumped slightly. "I'm sorry?"

"Nothing has changed, has it? Officially? We still use the eagles?" He slipped his finger over the glasses, turning them.

"But what are you saying!" cried Nabucet. "My goodness! You're not thinking we should hang the Maximalists'[7] flag in here?"

"Of course not," said the dean, chastened. "I didn't say that."

"Lenin's flag! That miserable red scrap! See, my dear friend, officially nothing has changed. Officially, we have to keep the eagles."

"Very well. Besides, it's obvious, and that's what I was saying... If it's a red flag," he continued, waving his arm vaguely...

"You doubt it?"

"Me?" He read the papers, of course. He wasn't that dumb. Who did he think he was talking to? "I know—"

But Nabucet interrupted him: "Because," he said, pointing his index finger, "if you had any suspicions in the slightest, there's someone here who could tell you all about it."

Nabucet's attitude, the ambiguous way he said it, the look that accompanied these words—the dean's ears pricked up.

"Here?"

"Even here."

"In this institution?" Where was all this going?

Nabucet spread his arms, lifted his palms—a priest's gesture, which made his manner of half closing his eyes even more emphatic—and said with a sigh, "I didn't want to believe it either. But I had to pay attention to the evidence. *Amicus Plato sed magis amica veritas.*"

"But really, what do you mean? That someone's writing defeatist propaganda here?"

"Yes."

"Who?"

"Since you ask," replied Nabucet, "I think it's time I told you that it's Francis Montfort."

"Are you kidding?" said the dean, bowled over. He knew Montfort was a weirdo, but to go so far as to call him defeatist?

"He's a problem," Nabucet continued. "He spends his time writing so-called revolutionary poems that are about nothing. But the serious part is that he reads them to the students."

"You don't say." The dean turned purple. Things were definitely going poorly.

"Would I lie?"

"And I wasn't informed!" cried the dean, raising his arms to the sky. "That's unthinkable! Unthinkable!"

Nabucet poured some salt in the wound. "By all means," he said. "Even more so because it's a source—I'd almost say—of scandal."

"But see here," exclaimed Monsieur Bourcier, "that goes without saying. If he truly read the students defeatist poems..."

"Their parents would have a right to complain."

"That's clear as day."

"As for the rest," said Nabucet, pulling a paper folded in four out of his pocket, "read this."

"What is it?"

"Read, read! That's the damning evidence."

The dean took the paper, adjusted his pince-nez and read:

"Comrade, soldier, brother
Hear the bugle call!
Rise, soldier, rise, RISE!
Take your gun and roll
YOUR cannon: and FIRE
On the REAL enemies.
Sever your ties
shackled like slaves
By your own hands
Around your Hercules neck
Or would you rather die AGAIN?
Again and again your blood on the field.
Your chest hacked open.
Your fist ripped off.
Your kidneys burned.
A clod of earth between your teeth,
With a cross of honor?
RISE! RISE! RISE!
Soldier, my brother,
That's the wake-up call ringing
FOR YOU. FOR US ALL.

"I throw up my hands," sighed the dean, handing the poem back to Nabucet, who put it back in his wallet with the trembling gesture of a miser hoarding a bank note. "And he read that to the students?"

"Exactly."

"When?"

"Yesterday."

"Where?"

"In study hall."

"But my dear Nabucet, how did you come to have this paper?"

"Oh! Our glorious revolutionary is also a glorified blockhead. He leaves his masterpieces lying around. Others collect them. Masterpieces! The poor boy thinks he's talented! A new modernism! What a fool."

"We have to nip this in the bud," said the dean.

"I think so too. By the way, the principal has been informed."

"Oh yes?"

"Yes. I don't know how he found out . . . since yesterday, he was in the know. And I know he means to have a word with this young . . . idealist, maybe even today."

"Perfect," said the dean in a glacial voice. He was outraged. They acted without him, they hid things. Well, God knows, if they wanted things to work under this roof, they had better decide to act in agreement with him. "I'm going to go find . . ." He quickly stopped himself.

"What was that?" said Nabucet, all ears.

A huge burst of laughter shook a nearby classroom.

"My word," the dean muttered, "there's a real ruckus for you."

"Does Merlin have class this morning?"

"Yes, but later."

The laughter increased. And since Merlin didn't have class then, the ruckus could only be coming from the English teacher Philippon's room, or the old astronomy teacher, Monsieur Laplanche.

"That must be Philippon," said Nabucet. "Poor man! He can't control the class anymore."

"I'm going," said the dean. Everything really was heading toward anarchy.

AFTER Étienne left, Cripure threw himself on the sofa, in the grip of a fit of fury. In his rage, he chased off the little beasts, who were shocked to find him so brutal—he was usually so kind, so tender with them, capable of petting them for whole hours at a time and murmuring all kinds of sweet nothings in the pretty spaniel's ear, words he wouldn't and couldn't have said to any human. But even pretty Mireille hadn't been spared. She had gone, ears drooping, following the cortege of the others to the end of the garden, meditating on the passions of humans. Cripure rolled around on the couch, suppressing his cries with great difficulty, crazed with helplessness.

Who on earth could keep his sangfroid after learning that such a plot had been hatched against him, since he was neither a slave nor a tyrant—and no Socrates either—and that this murderous impulse hadn't come from jealousy or vengeance, and barely from hate? He was sweating and trembling at the thought of that fall—as surely fatal as dropping from the basket of a hot air balloon, or from the moon—which had been avoided by such a lucky coincidence. And yet, and yet! What better death could there be for him: killed, rejected in both soul and body, spat out, spit up by society in one giant gob of blood. A splendid death. To think that if, even in the instant it was occurring, he'd still been capable of a flash of consciousness, such a death would have seemed without a doubt—without a shadow of a doubt—like a compensation that was a thousand times too generous for all he had suffered in his life, the proof to end all proofs that this band of dunces . . . "But that's just it," he cried in his fury, getting up—Maïa was in her kitchen, and he spoke only to himself—"but that's just it, not a simple scheme, was it? But a scheme in the first degree. They had ringleaders . . . a ringleader: Nabucet, not a shadow of a doubt about that. Oh! That man!" And to be unable to speak, to be unable to tell anyone, not even Maïa. Since he had read so clearly in others' eyes that they took him (yes, Cripure!) for a poor sick man caught in a delusion of harassment.

Drunk with sorrow, his head in his hands, he began spinning around the office, crying "Maïa! Maïa!"

What? What did he want now? This comedy wasn't done yet? Couldn't she get a minute of peace, to finish working on his dressy clothes? "What? What's it now?" When he saw Maïa, his bout of rage took on a whole new life. He had cried, threatened, spoken of a faction—just what was that anyway?—determined to destroy him, of a black fist . . . Maïa hadn't lost any time. She took him solidly in her grip, and run along, there's a good man, let me help you get a move on. He wasn't such a loony as all that? A black fist? What was the point of going looking for gobbledygook like that? Go on! Get along my man . . . enough of that trash! And in less than ten minutes, faster than ever before, Cripure found himself washed, dressed from head to toe, brushed, polished, wrapped in his goatskin and sent on his way with marching orders, a prediction that the fresh air would set him straight, and a word of advice, repeated a thousand times, not to say all that nonsense if he ran into anyone. After a few steps, the air had its desired effect on him, in just the soothing way Maïa had predicted, and he wasn't ten minutes into the walk when he started to see the story in a completely different way. In the end, he'd perhaps been wrong to get carried away. That Nabucet was a cunning one, it was true, a real rogue, and they'd be decorating him one of these days too, but all the same, to think he was a criminal! Yes, perhaps he had been mistaken. It wasn't reasonable, wasn't wise. Nabucet must have other things on his mind besides bikes. He must be thinking of his theater company—what a good excuse to feel up the girls!—and the next productions he'd put on to benefit "our dear wounded." He must be thinking of Madame Faurel. The bastard! *And to think that I once wandered into his living room!* For hadn't he also hosted a salon in the years before the war? Of course, he hadn't waited for deputies' wives to decorate in order to exercise his zeal. Everyone in the town—Nabucet called it the city—who counted as literary, artistic, or even scientific characters met at his place every Friday from five to seven. Nabucet was trying to prove that Paris didn't have all the culture, he wanted—so he said!—to combat the dangerous centralization that would make all the provinces into poor relations, since they were just as capable, if not more capable than Parisians when it came to independent thought, and Cripure had heard that the motto of that bootlicker was: *Others over self.* It was enough to make you writhe, to make you die laughing ah, ha, ha! And this was supposed to be doing his part.

In fact, Nabucet had played one. Cripure felt the effects of that salon. Over a cup of tea, in winter, before a crackling wood fire, what "charming" gatherings! The school inspector had regaled them one evening with his theory of Spain, which he'd rushed through on his last vacation, alas! without having the chance to participate in the running of the bulls (*corrida*). Another evening, Doctor Blanc gave a whole lecture on the ways to prolong your life that was so convincing, it had seemed to everyone afterwards that living forever was, as the doctor had put it, only a matter of *technique.* Finally, one evening Nabucet had watched Cripure himself arrive. Awkward and timid, not even thinking to remove his goatskin, he sat defensively on a chair like a huge porcupine. What a victory, what a triumph for Nabucet to have brought this rebel to such a place! It was like he was laying down his arms. Cripure came of his own volition, uninvited, and, all things being equal, he could have easily had the pleasure of turning him away. Nabucet had considered it for a moment, entertained by the thought that such a perfect chance for revenge had arisen, and from whom? From the victim himself. But he had decided it was better to host this loony at least once, to let him show his true colors. Excellent strategy. Cripure had disappointed them all by speaking too excitedly about a foreign writer, a certain Ibsen he was totally obsessed with. Even then, as was the case these days, praising a foreigner like that had seemed inappropriate to them. It indicated feelings of hostility toward French culture. Why the hell should they have anything to do with the Swedes and all those other hacks? "Thank goodness," Nabucet had exclaimed, "we've got everything we need within our borders, and we've so far surpassed these barbarians who have nothing to teach us." But why argue? Wasn't it true that in literature, as in everything, these people were just dull copycats of France? Didn't the French always innovate and other people profited from those innovations? What! But really now. He'd had the bad grace, that Cripure, to talk about a certain Nietzsche—a German— which had made Monsieur Babinot's ears prick up, as it always did when anyone mentioned "those barbarians" in front of him. In short, Cripure, who had doubtless made his way there under a spell of ennui that was worse than usual, had been defeated in the bloodiest way possible under the watchful eye of Nabucet, who let Cripure dig himself in deeper and deeper. And he'd do the same thing at this party if he got the chance, thought Cripure, walking down the street.

With his little cloth hat sagging over his eye, his goatskin cape floating, his cane clutched like a sword, and the so painful effort he made with each step to pull, as though from sticky mud, his wide cripple's feet, Cripure had the air of a sleepy tightrope walker. His nearsightedness exacerbated the shocked look on his face, giving his movements the hesitant indecision of a drunk or someone playing blindman's bluff. He always seemed to be battling a gust of wind down the sidewalk, running his hand over the walls, the point of his beard like a spur, his cane whipping the air behind him as if to keep the invisible monsters on his heels at bay. His lips trembled like those reciting prayers, or even exorcisms. And beneath his elbow he held a black satchel, his old schoolboy satchel, which had become a teacher's briefcase, a precious object, which that morning held not only student papers and necessary books for his upcoming course, no not only those, but also the bonds he was going to take to the bank, and a pile of banknotes. Though Maïa had really made him move it, he'd managed to remember the precious satchel, packed last night it was true, and he hurried, wanting to pass by the bank before school. But try as he might, today wasn't the day he'd be spared the torture of hearing people walk up behind him, come close, and pass him by. If they came from far off they always passed him anyway, even the old men. Oh Christ! Maybe—since he'd have to leave the bikes alone now—he'd decide to buy a little car, an alibi on wheels. Hum...which could be stalled no doubt by similar tools. But the idea was tempting, provided of course that someone who knew about these things, Basquin for example, could check the engine beneath all its covering, and failing that—otherwise he'd let himself be fooled again like a poor sucker— he'd have to look into it. And in the meantime, he could afford to pay a cab, make an arrangement with the old coachman, Père Yves. He was the only one left in town. Père Yves could come drive him to school in the mornings. He'd really be playing the pasha then, would he? The tsar in his sled? Then what? Then at least he could stop fighting these streets—dear God!—these sleepy streets, breeding grounds for cloppers, factories for woodlice, the sight of which sometimes seized his heart like a bout of shame, which threw him into total panics he would wake from as if from a dream, but to real unhappiness. The grass grew here at its ease, as it did in ruins or prison courtyards; and no doubt the hearts of the people who lived behind these blind façades were also overgrown. Two men playing cards in silence behind a half-closed curtain. A street gray with rain, and at the end of that street, the furtive shadow of a louse. Somewhere, behind tight-shut blinds, the high voice of an older woman singing Gounod's "Ave Maria," her "young" daughter accompanying her on the piano, while in the kitchen next door you could hear the silverware falling piece by piece into the drawer as the housemaid polished it! It was enough, some evenings, to make him almost shiver with horror, almost weep before this forsaken squalor.

Oh, why couldn't he let it go! Break his chains! But for a long time he'd been beaten down, bound like the others. Very unlikely he'd ever have the guts to break away. Here, nothing encouraged happy, liberating bravery—everything pushed for a more desperate courage, or death coincided with the end of captivity. A finite world. Worn until threadbare. Ah! Yes, to escape! To shove off for the Dutch East Indies or elsewhere—*To study Your blue, o equatorial sea!*—to burn away the politeness of this so-called civilization, the Just War and all this reverential muck. To escape, to forget, to start over!

Others he admired had that courage. From one day to the next, they had broken the bonds of disgrace, had cut the mooring that tied them to a present, a past, a future, all equally dishonest. Free, they had placed their bets. As for him ... *But me? Does one escape? Java is far!* He'd never get farther than his little cottage by the sea, where all day he'd hunt, go shell fishing, browse for books if the fancy struck him. He swam alone, untroubled, but for how much longer? The water would be warm ... *Free man, forever you'll treasure the sea ...* Another year before retirement.

How many weeks until break? Before he could go roll in the sand and chase curlews, he had to put one foot in front of the other and dispense lies! And to top it all off, to really toss in the anchor, he had to give those little gentlemen their exams, poor robbed kids, shamefully duped. He'd lent his efforts to this comedy, he wasn't exempt. And he even made money from it. He didn't mean only the laughable sum of a few francs allotted for each corrected test—not ever a huge amount of money, but in the end, always good to have—but an even bigger bonus: he would, as usual, take a room at The Alcazar. Every year at the end of term, when he had to go to Sernen to administer a few days of oral exams, he would take a room at The Alcazar, which was to say, at the brothel. He'd write to the Madam in advance so they'd save him a room, and he'd spend the three or four days in the company of girls who, it was true, had a primordial advantage over other women and over so-called civilized society: that of being absolutely real. He didn't sleep with them much. What he liked was the atmosphere, the smell of the brothel, the *brotherly* rapport he had with the women who didn't think of mocking him or pitying him. Nowhere else was as restful as The Alcazar. For him, it was a Java within reach. A break from *their* way of life. Cripure openly took a cab there after the exam sessions, sometimes with one of his colleagues, another woodlousy philosophy teacher, who also, in his faraway hole, limped from one end of the year to the other and looked forward to the exam season in much the same way Cripure did.

Would that big brunette from last year still be there, the one who had really wanted him to explain what "true philosophy" was, the one he'd bought a glass of champagne for? If she was, he'd tell her about the bikes, just to see—

These streets. He stopped on the sidewalk, reciting this dictionary definition to himself: *Woodlouse. Vulgar noun applied indistinctly to isopod crustaceans of the family* oniscidea. *Almost always land-dwellers (in temperate climates), living at the edges of the ocean, under stones and in rock-crevices or in damp, dark places—caves, cellars, under moss and old bark. Many have the ability to roll into a ball at the slightest appearance of danger.*

Was there anything truer? More relevant? Since he'd paused there like that, the little hunchback and her yellow dog appeared at the end of the street. She skipped along, seeming to lead a procession of recruits who were singing arm in arm, a huge flag batting their heads—or were they chasing her? Cripure recoiled, hiding in a doorway. Oh what a sight!

The conscripts swarmed over the pavement, apparently harassing the hunchback and shouting from under their cockaded hats, flamboyantly ribboned—they also wore ribbons in their buttonholes. What he wouldn't give to stuff a spring of parsley up their noses! *Oh evil herd, you deserve your fate! All those young people who let themselves be fooled. How ugly and foolish humans are! Why didn't they revolt?* And burning with anger, Cripure left his doorway and came down the sidewalk as if to meet them. Alas! His pince-nez fell off. Shadows.

Lost, he waved his arms in the air, dropped his cane. The recruits passed him shouting wildly:

> "We will get them
> When we want them.
> Dirty Kraut
> You'll come out
> Of your stinkhole like a rat."

A gust. Cripure swung his arms, feeling around with an uncertain hand for those idiotic pince-nez that never did anything but fall off—the conscripts were already far away and he was still there, like a swimmer in great danger, stuck in an undertow. A hand grasped his—a hand that was at least as energetic as Maïa's had been earlier, and without a word he was back on the sidewalk, his pince-nez in one hand and his cane in the other. "Thank you, thank you!" he stammered, putting his pince-nez back on. There was no response, and to his amazement, Cripure, able to see again, discovered that his mute and mysterious savior was none other than the mayor himself, who had come gravedigging this way. The mayor clearly didn't have time to stop. He gestured as he hurried away, a little movement of his fingers to say "No time, my friend, not a minute to spare ..." And he went off in the same direction as the hunchback. A curious carousel. Very odd clockwork. "If it goes on too long like this," Cripure said to himself, "I'll be crazy before the end." And he marched on, waving his cane furiously, whipping the monsters at his heels more fiercely than ever.

Already beat, after at most a half-hour's walk. For a while now he had been putting on weight, but not what you'd call healthy fat, a pale flabbiness that had started to look suffocating, sickly, giving him more trouble than ever as he went along the streets. He sweated under his goatskin. A sort of pale sun emerged through the humid, almost lukewarm air. And the goatskin stuck to his back. The few woodlice whose shadows shyly appeared now and then in the strangled streets seemed to look at Cripure with an astonished amusement that was different from usual. Were they spying on him? They wanted to know where he was going? Hmmm ... why should they need to know if he had money or not? That wasn't their fish to fry. It was hard enough for him to discuss such ... intimate details with some employee or other without everyone else spying and poking fun at him right under his nose. *Oh that old anarchist, he's got savings in the bank and owns property no less!* And so what? What then? Did he owe them anything? Wasn't he free to contradict himself? Oh, anyway, it was crazy how prickly they were on the topic of money and real estate, as if that had anything to do with being upstanding and honest.

He gave a careful glance around him before going into the bank, deserted, polished, silent, despite the whispering of a few woodlice at the teller's booths. He didn't need to see their faces to recognize them—he knew who they were by their backs. People he'd never spoken a word to in his life were like intimate friends to him. He knew so much about them! By what strange path had they reached him, these revelations about lives that were always so sad? Was it impossible for people to conceal the secret that everyone was his own best snitch? He sat down at a table and put his satchel in front of him. Murmurs like prayers or confessions. A temple? Oh, that was a little too easy. A Temple of Gold. An idea which often ran through the little anarchist pamphlets he read in his youth. What fools! Ah! To no longer be a poor sucker, but a king of finance, at the top of the world like a few were—a Rockefeller, a Zaharoff, a Pierpont Morgan, aces, those men, fellows making a difference, magnificent specimens, weren't they, handsome predators, not at all in the same class as this Monsieur Pinche who came toward him asking what was new. How was his health? Very well, thanks, and yours? This Monsieur Pinche had the head of an old mangy bird, sunk into a long neck. He was coming back from the market, a net bag full of groceries on his arm. Oh and glasses, he wore them too! He had turned sixty-seven years old yesterday, ha! But solid as the Pont-Neuf, you know! Ha! As for that . . . since he'd been retired, he kept himself fit. What did he do before? Worked for a registrar.

"Between us, I've been writing, I'm putting together a little novel. It entertains me to make up characters."

He had also written a long poem in the style of *Jerusalem's Deliverance*, but shorter, about a thousand lines.

"I write for my own amusement. My heirs can do what they like with it, you understand?" A pause and Monsieur's mouth opened wide, his cigarette butt sticking to his lip. What a sad look! At the end of his arm, the bag seemed to weigh on him like an iron. "You've got to be protected against circumstances." And forgetting that he only wrote for his own pleasure: "I'd have liked to make a little printing of my poem." It wasn't expensive—two thousand francs for an edition of a hundred. Did Cripure think that was a good rate, since he was in the business? Cripure didn't know, couldn't say. He'd published a volume a long time ago, on a fellow named Turnier, and another on the Medes but . . . "not the sort of volume paid for by the author." Really, for what it was worth, Monsieur Pinche would have published his poem if his wife had let him.

"But it's always the same story, my friend, it's hard to avoid—the intellectual vs. the stewpot, you know. Madame Pinche said to me, 'Write verses if it amuses you, I'm even glad about it, and it doesn't bother anyone, but to spend our pennies on that! Go chase your tail somewhere else.'" Another pause. Another yawn. The cigarette butt looked like a huge wart. "But if I'm ever on my own again," said Monsieur Pinche. And that was all Cripure heard. Monsieur Pinche disappeared like a ghost, burying his head in a teller's booth like an old horse at his feed trough.

Just as well. There was nothing to say. It would continue. That Monsieur Pinche must have been married for forty-odd years—married love was a beautiful thing, the kind of love which, of course, went unspoken between them, but which was understood to lie below the surface, just as death lies below the slab. What made them stay together for a whole life? A fascination.

"Your turn, Monsieur Merlin."

Deliverance. Time to put his own head in a teller's booth. And so? Had the market been good? Nothing much to complain about? As often as he had done it, he never went up to a teller's booth without trembling. But for once, it was fair to be pleased. Sales had gone well. He'd made about a thousand francs. A thousand points higher! *Bono, bono,* that would put a little heart in him. He deposited his titles and the bills he had in his satchel, gave instructions for new trading, and left the bank almost festive. A thousand francs, that wasn't a huge sum, but it was quite a bit. You could do a lot with it, get pretty far. A ticket for Marseille didn't cost that much, and those were expensive.

Time to hit the road! But to school.

THE HABIT of these gentlemen teachers in the short recess periods between classes—which Nabucet called "a bit of air, a little breath of oxygen"—was to meet beneath one of the galleries in the Honor Court and stroll there, chatting. They went along at a calm, measured pace, as they did on the post road, usually in one line, but in pairs if they were all together. In the second case, the two lines faced each other, as if they were doing a quadrille. They called it "doing the Lanciers." They'd all known each other for so long, they were so used to each other's steps and gaits, that the Lanciers formation was executed with unhesitating precision, without a word or even a glance. Another formation, which wasn't quite the same as the Lanciers but evolved from it, was the Drum Major. When there weren't quite enough gentlemen for two lines, but too many to walk under the gallery in a single row without crowding, one of them, usually the one who was speaking, would step out of the line and keep talking while he walked backwards, which would give him the air of a drum major, especially if it was Babinot.

It amazed the schoolboys that there were never any accidents, that Babinot never stepped on Nabucet's feet or Cripure's, that the dean never fell on his ass, and neither did the principal. Nothing like that ever happened. Instead, everything was so orderly that even the unfortunate Cripure could take part in these little strolls without worrying, on the condition that he never had to walk backwards. His colleagues modeled their economical steps on his hobbling ones, and though he couldn't walk two feet in the road without remembering his disability, he was able to forget it almost entirely here.

Cripure shook hands and joined the rank. Monsieur Babinot was playing the role of drum major. With his huge nose, his goatee rusty as an old lance, his authoritative mustache cutting a straight line across his face like the hilt of a Gaulish sword, his hands folded under his coattails, a bowler hat tipped back down his neck, he made his iron-soled shoes resound on the stone slabs, holding forth in a nasal voice:

"In France we have so many heroines behind the lines, masses of them, from all walks of life. On the one hand, Madame Faurel, who will soon be given her due recognition. But let's not forget the poorer women who work tirelessly, day and night, at the rough, sometimes very rough, jobs in munitions factories. I read somewhere recently, such a moving story you know…"

The gentlemen slowed their steps.

"Yes," Babinot continued, "I read a story about four hundred young women in a factory somewhere or other in the provinces, whose job it is to manufacture, you know," he winked, "that explosive chemical called picric acid. Whoever is around it for a few days turns yellow as a lemon. Well that little detail didn't frighten away our pretty workers. The most beautiful girls in the area, you know, made a point to push forward with the war effort, to do the work that left them 'saffron' for six months after fighting had ended. What's more—they were proud to have gained something in common with their faraway Japanese allies, and their cute little joke was to call themselves—can you guess?"

No one answered.

"The canary club!" cried Babinot, laughing delightedly.

"See, see!" said one of the gentlemen, scratching his nose. It was the rhetoric teacher, Monsieur Robillard. "That's heroic spirit. A wholesome pride."

Babinot agreed.

Robillard went on: "Do you know what I gave my class for French homework? No? Well it was just this kind of thing about pride. Comment on these lines from our great Alfred de Musset:

"pride
it is the little beauty in life that remains for us,
the modesty of the poor and the greatness of kings."

That was just it. They all agreed. That was right in tune, wasn't it . . . Monsieur Babinot took his hands from under his coattails and applauded softly. "I say, bravo!"

"Oh," said another, "it's remarkable. Anything more would take it too far."

"But that's it, that's just it," said Monsieur Robillard. "The important thing is to . . . insinuate. Not to attach too much importance to some fact or other but to open their minds, make them curious."

"And to guide them," someone said.

"But of course. Listen, for next time, I've got two lines in reserve:

"Let us defy fate and be on our guard
after the victory is won . . .

"what do you think of that, Monsieur Babinot?"

"Why," said Babinot, "it's excellent. Our young men will be in charge, leaders of men. It's good to help them develop healthy ideas."

The principal passed by the group looking depressed, already dressed up and ready for the afternoon's party. He walked over to the little group and shook hands.

"Have you heard anything, Monsieur Principal?"

He shook his head. "Still nothing."

"Ay, ay!" cried Babinot.

"Terrible," murmured Monsieur Robillard, but aware he had misspoken, he continued: "but see here, Monsieur, it's no good to believe too quickly that he . . ." He was about to say the worst possibility. Another error. "My son," he said, "went two months without writing. Well, he'd simply lost track of time."

"I know, I know," said the principal. He also knew why Pierre wasn't writing. What a letter the last one had been! *It's you who've sent me here, you and those like you. Even if I survive, I'll never see you again. I'll never forgive you.* That's what his letter had said. He sighed. "Leave it be, gentlemen."

Babinot was forward enough to pat his arm affectedly, relinquishing the role of drum major. "We must drive out dark thoughts," he said. "Do you know what my son wrote me? It's a story passed down the trench. Eleven in the morning. The captain was sheltering in his post, when a volley of shells came. Everyone had their heads down, then they saw two cooks who came carrying breakfast in a huge vat, moving along calmly, without hurrying, through enemy fire. They entered the shelter like nothing had happened, and of course, the captain reprimanded them, 'Are you crazy to walk out in this? Couldn't you wait until the volley was over?' And then, do you know what the cooks said? Ah, ha ha! 'But it's kidneys, sir, it's kidneys,' they both cried at once. 'It couldn't wait!' Ah ha ha! Kidneys! Kidneys they said … Don't you think that's wonderful? You know, it was just yesterday I got a letter where he told me that those men, in a …"

"Excuse me, dear Babinot," said the principal, "I've got to get back to my office to … work. Forgive me."

"But of course," said Babinot, "God forbid I keep you from working, Monsieur."

The principal left.

"He seems very upset," said Monsieur Robillard. "Is it fifteen days that he hasn't had any news?"

"Something like that."

"That's hard, that's so hard!"

"What was I saying?" said Babinot. "Ah, yes! Another story I got from my son. You're aware that …"

But Babinot had no luck that morning. He was interrupted once again. The principal had barely turned his back when a curious couple appeared at the end of the gallery, a couple for comedy's sake, the pair formed by the tutors Glâtre and Moka, inseparable. *Arcadian lovers*, the wicked Nabucet called them. They hurried toward the group.

Since nicknames were all the rage at the lycée—where Merlin was Cripure and Babinot was Henri IV (because of his goatee and his love of that farcical king and his chicken in every pot), where Bourcier the dean was Wolf-in-Sheep's-Clothing, Nabucet was Cherry-on-Top or Isn't-It-So, where Glâtre was Monsieur Abbot—Moka had the privilege of two nicknames, so that the name on his birth certificate was entirely forgotten. They called him Moka and What-Would-Jesus-Do. Moka was the name of his dog, a crying runt of a fox terrier he took everywhere, just like the horrible hunchback. Noël looked after the dog when Moka was tutoring. As for the source of the moniker What-Would-Jesus-Do? you only had to ask the question to see him touch his forehead in a particular way.

They approached together, Moka gesticulating, and his companion the opposite—very calm, hands behind his back, thinking. There was something in the character of Glâtre, small and round and fat, to justify his nickname—a hint of the seminary, where he'd supposedly spent his youth. Defrocked or not, he wore a black suit, a stiff collar, big shoes, and a bowler hat. But more than a defrocked priest, he had the air of a poor old man keeping up appearances.

As for Moka . . . thin and tall, he towered over Glâtre by a whole head. He too was already dressed up for the party, magnificent in his tux, a nice tux made for someone else's marriage and smelling strongly of mothballs, which made Cripure grimace. Moka wore a snowy placket-front shirt and, like a real groom, a white rose in his button-hole. When he tipped his hat to the gentlemen, a superb crest of red hair appeared, falling over his milky forehead like a gas jet. He bowed especially low to Cripure, his old master, and the red crest fluttered like a clown's tassel when he's about to jump through a hoop. It fell in his eyes, hiding them. Eyes that were too blue, a girl's eyes.

"We have a plan," he said straightening up. His voice was curiously musical. "Yes, a plan . . ." It must be a very important plan, since Moka's eyes were glowing with mischief.

"Aha!" said Babinot. "Can we hear it?"

Moka turned to Glâtre, as if for a final consultation, but Glâtre shrugged. "We were thinking," said Moka . . .

"What!" Glâtre broke in. "What do you mean, we? It's your project my friend, take responsibility for your own actions."

"Oh?"

"Why yes, yes."

"Oh? Well then." He cracked his knuckles, and began, "I had thought we could organize a kind of little museum, you see, where we could exhibit photographs and things from the front, you understand—"

"Things like shell casings and helmets from Boches," added Glâtre.

"We could do it in the parlor," said Moka.

"By the hair of my chin," cried Babinot, who grabbed Moka's arms with an affectionate brusqueness, "that's a lovely idea, you know. Well! Do you believe it? I had thought a little bit about that, a while ago. I can't rightly remember," he said, scratching his head, "why it came about that the plan didn't happen . . . it's true we have so many things bouncing around in our heads! But in the parlor, just as you were thinking."

Moka was delighted. "Great minds think alike," he said.

Suddenly Babinot frowned. "Ay yai yai!"

"What? What is it?"

"Oh, it's such a shame!"

"But what is, dear Monsieur Babinot?" said Moka. He thought everything was ruined and his plan was out the window.

"Oh, what misfortune! What misfortune, my friend," replied Babinot. "You might have been able to speak to the general about it today, you understand. Oh! What bad luck. You know he's been ill, don't you? He won't be with us this afternoon. Tsk, tsk."

Babinot dug a pinky into his ear and closed one eye. His hand wriggled vigorously.

"Too bad," he said. "We'll do it another time. We'll speak to Nabucet about it right away."

"Great."

"He's just the man you need," said Monsieur Robillard.

"Exactly. Totally agreed. The general will come, we can have a grand opening . . . It'll be perfect. Oh you know what else I was thinking?"

They had formed a circle around him. Cripure hung his head, his hands stuffed into the pockets of his goatskin.

"You'd like, wouldn't you," Babinot asked, "to basically recreate the atmosphere of the front, to put an image before the eyes of our students, isn't that so? Yes? Perfect. But do you know what I'd like to ask the general? Can you guess?"

No one replied.

"No guesses?"

"No."

"What if, outside the museum," he said, rubbing his hands together, "to complement it...you still can't guess?"

They all thought about it, even Cripure.

"Look at this courtyard," said Babinot, "doesn't it seem strangely empty?"

Actually, there were students scattered under the galleries and in the doorways. The bell was about to ring for the end of recess.

"A barren waste!" said Babinot. "Well, do you know what I'm going to ask the general for?" Babinot paused and raised his index finger. "A little cannon," he finished. "Aha! None of you thought of that! A handsome little seventy-seven taken from the enemy, that's what I'm going to ask the general for." And he ran off, laughing and shouting to Moka, "Think of the cannon, my friend!"

Of course, Cripure loved his country, and that patriotism was perhaps the most authentic feeling in him. But in the end, it wasn't right to confuse, as Babinot did, that love of country with a love of militarism or, as so many did, with a love of death. Most of all, it wasn't right to confuse it with a flat acceptance of conforming to others. But the way things were, Cripure had to hide even here. Despite his love for his country, which went deep, he couldn't bring himself to express it like the others, since he wasn't at all in agreement about their way of loving. And in a moment when patriotism was on everyone's lips, when from morning till night there was only talk of France, Cripure alone was unable to speak, and he suffered for it, brushed off, here like everywhere else, into loneliness or comedy. He certainly had to pretend to love France their way. It was too dangerous otherwise. He had even—and this memory was more than painful—forced the note once. He had proven himself more chauvinistic than all of them put together. No one had forced him to say what he'd said, last year, on prize day. He very well could have limited himself to necessary banalities, stuck to pedagogical generalities, idiotologies as he called them, instead of launching into such a crude praise of heroes. They hadn't asked for all that. So why had he painfully composed a speech that would have suited a lower-level politician and spoken for a whole hour by the clock about the monuments they would raise to the eternal glory of the poilus? Why had he prostituted himself? Once again, he could have skipped it. No one expected anything more from him than agreement. But far from opposing them, far from scrutinizing the war, he had glorified it instead, spoken of it as a grand and terrible source of heroism and even beauty, had forced himself to find a moral in it. The speech had created a little sensation, but not at all the way he had hoped or expected. They hadn't much liked what he had said, precisely because he had forced it. For some, it had seemed natural for Cripure to fall in line and practice the sacred politics of unity, and that was all they had seen. But others, like Nabucet, had perfectly understood the insincere side of his flattery, like that of a valet who exaggerates his master's praises, and they had turned their backs on him, so completely that poor Cripure was once again deserted, despite his efforts. Trouble for nothing. *Now go teach ethics.*

LUCIEN Bourcier roamed limping through the streets, his suitcase in hand. He could have hired Père Yves's cab and gone straight to the port, a handful of kilometers away, where the *Devonshire* had been anchored since the day before. But the *Devonshire* was only a small cargo ship that allowed a few passengers, and it didn't have cabins, just berths. So the passengers weren't allowed to board until an hour before the scheduled departure. The *Devonshire* would weigh anchor tomorrow at seven a.m., with the tide, so Lucien couldn't board until six. Left to find a room for the night. And for the day. He was determined to stay out of sight. Alone. He carefully avoided taking a room in a hotel—he knew too well that his mother would be frantically searching until she found his hiding place, so she could harass him one last time. She'd send messengers to all the hotels in town—messengers who were more skillful than policemen. But maybe they wouldn't imagine that Madame de Villaplane's rooming house could take him in for such a short stay, and he guessed her house would offer the peace he wanted. He headed that way.

He didn't regret anything. Tomorrow he'd be in London, a few days later in Sweden. Then he'd figure out how to get farther. In the town square, all the stores were open. A tarp was stretched between two posts, making a stand that sold whistles, cockades, and flags to conscripts. And drinks and food as well. They fried cod in the open air, and sausages, which the conscripts scarfed down with rough wine. On the steps of the town hall, a policeman called the roll.

Lucien circled the square, wandering from one stall to another, fascinated by all these young men he stared at as though he were looking for someone he knew. For the most part, they were young peasant boys who had come on foot that morning, in groups led by a fiddler. The ones from town never stayed in the square. Cod, black bread, rough wine, that wasn't for them. They were in the cafés or had already gone home to take the news to their parents: armed service or deferral. No alternatives. These malnourished kids already wore on their hats the sign of death to come. How unwarlike they seemed, and yet, how unready for death. How little they appeared to think about it! Nearly all the young faces, even the toughest ones, had some confidence in them, a childlike trust, a pathetic ignorance of lies. They hadn't yet learned someone could betray them. They were ready to hold out their hands, to be led, as long as the promised fairy tale proved to be lovely and noble. They didn't have conditions, it didn't seem to occur to them to demand to know what, at the other end, would make up for the loss of their young lives, and if this in-nocent acceptance of pain and death would at least allay the sufferings of the world. But did they accept it? Had they internalized this debate, or were these thoughts his alone, as Lucien suspected, the reasoning of an intellectual? But no, no. That would mean he believed these young men were incapable of a single thought. Lucien fiercely rejected that—his whole self rebelled against such a dark view. No, a thousand times no, until death, no! Thinking wasn't and couldn't be the priv-ilege of only a few, and if it was, what was it good for, this thought that justified a scorn for life? And justified the shame men felt—im-posed by other men? For better or worse, they had to break out of this savagery, to give life back its value. Not life as it was for most people—crushed, mutilated, denied, stolen—but life as it could be created. Here, in the square, among the fryers, the atmosphere like a carnival or even a party, there was enough pure and noble life to make a world. He caught, in the passing gestures and glances, how this world could appear in its simplest and most essential qualities. In the delicate, brotherly gesture of two men sharing bread, it was there, ready to burst out, blazing from uncorrupted hearts, a will that was sleeping for the moment, but which would wake one day for all time. They didn't seem to suspect what they were capable of, but everything in them was prepared for awakening and change. There was no hope except in them, in their youthful energy and freshness.

So he thought as he continued to wander among the groups. Yes, there was no hope but in them, once they finally broke the spell—which hid them from their humanity, still so visible under this pageantry—and got a glimpse of joy. Then, they would fight for it, they would know how to seize it. Humanity hadn't said its last words. It was cowardly to pretend, as Cripure had the previous day, that it would sink, drowned in blood. No. No. Humanity had barely uttered its first cry. After so many early horrors, it would end by seeing life as a prize, as a thing to be respected, a real brotherly love. The question wasn't what that life would be like, the real question, the only one, was: What can we make of living? We could do anything, on the condition that we don't begin by repressing vitality. It was a massive revolution, not, as Cripure still believed, one that required all thought to be suppressed, but the opposite—that all thought would be released, that the chances would be on the side of life and not of death. And if it couldn't happen without violence, they would use force. Where others used deaths for dying, they would use them for living. And if it was true that most people were nothing but drudges, then it wasn't more difficult to impose life on drudges than to impose death. You could make a free man out of a living drudge. Then they'd at least get rid of some evil. But a dead drudge? All the revolutions up to this point had begun within a certain circle. Now it was time to break the circle, to make a new start, as the factory workers and peasants in Russia had just done, men who were brothers of these little conscripts, their first comrades. How long would he wait before the others...

He sat on a bench and stayed there, even though it was cold. His thoughts took a different course—toward those comrades, whom all these little peasant boys would so much resemble before long, when they had lost that confidence and become shocked in their turn. He remembered his last meetings with his two friends, Pierre Marchandeau and Louis Babinot, his classmates who, before deployment, had been so taken by the year they had spent in philosophy class with Cripure. When he'd seen Pierre for the last time, he could barely unclench his teeth. They had spent an afternoon together. Pierre hadn't opened his mouth except to say that they had messed him up. That day, they'd understood each other completely. The meeting had happened when they were both on furlough together, in a country of fields and sun. If Pierre survived, Lucien knew he'd find him again one day; they'd find each other at the start of a new battle. The last time he'd seen Louis Babinot had been very different. At night. In a train station. He remembered the scene perfectly.

Gas lamps had been shining through the windows of the offices, and flares illuminated detachments and groups of lone soldiers who were waiting on the platform for the train. Some artillerymen arrived, under the command of sergeant—they were returning to the base to regroup their formations, and the prospect of passing through Paris was exciting to them. A police sergeant with a chinstrap was on duty.

The train had been late. Lucien and Louis went into the waiting room, a murky lean-to, with an unlit woodstove in the center, and, to one side, a pile of straw bedding where twenty men were stretched out. Bags, weapons, helmets, everything was heaped in chaos. The men were sad—they had been called back up. The next day, the supply train would deposit them at the front. Oil lanterns glimmered through the room filled with pipe smoke. Outside, every ten minutes, troop trains passed, further delaying the civilian train the artillerymen hoped to take. Endless convoys of forty or more freight cars followed one another. On flat cars, cannon, camp kitchens, regimental freight, and ambulances scrolled by, and ruffled heads appeared in the windows of rare passenger cars. Everything was going back "up there." In the waiting room, the soldiers were sleeping. An officer called the roll, picking out each of them. A wake-up call. Fumbling in the dark, the men gathered their equipment. A rifle fell. The officer with a lantern in his hand continued the roll call, and the men grouped themselves into little units. "It's time," Louis Babinot had said. He was getting on that train too. Lucien was coming back from the hospital, he was being sent home to convalesce, and he had only come to see Louis Babinot. The officer, convinced all his men had been called, took the lead of the little group and started toward a chain of dark railway cars they would soon attach to the supply train. Policemen—from where?—arrived, carrying their canteens.

He remembered all that like something glimpsed in a cave, like images of a world where everything took place and nothing happened. They'd stayed a few more minutes on the platform, and Louis Babinot had started to talk, in a dull monotone, a quiver in the back of his throat. "You tell them…" Trains groaning, the loud buzz of an airplane flying over made his voice go in and out. It wasn't cold, it was lovely, and a nearby garden gave off the smell of wet earth. "For my father's sake, I'll have to die at the head of my battalion, leading my men in the assault. It's so simple. You'll go see him. You'll tell him, ok? Tell him I was always the brave soldier. Remember that. It's what will make him happiest. In the end, you'll figure it out—how much truth to tell and how many lies. Everybody gets what's owed to them, or maybe what they can bear," he added in an even lower voice. "You don't have to tell my mother anything. I think she understands…"

Lucien had promised.

The very day he got home, he'd gone in search of Babinot. As it was a Thursday, Babinot was at the town library instead of the school. He combined the job of town librarian with his duties as a teacher, and he worked there every Thursday and Sunday. A rotten place, that library. And it wasn't even really a library, just a reading room. As an adolescent, Lucien had always hated going. Two or three old biddies out of a Goya painting, with high, whalebone collars and sharp snouts, reading the *Revue des Deux Mondes* with little glances through their pince-nez. And here and there a few invalid men, satisfied with drooling over the local paper. At the back of the room, in a glass booth, was Monsieur Babinot himself, wearing a tailcoat and smoking cap, lost in some scholarly and recently acquired book, something along the lines of *The Yellow Peril* or *Oberlé*. That was the scene on peak days, but there were empty ones too, and Lucien had arrived when it was quiet. No one. Not an old spinster, not even an invalid's cane… Monsieur Babinot was alone there, and… he was fighting! Fighting with his shadow. Armed with a glittering foil—he must have spent hours polishing it—he was doing impressive thrusts, feints, and parries, so absorbed that he hadn't even heard the door. In his jacket and cap, the big checkered handkerchief hanging down out of his pocket looked, from behind, like a third coattail. One of his pant legs had ridden up almost to the knee, revealing big woolly blue socks. Lucien had delicately left the room. The folly of these little gentlemen had something oppressive about it that left little room for comedy and many reasons for anger.

The policeman on the town hall steps continued his never-ending roll call.

From the other side of the square, Francis Montfort ran over. In the wind, his hair was blowing more wildly than ever beneath the bowler hat falling into his eyes, and his books were still pinned beneath an elbow. The corners of his jacket flapped, and one of his untied shoelaces was dragging dangerously. He arrived at a group of conscripts and stopped running. About to hurry into the town hall, he caught sight of Lucien. His face lit up, and he approached.

"Aren't you a bit late?" said Lucien.

"That's no problem," Francis said, out of breath. "I was hurrying in, but since you're here . . ." He put his books down on the bench and sat. "Do you have a minute?"

"Of course."

"I don't know why I ran. A habit." He lifted his hat and pushed the hair back, looking around with astonishment. "You'd think it was a fair."

"So true."

"It's like it hasn't occurred to them. Weird, don't you think? It's like this is for fun."

"They don't come to town very often."

"Yes, you have to take that into account. It's funny how there's a vision of life here that hides the life itself. Like life crusted over. Do you see it? You think things are what they appear, but it's a silly mistake, isn't it?" Francis said.

"Definitely."

"I agree with you. And then, I used to believe a long time ago—" Lucien smiled at that "—I really thought that peasants like this were very different from me. I didn't think I could ever become friends with a peasant. It's strange isn't it? And the only evidence I had was that I didn't believe I could love them."

"Are you in love with a peasant?"

"No. But I could be. Why not?"

"Good man," said Lucien, putting a hand on his knee. "What used to turn you against peasant girls?"

"I don't know... Really, I didn't think about it. They didn't seem very attractive to me."

"And peasant boys?"

"Naturally, I thought they were all a bit dumb and without... polish. But all this was when I was too stupid. I've changed a lot."

"You mean you've become smarter?"

"Yes. Why not say it?"

"Why not," said Lucien, "since it's true."

"It's possible to figure it out on your own. You can tell down to the minute when the transformation takes place, don't you think? All of a sudden, the things you missed yesterday have become obvious. You must know what I mean."

"Yes. But what became obvious so suddenly?" Lucien asked.

"Oh!" said Francis, laughing, "first of all, that I was pretty dumb. That I had fallen into step."

"And you're not marching anymore?"

"No."

"Why not?"

"Because. I like living."

"Short as life is?"

"No. The love of life... a real life, you know," he said, conscious of being inarticulate. "They've betrayed us too much. Oh!" he said all of a sudden. "Will it bore you if I read a poem?"

"Not at all."

"Really?"

Francis took a little notebook out of his pocket and read:

"You've wronged me
Lied to me
Jackets and glasses
Shoes polished
Bowler hats
I thought were all that!
Can you show me a bit
of your immortal soul?
I've perceived
nothing but wind
falling on a hundred thousand bodies."

"I wrote that in five minutes."
"It's good."
"Good?"
"Very good."
"May I read you another? Since it's just right here in my notebook …"
"I'd be happy to hear it."

"Sir, at your house
All is straw
At the straw man's
Your place, Madame, is just a haystack
The mill is stuffed, the clogs are stuffed
Hay and straw
Inside and outside the heart
like a hat."

"Not bad, not bad at all," said Lucien, laughing. "And how long did it take you to write that one?" He might as well play along a little.

"A flick of the pen."

"Oh! Impressive."

"Yeah. That one is hilarious. I spent part of last night copying them into this notebook. It's so I can carry them with me—on loose sheets they disappear. I lost one that was really good, much more revolutionary than those two!"

Lucien smiled again, and Francis continued:

"I can't put my hand on it. It's strange because I had it just the day before yesterday—I read it to my old classmates, in study hall."

"What?"

"They asked me to."

"And how did they respond?"

"Well, they seemed pretty surprised. I don't think they liked it. You know, it was a pretty straightforward call for rebellion, that poem. They must have told on me. Nabucet had a word with me just now, telling me I'd be called in to see the principal."

"Marchandeau is a good man. The other is an accumulation of all the worst possible qualities the category has to offer... and I've known him for a long time. What will you say to Marchandeau?"

"I don't know... I wanted to show you the poem."

"They've stolen it from you."

"You think?"

It was clear—the naive boy had fallen into a trap. "If I were in your shoes, I'd keep a sharper lookout."

"But I'm so careful!" Francis thought he was a concealment expert—you could see it just by looking at him.

"Well. We'll see."

"What does it matter if Marchandeau snaps at me? In less than half an hour, I'll be called up into the armed forces."

"That's one view. What do you think about going up there?"

"It's filthy. But I'll have brothers there."

They didn't say anything for a moment.

"You're not worried about keeping them waiting?" Lucien asked.

"Who?"

"The draft board."

"It's no problem. I'm in no hurry. And you?"

"I've done my time."

"Do you know they tried to kill Cripure?"

This incredible segue bowled Lucien over.

"Is your head all right, my friend?"

"Perfectly ok. Better than most."

"To kill Cripure?"

"Yes."

"Who?"

"The kids at school."

Lucien shook his head. Cripure had never been more than a joke to the schoolboys... "It's not serious?"

"But I'm telling you, his life was hanging on nothing but a ... bolt. Cripure always bikes around, you know. Yesterday the boys found a way to unscrew the bolts on the forks."

"Tell me more."

"I warned him. I had a note taken to him this morning, by my friend Étienne. I just saw him, and that's why I was late. Cripure screamed."

"But finish the story!"

"He shouted a lot. He went crazy when he read my note. Other times, I've ignored what's gone on between them, but Étienne couldn't stop telling me Cripure's a crook."

"Tell me the story," Lucien said, losing patience, "tell it a little bit clearly why don't you ..."

"All I can tell you," said the young man, "is how I learned of the plan. It's very strange, as you'll see. Among the students I supervise is a certain Blondl. He's a boy of twelve or so, a little wily one, a bootlicker, very conscientious. Rich. A future Nabucet. So, that morning in the dormitory, I went by to check the boy's comb. He'd lost his and was looking for it ... while crooning to himself." Francis paused. "Singing in the dormitory, that's an offense. Coming from someone else, I wouldn't have been surprised. But Blondl! I said to myself right away that there must be something behind it, especially because he was singing while puttering around, clearly trying to attract my attention. I went over to him. I saw his comb right away, of course, but Blondl wasn't interested in that, and the singing didn't stop. I took the comb," said Francis, getting up to demonstrate, "and examined it like this, turning my back to Blondl. I was, you understand, convinced he had something to tell me. His song sounded like something improvised by a daydreaming kid, apparently unaware. It wasn't until I heard Cripure's name repeated over and over, mixed with a story about bicycling and loosened bolts that I started to understand. Then, he told the whole story, clearly, while still singing. I turned around to give him back his comb, and our eyes met...his looked like the eyes of someone in love."

Lucien had listened to the whole tale with intense concentration, completely forgetting about Cripure, so astonished at what Francis had described—the troubling image of this sweet, rotten boy. He didn't doubt that Francis had told the truth, even though the story had an artful quality. But he had to ask, "And you're sure things happened that way?"

"You don't believe me?"

"I do."

"I've never seen anything more—how to put it? Characteristic. But I'm well versed in the behavior of those little pricks."

"That's all to the good."

"He'll be a policeman someday and never look back."

Something else was bothering him. "Poor Cripure," Lucien muttered. "He doesn't deserve this. It's strange—" his smile was almost timid "—It seems so much like..." He stopped, a sad look on his face.

"Like?"

"Nothing. Perhaps some kind of sign, if you know what I mean," said Lucien, brightening. "A warning. But let's leave it. Poor Cripure! We had a depressing conversation yesterday. In some ways, Cripure's a fallen man who has nothing left to cherish but his fallenness. But again, let's leave it, my friend. This isn't the time to tell you about that," said Lucien, getting up.

Francis took the offered hand. "You know," he said, not without a certain quaver in his voice, "you know, I love him too."

"I know it," said Lucien. "Even though he's a crook?"

"Yes."

"Well then...you must know how hard it is to love someone who has to disappear?"

"Has to? Is that what you think?"

"That's what I'd wish," said Lucien. "And now, I have to go. I need to be alone. Good luck," he said, "try someday to find brothers who aren't your enemies and neither are you theirs."

MADAME de Villaplane was an astonishing old lady. If she imitated life, the imitation was perfect. Who would have guessed, seeing her full, supple features, that she'd just turned sixty? Her well-formed nose, her still-lovely mouth, and from her oval face, under the clips which held back her barely whitened hair, the pressing look of those dark eyes—what a sensation she must have created at twenty! Her high yet refined voice was still loud enough during arguments to be heard from the basement to the attic, and even by the neighbors. Besides her way of appearing and disappearing as if she could walk through walls, what gave Madame de Villaplane the air of a marionette was her jerky step and her great artfulness in falling suddenly into someone's arms—stiff as a board, not breathing, lifeless—so convincingly that you had to ask yourself whether it was really a corpse you held, or a wind-up toy at the end of its spring. She had already fallen twice into the arms of Kaminsky, her lodger.

Madame de Villaplane was a noblewoman fallen on hard times. She'd spent years trying to sue her children, but because she was "too good" and "too lenient," she'd lost everything and there was nothing left now but a "pretty penny"—this little house, which had become an inn. It was her rock, she said, her island of Elba. Once, the house belonged to the Turnier family, whom Cripure loved and hated in turn. She'd inherited some of Turnier's father's wealth, and this was where the son had returned after his unhappy adventures. And he'd left from there, when Mercédès didn't come, to throw himself into the sea.

It had been a solitary spot, but since then a whole new neighborhood had grown up around it—Turnier's house was no more than a house among others. No one (besides researchers and curious locals) knew the story anymore. One year, it was true, she'd lobbied the municipality to put a plaque on the front of the house in memory of the great departed man, but she'd come up against the brusque refusal of those gentlemen, who, since they were mainly clerics, wouldn't hear of honoring a suicide in any way, no matter the circumstances. It must be said that Cripure had, for his part, refused to support it, due to other objections of course, which were mainly that it was best to leave men like Turnier in peace, since he had been abandoned during his lifetime. And so it was that the gray façade of this boarding-house had no markings on it—save for a wooden crest over the door. The house had an air of poverty, which never ceased to embarrass Madame de Villaplane, born Blanche d'Elloudan, granddaughter of an imperial colonel, daughter of a prefect! And what a colonel, what a prefect! She liked to bring up, as a particularly appropriate example of her father's good taste and sense of duty toward his position in the government, the fact that he would never tolerate clipping his wig to his hair with fasteners that weren't silver. A great man, that prefect. If there was any doubt, you only had to see his portrait hanging in the dining room, next to the portrait of her grandfather, another great man it was impossible not to notice. No portrait of her former husband.

Regarding this fellow who had vanished many years ago, Madame de Villaplane exercised a discretion that was fairly suspicious. She never shut up about her children, whom she accused of all sorts of crimes, but as for their father, not a word. It was so bad that you might have thought he had never existed, if it weren't for certain people, scattered around town, with good, faithful memories, who could recall the scandal of yesteryear which had resulted in the inexplicable flight of Monsieur de Villaplane. So Madame de Villaplane wasn't a widow, as one might have thought, but an abandoned wife, one of these martyred women plagued by an evil husband. All this was more than twenty years ago. No one could say which particular vice had led Monsieur de Villaplane to all of a sudden break the sacred and charming bonds of marriage, and without the normal recourse to divorce, he had resolved it by disappearing completely, without leaving even the shortest letter behind on his ministerial desk. Nothing. Not even a scene. No tears. He hadn't fled. He'd simply left. He'd taken the train, carrying a few thousand francs with him, which meant he had only enough money for the time being. A motiveless man. Since then, no one had heard from him. Madame de Villaplane certainly tried to play out a farce of great sorrow after her husband's disappearance, but she'd gotten sick of the role, discovering nothing inside but indifference. And the absence of her husband in the dining room, next to the two other portraits, could easily be explained this way: she'd never thought to put him there.

All of that had little importance compared, for example, to the slightest quarrel with one of her boarders, and these quarrels were frequent. Madame de Villaplane was rightly considered extremely straitlaced in matters of deportment. She was a strict landlady. As soon as a new lodger arrived, she'd check his luggage and try to figure out what kind of a background he came from, what his religious and political opinions were, and, if he passed this inspection, she would detail the rules everyone had to follow under her roof. *First*: she only took male lodgers. She wasn't silly enough to rent rooms to those ladies of La Poste and other fast girls who'd get nothing but bad reputations. No scandals. *Second*: it was to be absolutely understood that the men swore on their honor to never bring women home, even for tea. No woman, except the maid, could cross the threshold of her rooms. Whoever broke that rule was kicked out immediately. *Third*: you had to be home by nine in winter, ten in summer. No making noise. Keep the bathroom clean. She didn't think she had to mention that cooking or washing up in your room was forbidden, that was an obvious general rule, etc. All these rules were copied out by her own hand onto large sheets of blue paper that she hung over the bed in each of the rooms.

It was also true that Madame de Villaplane's rigorous judgment of her lodgers enabled her ambition to only rent to guests who were distinguished enough that she could entertain them for tea at least once a week in her parlor. The boardinghouse would then become a sort of country estate, where she could receive visitors, as she had in better days. Then she could forget that she had fallen on hard times, she would find a way out of herself by telling her story, which she was only able to do in bits and pieces, when she got the chance. Unfortunately these timid soirées never added up to much, and had occasionally even resulted in painful scenes and evictions.

Madame de Villaplane had succeeded in creating such a reputation for herself in town that these days her boardinghouse was nearly deserted. The only lodger who could manage to stay was Otto Kaminsky. But didn't they say she was in love with him?

Of course, Madame de Villaplane's secrets were not protected from what one might call harmless indiscretions, for lack of a better phrase. Just as everyone in town knew the smallest details of Cripure's most private (or what he thought was his most private) life, so too did everyone know that for a year now, this crazy old lady had thought of no one but this soldier, so un-martial it was true, still such a man of the world under his uniform. For once, Madame de Villaplane had the chance to fall for a distinguished guest, a boarder who was young, rich, well educated, curious about art, rather well built—in short, the person she had been dreaming of all these years—and he even spoke multiple languages. It was because of his language skills that he'd been appointed to the prefecture as an interpreter. It was his job to read the correspondence of enemy aliens. A trusted position, you could say.

All these features made Kaminsky extremely attractive to Madame de Villaplane. In such circumstances, who could be surprised she'd fallen in love? He was an excellent fellow, so Parisian, and who also had the advantage of being foreign, exotic. He was Jewish, but to Madame de Villaplane, who hated Jews without knowing exactly why, he was just Polish, which meant: Slavic.

And here was one who, from the first day, she could entertain for tea! She had explained to him that her grandfather, who had earned a title after Austerlitz, had pursued a career quite parallel to the Baron General Marbot, who had been his friend. "Since you're such a great reader and intellectual, it can't have escaped your notice that the Baron General Marbot wrote at length about my grandfather in his *Memoirs*. He gives a long account of his soldier's skill and his courage, etc."

They were sitting together by the lamp, he smoking oriental tobacco and she crocheting an aviator's face mask. An intimate little evening, with a good fire in the grate. Even if it was true that the emperor himself had, from the depths of his exile, encouraged the memoirist to write up his accounts for the glory of the French army, Kaminsky must realize that the baron hadn't always spared his old army buddies. Quite the opposite. The tales he told about the campaigns in Spain and Portugal, which had failed due to petty squabbles, celebrated the courage and fortitude of the imperial army, admirable as always, but cast a bad light on the worthiness of certain leaders and their ability to make decisions. According to Madame de Villaplane, her grandfather had saved the day countless times during those campaigns. "God's honest truth..."

Afterward, she talked about her father, the prefect. And, of course, she didn't care to leave out her issues with her children. Madame de Villaplane loved to be pitied, and she went on at length about the saddest part of the story—the deceptions of motherly love. Kaminsky had lent a more than attentive ear to these tales—he was taken in from the start, by the character of the storyteller much more than by the stories themselves. Certain traits of hers had really struck him. Hadn't she made him swear his soldiers' oath not to repeat what he heard before telling him the most banal details from a lawsuit? He had given the easiest oath in the world, without cracking a smile. Then she had told him, with much ceremony, the story of Turnier, explaining how the very same house where they were sitting had once belonged to the philosopher, and how he had left it one day to throw himself in the sea. Kaminsky had wanted to hear about it in more detail, but he'd run into Madame de Villaplane's curious reserve, and she'd begged him not to ask her about that painful story. He hadn't pressed her, and the evening had come to a close.

The next day, Kaminsky brought Madame de Villaplane a beautiful bouquet of flowers, a gesture that, since her youth, had become so unfamiliar that she was moved to the point of almost fainting with joy.

From then on, Madame de Villaplane's life had taken a new turn. As psychologists have it, a fixation is a conviction that goes unexamined, and so they define madness. By that reckoning, Madame de Villaplane wasn't at all crazy, since she was totally aware of the obsessive desire that took hold of her: to run away with Kaminsky. To leave everything behind. She didn't know which she wanted more—to be with Kaminsky or to leave town, but she knew that one was unthinkable without the other.

In the person of Kaminsky, she had created a whole kingdom that appeared like a promised land where they would be reunited one day. That she'd be an old woman didn't occur to her. She didn't ask herself whether Kaminsky would consent to take her away—she was convinced she could compel him.

Since Kaminsky had arrived in her household and prompted this dream, Madame de Villaplane had become more conscious of her past. She was horrified to contemplate what her life had been, and something like a demand for justice mixed with her love for Otto. It wasn't possible that a woman's existence could consist only of what hers had been. The idea of dying like that, with her hands empty, terrified her so much that she trembled, alone in her room. He had to take her away, she had to live with him for her last years, or else something would be wrong in the universe. Every being had to love, to be loved, or else ... To love and be loved sooner or later. The sharp pinch of a wasted life, of lost time, gave her desire a pathetic force.

Kaminsky, for his part, had suspected nothing. He saw nothing in her but an old woman who was a bit loony, and for a long time he continued to be an attentive guest, a man of the world, well-read, an art enthusiast—what he'd been from day one. But the day of Madame de Villaplane's first scene he'd begun to open his eyes.

One evening, without any justification for such treatment, Madame de Villaplane had burst into his room all of a sudden to ask him point-blank if he thought he was living in occupied territory and did he mean to bring all the worst of barracks behavior under her roof?

It was so unexpected that he hadn't known what to say, but he started to watch her closely. After the deluge of reproach she heaped upon him, he finally understood that she found him guilty of a serious breach in her house rules—because he had gone down to the kitchen in the middle of the night to scrounge a crust of bread. He admitted that he'd developed a craving right before bed. What could be more natural, more innocent in those circumstances than to go down to the kitchen? Madame de Villaplane didn't want to hear it. In response to these explanations, she only yelled louder. Did he want to complain about her usual provisions? Did he, by any chance, think she starved her guests? And so on and so forth. And in the end she'd fallen into his arms for the first time, in a dead faint. He had to carry her all the way to her bed.

Anyone else in Kaminsky's place would have been in a hurry to leave the boardinghouse, but the fascination sparked by the scene kept him there. In any case, all had been forgiven the day after. But something fundamental had shifted in their relationship, and at the bottom of her heart Madame de Villaplane believed she had gained an advantage.

It wasn't until later, much later, when everything had become clear to Kaminsky—for the simple reason that she had told him everything—that he'd understood the reason for her curious outburst. The snacking incident had nothing to do with it. What mattered—after certain calculations he was sure of it—was that Madame de Villaplane had just learned about the affair he was having with Simone Point, the notary's daughter, and about his rental cottage, by the sea, where he went almost every day with Bacchiochi, the surgeon general, in the prefect's very own car, driven by his chauffeur, Léo. And so it was a fit of jealousy, no doubt about it.

Since then, there had been ups and downs. The scenes continued, and they took a new character, often leading to periods of sulking that lasted entire weeks.

Nothing was more comical than the way they worked around each other. It was silently understood that they wouldn't meet, wouldn't even see or perceive each other's presence in the house they shared.

Madame de Villaplane therefore arranged to eat her meals alone, and sometimes she even had them carried to her room. But in the morning, when he left his room to go to the prefecture, Kaminsky would stand at the top of the stairs and call out: "Watch out! I'm coming through."

And for all the money in the world, as funny as he thought it was, he wouldn't take another step before hearing Madame de Villaplane say, "The coast is clear!"

For the moment, they were in a relatively calm period. It had been more than fifteen days since her last big scene, though it had to be said that this one had ended with a complete confession. She had, with an expression he was surprised to hear come out of her mouth, "let the cat out of the bag."

He'd listened to it all without protest. Afterward, he had given her a chaste kiss. Then he'd started to explain his view of love to her. It was exactly the same as Madame de Villaplane's view. How intelligent Kaminsky was, how well he understood people! What an open mind, what a free spirit! Not for a second had he considered it ridiculous for an old woman to fall in love. He'd understood her, that was undeniable. On the question of running away together, he hadn't said yes or no. "We'll see . . ."

They'd left it at that. Since then, they hadn't spoken more about it. "Just a little patience."

But patience wasn't Madame de Villaplane's principle virtue. Wasn't patience the same as watching the days go by without doing anything, like watching blood flow from a wound without even thinking of stanching it? She had no more time to lose.

Since the day before, an anxiety had crept up on her, an inkling that everything wasn't going as well as she'd thought for the past two weeks, that there was a threat. From certain surprising signs, she guessed Kaminsky was hiding things from her. The previous day, he had a funny smile when they parted after lunch. And he hadn't come to dinner. He hadn't come back from his cottage until very late that night, driven home by Léo, as always; she'd heard the car. What orgiastic scenes must take place in that cottage! If Kaminsky went there to meet his mistress, the others—that Léo and Surgeon General Bacchiochi—must also bring their girls. And not always the same ones. It was said that the good little bourgeoises of the town took turns going to assignations there. And wasn't it also said that a certain Basquin, who had God knows what role at the camp for enemy aliens, furnished them with women chosen from the youngest and prettiest of the prisoners? And all this while she wasted away in her deserted boardinghouse, the devil take it. What time had he come home last night? Two a.m.

Usually, when he was out, he stayed out all night, slept over in the arms of that little slut Simone Point. Why last night? And she couldn't say anything about this breach of her rules. Hadn't she, in a moment of folly, lifted, for him, the particular rule that required boarders to be home at nine—and even worse—hadn't she given him a key?

He was still sleeping, no doubt. In any case, he hadn't come down yet, even though it was late, and Madame de Villaplane wandered, sighing, around her house. What could she do? She had her breakfast served, the breakfast she had wanted to share with Kaminsky.

The maid came in, brought the coffee, checked that everything was in order—the bread, the butter, the sugar, the jams—and went out.

Madame de Villaplane ate with a ravishing grace. Her little porcelain hand lifted the toast with the delicacy of a cat. But her chest was tight and it seemed hard for her to swallow.

The sky darkened, and everything in the dining room became even more somber, more boring. In their gold frames, the portraits of the colonel and the prefect seemed to scowl, as if in the depths of their deaths the father and grandfather had been dreaming and finally understood what life should have been. Madame de Villaplane discovered that the coffee was bad, too weak, and that the toast was not grilled, but burned. "God! Will I have to go on like this for much longer?"

She went up to her room.

Madame de Villaplane carefully closed her door. Then, pulling back the carpet, she stretched out on the floor and put her eye to a convenient hole. Kaminsky's room was just below.

In Madame de Villaplane's defense, she hadn't made the hole, or had anyone else make it for her. She'd simply taken advantage of the sorry state of the floor. One day, when Kaminsky was at the prefecture, she'd stuck her umbrella in the hole and poked away the thin film of plaster that plugged it. This was the extent of her guilt. To Kaminsky, who complained the next day about finding rubble in his bed and sarcastically asked if he should be expecting the whole ceiling to cave in on his face one day, she replied that he could move out if he wasn't happy. It wasn't her fault that the house was so old, that it had previously belonged to a man who'd never cared to pay for even one sou's worth of repairs, that, after his suicide, it had been empty for years. Which was to say it had been in a state of total dilapidation when she'd acquired it, and to get it into some sort of shape had taken the very last sous that her children had seen fit to leave her. Voilà. If he wasn't satisfied with that, he had only to say so.

He was careful to keep quiet. Not for a second would he dream of finding a room elsewhere, even if he'd understood what it meant that this little hole had suddenly been poked in his ceiling. But he hadn't figured it out, and Madame de Villaplane was the only one who knew about this vantage point. Even the maid was ignorant, since Madame de Villaplane cleaned her own room, and the maid only entered to bring meals or groom her mistress.

Madame de Villaplane hadn't thought for a second that it was dishonest and horrible to spy on Kaminsky. This habit became one of the costs of privation. She didn't have an ounce of remorse. Spying was her vice. It bears noting that she surrounded herself with luxuries when she kept watch, as she put it, through the crack. Her watches went on for a long time, for hours. She'd even taken the care to arrange a whole assembly of blankets and cushions on the floor next to the peephole, so that she could stretch out there almost as comfortably as she did on her bed.

Perhaps to a watching stranger, or to an abler spy, surveilling her in turn from a perch on the roof, this nice old lady would have provided quite a spectacle—stretched on her stomach in a nest of cushions, not moving a muscle! What a shiver would have passed through that stranger, if he could have seen the astonishing smile that sometimes crossed Madame de Villaplane's face. But there were times when even the most talented spy wouldn't have been able to see anything—when Madame de Villaplane darkened her own room and stayed at her lookout, still and scarcely breathing, her eye pressed to the bright pastille the hole made in the darkness, a clot of shadows in shadow. Then the watcher would be left to come to terms with his own suffering.

That morning, Madame de Villaplane was in a rush. She threw herself down on the floor without thinking of her usual comforters and cushions. It wasn't just for pleasure—not a job for an amateur— this was about knowing.

She didn't immediately understand what he was doing. When her gaze plunged straight down into his room, he was right below her, Kaminsky's skull like the weight at the end of a plumb line, his handsome black head like the plumage of a crow. His hair combed, shiny with brilliantine, and parted down the middle like two wings. He didn't move. Standing in the middle of the room, he was thinking, rubbing his hands together softly as if lathering them. And he was crooning. She hated it when he sang. She found it vulgar, and she grimaced. She was annoyed she couldn't yell at him to be quiet. She shifted her position and pressed her ear to the hole.

> "To see it again, Pana-me
> Pana-me
> Pana-me . . .
> The Eiffel Tower, the place Blanche
> Notre Da-me
> The boulevards and the pretty Mada-mes . . ."

So he was singing that, was he! She quickly looked in again. Standing now in front of the open doors of his wardrobe, he was singing loudly enough that Madame de Villaplane could hear him without turning her ear to the hole. She thought he must be looking for something like a hat, since he was dressed to go out, wearing his uniform, with only the jacket off. To her great astonishment, it wasn't a hat he took out of the wardrobe, but its entire contents. And still singing. That vulgar song about Paname gave a rhythm to Kaminsky's gestures as he threw all his linens onto the bed along with his clothes, his books, magazines and newspapers. What had got into him? Had he decided to undertake an inventory of all his possessions? Did he think someone had robbed him and that the boardinghouse was a den of cutthroats? Madame de Villaplane didn't understand at all what he was planning, and when she saw him bend down and pull his suitcase from the bottom of the wardrobe, she couldn't bear to realize. But she felt herself stiffen and die at her lookout. She even stopped watching for a moment, closing her eyes, filling herself up with shadows. *He's leaving.* This was what had been looming for the last two weeks! This was why he'd had such a funny smile the night before. Now the carefully kept secret was revealed—the cruel executioner! Since when had he been planning this blow? From the very beginning no doubt, the very first bouquet he'd given her—poison under the roses. Oh the traitor, the liar, the two-faced man! Crazed with rage she rolled over, contorting on the floor like an epileptic in a seizure, her hands clenched in the rug. Then she glued her eye to the crack and didn't move.

Still smiling, Kaminsky packed his suitcase with linens, clothes, and books. He ripped the newspapers, glanced at the magazines before tossing them in the bin, and looked around him, making sure he hadn't forgotten anything. And still the same song. Forever and always that Paname tune of a party he was undoubtedly headed to, maybe even that day. Where did he get the nerve? How was he, a simple soldier, going to escape the laws that held every man to his post? There must be exceptions for traitors then, but was every liar going to be allowed to carry out his evil scheme, despite the war? What friends in high places did he have to escape the usual laws? Surely he wasn't going just for a short leave. She'd seen him go off duty before without that aura around him. And he hadn't hidden the other trips from her. His silence, yesterday's smile, his secretive-ness, other bits of evidence—what additional proof did she need to know he wasn't coming back? She'd been betrayed, fleeced, thrust back into her prison—she who had been hoping for so long, who had put her trust in him! And he was singing! So he had forgotten her? At least—this supplicating thought arrived—he was perhaps only singing so that she would hear. He was certainly capable of it!

His suitcase buckled, he left it on the table and went out. Quickly, Madame de Villaplane got up and ran down the stairs, and as he reached the vestibule, she called out, "Monsieur Kaminsky!"

He turned and smiled, calm, innocent, friendly, a hand resting on the banister. His long olive-skinned face, his big nose, his fat lips, his full cheeks gave off a happiness he made no effort to conceal. He waited. "Madame?"

She had her game face on this morning. Literally overcome. He made a movement to look at his watch, ostensibly checking the time.

"Oh, really?" said Madame de Villaplane, paling. She came down a few more steps. He still didn't move. She said again, "Really?"

He stopped smiling. "What do you mean?" he said.

"Are you in such a rush?"

He thought about it, then shook his head, "No, after all, no."

"Let's go into the dining room."

He diagnosed her: maximum level of agitation. Big scene ahead. "But of course," he replied, at the bottom of the stairs. She followed.

They entered the dining room like two accomplices, and he thought, with a little pleasure, of the loony scene that was brewing. Madame de Villaplane carefully closed the door.

As soon as she did, her manner changed. She looked Kaminsky up and down with disgust, moving away as if she feared his touch. "I must tell you," she said in a shrill little voice, "I must tell you, Mon-sieur, that you would do well to find another place to stay!"

Damn it, did she really have to go to all this trouble just to tell him that? She was a cunning one, wasn't she! "Come, come," said Kaminsky, almost inaudibly.

But already Madame de Villaplane continued, "What! This disrespect on your part—what time did you come home last night?"

Kaminsky's smile returned. "You want me to tell you, dear Madame?"

"I demand that you reply."

She was trembling, poor little old lady, she was alive with anger.

"But," Kaminsky continued, in a voice of true gentleness, "you astonish me. What time did I get home? Come now, it's you who are about to tell me, Madame. Why don't you try to remember, attempt to put a finger on the exact moment you woke up? I am in fact in a bit of a hurry, but if this must continue—I can spare five minutes—will you permit me to take a seat? And would you perhaps take one too? It seems to me that you're a little tired this morning. May I inquire—how is your heart?"

While he spoke, he pushed a chair towards her. With two glaring eyes, she watched him do it, the whole bottom half of her face frozen into a grimace that must have been quite painful. Her two hands were clasping, refusing. "Leave my heart alone!"

"But allow me," he said again, "I must insist."

"Otto!"

He let himself relax. "Ah! That's better...yes, I like that much better. Finally you're looking more like yourself. Yes, much nicer now. What has upset you so, my dear...Blanche?"

"My God!" she murmured.

He pretended not to hear. "Once more, are you sure you won't sit down? No? You refuse? In that case, I must ask your permission to seat myself. I'm a bit tired...after a night like that!" he finished in a tone that made Madame de Villaplane tremble from head to toe.

"Are you truly the devil incarnate?" she cried.

He widened his eyes, apparently shocked. "That's quite strong!"

"But don't you understand—"

Her sentence went unfinished. Madame de Villaplane leaned on the mantel, as if to put herself under the protection of the two portraits of father and grandfather. She was shockingly fragile this morning, so vulnerable, as Kaminsky of course realized. Usually, she reserved a different violence for these scenes—and often, she was the one who controlled them. But this morning Kaminsky was in charge.

"May I smoke?" he said, taking a packet of cigarettes from his pocket.

A moment. Then she replied, "May I kill you?"

He burst out laughing.

Madame de Villaplane's arms fell limply on her black dress.

When he had finished laughing: "Let's be serious. I mean," he said, crossing his legs (he had put a cigarette in his mouth but hadn't lit it), "I mean to invite some friends over for tea this evening. Would that be an imposition do you think?"

She didn't answer.

He continued calmly, "There will be five or six of us, no more. Would that be possible? Do you have everything ready? I would like... Oh! Don't make that face. When you want to, you still know how to be pretty!"

She didn't flinch.

"Say something. Answer me!"

"Who was in your bed last night?"

He looked at her with great astonishment, as though she'd asked him if his name really was Otto Kaminsky, if it was true that he was a man, and not a bird.

"Why, Simone."

"And Léo drove you back here?"

"Who else besides Léo would it have been? Yes Léo. In the prefect's car. As usual. Why do you ask?" No answer. He shrugged. "You're acting funny this morning."

"Do you think?"

"Yes. Standing there, leaning on the fireplace, not moving. You—excuse the comparison, but it's because of the fireplace—and you're so little! You look like a log, like a little stick of kindling."

"Mostly charred?"

He considered this.

"Yes. Because of the black dress, no doubt. Why do you make me say such things? I don't want to. It's funny—there's something about you that makes me cruel."

She closed her eyes.

"And what's more, I have, towards you, Blanche—must I tell you? Do you want me to tell you—"

"Be quiet."

Her eyes still closed, her little mouth in a tight line, her fingers clasped together over the black dress so tightly they could crack. "You're worse than I am, Otto."

He gave a strange answer: "I'm doing my best."

Silence.

Kaminsky balanced delicately on the chair, which creaked. He decided to light his cigarette. "Let's get back to business," he said, tossing his match into the fireplace. "I told you I mean to have a few friends over for tea this evening. Basically, I'd like to give this little gathering a—celebratory air. For example, I would like this dining room—which between us, no offense, is rather depressing—to be decorated. Couldn't there be some flowers? And candles, that's what I would like. It is, I admit, a little bit romantic on my part, but in the end—how much would that be?"

She seemed not to have heard.

"How much? Don't forget that I'm a miser!"

For the first time since this fight began, something resembling a smile flitted over Madame de Villaplane's face.

"—all the money in the world," he heard her say. But it was barely audible.

"What was that?"

"Not for all the money in the world!"

"What! Really? How could you refuse?" he said, tipping back against his chair, his cigarette left to burn between his fingers. "Is that so? And I thought it would cheer you up, I thought you'd like to be among us!"

"Me!" This time, Madame de Villaplane had shouted. Not only that, but she'd torn herself away from the mantelpiece and stepped toward Kaminsky, who stood up. She yelled into his face, "Bastard!"

He gently took the old lady's frail wrist between his fingers. "You're getting yourself all worked up. Why so angry? Whatever I say, you always hear God knows what subtext. Don't you know that—that you're my best friend?" he finished in a tender tone, leaning in towards Madame de Villaplane's face.

She pulled away. "Let go of me."

"Why?"

"Let me go or I'll scream!"

"Don't sound so childish, my dear Blanche. Scream? Why would you? After all, if you feel like screaming, you can go ahead. They say it's calming. You'll scream, someone will come, and I'll tell them—"

"Is there anyone on this earth more disgusting than this man!"

He pushed her away. "I am what I am."

The silence returned, heavier, thicker. It was dark inside the room. Outside it rained.

"So it's settled then?" he finally said. "The answer is no?"

She didn't understand right away. "No what?"

"About the tea?"

She shrugged clumsily, with a childish, sulky little frown lurking on her lips. "What more could that do to me?"

"So it's all right?"

"Why not? What do I care?"

"With flowers?"

"All the flowers you want. Tell the maid so she'll take care of it—"

"And a big wood fire in the fireplace, of course?"

"Naturally."

"Then we're agreed. And you'll be there, won't you?"

"Otto!"

"If you start screaming again, I'm leaving. I—I've had enough. I can't stand to hear you scream like that. You have to be there. It's a little—goodbye party."

She looked for something to lean on. Her hand found the back of a chair.

"Since you're kicking me out," finished Kaminsky, looking her straight in the eye. "Since—"

But this time he didn't have the chance to say more. Madame de Villaplane left the dining room like an arrow that's been released.

In the vestibule, the maid was talking to Lucien Bourcier.

"A room, sir?"

"Yes please."

"For one month?"

"For one day."

"But we don't rent rooms by the day, sir." And seeing Madame de Villaplane come into the vestibule looking like death, the maid cried out, "Madame! Madame!"

Madame de Villaplane paused.

Kaminsky appeared and said, "Madame de Villaplane isn't feeling well this morning, Ernestine. Would you—"

"Mind your own business!" Madame de Villaplane interrupted in a bitter voice.

He smiled. "You've surpassed yourself."

"Enough!"

"Fine. As you please."

"Be satisfied with giving orders for your . . . tea," she said. "And by the way, yes, you're right, I'm not well, it's true. Ernestine, see what this Monsieur wants, if this little scene hasn't given him reason enough to flee. What, sir, would you like a room here?"

"For a day," said Lucien.

She gave a burst of nervous laughter and staggered toward the stairs. "For a day! For a day!" she cried, "Oh why not for a day! Ernestine, give this man a room. For a day! Nothing but a day!"

They listened. She didn't stop laughing and crying "for a day!" as she climbed up to her room. A door slammed. Then nothing.

CRIPURE was dictating to his class.

Sitting under the window, he looked enormous in his goatskin, like a bear. His tapered hands rested on his thighs.

"Morality, you see, is a science, you see, or an art. Write that down!"

"A what?"

"An art," came the whispers from various sides of the room, "an art!"

"Silence!" he snapped, in a sharp voice, exasperated. They laughed; he threatened, "Enough! The first boy who acts out will be kicked out of class immediately. For good, with the additional bonus of a four-hour detention." He hurried on with the dictation, "Morality is a science or an art which teaches men how to conduct their lives. Write that down!"

The pens scratched. But even the scratching wasn't a simple sound, but instead something like the scrabbling of an army of ants or spiders on sand—

He took his watch out of his pocket—another fifteen minutes. How his classes dragged on, how everything dragged on! They could hear, from the neighboring classroom, Babinot's nasal voice, "Is Le Bars a bad student, mes-si-eurs?"

The class answered together: "Yes!"

But Babinot said, "Nah, nah! I'm telling you nah. And why mes-si-eurs do I say nah? Because if Le Bars were a bad student then he would also be—go on, mes-si-eurs, go on! What would he be?"

"A bad Frenchman," the students chorused.

"That's what I wanted you to say! He'd be a bad Frenchman. And is Le Bars a bad Frenchman?"

"No!"

"*A fortiori* then, mes-si-eurs, our friend Le Bars is a good student, and he's going to recite the lesson for us. We were saying, mes-si-eur Le Bars, we were saying that Verdun—"

A sound of footsteps, then silence.

"I congratulate you, mes-si-eurs! Have a seat!"

Footsteps again. And Babinot continued: "Verdun underwent eleven sieges. They were?"

A childish voice began: "In 451, Attila—"

With a sigh, Cripure lifted his head. His own students, pens at the ready, had only been waiting for that signal to burst into laughter. He realized he had completely forgotten them.

"Silence!" he shouted in a shrill, cringing voice. But they only laughed harder and he rose from his seat, fleeing his suffering, recognizing his helplessness once again. On his feet, he was grotesque—no longer a bear but an ape, a paralyzed orangutan, sagging on too-long thighs. The impression hovered over the reality like a more menacing real. He gave his students a terrified look, and their joy grew.

From year to year, it got worse. Would he end his "career" senile, being the lookout for these dunces as they played cards? Or as a louse?

"Silence, you dunces!" He banged his fist on the lectern, and it echoed like a barrel. They were quiet. *Perhaps it was a false alarm*, he thought.

At his desk, a student was noisily cracking his knuckles.

"M'sieu!"

Cripure took his chances, casting a fierce look at the little scoundrel's face, which was puffed with laughter. "What do you have to say to us, Monsieur Gentric?"

Gentric got up, and said in a rush, "Is it true m'sieu, that Immanouel Kant, the immortal author of the *Cripure of Tique Reason*—"

A pure delight seized the class. They didn't content themselves with just laughing, but clapped their hands, banged their feet under the desks, cried out "Creep, creep, Cripure!"

Cripure closed his eyes.

"—Is it true he was a virgin?" Gentric finished. The more cowardly— a large number—sank into their seats. Gentric looked back and forth like an overgrown bird. To their surprise, Cripure also smiled, then laughed outright, his watch chain bouncing up and down on his vest. *Oh! It's all to the good, understandably, this irreverence for idols! All the same—*

"A little too spirited, don't you think Monsieur Gentric, and a little too Rabelaisian at that. Let's drop it." He laughed even harder.

Gentric exploded. The others, seeing that he'd get away with it, picked themselves back up and joined the chorus. So much coward-ice disgusted Cripure. Truly the worst human quality, at all stages of life, was the hypocrisy that came from this unwillingness to take a risk.

"Fools!" he cried, "Shut up, you fools, you herd of bootlickers, daddy's boys! Filthy little bourgeois! Why do you even come here? For culture? Let's talk about that, then, you band of—scoundrels! You're nothing but—" He bit his tongue on this risky insult: killers.

They must be hiding somewhere in the crowd, the two or three little bastards who had loosened the bolts on his bikes. They must be shaking with fear, just then, with the idea that they'd be in detention for a whole Thursday. What disgust! And disgust with himself too, since after all—

Since after all, he'd done himself in. And the proof was that he'd barely thought of the affair, that he still didn't know if he'd complain to the principal—

There was a knock. At the same time the door opened and Mon-sieur Bourcier entered brusquely. Cripure, crimson and sweating with anger, held his breath. He lowered his raised arm, and even attempted a smile (which went undetected) in response to the dean's greeting. But it was the guilty smile of someone who's caught in the act and begs for mercy, and the joy—yes the joy—of the threatened passerby who sees the police rushing in.

The students were fixed in an attitude of false respect, but they were laughing under their breath. They knew well that, in the eyes of the dean, Cripure was the guilty one, not the other way around.

Monsieur Bourcier glanced over the class with a look that was sad, unreadable, and stood there for a while without speaking, his eyes moving from one to another, as if hesitating over his choice of victim. He created the atmosphere, but his victim was obvious to him, and finally he settled his heavy gaze on Gentric.

"Monsieur Gentric?"

Gentric straightened up like a soldier on guard, and his heels clacked disrespectfully.

"You're put in detention for all of Thursday," the dean said slowly. And his eyes widened under his heavy eyebrows.

Gentric smiled. Monsieur Bourcier looked at Cripure, who shrugged slightly.

"Very well, Monsieur Gentric," said the dean in a changed voice, one ready to shout, "Since that makes you smile, you'll have two days detention instead of one. Are you smiling now?"

Furious at being beaten, he could barely contain himself. "No, Monsieur Dean."

The insolence of this reply was made even greater as Gentric fought the crazy urge to burst out laughing.

"Watch yourself, Gentric—the next step after detentions is getting kicked out of class, do you understand?"

"Unequivocally, sir."

"All right, that's the last straw!"

Gentric gathered his things, and made a show of leaving the room, closing the door calmly behind him.

"There's a fine one for you," Monsieur Bourcier finished.

He turned toward the others and threatened harsh punishments at the slightest sign of disrespect. He would defeat this detestable attitude of insubordination and unruliness that was spreading among the youth and—be warned! He would show the ringleaders no mercy.

He finished his lecture by reminding them of the sorrowful circumstances France was facing.

"It would be cowardly for you all to abuse the liberty granted to you in your fathers' absence." That sentence, which these dunces had heard a million times, signaled to them that the harangue was over. *Ite missa est.* The dean turned toward Cripure, who lowered his head.

"Crack down on them, Monsieur Merlin." And he went out quickly, without ever taking off his hat.

The silence stretched out for a moment after he left. Then loud, ironic *oufs* brought Cripure out of his reverie. "Where were we?"

"... an art which teaches men how to conduct their lives."

"Fine. Let's continue. Title: *Individual Morality and Social Morality.* Write that down!"

His back arched, his hands deep in his pockets, he continued the dictation in a voice that was jerky and irritated, a tone that went against everything he said. His eyes, dull behind his pince-nez, looked toward the light like a memory—as if he were a fat, trapped fly bumping against a window. In the silences of the dictation, his mouth tightened, and his thin lips seemed to vanish, swallowed by the lifted point of his chin. The pens scratched. He continued: "A question arises: that of knowing whether individual morality should be subordinated to social morality, or vice versa, the social to the individual, or if both moral standards should be juxtaposed to benefit each side equally. For some philosophers—"

"The bell's ringing, Monsieur," one of Gentric's followers interrupted. And without waiting for Cripure to give the word, the schoolboys raced for the door all at once in a furious mob, jostling him as they went by so they could stealthily pull out big tufts of goat hair.

He rubbed his temples with the tips of his fingers—the tic—adjusted his pince-nez, and, with the hesitant movements of a man who expects the roof to fall in at any moment, he left the classroom, double locking the door behind him. Monsieur Babinot, his hands crossed under the lapels of his jacket, his head bent, his big spiked boots ringing out on the flagstones, was grumbling to himself. Seeing Cripure, he rushed over.

"Guess what?" he said. "Can you guess what I'm thinking? About me! About that horrible *I* the philosopher speaks of! Well then, when I say *the I*, it's a missing person I'm talking about. The war effort, the danger to France, the national resistance—"

Cripure was already far away. His direction: the bar.

Streets, for a change. Familiar torment. It would take him half an hour more at least to reach Café Machin. Dragging along. He hated the houses. *Man's great struggle for so many centuries just to build these hideous boxes! What prevented them from putting fountains everywhere, and gardens, and palaces? Why not the palaces from* A Thousand and One Nights? *Why can't I at least be blind?*

He was only nearsighted.

Someone passed and, seeing Cripure, murmured his pity.

And deaf!

He bravely continued on his way.

As he passed, he glanced at the prefecture—a spiritual monument in its way. He always trembled when he had to brave those bars, as if he worried they would close behind him, finally taking away his escape.

Flee!

He went on towards the square.

Somewhere a horn was blaring endlessly—it could have been in the Square, or maybe on the moon. Cripure was still walking when, realizing there was a car rushing at him from less than a meter away, he leapt, jerking aside, almost knocked flat on the ground.

The effect was undoubtedly quite comical, since, as soon as he regained his senses, still panting, a great burst of laughter rang out. He turned around—the car had paused. A young officer in fancy dress was holding the wheel in both hands.

Cripure was breathless with anger. But before he could say a word, an officer with a monocle and soft leather boots got out of the car with his gloves in his hand and came toward him.

"Faurel!" It was the deputy, no less, a staff officer.

"Excuse me my dear professor," said Faurel. "I had nothing to do with this odious joke. I was half-asleep in the back of the car—we were traveling all night. And then this trumped-up idiot woke me with his brakes. I didn't have time—But just look at him! What a laugh! Corbin!"

At the wheel, this "trumped-up idiot" smiled behind his hand.

"That's enough," Faurel ordered dryly. "Come excuse yourself." He turned to Cripure, "Please forgive him, my dear professor. He's still a kid. It hasn't been long, you'll remember, since he was your student—"

Cripure slowly pulled himself together. He adjusted his pince-nez and glanced toward Corbin. Oh these bastards—this was how they wanted to crush him! It had reached a new level—first the bikes and now a car.

"As a matter of fact, I remember Monsieur...Corbin quite well," he continued, looking at the chauffeur who had finally come down from his seat. "But I wouldn't have recognized you in that astonishing uniform. No I wouldn't have seen anything of my old philosophy student in you—it's been what, two years?"

Corbin, standing as if on guard, replied, "That's right, Monsieur Merlin." Not a wrinkle had moved in that knife-blade face.

"Well then?" said Faurel.

"My dear Monsieur Merlin, please pardon me. I didn't mean to cause harm. It was just my excitement at seeing you again."

Faurel raised his eyebrows. "That's all?"

"I only make fun of people I respect—or love."

This outrageous lie didn't prevent Cripure from shaking Corbin's offered hand. He smiled. "Youth does have its privileges."

"For now, it has the privilege of putting the car away," said Faurel. Corbin saluted and disappeared.

Cripure and Faurel walked on slowly, the deputy taking the arm of his "dear old teacher."

Faurel's face showed traces of weariness that weren't only due to his long journey, but which had been intensified by the trip. His cheeks, carefully shaved, were slack, gray, and framed with crows' feet; his big eyes bluish and troubled. His mouth, below a thin, still-black mustache, expressed the kindness typical in men who value pleasure—and don't always encounter it—and made up for the raw sensuality of his aquiline nose and the tic of his constantly twitching nostrils. His body beneath the uniform was slender and energetic as ever. But whether he wore his uniform or civilian clothes, everything about him betrayed Faurel as a man who'd spent his life among women.

"This is a strange place to meet you, my dear professor," said Faurel, in the tone of tactful distance which was natural to him, but which signaled a sincere respect for Cripure. "These aren't your usual haunts, these bastions of government," he said, gesturing toward the prefecture. "And how is Madame Merlin?"

"Why, very well," Cripure replied, genuinely touched that someone had asked after his companion. That happened so rarely!

"You'll give my best regards to her?"

"You're too kind."

"We had such good times at your cottage," replied the deputy. "I remember it like yesterday." Faurel thought of himself as someone who loved ideas, and he was curious about people. He recognized Cripure's talents, and was always asking him about his little projects, especially *The Wisdom of the Medes*. That book had astonished Faurel. He also loved to ask Cripure about the intricacies of Sanskrit—the deputy would have loved to learn Sanskrit!

Fortunately the conversation took a different turn. "You're still hunting?"

"Once in a while—"

"That cottage!" murmured Faurel, turning sentimental.

"Yes," said Cripure, smiling to think about it. *His little cottage!* He spent the summers there and long stretches of the winter as well.

"The winter is just as lovely."

One evening, with Faurel, they'd walked up the road. They'd climbed to an inn where two paths crossed, arm in arm, as they were that moment. What had they talked about?

"Do you remember that conversation about Rousseau, Professor?" *Did he remember!* "I do, as if it were yesterday. Before going out, we reread that astonishing page together, you recall, from the *Dialogues*, where he's about to take his manuscript to Notre-Dame. Such a moving passage—maybe the most intense pathos in all his work, including the *Confessions*. Such beauty—electrifying, wasn't it?"

He must have said the same things, that night. Faurel pictured Cripure's gesture, standing in the street. He'd stretched out his arms, as though to measure the spaces of shadows. The waves echoed in the distance.

Cripure remembered it too. The voice of the sea, mingling with theirs like the chorus in theater, had shaken loose a tenderness. Precious moments when his inner voice, suddenly freed, had found its match in the voice of the world—or in a face!

"Times have certainly changed," he said.

But even that night, there had been some ugliness. They'd touched on the prickly question of bastard children. Cripure had stuck with Rousseau and Faurel had gotten angry. True, Faurel hadn't abandoned Corbin, as Cripure had abandoned Amédée.

This unhappy memory broke through the charm.

"Yes," said Faurel, "they certainly have. What do they think of the war here?"

"From this point of view, you know, it's nothing but a fairy tale. A bloody fairy tale, but a story all the same."

The deputy closed his eyes and shrugged. Scornful and resigned. "Pathetic human psychology," he said.

"Biology," said Cripure, forcing a laugh.

"When it's going so poorly!"

"Truly?"

"Oh! If I could tell you—"

Bah! thought Cripure, *when are the depths of war really known?* Was it possible to comprehend the details of something so fucked? Maybe he didn't want to. Not only did he want to be fooled, but with an air of mystery. "What can we think of a human race completely engrossed in destroying itself?"

"It probably doesn't deserve anything better."

That made Cripure laugh, genuinely this time. Confronted with that thought, he felt right at home. "Humans aren't necessary," he said.

Another pleasant idea. His eyes shone with the malice of someone who's just uncovered a plot.

"One couldn't say it's going very well, but it's going all the same," the deputy continued. "We'll soon redress the moral wrongs, but what a cost!" He looked skyward.

"It seems we may be quite close to a revolution," said Cripure.

"Right on the verge. It's almost come to that," said Faurel, clicking a nail under his tooth. "Inside the lines, there's nothing much going on anymore. Some very small incidents, some noise at night on the trains for furloughed men. Nothing next to what we had seen! Not even close. The major-general asked for carte blanche in dealing out punishments and setting examples."

"Many?"

"Alas! You know, my dear professor, I'm a little bit of a revolutionary. At heart I am, and I've always been a good liberal, a good patriot. But to see that! There have been horrible things. Even so, that's too much. I know how serious the situation is, and that we can't let the army go to waste. Keep the spirit alive, my friend, but know that there were five whole divisions almost completely contaminated."

"As many as that!"

"Maybe more. I told you, the situation was extremely dangerous. Especially if you take the political climate in Paris and within the region into account. May first, there was a strike in Paris. June second, more than three thousand women on strike demonstrating for over two hours on the Champs-Élysées. The Tonkinese fired on the crowd at Saint-Ouen.[8] And then others. And to think that no mutineers have been pardoned."

"And of course," said Cripure, "those are the purest of them, the ones with integrity who take the blame for it."

The deputy let his arms fall to his sides in agreement.

"Not one pardon!" Cripure continued. "But—Poincaré?"

"You don't know that man. When Painlevé asked him to pardon

two mutineers, he replied that 'this wasn't the moment for weakness.' God, when will this end?"

They both sighed, walking a moment side by side without saying anything.

"That's all so tragic," said Cripure.

"But all the same it has a comic side—would you believe that Pétain asked Madelin to research cases of mutiny from the Revolution before coming up with ways to repress the current trouble? And then he consulted that grammar buff Henri Bordeaux!"

Cripure burst out laughing. "Priceless, that's what that is," he said, "ah, ha! I couldn't make up a more cheerful story. All the same, this loony stuff does some good."

And the conversation took a joyful turn, almost fanciful.

"I heard that they're decorating Madame Faurel?"

The deputy frowned a little. He knew what Cripure thought of decorations and how they were gotten. "I've got to howl with the pack," he said.

"But, it's very nice," said Cripure.

"What is? That they're decorating my wife?"

"Yes, exactly."

Oh, all right—in that case, if Cripure was going to take it that way.

"Between us, my friend, I'm more towards your point of view. It will be one well-deserved trinket. But it certainly isn't necessary. They insisted, you know. And my wife, good sport that she is, didn't want to tell them that she couldn't give a—damn. I was about to say something even less—academic."

"Come now! When someone exposes themselves to risk as she did—"

"Yes, that's true."

"I'll make a point of being there."

"Why, that's very kind. I'm touched. I mean it, you know. And she will be too. She cares very much about you. I'm touched."

Cripure took his hand. "Come, come, my friend."

"But I am. Very much—"

"I wouldn't dream of missing it."

"It's this—decoration that brings me back here," Faurel continued, "and the need to recover, to forget a little. The horrible things one sees! I'd like to go lie down in a field, to nap in the good air for a while. But I've got to pay a visit to my tenant farmers. That'll be a rest. I need one. Oh if only I had a little more time. I'd ask to stay in your little cottage for a day or two. But I'll have to be happy with what time I've got. Isn't it already so wonderful to run into you just as I arrive, even though," he said, pointing to the prefecture, "we're nearing a place where you never set foot? These official buildings!"

"You mean, don't you, that I avoid them?"

"You're a wise man, and I don't just say that to flatter you. No!" and Faurel made a gesture to indicate that he was through with all the flattery, all the intrigues he'd fought through all his life, that he was simply tired. "Yes, what I wouldn't give," he continued, "to spend a day with you at the cottage, as we used to do, to talk over a few ideas. But it's impossible."

"I know, I know, my friend."

"I sense you doubt it? Farewell my friend! You're the only man I'll be pleased to see here, but it's the prefect who's expecting me. He's not expecting you, I hope," Faurel added, finishing the conversation on a joking note.

And he disappeared with a wave of his gloves.

NOT FAR from Simone's house, the prefectural chauffeur stopped. Léo turned toward the backseat, his face battered, copper-colored, with almost no nose and a Buddha's lips. His eyelids, with their strange, white lashes, lifted to reveal murky gray eyes.

"Getting out?"

"Just a moment—"

And Kaminsky, still holding Simone's hands in his, continued, "My darling—what will you think of me if I ask you to consider things a bit more before making such a serious decision? If I turn into Father Prudhomme[9] and start giving you wholesome advice? To leave your family! And go to Paris with your lover! That's called throwing your life under the wheels. What do you think?"

She laughed. Her hands quivered in Kaminsky's.

"I think—I think the same thing you do."

"And that means?"

"That you're teasing me."

"Why not at all!" He cried. "Not for a second. How could I? Coddled as you are by your father, by your mother—in light of the jangling pockets of comfy notaries. You have everything you need to be happy, my dear Simone. Won't you think about it?"

"That's all I'm doing!"

"Bravo! Show me your hand?"

She held out her hand, palm up.

"No, the left hand."

He bent over it. Simone smiled. Léo, indifferent, lit a cigarette and threw the match out the car window.

"*Primo*: you will live to be very old," said Kaminsky after a long moment, "*Secundo*: you'll never go crazy."

A pause.

"You know I'm not actually seeing anything?" he said, raising his eyes.

"Keep going anyway."

"Date of birth?"

"August 1899."

"August: great men and great murderers. You'll succeed in your endeavors."

"In murder as well?" she asked, bursting into laughter.

He didn't answer, but approached her open palm with his lips, placing a kiss there.

"Will I have money?"

"More than you'll know what to do with. In sum, everything looks good. August 1899—that means you're a little over eighteen today. Not much of a wait, but it's time. You only get one roll of the dice—"

She knew it.

"Well, then it's understood," Kaminsky continued. "After lunch, Léo will take you to the cottage, with Marcelle. At five, we'll join you with Bacchiochi. Then we'll go have tea with Madame de Villaplane. Ok?"

"Why do we need to go to Madame de Villaplane's?"

"It will give her so much pleasure!" Kaminsky replied with a bitter smile.

"Ok, fine then."

"Settled," said Léo.

"Drive slowly—"

Léo braked. The notary's house appeared, at the end of a grassy lane.

"Incredible, isn't it, how this house resembles a piggy bank," said Kaminsky. "Doors, windows, chimneys, skylights, crevices, everything looks like a coin slot. Who'd they steal this little shack from?"

"Two old ladies."

"Dead?"

"They became dead. He even nabbed their parakeet, which he had stuffed and put on the mantelpiece. You don't know my father! Here's good, Léo—stop!" He pulled over to the sidewalk.

"See you here in an hour."

"I know it." She slipped out of the car. The two men looked at each other and smiled.

"Eh?" said Kaminsky, with a wink.

"I get it."

"She's a determined woman. She'll do just what she wants."

"That's rare."

"Very rare. And at eighteen, no less. But that, my dear Léo, is like talent—you have it or you don't. And when it's there, you notice right away. Later on, you can perfect technique—"

Léo put the car in gear.

"And prettier and prettier besides," Kaminsky continued. "Go ahead, she's gone inside."

A little acceleration.

"Not my type," said Léo. "Too brunette for me. Legs too long. Eyes too dark. Not much chest. Me, I like a blond with blue eyes—" He sped up. More pressure on the accelerator. "Some meat on her bones—"

Simone went upstairs to her room. She threw her coat on the bed and thought for a moment. Then she went back out, leaned over the banister and yelled, "Rose!"

No response.

Of course, Maman had taken up all Rose's time once again without thinking of anyone else, without asking if—

From below her mother's dry voice replied, "Is that you, Simone?"

"Yes, it's me." She'd recognized her voice, hadn't she?

"Who are you calling?"

"The chambermaid, Maman."

"Why—what do you need her for?"

"Tell her to come up."

"But—what for?"

"Oh!"

Simone gripped the banister, shaking with rage. It was murder, this mania her mother had of always getting into everything, of asking endless questions about the simplest things.

Her mother, at the bottom of the stairs, spoke standing up, without raising her head, her face to the wall. Simone caught sight of her pointed bun, her thin shoulders.

"Tell Rose to come up and make me a fire, ok?" After all, this was the last time she'd have to participate in one of these never-ending, exasperating exchanges—

"Are you cold?"

Simone gritted her teeth. "Listen, Mother—why don't you just tell Rose to come upstairs."

"But I don't know where Rose is!"

Simone went back into her room and violently slammed the door. She couldn't possibly have told her right away that she didn't know where Rose was! That would have killed her, wouldn't it? And to think it was like that every day from morning to night—*she'll drive me insane*—

She opened her little desk, took out some papers and put them on the table. *All that needs to be burned.* It would have been smarter to look at each paper, one at a time—that's what she would have done if she'd had a fire. But what for, were they really so important—letters from boys, photos—she'd burn it in bulk.

She grabbed a scarf and hung it from the doorknob, covering the keyhole. That way, her mother could peek as much as she liked. Then she went back to her papers, emptied out all of her drawers, made a pile of everything that needed to be burned, and sat on the floor. A match. Big flames roared up the chimney. *Why did I even get angry?* Once again, she'd been forced to march to their tune. But it was always like that. Not a day went by in that house without angering her. *But that's it. I'm burning everything. I won't bring anything but money, if I can get some, in a minute.*

She looked at the fire and smiled.

When he thought about Simone, Kaminsky felt an immense self-satisfaction at the remarkable progress of his student, which he attributed to his experience and his energy, forgetting that he had given her *Lamiel* to read. This attribute of her mentor hadn't escaped Simone, but she was careful not to let it show, and she even encouraged him to take all the credit for what he called "a revelation." She did this out of sincere recognition and because she had resolved a long time ago to use him in getting around the last, most difficult obstacles which still barred the way to freedom and riches. If he would only bring her to Paris! She wouldn't ask for more than a few months of support from him once they arrived in the capital—another word to eliminate from her vocabulary! The rest was her business.

She'd been careful not to breathe the slightest word about this plan to anyone. A strong instinct warned her to keep silent until the moment came, and this was it. When it came to outfits, manners, things you could learn, she left Kaminsky the flattering thought that she'd gotten it all from him. But as for her *understanding*, she'd always been very careful to keep quiet, and Kaminsky—deep thinker, subtle intellect that he chalked himself up to be—he hadn't suspected anything.

In such a vulgar scene, where ambition itself was vulgar when it existed, Simone had been on her own growing up, and it had taken so long to recognize the dangers around her that she'd been close to letting herself be engaged to the son of one of her father's colleagues, as if the idea of becoming the notary's lady wife in her turn, being a faithful spouse and a good mother to her family, had given her any happiness. That mistake hadn't lasted long. The suffering brought on by the engagement was a wake-up call, causing her to break off the deal and wait until she could cut the anchor. She'd soon understood what it would mean—they'd started talking to her about happiness and everything else their immense hypocrisy used to cover up the dead, more than half of whom had been murdered. Yes, they knew very well how to kill, and they didn't need daggers or poison to do it—their methods were subtler. What she owed to Kaminsky was the discovery of certain things that she would have otherwise discovered much later, probably too late. He'd given her a ten-year head start, which meant she could have a life. She wouldn't be a *victim*. From the moment she made that resolution, she'd never stopped thinking about her strategy, all the while remaining the provincial girl and continuing to go to mass. This way, hypocrisy had become a foundational concept for Simone, and it was on its way to becoming a science. She didn't try to justify it. Among the remarkable lessons she had acquired from Kaminsky was the understanding that justifications were always weaknesses or mistakes, and that between working for hypocrisy (which was considered one of the fine arts) and the possibility of getting one's throat slit, it would be shameful, crazy to hesitate, even for a second. When it came to the supposed "freedom" of young ladies during the war, what a joke! Just because it was easier to sleep with men—and was that even true?—didn't mean they had suddenly become liberated. That wasn't all there was to life. Simone's progress was so great that she could no longer conceive of a freedom that depended on circumstances or even manners. She only wanted to keep it within her.

Nothing left to burn. In the fireplace the letters, the photos were now a little pile of ashes she stirred with a poker. Fine. They were welcome to sift through it when she was gone—that was all they'd get for their trouble. And anyway, what did she care?

"Isn't it great to start a new life?" she said to herself, getting up. She looked around the room where for so long she'd been chewing on her leash. "It's so easy! All you have to do is act and see your actions through."

Action, for the moment, meant going upstairs.

The books. She took a luxurious edition of *Dangerous Liaisons*, a gift from Kaminsky, wrapped in a removable Moroccan leather cover. She lifted the book, put it on the table, and taking the cover, soundlessly left the room. The door barely squeaked. She paused to listen. Nothing. Rose, no doubt, was still nowhere to be found, and as for her mother, God knows what she could be up to!

Cautious all the same, Simone listened again. Then, sure that no one would catch her, she tiptoed upstairs.

The rug muffled her steps. She was very calm.

A kind of anger came over her when she entered her father's study. It was full of his smell, of his disgusting essence. Stale whiffs of tobacco, cheap cologne, other, unidentifiable sleaze. The ceiling was low in the room—a sort of attic turned into a study, with big windows covered in thick curtains, making it dim. Books, heavy furniture, paintings, leftovers from clients.

Resolved, she crossed to the desk. There was a drawer on the right, and within it, his money. Idiot! He hadn't even bothered to lock it. All she had to do was pull—the bills were there, safer, he thought, than in his strongbox. They were all the same. They all took great precautions against thieves, without even thinking for a moment that their own children … She smiled scornfully as she took out two bunches of thousand-franc bills. Should she count them? Why not? She counted them calmly, checking that each wad contained fifty bills. She made a bundle of it all, which she tied up and hid in the book cover. Then she left the room just as calmly as she had entered, not without closing the drawer and first checking that there was no more money lying around.

Robbery! Was that all there was to it? She was surprised it had been so easy, and, when it came down to it, so—logical. Yes, there was logic to all this. *After all*, she thought, *how could they imagine I'd arrive in Paris empty-handed and look for work?*

"Simone!"

She ran to the railing. "Yes?"

"Lunch is served!"

"Already?" It was barely noon. For some bizarre reason, lunch was early today of all days.

She went downstairs, her book under her arm. Her mother and father were already seated. They greeted each other pretty rarely in that household.

They ate in silence—apart from the loud ticking of the old grandfather clock, inherited from some forgotten peasant of a great-uncle, and the sounds they made as they gulped, breathed, clinked their knives and forks, fidgeted, and moved their chairs around on the polished parquet. Monsieur Point read his newspaper, which he had propped on the bottle in front of him. Madame Point looked like someone playacting a picnic, swallowing tiny bits of meat she skewered with the point of her fork as if in protest, with the expression of a convict who knew her punishment and fought, with what little she had, against the usual prison schedule. Simone had put her "book" next to her plate and glanced at it from time to time and smiled, inwardly replaying, "*N'est-ce plus ma main—*"

What else could you possibly hum, when all you had to look at was the sideboard, that masterpiece of pure Henri II style, with its gleaming sculpted figures on the middle door, that young actor in short breeches and a lacy ruff who for an eternity had been holding out his hand to the leading lady in a long dress and also a ruff, but a low-cut one—oh là là!

> *N'est-ce plus ma main que cette main presse*
> *tout comme autrefois?*

A head of white hair, speckled with dandruff, a big red forehead, and two bushy eyebrows peeked from behind the newspaper her father was reading. In his heavy, boxy hand, he held out a glass without looking up. Simone poured some wine into it. Glug, glug. Tick-tock.

Wasn't it always this way in the notary's cozy home?

With a prissy gesture, her mother dried her lips. Why? She'd certainly left nothing on them. *What a joke*, thought Simone. Every bite her mother swallowed must be neatly stacked in her stomach like the shirts in her closet—starch shelf, beef shelf. *That's my mother for you!*

Gray, ash-colored hair, whitened as if with powder, and below her squished forehead, two yellow slits for eyes, two blotches of plaster for cheekbones, set on her brick cheeks. She had read, dear woman, in the correspondence section of *Women's Style Weekly*, that combining one part glycerin with one part plain water was better for the face than the most reputable creams and a third of the price. Applied in the morning, with a coat of powder: set for the day. But she always put on too much, and the powder congealed like starch. Only fallen women knew the art of applying makeup, and she certainly didn't envy them! Her economical little recipe and her baby powder—she didn't allow herself anything more, and her wrinkly mouth had never known rouge, even in the long-ago days of her youth, when she must have been in love, when she must have thrown herself on the neck of that mister who was so profoundly absorbed in reading his paper, crying "my superb and gentle lion!" like in Hugo's *Hernani*. Her shiny chin, hard as a polished pebble, joined the girders of her jawbones and the massive padlocks of her ears to make one block. As for the rest of her, Madame Point the notaress wore a black dress that went from her neck to the tips of her toes, which were invisible under the table. She was a thin and scampering person, mechanical, a little hunched, since her hand (which by some mistake was rather fine) was occupied just then with endlessly sliding a gold pendant the size of a lapel-pin back and forth across her flabby chicken's neck. The notaress's character had one quirk, which was perhaps quite rare—that her silences were as considered as her chatter, which made Simone think not only *Maman is quiet* but *Maman is working on quietness*, or even *Maman is counting*. In fact, when the notaress was quiet, as she was just then, her face immediately looked like that of a child who is determined to count to ten thousand before taking a sip and really doesn't want to be interrupted. It was impossible to get a word out of her—not by joking, not by surprise. She responded to everything said to her with a stony glance, haughty and reproving, the same look she'd use to bury any impudent person who whispered a vulgar suggestion in her ear. The Pope, whom she adored, would have lost his seat.

Tick-tock—

Simone's hand found its way to her book, and rested on top—the feverish touch of a believer on her relic, the superstitious on her charm for conjuring hate.

A recent memory: her mother, in the kitchen, with her back turned. She was drinking a glass of milk. Simone came closer. Her mother hadn't turned around. On the table—basically in her hand—an enormous knife. A ten-inch, triangular blade. In a momentary flash, Simone had *seen* the place to strike, between the shoulders.

How could she escape from that? How do you avoid chance? Simone came to herself in her room a minute later, trembling at the idea that she could have ruined everything that way.

She raised her eyes, peeling an orange at the same time, and gestured as if to say something. Her mother must be in the two thousands at least; her father in the classifieds.

Enough of this!

"Father?"

He lowered his paper, and gave his daughter a slanting look from only one eye. He closed the other as if the light were bothering him. She smiled, impish as Lili, at that barren face. He looked like the mayor. An illegitimate brother? It wasn't impossible. You never could guess how they arranged their beds, and it was true that in town, you started to notice certain strange resemblances when you knew people well. Everything would be clear fifty years down the line—

"What do you want now?"

Oh! That snout! Puffed up and bloated—a real balloon. A red piece of beef with white bags under the eyes, the flesh of his neck puffing over the collar. Big, fat, pompous, decorated. *That's my father for you!*

She scratched the tablecloth with the tip of her index finger, head bent, absorbed. Her father! A fat man in a bad mood she saw at noon and at seven. Get to the table, eat everything, and drink, smoke his cigar, read his paper, write anonymous letters, steal from his clients— he hoped it would last a long time, after which he'd make sure his corpse was as heavy as possible, just to burden the pallbearers. Usually, when he came home, he went to find his spouse and kissed her on the forehead. She'd give him one in return, on the cheek—an unspoken story. Once a week, without fail, Madame Point would shrink from the approach of her lion, roll her eyes like a maniac and cry, "I can still smell her on you!" He would shrug. All these years he'd been going to the brothel once a week, and though he might shuffle the day of his visit like a pack of cards, she never once guessed wrong. *That's my father!*

"What do you want?" he asked, in the exasperated tone of a sick person, bothered just at the moment when he was about to rest.

She asked innocently, "Do you still remember what you learned when you were young?"

He took his time. "Why are you asking me that?"

"No reason. Just curious."

What did she want from him, the little brat? He saw through her. Did she think she could manipulate him? "I went to lycée like every-body else. Then I got my certification. I don't see what this has to do with anything—" He certainly couldn't see why anyone would disturb his reading to ask such silly questions. His murky blue eye fixed Simone with a suspicious look. What had she gotten into…

"You didn't learn English?"

Was she going to insist? He put the newspaper down on the table. Sometimes you had to seem like you were at least pretending. "No, when I was your age they didn't think modern languages were as important. I think I remember having learned a bit of German, but as for English, nothing."

A two-sentence reply! That was a record for the end of a meal.

"That's too bad," said Simone.

"Well, you can't learn everything," said the notary, who in fact had never learned much.

She played with the orange peel cut up on her plate. "It's such a wonderful language, so marvelous!"

"And a very useful one—"

"I was going to say that—but also, it's so musical, Father. Listen to this."

And she put an elbow on the table and recited in English:

> "Ship me somewheres east of Suez, where the best is like the
>   worst,
> Where there aren't no Ten Commandments an' a man can
>   raise a thirst…"

Simone's eyes were shining with feverish malevolence. What had possessed her to say that? A curious sickness had come over her, like some kind of desperate love.

"What was that?"

"A riddle."

"Huh?" Was she toying with him? He raised his eyebrows. She'd been behaving strangely for a while now. "Is this a joke?"

"Not at all, Father, come now! It's by Kipling."

He didn't want to seem totally uncultured. "Ah? And what does it mean?"

"Untranslatable." She looked him straight in the eyes. "This too, is untranslatable, and it's a pity since it's very beautiful"—she began speaking in English—"*You bloody sinner, I'm leaving you and the old witch tonight forever, eloping, I mean, with my lover and I stole your quids just a little while ago*—Yes, very very beautiful," and she let out a burst of nervous laughter, pushing the table away, the nape of her neck resting on the chair's back, her hands flat on the table.

Two little clinks of a fork on a glass—her mother. "That's enough silliness!"

Rose entered, and bent fearfully toward the notary's ear. "Monsieur Couturier is here. He would like a word with you, sir."

"Again!"

The notary slammed a fist on the table. "I've said, repeated a thousand times, that I expect to lunch in peace. In peace! Do you understand, Rose? I'm talking to you."

"Yes, Monsieur."

"You don't seem to understand."

"I do, Monsieur."

"Well then, try not to forget it. It's the last time I'll tell you—I'm warning you, at mealtimes, I won't receive anyone. Not anyone. And certainly not my employees, come on, that's outrageous! Is that understood? If this ever happens again, you're the one who will be sent packing."

"Yes, Monsieur."

"Tell Couturier that I'll see him in a bit, in my study."

"Very well, sir." She went out.

"One moment!" said Simone. And turning to her father, "Surely you must find out what he wants in any case. Since he came to look for you now, even though he knows your habits—"

The notary choked in his stiff collar. "Why are you interfering?"

"His son goes back to the barracks tonight."

"His son?"

"Étienne."

"All right," said Monsieur Point, raising his eyebrows, "have him come in, but make it quick—" He was still grumbling when Monsieur Couturier appeared. "What is it, Couturier?" he said without raising his eyes. He took an apple to slice and was peeling it, his elbows on the table.

Bird-like, little, thin-shouldered, Monsieur Couturier looked like an adolescent with a head of white hair. He fidgeted, looked at the ceiling. His hand wandered in front of his beard, as though he were chasing a fly. Finally he lowered his troubled, wino's gaze, letting it fall on the notary as he mumbled something inaudible.

"What was that?" said the notary, still peeling his apple.

"Monsieur—Boss, I beg your pardon," said Couturier in a wheedling voice, "I came to ask a favor from you—in a word I would like—and be assured that if I'd been able to ask you this morning, I never would have come to bother you at this hour," he continued in the tone of a student reciting his lesson, "but—"

"You'd like to take off early?"

Couturier stopped prancing. His hand fell to his side. *You could say he's trembling*, thought Simone.

"Yes," he murmured.

"And your excuse?" The notary still hadn't raised his eyes. The apple.

"My son, Monsieur—Boss. In a word, I'd like to leave the office at five—instead of at seven. I—I'll make it up—I'll—"

He was fidgeting again, playing with his handkerchief.

"In principle, I don't really like it when people leave early," said the notary. "But I can't stop you from seeing off your son. He has to go back to the barracks tonight?"

"Yes, Monsieur."

"Understood. You'll leave at five."

Couturier was speechless. The silence made the notary raise his eyes and their gazes met. A look of intense sorrow covered Monsieur Couturier's face—once again he gave the impression of being a man who had endured a hardship, perhaps that of becoming a drunk.

"You may go."

He went out on tiptoe, still prancing, after babbling a thank you they could barely hear.

The notary plunged back into his paper. As for the notaress, she was still counting. It seemed as though she hadn't noticed Couturier's arrival. Simone, once more, put a hand on her "book."

The maid came back, bringing the coffee. The notaress drank hers in one swallow. Afterwards, she dabbed her beak, crossed herself, and mumbled prayers for herself alone.

Oh! It was still too early to meet Léo, but it wasn't too early to leave.

Simone got up, took her "book" under her arm and went out. On the threshold she turned, curtseyed, and said:

"When shall we three meet again
In thunder, lightning, or in rain?"

THE HEAT, the smoke turned the windows of the café the color of milk. Cripure found himself seated in a chair before he'd decided to go in.

"Waiter!"

"Ready, aim?"

"A glass of Anjou."

"Fire!"

That overused joke hadn't made anyone smile in a long time.

Sitting at the Café Machin—he could say seeking asylum—nursing a glass of Anjou, or two, or three, without doing anything but drinking, without a thought in his head, *forgetting*, like the most ordinary fellow, that was maybe sensible. Maybe! In this world that they'd allowed to come to nothing, he didn't have anything else to do. They being those "gentlemen scholars" as Babinot might have called them.

In any case, they could have made something of it without too much effort. In this world they were given only once—and they said it was God's work!—they'd managed to make a situation that was probably worse than despair—why? Why?

As for the rest, it wasn't a world that was given only once—but a life. What a difference!

"Oof."

If you looked closely, the Café Machin was as good as any other, and better than any other, since it was ridiculous, and in Cripure's eyes, ridiculousness was more valuable than anything else. *My dear old bar!* His old spot, with its busted barstools, dented tables, and dirty windowpanes, he loved it with all his heart—through the effects of long fidelity, by becoming one with that atmosphere, blackened like an old hearth where he'd come to rest so many times.

He looked around.

Who were those men playing manille?

Through the smoke from pipes and cigarettes they looked like shades—laughing, slapping each other on the shoulder, throwing down their cards with big whacks on the green felt. Sitting at the cash register as if it were a throne was a fat blond woman armed with a coin rake she wielded like a scepter, looking around the gathered company with the air of a laying hen. Now and then someone would get up and approach her. She held out a hand—a paw—as if from the height of a perch, perhaps expecting a kiss. The waiter, a napkin slung over his shoulder, went endlessly back and forth between the tables with the air of a nurse, which was complemented by his white uniform. Everything seemed in order. Everything basked in the light of an eternal—simplicity, for lack of a better word.

What bothered him about it was that the grocer always stayed the grocer, the lawyer was always the lawyer, Monsieur Poincaré always talked like Monsieur Poincaré and never like, for example, Apollinaire, or vice versa—

And Cripure was always Cripure.

He was monologuing:

I could see through the lie, but that's as far as my courage went. I didn't know how to act, didn't know how to keep Toinette. And now, I'm old, ugly, sick, alone in spite of—the other one. Beaten hands down. Yet do I even have the right to say beaten if I never put up a fight? I don't have a right to anything. I'm nothing. Nothing but one of them. He raised his eyes to the drinkers and murmured, "I'm one of them!"

His eyes half-closed, he recited a line from one of his favorite professors, *"Amor fati*: let that be henceforth my love. I refuse to go to war against ugliness. I don't want to accuse, I don't even want to blame the accusers. To look away will be my only fight."

A sigh. He murmured, "God that's beautiful."

That was exactly it—he hadn't looked away. And then what, embrace his fate? What a joke, what a load of garbage. What courage must he have then—

Did the Clopper have courage, with his chin to the ground and his iron feet, one shoulder higher than the other and his solemn cane like a shaman's scepter? Yes, of course, o coward, kissing the hangman's ass!

"Waiter!"

"Ready, aim?"

"A glass of Anjou."

"Fire!"

This is only the second glass, Cripure told himself with a bitter smile. *Maybe I'll think seriously about the* Chrestomathy *over the third—*

This *Chrestomathy* would be much more serious than his little tales of the Medes from before. The Medes! He didn't give a damn about the Medes. And to think that back then, they'd listened to him, they'd practically taken him for a great man! That told you something about them in any case. *The Wisdom of the Medes,* God they were gullible. It was better than the thinking of his colleagues, who never thought about more than declensions. If he succeeded in finishing his *Chrestomathy,* it would be something else. No longer their so-called opinions, but a whole philosophy of opposition and sorrow. He would say—

"Bah!" he murmured. Reading and writing, what silliness is this? When it comes down to it, their literature tortures me with its exaltation of suffering. To make suffering into a value! Fatal ridiculousness, carefully crafted by poor fellows all crazy with pride, all writing to prove they're more intelligent than others, that they have more heart, that they've suffered better or more than the average man who croaks, as if that had any importance whatsoever! Ah! Since there have been those men who think, or pretend to think, it's all the same—

He snickered softly into his handkerchief. This life, though! And he drank his glass in one gulp.

"Waiter!"

"Ready, aim?"

"A glass of Anjou."

"Fire!"

"And—a newspaper."

"Which one?"

"Oh it doesn't matter. And something to write with."

"That's it?"

"Yes, thanks, that's it."

"He wouldn't notice," said the waiter to the woman at the register, "if I brought him the phone book or the map. And sometimes maybe not even the chess board." The cashier laughed softly on her throne.

The waiter brought the wine, the notepad, the ink, the paper. Cripure sipped the wine, opened the paper and looked at it vaguely. *Ah, yes! Still news of the war, eh. Let's see what's on the inside—*

The news inside was also about the war.

He was lost in thought.

"Dear God! What am I still doing here?" he mumbled after a moment. He was reading the local features. But he never would have admitted that he read the local news with the secret hope of learning of the death of the blond officer, his rival. A mania of his, for years now.

He sighed, turned over the page. *I'm a bastard, aren't I.* And hunching over the table, he opened the notepad, dipped the pen in ink and wrote: "*Note for the Chresto*: To love T—and all she was destined for, including what I've referred to as her betray—*I understand that.*" (He underlined it twice.) "If only I could have been capable of such a love! I could have conquered her for all eternity."

He underlined *and all she was destined for* another two times and put down the pen. He thought, *it's not true that I've never wished for the other one's death.* Each time he read the local news, he repeated this thought. Out of remorse, he wanted to like the blond officer. It lasted for as long as it lasted, usually not very long. The slightest chance, a surprise meeting, a word taken the wrong way, a dream—and he would fall as if from the top of a roof into an anguish of jealousy.

Ridicule had marked out his destiny with its snide, nasty smile. It was true that the great love of his life had been a petty bourgeois girl, Toinette nonetheless! And by some sort of inverse perfection, hadn't the whole affair begun and taken its course in the most boring town in France—and perhaps in the whole world? Angers: a town with no mystery, under the most banal skies. They had told him a thousand times that it was a town full of music and flowers, and he, imbecile that he was, had daydreamed about it, only to find, in the end, military music and rosettes united on the promenade. Surely, France had no better examples of this sordid kind of town that had been so highly praised. If Bordeaux was where he'd seen the most top hats, Angers was where he'd seen the most fur-collared coats. Nowhere had he encountered a bourgeoisie that was more self-satisfied or more rigidly dull. No surprise that the counterrevolution was always alive and well there! And it was in such a place that he'd spent four years in the prime of life, eventually falling in love with Toinette like you fall into the sea.

Everything happened as though he'd had no other possibilities, as though he were filling a canvas that had been predetermined and given only once. He'd always known in advance how things would be, not only with his love for Toinette and his marriage, but also when he'd attempted to make the Sorbonne accept such an arrogant thesis, when, under the pretext of studying Turnier, he'd made such rebellious arguments and dragged so many people through the mud. And that thesis, he'd known they would fail it, they'd warned him in advance. He'd even been bold enough to visit the professor in charge of evaluating his creation, and the man told him they wouldn't pass it, that he wouldn't even be allowed to defend—his work was decidedly too incomplete and fantastical, however brilliant and worthy, like his *Wisdom of the Medes*, of the attention of the literary public.

Cripure had shown the professor an infinite courtesy, more than courtesy—he had been timid, maybe dull. That hadn't stopped him from acting surprised and indignant when the thesis was officially rejected.

Those who knew him at the time remember seeing his face disfigured with anger, waving his arms and shouting that he was "stronger than them," and that he'd get his revenge. He'd played his role admirably, perhaps without knowing he was playing one, as a man who plays with fire only realizes when he gets burned that it wasn't fun and games. And he was well aware, without admitting it, that he'd courted this blow to his pride, as in his marriage to Toinette, when he'd voluntarily courted the greatest sorrow he knew. But willing or not, the hurt pride and the sorrow were there for the rest of his life.

That all this was absurd didn't offer any consolation, except through certain delicious thoughts of how indifferent he'd always been to having a Ph.D. from the Sorbonne, and that even Toinette had never been more than a petty bourgeois, by now a lady, no doubt, the sort it was easier to hate than to love. At least, he liked to think so. But this hatred of the bourgeoisie that he thought was so natural in him and so well founded was perhaps nothing more than a way to deceive himself and to compensate for a certain love of things that were easy and low—in short, a pose.

He hadn't, in fact, found it insurmountable to drag his love before the mayor and the priest, like all the rest of them, and in the living rooms he'd frequented, under the patronage of his father-in-law the magistrate, Cripure hadn't felt too ill at ease. No, he'd even felt a certain flattery in being invited into that posh circle where his colleagues couldn't follow. They'd received him with respect, like a man whom they would eventually come to count on, like a choice intellect, and everyone had set about forgetting his disability, which had caused so much gossip during the engagement. Toinette could have easily made a better match! It had been so painful for them to resign themselves to a marriage for love. Harder than accepting a death.

In the dizziness of the honeymoon, Cripure felt like everyone's equal. Fleeting happiness. Too soon his suspicion had regained its tyranny over his life. From then on, the long torture which might never see an end had begun, well before he met the blond officer, one evening when, entering a parlor where he'd come to look for Toinette, the people there had smiled at him in a peculiar way when they saw him appear—at least it had seemed that way to him. Toinette was there—so young, so bright, so happy! But what a sickening happiness! What were they hiding from him? Who had they seen her with? Powdered, her lips rouged, she was sitting next to a man—a young man—she'd taken off her hat and her hair fell on her neck. Her arms were bare. When she leaned in to listen, she surely brushed against the young man, and he could surely see the tops of her breasts. But all that was nothing.

What was more serious—was one evening when he'd come home to find, not the young man from the parlor, but the blond officer, in person, become a friend of the family. What did it matter that the blond officer should be there? He'd been there many times before. But in response to an insignificant question Cripure had raised—about a pair of curtains—Toinette had smiled such a crooked, calculating smile, and she'd given him so many useless explanations. He'd been horrified, unable to speak. It was certainly a question of curtains!

Then, later on, a colleague had talked to him, one of those officious people charged with the comedy of opening eyes, that's to say, gouging them out. Cripure had left. He'd left that very evening—it seemed like yesterday. Fled. And without challenging the blond officer to a duel. Maybe he'd only fled so quickly to avoid having to fight a duel and being killed. And maybe Toinette hadn't betrayed him after all, maybe nothing had happened between her and the blond officer, and his colleague had lied?

He picked up his pen once more and wrote:

Another note: Once again I find in my heart, without the slightest surprise, without even the shadow of disgust, feelings that I truly believe I would hate in others—a kind of fear that might be called cowardice, and confronted with those whom I've always thought were my enemies, a certain flattery, and worst of all, a flattery that borrows the mask of irony and independence.

A pause.

He wrote again: *But that cowardice, that flattery, these are things in me that are foreign to myself. Not feelings I need to be ashamed of—but equations considered and contemplated among others.*

He crossed out *contemplated* and wrote *confused.*

He put down the pen.

He raised his eyes, rubbed his temples with the tips of his fingers, adjusted his pince-nez—the tic. "Hum!"

In that room, where the mirror-covered walls looked like an aquarium, there was no face, no object, which could persuade Cripure in some decisive fashion that he should honestly get up and leave.

Another look around. The manille players were still there. Who were they?

And who was he to them? Nothing but poor Cripure, ill and crazy, inept lover of a sailor's lass. But if they only knew—

If only!

"Waiter!"

"Ready, aim—"

"A glass of Anjou!"

"Fire."

If they only knew how I envied them!

It was simply as though he'd never existed. Once more his spirit had renounced and humiliated itself for nothing. No use—no one needed a fourth player for manille.

Leave? Go home? What for and what good would it do? Here or else-where—"forever and always lower," he murmured, emptying his glass. *Rolling to the deepest depths of vulgarity, down where the last human ties finally unravel and rot—maybe there he'd find an equivalent—this drunkenness is starting to interfere,* he thought with a smile, pointing a finger at himself. *There were good times when I figured out how things would go for me—crafting stories for myself, lying, lying to others! How*

I lied to her! 'Where were you? I was worried sick…' 'Oh, here and there,' and I'd smile sweetly as if to show her, 'See how I am, a real dreamer, a poet! What do the hours matter, why does it matter where I go? I myself couldn't tell you—' In truth, I knew all too well. If she happened to complain, I'd kiss her, saying, 'This is how I am—Would you rather have a husband instead of a lover?' Me, a lover! She would listen and I'd smile. 'How easy it is to fool her,' I'd be thinking. And I unspooled my lies. What joy in lying! What a lovely cord to hang myself with! I threw myself into her arms, feeling a weight on my heart, as if I were maybe about to cry, and in fact I'd only muster a little hiccup. 'My sweetheart, my dear!' she'd say to me, running her fingers through my hair. Then I'd often feel an irresistible desire to laugh, which I'd try to stifle. And she'd think I was sobbing! 'My sweetheart, darling!' My head rolled on to her breast, living it up in style, throwing myself at her feet. 'Forgive me, oh, forgive me for everything'—'what's wrong with you? but what is it? What do I need to forgive you for?' she asked me, weeping. I was starting to feel better. 'I must go out again.' Sadly, she'd hand me my overcoat—the goatskin came later. And outside, everything would be different, I'd light a cigarette. I could smoke without getting a migraine in those days. 'Eh, what does it matter,' I'd say to myself, 'what does it matter to me, what do I matter to me?' I'd feel a dirty smile on my face and I'd go drink just like I am now. I'd snicker: 'Forgiveness! Who gives a damn about anyone's forgiveness!' And I'd gather myself in, taking a vain pleasure in what I called my 'largesse.' At least I wasn't a fool. Oh my God, is it possible? Is it really possible, having been that person, is it possible that I'm not deluding myself today as I did then? Did things really happen that way? No, no, it wasn't all true. I remember other things. But everything's mixed up, everything's lost— and, and—

"Waaaiiter!"

"Ready, aim—"

"A—glaaass of Annnnjou, if you please."

This is starting to get interesting, thought the waiter, bringing over the wine.

It was maybe his eighth glass.

Cripure frowned at his glass without sipping it yet.

Half past noon.

The café was emptying. One after another, *they* were going home. Lunchtime was no joke and precision was—what? "I'm not here anymore—"

He raised his head—facing him was a mirror.

"Hey, look!"

Was it the smoke from when the room was full or the fog on his lenses? He couldn't really see the person who was talking to him. He heard a sharp, unexpected noise, but somehow he wasn't startled.

"Excuse me," said the man, "but this coincidence is just too funny."

Cripure smiled. "Have a seat," he replied. *It's odd*, he thought, *you would think he had stolen my hat.*

"Yes? Why thank you," said the man, slipping onto the stool.

He put his glass on the table, lifted his eyepiece, rubbed his temples, and murmured a few words that Cripure couldn't quite hear—something about solitude. He talked too, about something that had hit him "right in the face."

"What?"

"But—my love, you see!"

"Very odd," Cripure replied.

And the other man said, "You're a good person. I can see it in your eyes. It was a woman who killed you, huh?" he said, winking.

"Killed?"

"You and I both know what I mean. Her name was Toinette too," he continued in a whisper, turning his head right and left to make sure no one overheard this confidence, barged in on this holy secret. Cripure copied him, looking around, and an ecstatic smile lit up his old face.

"My friend!"

"They didn't hear us?"

"No. Come closer. Say it one more time—"

"Toinette," said the voice, very low.

"Toinette, Toinette—"

Cripure closed his eyes.

"What's come over him?" the cashier asked.

"Dunno. He's plastered," said the waiter.

"He's not actually going to fall asleep here and start snoring?"

"It's already happened once, not too long ago. I had to put him in a cab. What a chore. I wouldn't want to be one of the pallbearers who carries his coffin. Especially since people weigh more dead than living, that's a fact." He yawned. He was hungry.

Cripure reopened his eyes. *The other* was still there.

"*That's how it was for me. I was afraid of being killed. And I ran away.*"

"*To Paris, you too?*"

"*Exactly. And got involved in a thesis on Turnier—you know, that other befuddled one.*"

"*I know!*"

"*In truth, I wrote a bomb—*"

"*I have to say—I felt like I was imprisoned in a dungeon, and I had a companion chained to me, some kind of dwarf—I don't know why I'm telling you this—sometimes he wore one face and sometimes another—revenge, revenge—*"

"*Eh! Eh!*"

"*Taking stock of the fallen world—alone and criminal. I shouldn't have fled,*" Cripure muttered.

Silence.

"*I—I saw the pope in a dream. Yes, His Holiness. He looked like Louis XI in my little history primer, when I was a kid. And he was drinking a ton, like a Viking, my friend, to the health of a hanged man. I could only see the feet of the person who'd been hanged, feet in very elegant dancing shoes. Yes. And then later on in the dream, I realized that the person I thought was the pope was really only the nuncio, old friend. As for the hanged man, he wasn't dead, not dead at all. They'd taken him down, laid him down on a bed, and a young woman gently wiped the sweat from his pale, pinched face. Do you follow?"*

"I know exactly what you mean," said the other.

"Well then, let's not dwell on it. Would you like anything else?"

"A little glass of Anjou."

"Waaaaiter!"

The waiter didn't budge, and for good reason. Not even the smallest sound had come out of Cripure's mouth. And anyway, Cripure hadn't touched the glass in front of him. He must have thought the waiter had just brought it, since he seemed satisfied.

The other continued, "Know yourself!"

Cripure jumped. "But for the love of God! Does self-knowledge ever go beyond—the, the facts of life?" he said in a changed voice. "It's not that we die, it's that we die cheated."

A pause.

"Yes," said the other, "But they kiss the blade that kills them. And that reminds me, how's the Chresto?"

"Bah!"

"In your place, I wouldn't say bah, I'd write the Chresto. You have to tell the truth, my dear, even if the truth is your poison. Are you afraid of dying?"

"Indifferent."

"Liar!"

"I can't hide anything from you," said Cripure. "But what's the point of writing the Chresto? Depicting dead souls, isn't it, or more precisely: murdered ones, and we should count ourselves among them, all arrogance aside."

"I was going to say that! Listen, I've got a new title, Bouclo et Pécuporte, *otherwise known as* Boucri et Pécupure.[10] *Our dear brethren! Otherwise called:* The Shades of the Prison. *Yes. I'll write that clunker. I've never held back my intellect."*

He burst out laughing. "Oh, ha, ha! I'm dying—"

"And what will become of Toinette in the work?"

"Don't think, though, don't think I've forgotten her suffering. Every

day. Every hour of every day, the poor woman, and for so many years! A whole life without her and I'm still faithful."

"Are you leaving something out?"

"Why would I?" Cripure stammered. "Intellectually, you know, we're not the cowards."

"So talk to me about the alimony!" And he banged his hand on the table.

"Oh, they hit you with that too?"

The man lowered his head. He replied in a sad voice, "Yes, they dealt me that blow. I lost the divorce suit, go figure. Excuse me, I'll explain," he said, in response to a gesture from Cripure, who looked like he might be about to interrupt. "Having lost the divorce case, I was ordered to pay alimony, because of the child—"

"The legitimate one?"

"Oh, so you know about the other one—I see you're up to date on everything. So, after the divorce—"

"You're going to tell me that—that she never stopped hounding you, demanding that the alimony increase in proportion to your salary. Was that it? You're a teacher, right?"

"Philosophy."

Cripure sat up straighter and gently touched the brim of his hat. "My dear colleague—"

"My dear colleague," the other repeated, straightening up and touching the brim of his hat exactly as Cripure had just done.

"A pleasure."

"A pleasure."

Cripure continued, "Philosophology, jokeology, hypocrisology—European philosophy—between us, my friend, what an idea to spend a whole life with that bucket of shit at the end of your arm! Enough! But tell me—do I take you to be a Clopper?"

"Why not at all! Come on!"

"I can prove to you without a doubt," Cripure's wheezing voice continued, "that all the notary's letters are fakes. Yes. All of them." And his hand banged the table in just the same way the other's had, just a moment ago.

"Did you send the money? Yes or no."

"That's not the question."

"Good. Excellent. Back then, I suspected as much. But it's better this way."

"Ghosts have a favorable instinct," said Cripure, quoting Rivarol, *"they only appear to those who believe in them. Think on that."*

"I'm not fooled, not onnne seconnnd," said the other, *"Goodbye. I'm going home to Maïa. Let me go, don't try to take me with you.* No, I said I'm not going! Get your paws off me or I'll call the police!"

"But Monsieur Merlin," said the waiter, "It's almost one in the afternoon. Madame Merlin will be worried. Be reasonable. Do you want me to call a cab for you?" And without waiting for a response from Cripure, whom he was moving heaven and hell to lift, he jerked his chin at Père Yves's waiting cab, murmuring in the busboy's ear, "dead as a doornail—go fetch a hearse."

DRUNKENNESS was nothing but a question of consent, and the fresh air, the wind in Père Yves's cab, succeeded in sobering him up. No way to escape, even in wine! Always a spectator of his own life. As for these games he played with imaginary friends, he knew what that was about. An old habit. The cab rolled.

It was an old cab, a real relic, a ruin of a carriage, the only vehicle of its kind seen rattling down the streets, driven by Père Yves, this old man with teary eyes, with a soft, dreamy little voice. The cab was dirty enough to be repulsive. Not only had it been years since anyone painted it, but, more importantly, it had also been years since anyone had brushed the seats. You could guess that once upon a time they'd been blue, but the dust from streets and boulevards had made them gray and black for eternity. Seeing how rust had eaten the iron parts of the cab, you could understand that Père Yves's business had declined and that it was useless to ask if he spent most of his time stationed at the town square or the railway station.

In spite of all that, it was an excellent cab, not too bumpy, and if you weren't afraid of dirtiness (as Cripure wasn't), you could relax as you took a nice little drive. Pompon, who pulled the carriage, had nothing in him of the classic cab horse. Quite the opposite—he was a young, energetic animal, well fed and cared for, capable of the occasional frisk.

Cripure let himself sink into the back of the carriage and, since he couldn't play with his imaginary friend anymore, he played "Monsieur" another way of pulling the wool over his eyes, but taken down a notch.

The same way soldiers who have no one to write to will send themselves letters, Cripure, who had no one to confide in, created a phantom confidante whom he called "Monsieur." And from time to time, when the fancy came over him, when he wasn't drunk enough to play with his imaginary friends, he'd ask "Monsieur" a few questions.

"What do you think, Monsieur?"

The horse trotted, the coachman clacked his whip.

"I'm considering. It would be so easy to leave, to live out the rest of my life in the sun, among simple savages, far from this garbage."

"Java, again?"

"You've thought about it all your life."

"But my dear sir, I'd kill myself getting there! Java! Might as well be Eden. But that's not possible anymore, no point in thinking about it. Let's talk about something else—let's talk, for example, about punishments for the guilty—what a joke history plays! Unbelievable hypocrisy. And all this will end how, by figuring the allies will be victorious? Well then, old friend, they'll probably send Kaiser Wilhelm to write his memoirs in Java, that paradise! The world is going to die from morality, I should say moralicide, old friend. What would Nietzsche say? And what can we say, as others, the Antis?"

Monsieur didn't respond. Cripure was getting tired, he recognized it, and his game wasn't as fun. He forced himself to tell Monsieur, *"You're not getting any more accustomed to being alone, are you?"*

"But I've always lived alone," he replied, *"completely alone. I wouldn't be less alone among the Eskimos."*

"Will you die alone?"

"I'll die alone."

Sober now, he stopped playing with Monsieur. He recited poetry:

> "As I flowed down impassive rivers
> No longer guided by the crew
> Garish redskins used them for target practice,
> Nailed them naked to their colored poles"

And the carriage rolled on with a sound of harness bells.

What a joy to let himself drag along like this, to forget his body, his feet of clay! Yes, he would do it, he'd make a deal with this old coachman, he'd go everywhere in this old rig. To hell with the money. And when the carriage pulled over to the sidewalk and stopped, Cripure, before getting down, asked Père Yves, "What would you say, my friend, what would you say to us making a little deal? Eh? You'd come tomorrow morning at eight to drive me to the lycée, for example? Eh? And then each day after that? What do you say?"

The coachman turned on his seat, whip in hand, and nodded. "That can be done," he said.

"Good, good," said Cripure. "I'll make it worth your while," he added, getting down. He paid him. "Until tomorrow, old friend."

"At eight?"

"That's it. A little before eight, let's say. And again, I'll make it worth your while."

"Oh, everyone knows you're a good customer, Monsieur—"

"Then it's settled, my friend. Tomorrow, without fail," said Cripure, going into the house.

The old coachman was delighted. Finally, a regular!

They didn't seem to be expecting him. Even the little beasts didn't come out to greet him. But goodness, Maïa, Amédée, the little dogs, everybody was in the kitchen. They'd started eating without him.

He took off his goatskin and his hat, propped his cane behind the door in its usual place and said, "Hello! It's me."

No response.

He wandered into the study, threw the goatskin on the sofa, and looked through the glass door for the shadow of the two others. Once he was sure they hadn't seen him, he went back into the hall—time to settle a question of money, the thousand francs he wanted to give Amédée.

He'd carefully considered how to give the money and concluded that the best way was to slip the bill into the pocket of Amédée's overcoat, which was hanging in the foyer. It was an old, dirty coat, with blackened stains on the back—from muck or maybe blood? He looked at it for a long moment with a frown, like a consignment dealer, and took from his wallet a thousand-franc bill, which had been ready for days. He'd conscientiously recorded the serial number in a notebook, in case of theft or—simple prudence. He rolled it between his fingers, and hesitated. In his pocket? Too risky. Why not in his wallet? It was there. Cripure opened it to put the thousand-franc note in—letters fell out.

"For God's sake! What have I done?"

Overwhelmed, he surveyed the disaster. Had they heard him? They'd come and catch him with Amédée's wallet in his hands, in the middle of going through it. What would they think? Anything but that! He wasn't one of those species of cowards who listened at keyholes and stole secrets from people around him. He had to put everything back as fast as possible! But his legs were wobbling.

Everything was still quiet in the house, no doors had opened, and he controlled himself and got down to pick up the letters, with infinite care—he who wasn't capable of tying his own shoelaces. It took a long time. The letters had flown everywhere—even into corners that were hard to reach, under the stairs, behind the bikes, hmm. Were they all there? Yes, he thought, taking another look around him. "Thank God!" He sighed. "Thank God!" he repeated, grasping the letters in his hand, ready to put them back. But how did it happen? At the very moment he was finally putting the letters back in the wallet, he happened to take in a sentence with a single glance. *Don't do anything more than what's necessary. As your mother I beg you—I can't live since . . .*

Letters from the mother!

He put a hand to his face like a man about to cry. Overcome, he shoved the thousand-franc bill in between the letters, put the wallet back into the coat pocket, and tottering, went back into the study with a look of infinite scorn and pity for the image he recognized in the mirror.

"WHAT THE hell were you doing, eh?" said Maïa, seeing him come into the kitchen like a large black ghost. "Your soup will be frozen. And hey, why didn't you get your coat off? What's with you," she said, seeing his look, "you got the colic?"

He stood in the middle of the kitchen, his arms limp, like he was blind.

"No."

"Is it that business from this morning that's bothering you?"

"The bikes? No." He'd barely thought about that affair.

"Wait a tick and I'll help you," she said, getting up, "cause if I don't get involved you'll keep your nice coat on and get sauce on it, speaking of decorations!"

He raised his arms and let her skin him, "like a big rabbit," Maïa said, carefully carrying the coat to the study where she hung it on the back of a chair.

"And now what's it you need? Your jacket?"

"Yes Maïa—"

"What a layabout!" she cried with a burst of laughter. "Here, sit. Do you need me to tuck in your bib too? Like a kid!"

He let himself be pushed to the table, all the while putting on his jacket, and glancing sideways at the bottles. Was it the good wine?

"How are you doing?" he said, to say something. He looked at Amédée.

"Getting along," the young man replied.

Cripure ate, absorbed in his food like a sulky, brooding child.

Ignoring him, Maïa continued the story she'd been telling Amédée: "And so," she said, "when Pierre came and found Louise to say that he loved her and he wanted her for a wife, it's all right she said, but there's one condition—my sister Ernestine lives with us. And him, he said sure, he didn't want to separate the twins. You hear me?"

"Yes, Auntie."

"Fine. So they married. He was an overseer at the brick factory, and the two women did sewing. They did all right. Since they had no babies, they saved and soon they got a little house, see, right next door. The best-kept house you ever saw, and happily too. But gosh that Louise! She was always teasing. 'Can you imagine, my dear, that it took me more than a year to call Pierre by his Christian name? It's unbelievable, dear, isn't it? When he'd get sick, I'd ask if Monsieur needed a hot water bottle for his feet and things like that'—Are you listening?"

"I am, Auntie."

"Only, after working for forty years at the brick factory, they tossed him out on his ass, since he was too old. And not a scrap of the pension he should of had! They only gave him a stupid medal and then some certificate—'Would you believe that, my dear,' Louise said to me, 'after forty years of service, those bastards! And he cried about it, not over the money,' she said, 'but Pierre's the kind who gets attached. So we put a mortgage on the house. That gives us three francs a day for the three of us,' she said."

"They'd better not gorge on that, Auntie, they'd better not like chicken too much. Or ever get sick."

"Right. That means the poorhouse."

"To croak a little faster."

"And worse," said Cripure. But right away he regretted speaking and bent his nose over his plate.

Maïa continued, "Louise's a real homebody now. She won't come out of her corner. Ernestine is the opposite—always on the go. As soon as it's morning, the littlest ray of sun, she's up and out."

"And Pierre?"

"He goes out too. But they go their separate ways. He always carries his medal. About town, if anybody says 'how does it feel to be a pensioner?' he takes out his medal and says 'here's my pension!' And he shows 'em the medal. And it's not easy on him. Oh!" Maïa said, remembering all of a sudden, "I forgot to tell you." She turned to Cripure.

"What, Maïa?"

"Yesterday morning, I went in, over there, as I was going by, just to say hello. Louise was all alone. 'Come and have something, a little glass of wine.' Me, I didn't want to, but I didn't want to upset her so I said ok, only there was no place to put the glasses. The whole table was covered with postcards. There were piles on piles, more than I ever seen. 'You're wondering,' Louise said, 'Well, I'll explain. When you're old, you've got to think of everything my dear, you've got to have all your affairs in order. Someday everything will get sold. The furniture, God knows, there's nothing can be done, but the papers? I burned the letters a good while back. But the postcards! I said to myself—there are so many that we've got to go through them all three of us, if we want to get done. When they're divided into hundreds, each one of us will take a pile, and God willing, when it's winter we'll sit around the fire and entertain ourselves by burning 'em one by one. By God we started in on 'em the other day it was so cold. I got up a big fire in the grate and we got comfortable with our postcards on our knees. At first it went fine. We laughed, my sister and me, but Pierre, he didn't, the poor man! Sure as day the tears started comin' down his face! Eh! Pierre, I said to him, what's got into you? At first he didn't want to say anything. Then he said, 'It's too painful.' 'Well then,' I said to him, 'since that's how it is, we won't burn 'em, Pierre.' And since then, dearie, the cards have been on the table. No one says anything about 'em and no one can touch 'em either. I've got to do the burning all alone, I said to myself, and that's what I should have done in the first place."

The meal ended, the last one they would have together, him and Amédée. Once again, everything was as Cripure had predicted—all of them with a guilty unease, without acknowledging each other, without tenderness. And it was done. Nothing left for him now but to send his son to death.

A little dulled from having eaten and drunk too much, he sank heavily into his chair, his look empty, and turned to the window where, between two motionless paws, Petit-Crû's thin snout appeared like a vision of Saint Anthony in his better days.

The Russian soldiers, in their barracks, sang together at the top of their lungs.

Amédée smoked his pipe, his elbows on the table, and chatted with Maïa. He'd removed his jacket and rolled back his shirtsleeves. Maïa got up and was rinsing the glasses, like an old servant who'd be looked down upon if she lazed about before a messy table.

Red-cheeked, her eyes wet in her greasy face that was round and soft as a cheese, she glanced from time to time at the young man, her look filled with a jolly lust that Cripure did not miss. But why not, she could sleep with Amédée, if that's what would do it for her, yes, no doubt about it! He wouldn't be jealous!

An odd little laugh went through him at the thought, and Amédée gave his father a questioning look, which Cripure ignored. He took his cup in his hand, and with a smile of childish sweetness that made his face seem confused and modest, he asked, "Another little cup of coffee if you don't mind, Maïa?"

"Ha, you old wizard!" she laughed, "My God he's never got his fill! Here," she said, putting the coffee pot on the table. "And what do you want in your coffee, you wily old man?"

"You know exactly what I want," he said, in the same sweet voice, like a child who's owed a treat, "a little drop of rum."

"A little drop! Hang on, here's the jug."

He poured himself some rum, dunked his lip in the cup and didn't say anything, plunged, as he so often was, into one of those reveries Maïa no longer paid any attention to. She'd learned to respect the mysterious silences of her man, to treat him in these situations as she would have treated a sleepwalker headed toward the edge of a cliff.

The camp chorus was silent, only a lone voice, sweet and impassioned. A soldier longing for his love:

"Ya lyublyu,
Vse lyublyu"

Cripure closed his eyes.

His passiveness was incredible—what else could you call that patience? It made him crazy to think that Toinette existed somewhere, and he knew exactly where. Hadn't he always known? She had a life, habits, her own place. People saw her and talked to her every day; every morning she went to the market. Yes, or no, had she married the other one, the blond officer? Yes, perhaps, but also perhaps not. The blond officer, whom he hadn't dared challenge to a duel, maybe he'd gotten himself killed in Champagne or at Verdun, and maybe Toinette was now a widow?

Forgetting for once—just for a moment—his pitiful handicap, he daydreamed of disguising himself. Dressed as a laborer, he'd go back to Angers—fake beard, tinted lenses—he could see Toinette again, maybe even talk to her. The dream barely lasted a second, leaving him suffocated by rage and sadness when he remembered his feet. Two clods. *And those feet? And my feet?* His chin dropped to his chest in two nods.

"You'll fall asleep," said Amédée, still smoking his pipe.

Maïa touched a finger to the young man's shoulder. "Let him be."

Funny old fart, thought Amédée. But he didn't care so much, even if this was their last meal together. He shrugged. *Queer old bird.*

What shocked Amédée most was that they hadn't gotten beyond formalities. They had tried—but the more familiar words had stuck in his throat. Why? There was nothing wrong with his father being an old fogey, an eccentric. He was really a good fellow. But there was nothing doing—two or even three times in the beginning they'd addressed each other as "Monsieur," which certainly hadn't helped matters, and since then, to avoid returning to something so painful, they'd each in turn started to come up with elaborate ways to get around the taboo words father and son. With Maïa, on the other hand, everything had been easy.

"And about that," Maïa said, pouring herself another finger of rum, "do you think you'll be there tomorrow? Or the next day?"

"That depends, Aunt. My regiment might be off duty or moved. Got to go to the major's office to find out, then on foot or by a convoy to the spot for unattached soldiers. There's one in every sector. They'll stamp my leave papers, I'll be squared away, and then they'll send me to my new regiment. If my unit is sent out, I'll have to go back to the base to get my fighting gear. That could take a few days—"

"Drop us a line."

"Count on it."

"It's too bad you won't see your mom before you head out."

"Yep, Auntie, it's too far. She's at Nice for the season, you know, in a hotel. And even if I could go see her, we can't really spend time together—she wrote me that she's got too much work, her boss is an ass. But if I'm not killed, I'll go on my next leave."

Cripure didn't seem to hear. It wasn't the first time they'd discussed the slattern in front of him. They paid him as much attention as they would have paid a deaf man. For them, it went without saying that he remained a stranger to their conversation. They didn't judge him, didn't have anything against him, and had he interrupted, they would have expressed only astonishment, as they would if a Chinese person replied when they thought he didn't understand.

His head lowered, his eyes half-closed behind his pince-nez, he looked like one of those unacknowledged wrecks you'd sometimes find in the back rooms of dirty provincial cafés.

"So it goes—she's getting older, you know, Auntie. And what'll she do if I'm blown to bits?"

"Can't think about it," said Maïa.

Hmmm, thought Cripure, *she must be more beaten down, more worn and slatternly than ever, like one of those cleaning women no one looks at anymore in the street. Would I recognize her?*

A slattern! How quick he was to say it! Did he really think then, that there were slatterns who were no longer human? This ugly thought succeeded in making him disgusted with himself. *All the perfumes of*

Arabia couldn't sweeten this little hand! He got up wearily and, back bent, arms swinging, he dragged his feet across the cement of the kitchen, back to his study.

They followed him with their eyes. Through the glass door, they watched him drop into his chair and reach blindly behind his pile of books and papers, grabbing a white sheet of paper, starting to write—

A new note for the *Chrestomathy*?

How much he'd thought to scorn the world, how strong he'd been! But the world had gotten its revenge. Cripure realized now how easy it had been to take an adversarial position. From here on out, the pose made no sense. The human experience collapsed into suffering, into blood. And he, who had always pretended, like a nobleman, to live secluded from men and scorn them, he discovered that scorn was no longer possible, except for scorning himself.

In the obscure realm where most of his dreams played out, he searched for proof that he wasn't entirely cut off from the group, that he could participate in the general grief flowing from everywhere like hysteria, breaking down all the doors, hitting every face, a grief to which he had only the slightest, most delicate, and certainly ridiculous connection—his bastard son Amédée.

Guilty of what? Of believing himself to be guilty—his mistake was the depression that killed depth, a perpetual hypocrisy inseparable from greatness. Always, even in this moment, the corner of his eye was fixed on the spectacle and a wily smile appeared from beneath his anguish. But all humans want depth—not deep thoughts, but depth of being, which could be given to any old imbecile and even to the Clopper, ignorant depth and plentiful love which surpassed all insults. Toinette.

Twenty years!

In twenty years, how many days could he say were lost, taken from him, maybe, as if that were believable! Days he hadn't put up a fight.

He got up to escape this torpor and went over to the window, lifting the curtain to look at the empty street with one big blue eye, as if he were dumb. *All this . . .*

In these barren days, what had still sustained him was the hope that he'd finally write his *Chrestomathy*, like a speech for the defense, or better yet the prosecution, where he'd spoil the ending, let slip a truth so bitter, *something to poison them for a long time*. Yes, yes, he'd reveal the password to a universal conspiracy, one of Punchinello's secrets.[11]

He stretched out on the sofa.

He could certainly doze a little. There was plenty of time to put on his tailcoat, which hung from the back of a nearby chair, displaying a shimmering lining of black silk. He was about to close his eyes when he spotted the corner of an envelope sticking out of the inside pocket of the coat, a white triangle, almost glowing in the gloom. A letter? Yes, a letter he'd forgotten.

He remembered: it was a letter Noël had handed him the last time he needed to wear the coat. What was the occasion? When the Rector had come, it must have been more than two months ago. That letter—he'd accepted it with something like distaste, as always, and he stowed in his pocket unread. Later! Later! What good would it do to throw himself stupidly into something that would deceive him once again? Even in that moment, he hesitated to take it. At his age, he was unchangeable. From the depths of his Siberia, it was still possible to increase his loss—deprived of music, a lack, of love, a lack, deprived of everything—O Toinette!—not the lack and deprivation of letters, that would be too good to be true, but, what made the situation worse, letters that were nothing, as this one surely was, letters that were nothing but prospectuses or junk, the kind of letters sent by parents of his students, or from colleagues who had problems with their theses.

How many not even half-read letters lurked in the bottoms of his pockets or between the pages of his books! Those with some white space he filled with notes for the *Chrestomathy*, but more often than not, Maïa used them to light her fire. This one here would be like all the others, except for a little disappointment all the same, a little bit of curiosity quashed. He reached out an arm, took the letter: unknown handwriting, unreadable postmark. He ripped the envelope, unfolded the paper—

One simple look—the "Ah!" of someone who has been mortally wounded, his arm dropped back to the sofa, numb and heavy. The letter slipped from him. He picked it up, as if the contact of his fingers with the paper was a signal that all ties weren't broken, that there was still a solution.

Certainly, not everything was greatness of mind—he'd often played with imagining Toinette aged and ugly, transformed into one of those bourgeois women all in black with a white velvet ribbon around her neck to hold up her drooping jowls. One of those women in a bonnet and wool gloves, who didn't even have enough energy to applaud the lecturer from *Annales* on tour at the Municipal Theater. In his darkest hours when revenge got the best of him, he'd even played at imagining her dead. But how different this was from the blow of reality! There was no past, no future outside this sadness that seemed to have no beginning, which seemed to do nothing but open its floodgates.

Something was stuck in his throat. He wanted to loosen his collar—his swollen fingers couldn't grasp the button. He didn't fight. He let his hand fall back. His mouth opened. *This will pass—I only have to*—he only had to make himself small, give in, let go the cord—run away. But his throat tightened again. His hands, his arms, his whole body started to tremble. *It's nothing, I've got to slip away, pass under it.* Everything in him wanted to bow his head. *I've run away all my life.*

But all of a sudden—he wasn't expecting it—tears came. He felt their presence on his face before understanding they were coming. They flowed from beneath his closed eyelids, wet his face. How many years had it been since he'd cried? He'd lost the habit. He trustingly let the tears fall, but quickly they became bitter and were accompanied by little groans which surprised him, since he didn't right away recognize them, hallucinating for a moment that these groans didn't come from him but from some wounded person who had entered the room—Maïa or maybe Amédée? But there was no one else there.

Next door, in the kitchen, Maïa and Amédée were talking, paying no attention to him. *I'm the one sobbing—*

His sobs doubled. *I mustn't, I don't want to!* The idea that they'd hear and come in made him sit up and open his eyes. *Not for the world! They won't come, they won't know! Not now!* He well knew he'd betray himself one day, that one day, something in him would reveal it all. But not now!

That Maïa might be jealous wasn't an issue, of course, but she could come in, see him and judge, that thought made him tremble. His eyes watering, fully open, he stayed seated, repeating to himself, *I don't want to.* And all of a sudden, he collapsed, grabbing a cushion in both hands and burying his face in it.

Then he was free to sob as much as he liked. His huge back heaved in the murk like the carapace of an enormous turtle, and around him the little dogs growled, wanting, with their paws and snouts, to take the cushion from him. Doubtless in the kitchen they would think he was playing with them.

He worried about the nasty side of grief—vomiting. He was afraid he'd throw up, that he'd have to call for help, and that Maïa would make fun of him with a child's words and jibes, as she once had long ago when he'd started sniveling in front of her. He didn't remember why. He only knew that he was capable of comedy—strange! But nothing acted alone, and the comedy of sadness was yet another sadness. But this time, no, there was, and there would be no comedy. *It's getting stronger.*

This time, his hand shook so much that the letter escaped him completely and slipped under the sofa. He felt the worst come on and prepared himself, tensing his whole body like an athlete. *Wait. And definitely keep your eyes closed.* Maybe at the moment he killed himself or was put to death he'd discover nothing so cruel. And killing himself was possibly easier after all—throwing himself under a train, for example, gritting his teeth, or swimming out to sea as Turnier had done. But even that thought was barely formed, and soon he didn't formulate anything more. He had no more need for language, unless you counted the cries, but he stifled them.

On his sofa, he was silent, heavy as a stone and slowly, he dug his nails into the goatskin. All his thoughts floundered in a pit of over-whelming light, suffocating, without compensation. *Why* mattered little now. And could he even understand where such a moment had come from? That somewhere he'd have his moment of recompense, as he hoped? No. Nothing. Death, which he didn't want—

But this wasn't death yet. Soon, his clenched hands opened and stopped trembling. He took a deep breath and a kind of vague smile sketched itself on his face. He made a little movement with his arms like a sleeper who wakes, and the little beasts wiggled. He petted them. They wagged their tails. Mireille licked his hand.

In the murk, only the face of the alarm clock glimmered. Cripure searched for a comfortable position on his sofa. There was nothing left in him but a great lassitude without thought, without dreams, without anything, only the feeling of no longer suffering quite so much. He finally got up with the clumsy, weighted movements of a man who has done a task that crushed him.

He shouldered the tailcoat and tiptoed forward to the glass door. It was open a crack—he pushed it. In the kitchen, they didn't move. Maïa was sitting beside Amédée, and his head was lowered. They weren't saying anything to each other. At the encampment, the sad singer had stopped, and the choir had returned.

Though he couldn't see Amédée's face, Cripure guessed he was crying. He retreated silently towards the door, but not fast enough to avoid hearing: "I'm sick, sick of, it's sick—"

"But what's that, my poor Amédée, what's sick?" asked Maïa.

"It's sick, me leaving her."

"Who? Your mom?"

"Who else did you think it was?" said Amédée, raising his head. Cripure turned the doorknob, pretending he was just coming in, but he looked away. To hide his face, Amédée pretended to tie one of his shoelaces, drying, for better or worse, his face on the fabric of his pant leg.

"There you are," said Maïa. "Come, let's clink. It'll be leaving time soon."

He returned to his place at the table.

"Let's make a toast," he said.

They raised their glasses, drinking to Amédée's health, to the end of this filthy war, and ate a cake that Maïa had made herself, a pound cake that was golden at the edges. Maïa dipped her cake into her glass, brought it to her lips and sucked it without biting. It made an irritating slurping between her lips. But she didn't know any better and there had never been a parting without pound cake. A habit which must come from a long way back, from her childhood maybe, or at least her first marriage, since she had been with another husband.

What made him think of that? Because of the cake no doubt, which must have had pride of place on Sundays and holidays in that little household of laborers. He watched Maïa dismantling it. The wench's mouth opened to engulf the cake and a little bit of wine dribbled from her lips. Did she think of him sometimes? Why wouldn't she? *Why not, like I think of Toinette?*

Everything, after a moment, had passed as though through mist. He no longer wondered about the retreat of his sorrow. He was practically free of suffering.

"Want another little piece?"

Maïa, offering him an extra bit of pound cake. He took it. She was delighted he liked it so much. She offered some to Amédée too. "You won't get cake like this out there where you're going!"

Why did she say that? thought Cripure. It was sad to see the two of them eating the little ends of cake. *Well, and what about me then?*

When Maïa's first husband died, the neighbors had joked a lot. They had a tough time putting him in the ground, they said, because his cuckold's horns didn't fit in the coffin. What jokes would they make when it was his turn to die? But more importantly, what ugliness had surrounded Toinette's death?

He jumped up, putting a hand to his mouth as if something had gone down the wrong pipe. "One moment!"

He hid in his study, closing the door behind him, and gripping the bookcase with one hand, he closed his eyes and didn't move. *I wasn't there!*

How long did he stay like that? He didn't lift his head until he heard them moving in the other room. They'd finished eating and drinking. It was time to go. *Come on now!*

And to cover it up, in case Maïa or the other one came in, he stood before the mirror and pretended to arrange his tie.

All dressed up. It was foreboding. And what an outfit! What a tailcoat. He wasn't missing anything, there was even a decoration in his buttonhole. It wasn't, thank God, that Legion of Honor which so disgusted him, which he couldn't see on someone without wondering what evil deeds had paid for it. He was satisfied with the little purple ribbon from the academy, obtained when he was promoted into the old farts club. All the same, he was decorated. Not with a spitball—just a little drool.

He looked at himself once more, as if he doubted that the image was really his, and he frowned. All in black! From head to toe, except for his collar, cuffs, and shirt front. *I look like an undertaker—*

"God's good name! What's he been burrowing around in now? Would you look here, Amédée? What a pig! Come here so I can brush that coat. You weren't gonna go like that, were you, dirty as a dishrag?"

He turned. "What's all this about?" he asked in a sweet voice, rolling his eyes.

"What's the fuss! He asks! What with him all covered in hair from those blessed ungodly dogs, that Judas who's shedding all of his fur. Come here!" She picked up a brush and brandished it. Amédée came in, his hands in his pockets.

"Turn around!"

Cripure arched his back to straighten out the cloth and startled, grimacing, at the first blow of the brush, harsh as a punch. Maïa grumbled. The tailcoat had fewer hairs stuck to it than the pants, but there were plenty to go around, and it was God's thunder getting them off. Worse than anything. Got to pick them off one at a time, finger and thumb. "And when I had so much trouble makin' him presentable this morning and just look what he does. Some schoolmaster he is."

"Tsk, tsk, Maïa."

"No ifs or buts. This is worse than the chalk."

"Come! Come!"

Why did she need to bring up the chalk! He was well enough aware, without her, that the damned pack of urchins amused themselves by making big chalk marks on the back of his jacket. He was so distracted, and they were so quick! They'd drawn a cartoon of him one day; another day they'd pinned a card to his ass with a bargain price—Cripure on sale.

"Bend over now. It's the seat of the pants that's the filthiest. And lift the coattails."

He obeyed. She did it with a good heart, Maïa! She dared them to say that she didn't take good care of him. Everything else, but not that. They could say she was an old whore, fair enough, *and why not keep at it, I'll outlast you.* But to say she didn't know how to keep him clean, nor her house, or that her cooking wasn't better than those who bragged to high heaven—no way! And she scrubbed and brushed, Cripure suffocating, his pince-nez dangling into emptiness at the end of their thread like a fishing line.

He asked for mercy. "Won't it do like that?"

"Hang on a minute!"

"It's just that—all the blood's rushing to my head, Maïa."

"That'll cool off your rump. Give you some fresh ideas." And she kept brushing. "Ok, that's it," she finally said. "Get yourself up." She gave him a hearty whack on the ass, and Cripure straightened, out of breath, putting his pince-nez back on, and preening like a big rooster.

"I'd pay two more sous for you," she said, stepping back to admire him. She squinted, as though he were a family portrait—*nice paintings shouldn't be looked at up close.*

All of a sudden, she pursed her lips. "For God's sake! There's a button ready to jump right off!"

Ah! Here we go again! "No, Maïa, no!"

"It won't take long."

"Let it go—"

"Won't take two minutes."

"But we'll be late, Maïa."

"I told you it won't be long—you'd better believe it!"

No argument.

The workbasket that had rolled on the ground this morning—but neither of them remembered it—was summoned as if by an enchantment into Maïa's hands. In the blink of an eye, she pulled out thread, a needle, a thimble. She certainly kept her promise—it wasn't long, and soon she bit off the thread between her teeth.

"There! It's done."

But then she noticed something else—his shoes.

It was what was most noticeable about Cripure's clothing, a real sticking point. Since she wanted them to shine! This morning, she'd spent a half-hour polishing them. But since then! The rain had tarnished them, the mud had stained them. And he'd said nothing, the idiot. What was he thinking? "You've got no pride. Come here! Put your foot there—"

Why argue? He sat in a chair, and there was Maïa, shining his shoes.

"Give me a hand, Amédée."

On their knees before Cripure. Each with a boot to speed things up. Since Maïa ignored Science and Industry's progress—the luxurious polishes you put on with a strip of wool—there was nothing for her but the rough barracks polish every artilleryman smeared on his boots with the tip of a knife, and which he spat on. Maïa spat too, saying with a laugh that it was the balm of her heart. Amédée did the same.

This way and that, they got the mud off, brushed, covered his massive boats in polish and spit, brushed, brushed again, panting like runners.

"That'll do," she said, "dropping her brush. Show me your tie?" She adjusted his tie and now that she was on a roll, wanted to touch up his mustaches with the iron.

"It'll take just a sec—" She burned him.

"Owww!"

"Calm down! Beauty don't know pain. What if you see a nice little chickie on your way?" Finally, she let him go. But! "And the errands?"

Quick, a scrap of paper and a pencil. She had to make him a list.

"Write down: Potatoes, red ones, not too stubbly. A pound of butter. A bottle of nice wine. That's everything? Ok, off you go!"

She kissed Amédée. "Watch yourself, ok!"

"It's the wheel of fortune, you know that, Auntie."

"Hang back as much as you can. Make like you're sick."

"They'd shoot me, Aunt. They're all pigs, you know."

Cripure lifted the curtain. It was raining for a change. Well then: the goatskin.

BASQUIN, from behind his blinds, watched Cripure's house. He smoked a cigarette, thinking about business.

The camp in back, it wasn't such a bad deal. Because of the Croats. A hundred and fifty of those scarecrows there, who let themselves get picked up at Le Havre, since the start. They were coming from America. They thought to return to their country. Those idiots, they didn't even know France was at war! And what's more, they'd booked passage on a French ship. Naturally, they were trapped like rats at the port. They bundled them away in a fortress for two months, then brought them to the camp. Almost all of them were big hearty fellows who had worked in the gold mines of Illinois, Alaska, Ohio, odd little spots. The interpreter said they didn't know German but they did just fine in Anglish. As for French, zilch. But they knew enough for Basquin's purposes. He had understood right away they were a good thing. And he hadn't been mistaken. On weekdays they wore work clothes, blue coveralls and vests that came right up under their arms with matching suspenders and endless numbers of pockets. For Basquin, it was astonishing, he'd never seen anything like it. And on Sunday they put on their nice suits, which cost from thirty to fifty dollars. They bought drinks for the poilus, and they weren't cheap about it. A little while after they arrived, two representatives from the bank had come to change their American and Austrian dollars. Basquin had watched from close by, out of the corner of his eye, but still carefully. And he'd figured out the exchange rate. For twenty dollars, they gave ninety francs, for two crowns, eight francs. The Croats, who hadn't been able to buy anything with their money before, since the French banks hadn't changed it, had rushed over to the canteen and gotten drunk as skunks, and afterwards one of them was joking with an watchman and gave him a friendly slap on the shoulder, and the poor fellow, armed to the teeth as he was, had panicked and run all the way back to the base shouting "Help! Help!"

Basquin laughed again, thinking of it.

Afterwards things had quieted down a bit. Some of them had found a way to get passage back to America, but most of the herd had stayed. And this was Basquin's personal gold mine.

He had a stake in the canteen. And then there was the whorehouse. It had gone unnoticed for the three years it had been running. What had almost put all of this in jeopardy was the arrival of the Russians. Those ones! He couldn't make a profit off them. The fraidy-cats who didn't want to fight anymore. So what! There was only one way to fix that! Was it our job to hold the line all alone? And while we're at it, feed and house them? What dopes they were, no joke! What idiots! If only he'd been more of a greaser in the government, he would have put a stop to it, yes he would. The ones who yelled the loudest up against a wall, the rest in the training camps, en route for the front, and if that's tough on you, too bad! Ah! He'd have beaten the rebellion out of them. With his rifle butt, mm-hm. Instead of that, they'd had to make room for them here, kick others out to put them up since they didn't have enough space, basically to make a big ruckus for a bunch of backstabbers. The whorehouse had almost gone under in the takeover, and he'd been very conniving to save it, oh so tricky! In the end it wasn't too bad. The little business had its following, but no thanks to them! Those dummies. After all, they were allowed to go around town like princes finding their own lovey-doveys here and there. They could do anything they felt like, even fuck for free. Oh, it was all terrible management. They should have given him free rein over the camp—and then, pow! First, they wouldn't be allowed to go out. Second, they wouldn't be allowed to howl from dawn till dusk, sitting in a circle in the courtyard. What an idea! Singing, always singing! Couldn't they leave people in peace? Even if just for the sake of poor Cripure. Basquin was sleeping with Maïa, sure, but that wasn't a reason Cripure should be kept awake by the Russians. A man who worked so much in his head, not to mention his hat, needed his rest. He had to understand everything, to make it accessible to everyone. And then, and then there were the rows! Those imbeciles over there weren't always getting along. Sometimes, instead of singing, they gave each other whacks on the nose and big ones too. No, they needed a tighter rein.

Yep! There he goes with his kid!

He went downstairs.

Left alone, Maïa tidied up the kitchen a bit, made the bed, then went into Cripure's study with the idea of sweeping it out. There was no use cleaning in there when he was at home—he wouldn't let her come in there. She had to wait till he was out to make it even a little bit presentable in that pigsty and even then she wasn't allowed to touch anything, as if it was full of treasures too fragile for her rough hands.

With the end of her broom she retrieved the letter that Cripure had let fall under the sofa and swept it out with the rest.

The bell rang softly twice, and from behind the door Maïa asked, "that's you is it?"

"Well, who else?" Basquin's voice replied.

She opened the door. Basquin came in grumbling, a cigarette butt dangling from his lips, and went into the kitchen, sitting himself down.

"A little coffee?" she asked.

"If you don't mind—"

The coffeepot was still warm on the burner.

Maïa brought over two glasses, the rum, the sugar, and a little bit of pound cake she'd saved for him.

"A little duckling to start," he said. He poured some rum into the bottom of his glass and dunked a sugar cube, then sucked it. His puffy face was the color of old wood, as if it were polished. One eye was bigger than the other.

"And where's Elephant Feet?"

"He just left to see his son off."

"And he's coming back here after?"

"Not before tonight. There's some party he's got to go to, some decoration or other for the wife of that Faurel."

"Oh! Well then." Basquin doubted it. Sometimes Cripure left, supposedly for days, and came back ten minutes later. He took care to remember how things had happened that time he pretended to go to all the way to Greece! He'd talked about the trip for two years, and booked his ticket all the way to Marseille, all paid for, and he didn't even make it to Paris. He got off at the first stop, yep, and came back. He imagined they were following him, that there was a conspiracy against him, didn't they know about it—what foolishness!

"Do you know," said Maïa, "he gave him a thousand francs."

Basquin choked into his glass.

"Are you crazy?"

"Don't believe me if you want. But I'm telling you..."

"Ah! Well I'll be damned... a thousand bones!"

"One bill."

He looked at her as if he couldn't quite wrap his mind around it. "Couldn't you of—" He didn't dare finish. Maïa's face had changed. No, but really. He wasn't going to reproach her? It wasn't as if...

"What's that to do with you?" she said. "It's not your dough."

He didn't answer. It was true, what she said. It wasn't his business, but it did something to him all the same. A thousand bones! It was a thousand bones pissed away. Amédée wouldn't have time to spend it before he got to the front, and he could be killed that same day. And even without that—

"You're not watching him sharp enough."

"I do what I can," said Maïa, "but the cash is his. He doesn't tell me his business."

"Clearly not! I can surely tell how this goes. You're the fifth wheel on the carriage, eh. You don't count. It's always the same song and dance." And after a moment of hesitation, "He's got to marry you, eh?"

"Oh that's what this is about!"

It was an idea long held between them. Once they got married,

Cripure's cash would fall into Maïa's hands, and then—of course Cripure would die first. Basquin was thinking of the future.

"Listen," he said, crossing his arms, "you're nothing but a ninny. Huh! There he goes, sticking his bastard with a thousand bones, but one of these days another one will turn up, and what'll he give that one? And then, does he have children from his first wife?"

"Dunno."

"You'd better find out! Suppose he dies, God forbid . . . And you, you've got nothing to do but bury him, thanks, goodbye? You've been left out of the chapter, eh? And all those sous, you tell me, where will they go? It's idiotic! You can't be sure, with a clever one like him, how the cards lie. Some legitimate son or nephew will come out of the woodwork, taking the inheritance under his elbow and laughing at you all the way to the bank, my poor Maïa. And you, you've cared for him, washed him, pampered him like a little brat, you've made him fancy little dishes every day and this is what you get? Do you want me to say it? It wouldn't just be idiotic, it'd be criminal! What? You make me laugh the way you talk! Better think again, goody two-shoes! He's got to marry you, or there's no justice in this world."

She listened, head down. All this was reasonable. Basquin saw how things stood, that was for sure. But the other one wouldn't hear of it. As soon as she mentioned marriage, he'd blow up with anger. And how angry he got!

"It's not his plan," she said.

Basquin bent forward in his chair, his arm stretched out, one elbow on his knee. He clicked his tongue. "Tsk, tsk, you don't know how to handle it."

"And you, what would you try?" she said, looking him in the eyes.

He lowered his voice. "But, this is ridiculous!" he said, gritting his teeth. "Don't you see you've got him right where you want him?" He waggled his finger under Maïa's nose. "What would he do without you?" he said, bringing his face closer, his two hands on his knees. "Can you tell me that?"

They stared at each other for a moment, neither one of them budging.

"I know it," she said.

"So, then go for it," said Basquin, "take the upper hand. Give him his marching orders: You marry me or I'll walk out. You'll see," he said, crossing his legs, and digging in his pocket for cigarette paper, "you'll see if he doesn't hop to it." He shook his head, rolling his tobacco all the while. "A Godforsaken thousand francs!"

He lit his cigarette, stretched out his legs under the table and picked up his glass. "A thousand bones! If I went to the front, I'd come back rich, you can be sure of it..."

She didn't reply.

They swilled their coffee in little sips, sitting across from one another, without anything else to say to each other, without even looking at each other, like an old married couple. Basquin smoked. He poured himself another shot of rum, which he drank in one swallow, and stood up.

"Your man?" he said, touching his forehead, "he's cuckoo."

She still didn't respond.

Calmly, without putting down his cigarette, while Maïa rinsed the glasses, he took his clothes off.

"Is Madame ready?"

CRIPURE dragged along at Amédée's side. He scolded himself for not hiring Père Yves for this departure ceremony. It hadn't even occurred to him. It's true that in the moment, with ten glasses of Anjou in his blood—Well, he could still beat himself up for it. What's more, he was tired from the comings and going of the morning, Amédée's presence at his side, what a penance! They couldn't find a word to say to each other, and it was so slow, this advance toward the station—Amédée slowed his steps, but clumsily, and Cripure was dying to tell him to get out of there, slip away, run!

He didn't dare.

At least if he'd been in the cab, besides the benefit of being driven, and at a speed, he could have put on an act, pretended to be daydreaming, maybe sleeping, his usual strategy. Instead he'd had to start a conversation when they left the house about the rain and the nice weather, which had not taken them very far. And since then, nothing.

People were looking at them.

Oh, of course, he didn't give a damn about what they thought, but all the same! There was so much evil in certain surprised looks, such spontaneous hatred. And not only evil and hatred, but you could say certain people, whose faces he didn't even recognize, understood everything, guessed what was in the bottom of his heart.

"Are you out of breath, Father? Maybe we're going too quick?"

He hadn't realized he was panting.

"No—yes." When it came down to it, yes. What was the point of explaining all that? *Let's get this over with as fast as possible—*

"Won't you be late?"

"Oh that's no problem! I'm not in a rush to go get my face blown off, you know, Father."

He hadn't understood that Cripure was giving him an out. *If I'm honest with myself, I'd leave him* ... but wait. What had Amédée just said? Something about the front, about getting his head blown off. *If I'm honest with myself I wouldn't leave him, on the contrary. I have money. If I was honest with myself, I'd give him the money to desert.*

That was sensible. That was the course faithful to himself. Was he a revolutionary? Yes or no? He gave himself the impression of one of those sinister fathers who puts a revolver in his son's hand instead of going to the bank for the fifty thousand francs that would let him escape to Venezuela.

But Amédée hadn't asked for anything.

Cripure wanted to ask all the same.

"Haven't you—tell me, haven't you had enough?"

Amédée hadn't expected that question, it was plain to see in his face. "Well, yeah!"

"Everyone has, right?"

"You didn't hear about those mutinies?"

"Yes. But, isn't it true, the movement was crushed, wasn't it?"

"Yes. But it's too bad."

"Ah?"

"Sure. It could've been the end of the war, eh? The end forever. There never would've been another. We would've been happy. I can't explain it to you, Father, but I can feel it, in here, eh?" he said, banging a fist on his chest.

Cripure didn't say anything else. He'd had to wait until the moment of departure to find out that Amédée was an idealist in his own right, and moreover a character that would be pretty typical in a Zola novel! He looked at him with pity bordering on scorn. Bah!

"You maybe don't agree?"

Cripure made a face. "I'd like—" A monstrous thought crossed his mind: that he didn't need to regret not being able to save Amédée's life because it wasn't worth it. He was just one of the herd ...

To dare speak of being happy! To mutiny in the name of future happiness—as that young lieutenant had done yesterday—took an absolute ignorance of mankind! Once again, if they'd spoken of nothing but blowing capitalism to bits, that would be one thing. But the rest...

They didn't say anything more, and continued their painful advance. How long it was! There was so much of it, streets and streets!

Cripure stopped a little in front of the station. Rather than waiting on the platform under a car door for the train to leave. The pain would be worse in that moment—it was better to brush it off.

"Listen, my child, I'd better leave you here."

"Ok."

"You don't want me there, isn't that so?"

"What a thought!"

"Come here..."

The arrival scene didn't reproduce itself—not a sob, not a shiver, no drama. It was a polite goodbye, more like acknowledgment. Everything went smoothly.

"And so goodbye," said Amédée. "I'll write to you. And thank you, you know."

"Oh hush."

"You've been kind to me and all."

"Hush now."

"Oh you didn't have to do all of this, eh?"

"Go on, go on. Hush, my child."

One more word would spoil everything. Each of Amédée's words cut into him cruelly. But Amédée thought his father was being polite. He insisted, "I'll never forget it."

"Listen," said Cripure, bending to whisper in his ear, "I put something for you in your wallet. You'll find it. No, no, don't thank me. Go now. Goodbye."

He pushed lightly on his shoulder, Amédée still repeating, "You didn't have to. You're so kind!"

So kind!

He watched Amédée leave. *What do I know?* he murmured, sighing. And when Amédée had disappeared he continued on his way. *What can all this matter anyway—Toinette is dead!*

Monsieur Babinot climbed calmly toward the station. A cigarette after lunch, when his wife wasn't watching, that was his one weakness. So he smoked it in little drags, not hurrying, and all the while keeping an eye out like a magpie for some boy with a kind face who would accept one of his "pomes" and who, in return, might let fall some heroic anecdote, some sublime phrase for his collection.

While he walked he recited his poems to himself, as if he were humming, delectating his own work once again, delighted to find his memory intact.

No sooner had Cripure made a few steps down the road after leaving Amédée to his fate, than he was already ceasing to think about it, dreaming of being finished with that burden, when he found himself nose to nose with Babinot.

While he recited his poems, Babinot sent severe looks all around him, as if it was his job to ensure that all was going well in town. He felt responsible for the morals of its citizens, old patriot that he was. And this patriotism certainly wasn't a recent thing! He'd always given incontestable proof at every opportunity. Hadn't he always been one of the most faithful attendees of the military concerts in front of the officers club every Tuesday, and also in the little squares on Thursdays and Sundays? Of course he had! He beat time with his finger, listening to the quick-step march. At the end of each set, he clapped louder than everyone, so much that people would say his hands were made of wood. Often he even accompanied clapping with his voice, encouraging the musicians and the singers. But that wasn't enough for Monsieur Babinot. He also knew how to make sure the French army was respected, going so far as to knock off, with the tip of his cane, the hat of some interloper who was thinking God knows what, one had to ask, as the flag passed one 14th of July. A little tap of the cane, deftly applied, and hop! hop! The hat had popped off like a cork. A punch in retaliation, pow! And Monsieur Babinot had learned the cost of making others salute a flag that wasn't theirs. A little row had resulted. But oh well! The interloper had saluted all the same, and that was all Babinot cared about.

When he saw Cripure approach, his eyes downcast, his lip bitterly curled, Babinot accosted him with aggressive joy, extending his hand with the brutal gesture of someone demanding your wallet or your life.

And, stopping on the edge of the sidewalk, looking proudly at Cripure with the particular air of an examiner who is also the police commissioner. "How goes France?" he said.

Oh! thought Cripure, *so it already begins! Where could he escape? Where could he hide? They were tracking him everywhere.*

He bent down, his hand still imprisoned in Babinot's, not sure he had quite understood this time, or, if he had, he was sure Molière had been outdone.

"I'm sorry?"

"I asked you, 'How goes France?'" Finally letting go of Cripure's hand, he continued: "It's my idea that when we greet each other, we shouldn't ask after each other's health anymore, not just an ordinary 'How are you?' but once again with those words 'How goes France?'"

A deep sigh escaped Cripure's chest.

Really, he couldn't come to terms with them on anything. It meant becoming like this imbecile who was talking to him about France. All around, they talked about it in more or less the same tone, and it was unbearable for Cripure, who knew just as well as they did, and perhaps better, that it was only for love of their country. But it was harder to play out the comedy of agreement when they had that love in common—it would have been easier in the opposite case, when he simply could have disagreed. But had they understood?

"France? France bleeds," he said.

Babinot was taken aback. "Let's not be pessimists! No my dear colleague, let's not be bad examples! What we need to do and what I'll allow myself to recommend, oh oh! is a discreet joy. That our dear men in the trenches have laughter. Their laughter is heroic. We have smiles. The smile demonstrates balance—a calm spirit and a confidence in the future. Not for the world should we seem to whistle as we walk through the woods. Not for the world should we seem like those people who turn a deaf ear. To the French! Always for the French!"

He followed Cripure and continued, "the little power that's in everyone will thus grow and be amplified. Clarified. What's the secret? What's the method? To put together the best of what we have inside us, to tie together what we have that's most precious, to think together on what we have in our philosophy that's purest. That's why we all have to come together," he said, thinking of the party where they'd meet in a little while. "Each gathering must be a miniature portrait of our sacred Union. By the way," he kept on, "the general is cured!" Babinot trumpeted, as if he were addressing a deaf person.

The general? "What general?" Cripure had to ask, and then he quickly amended it with an "ah! ah!" that wasn't much of a compromise.

"Yes," said Babinot, "he'll be there later. It's Nabucet who's just told me." And two little pats from his hands made the lapels of Babinot's jacket tremble—plouf, plouf.

"The general," Babinot continued, still walking, "has very delicate lungs. The slightest breeze and—paf! And that's what happened. But now he's back on his feet." And once again Babinot's hands flapped like the back paws of a dog, and the lapels of his jacket trembled.

"Are you out for a stroll, my dear colleague?" Babinot asked.

"That's to say," Cripure replied, "that I just came from taking my little nephew to the train, you know eh...who's going back to the front."

"Ah! Perfect! Very good! I didn't know you had a nephew. But that's perfect, just perfect. Full of purpose, I hope?"

"Yes."

"They're all like that."

Cripure remembered Amédée, just now, in the kitchen.

"At the Chemin des Dames, the work of two artillery units," Babinot recited, "easily pushed back a few feeble Germans. In sum, we're on the favorable side of the war. Let's not unbuckle our cuirasses.

I'm laughing, you know, when I hear that they're demanding the allies make their goals for the war known. The goals of war! That the allies make known their goals for the war!" He shouted, raising his arms to the sky. "As if the goal of war was anything but peace! Let's not be sentimental. There are people too, who know very well what they're doing, trying to discourage us, who want to clip our wings, that whole group of bad Frenchmen who have Kienthal and Zimmerwald in their heads. But Clemenceau will insure us against that. The army is healthy, no matter what people say. It's not, it seems, a little noise around the trains for furloughed men that'll bring the morale of the army into question. They should stop supplying those idiots with alcohol. And as for the ringleaders—shoot 'em."

Cripure wasn't hearing well. He had a strange ability to turn a deaf ear to those things that deserved a slap in the face in reply. What better moment to repeat to himself that nothing was true, that everything was permitted, that life made no sense and neither did death. It wasn't lost on him.

Two off-duty soldiers were walking in front of them.

"Would you look at that," cried Babinot, "how limber! What nerve! And you only see men like that—martial!"

The two men turned and Babinot, leaving Cripure behind him, walked vigorously over to meet them, trying to imitate the hunter's steps of Monsieur Poincaré, and he took a bundle of his poems out of his pocket.

"Hang on," he said. "Yes—take it!"

"What is it?"

They were suspicious.

"You'll see later...You can read it on the train," said Babinot.

One of the men took the poems.

"It's probably nonsense," said the other. "Let's have a look," he moved to read over his comrade's shoulder.

"That's it," said the first one. "Some verses...the motherland..."

"Again?"

Babinot prickled. "What do you mean, 'again'?"

"That's enough! I've had it with them," said the man who had taken the poems. "You see your little poems, old man?" He gave a mean laugh. "Take a good look!"

And under Babinot's chin, he ripped the poems and threw the pieces to the wind.

They turned on their heels.

Cripure watched the scene open-mouthed. As for Babinot, astonishment froze him in place. "Excuse me!" he cried, running after them.

"The idiot. The hell with peace!"

"One moment! What you just did is very bad. Unworthy of the uniform that—"

"Shut your mouth!"

They hurried their steps. But Babinot could walk fast. He kept at it. Irritated, the poilus did an about-face and stopped. "Are you going to push it? You've got nobody, I bet?"

"My son is there," Babinot shouted, "and I'm proud of it," he said triumphantly.

"Bastard!"

"If your son is up there, he's like us: he's had it."

"Are you traitors to France? What regiment..."

"Oh a tattletale? The son of a bitch..."

An unbuckled belt whistled through the air like a whip. "Put that in verse!" Babinot heard. And he thought someone had ripped off his face. He whirled around twice, blinded and crying in pain. The two men hustled off.

"Help!" cried Babinot. "Help! I've got an eye dangling!"

Cripure made such a violent effort that he was actually running, his pince-nez held between his thumb and forefinger. "Here I am! I'm coming, dear Babinot—"

On the sidewalk, Babinot was prancing, holding his head in his hands. It looked like he was dancing drunk, but he was groaning too much for a dancer. "Owwwww I'm blinded!"

"I'm here, my friend! Here I am," said Cripure.

But without listening to Cripure, without even seeming to hear him, Babinot cried even louder, "My eye is gouged out!"

In his panic, Cripure circled around Babinot with his trembling hands outstretched. Which part should he get a hold of?

"Owwww ahlalala—I must have—I must have had an eye—Gahhhh—gouged out—"

"May I?" said Cripure, "Let me see."

Babinot stopped dancing and even stopped groaning. The left eye was terrible to look at—he would have to go with him. "If we went into a café?" Cripure suggested. "There we could bathe the eye..."

"No, no, no, no! No scandal!"

"To a doctor then. It's only prudent."

"A pharmacist."

"So be it. Can you see here?"

"Barely."

"Allow me...I'll take your arm like this."

"My hat?"

"Ah, of course...give me one second, don't move..."

The hat had rolled a long distance, and Cripure couldn't find it right away. Babinot grew impatient.

Finally, he found the bowler hat and brushed it with his elbow, returned and placed it on Babinot's head with infinite care. "There you are. There's the hat, old friend. Let's go now. Let's go to a pharmacist. Does it hurt?"

"It hurts," Babinot nobly replied. He was proud of suffering.

Cripure took is arm and they started off. "How is it now?"

"It's starting to stew."

They made a rather notable couple. Someone might have thought they were a pair of drinking buddies, a little tipsy, but a maudlin drunk, without singing. They didn't say anything else. Cripure's tall silhouette was a head taller than Babinot, who, with his jacket, his bowler hat, and his handkerchief wadded up over his eye, looked a bit like the Clopper, but a Clopper that was finally the prisoner of his enemy—a sniveling and reluctant Clopper being marched to his dungeon.

They went into a pharmacist's shop, Babinot still dabbing his eye with the handkerchief and leaning on Cripure. The pharmacist rushed over, and got the wounded man a seat—his eye certainly wasn't dangling. Luckily, the belt buckle had struck the arch of the eyebrow and Monsieur Babinot would escape with a magnificent black eye.

"Take good care of yourself, Monsieur," said the pharmacist. "One centimeter lower and you'd have been one-eyed for the rest of your days..."

"I'll make them pay," groaned Babinot.

The pharmacist washed it, dressed it, and wrapped a large bandage around his head. Then, he advised him to go home and go to bed. He should be careful—he'd surely have a bit of fever.

"But...what about the party?" said Babinot.

"What party?"

"What do you mean! Didn't you know that we're decorating Madame Faurel today? It's not this wound, I think, that will keep me away..."

And with all his bravado, proud as if his bandage were a medal, already forgetting his pain, which, to tell the truth, wasn't very bad anymore, he got up, paid, and went out.

Once he reached the sidewalk: "My dear colleague," he said, turning to Cripure, "I won't forget what you've done for me. Thank you, thank you! See you soon!" And coming closer to him, "This was quite a mysterious affair, but hush! We'll clear it all up," he murmured in his ear.

With that, he turned on his heel. God forbid he arrive at the party with a Cripure on his arm!

WHAT A lovely bow Nabucet made as he greeted the general! It was impossible to imagine a more delicate, more gracious, more devoted one, even if, instead of a rather weary general, it had been a ravishing young actress getting out of the carriage. The way he held out his hand to help him to the ground looked like Nabucet was offering his arm. My dear General, here, my dear General there...how moving! How delightful! Take your places! Stand back!

"Make way, please!"

To whom was he addressing that order? To two or three students who happened to stop there, by accident. They immediately let them through. The general came forward with a couple of officers, Nabucet leading the way.

Nabucet's eyes were shooting fire, seeming to threaten with the forces of hell the imprudent, the impertinent who didn't obey quickly enough; then, returning to the general's face, they became soft, caressing, full of soft smiles, searching that aged face for signs of his illness. But God be thanked, they weren't too deep. The general had good color, alert eyes, and his whole person emanated a sense of contentment and even happiness that delighted Nabucet to the core of his soul. Ah! Please God! Let the general remain well...

"This way, my dear General—"

A general!

Really, it was all too rare that one got to say "my dear General!" He came forward, twisting and turning like a dancing master, sometimes walking backwards, sometimes by his side, sometimes bowing deeply before the trio of military men, always smiling and flowery.

Ah! My dear General, could you please give me a boot to lick, just one! And if by great luck you happen to have an old one you don't need anymore, my dear General, honor me with it as a gift, so that I might lick it at home...

"Wonderful to see you," said the general.

"The honor is all ours," Nabucet replied in his most delicate voice.

He made another bow, pointing the way with his hand, delirious to the bottom of his heart with the pleasure of having beaten everyone, to have been there first—the first!—even before the principal, who was running over. Ah! He had them!

"My dear General..."

"Dear General, gentlemen, please forgive me," babbled the principal, who was also making a great effort to smile, and to excuse his lateness. The poor man wasn't himself.

"Not at all," said the general. He took the principal's hand and shook it with soldierly vigor. "Good news of your son?"

Monsieur Marchandeau's voice choked.

"Thank you, General."

"I've heard reports recently that he's an excellent officer."

"General..."

The other gentlemen of the faculty arrived—Moka with his embattled red forelock, Glâtre, portly and watchful, Surgeon General Bacchiochi, the bursar, among others... they saluted as one, and the little troupe marched together, the officers' sabers hitting the stone of the staircase.

Nabucet led the procession.

Then, suddenly, Werner the cook appeared. Too late to avoid him!

"Awkward kid!" murmured Nabucet.

Werner was frozen in salute against the wall. The general stopped. A pause.

"Here's a hearty fellow," he said. He looked him over from head to foot. Werner didn't budge.

"It's the cook from the hospital...one of the cooks, my dear General," the Bursar explained. "We borrowed his services for our little gathering."

"An Alsatian," said Nabucet.

"Hold on, hold on!" said the general, scratching his chin, "But, my boy, why aren't you enlisted? You came from the internment camp?"

"Yes, General, sir."

"Do you have family in France?"

"No, General, sir."

"And . . . were you part of any French societies?"

"None, General, sir."

"And were your parents French before 1870?"

"Yes, sir."

"Is there any way to prove it?"

"My dear General," said Bacchiochi, "he's been asked several times already. He even met specially with the prefecture and his file was examined."

"I can well believe it, but I don't see the reason in all this that keeps this boy from joining the foreign legion. What do you think about that?" he said to Werner.

Werner hadn't moved a muscle.

"I have two brothers enlisted in Germany, General."

"Ah! Ah! And they're in combat?"

"Yes, sir."

"On which front?"

"I have no idea, General."

"Fine, fine. Your scruples are honorable. But after all, your brothers are Alsatian like you. Why are they fighting against us? Yes, I know, the question is a delicate one, but in my opinion, since your brothers are fighting, young man, I don't see why you couldn't do the same. Isn't that so?" the general asked, turning to the others for assistance.

They all agreed, some with their voices, and others only with nods.

"Excuse me, General," said Werner, "I still have my mother and father to think of."

"Oh! At your age, you see, you're certainly old enough to bypass their opinions." He decided to continue up the stairs. Werner saluted and went downstairs.

"They don't keep a close enough eye on particular cases like that," the general concluded. "I must follow up on this business . . ."

I'm fucked, thought Werner.

What a magnificent group! The prefect in full dress uniform, his wife and associates, the municipal counselors, the academy inspector in white tie, Madame Poche, the president of Les Dames de France, Madame Rabat, the headmistress of the middle school, Madame Bourcier, Madame Marchandeau, Madame Point herself, the notary's wife, and Madame Babinot also, alone in a corner, looking like a blind woman in mourning. They all rose when the general entered.

"Our General!"

"My dear prefect, Madame . . ."

"General . . ."

"Monsieur Inspector, Messieurs, Mesdames, Madame . . ."

The fire crackled in the back of the grate.

When the excitement had died down, the general examined the space. "Well, well! Here's a marvelously decorated room. A very confident taste . . . very fine."

Nabucet blushed. "General."

"And very learned," the general added.

He sat down, the others forming a circle around him. The general made erudite comments about the decoration of the room, proving his education. He reminisced about secondary school. The prefect cited a Latin verse that no one understood. The academy inspector surveyed the scene with the smile of an evil priest. And the fire crackled.

Besides the principal guests of honor, Madame Faurel and her husband, they were waiting on Monsignor.

The mayor would come too, if he had a minute.

They suddenly heard, "It's nothing! Nothing at all! A lit-tle fly—"

They all turned—it was Babinot who entered.

When she saw the bandage, Madame Babinot opened her mouth and her eyes at the same time, becoming even paler in her black dress, without making a sound.

Babinot came forward, smiling. He waved his hand up and down in the air like a conductor who wants the bass to be a little quieter, and in his nasal voice he repeated, "It's nothing, nothing at all."

He was surrounded. A million questions.

"What! What happened to you?"

"What accident?"

"Monsieur Babinot is wounded!"

What happiness! What a beautiful moment for him! How proud he was of his bandage, even though the bandage didn't show so much as a drop of blood and he smelled of lavender!

"A little fly, maybe a winged ant that got into my eye while I was talking to a couple of off-duty soldiers."

Two men on leave had asked him to recite a poem, and he hadn't wanted to deny them the pleasure.

"So I was reciting when, paf! This devilish little fly went into my eye and planted itself there like a thorn."

Ah! Ah! he thought, *there's another story I'll tell a little later. Chivalrous! How Monsieur Babinot didn't want to frighten his wife, so he invented a little fly.*

They got him a chair. Did he want a something, a pick-me-up?

"A little chartreuse?" proposed Madame Bourcier.

"No, no…"

"A little Benedictine?"

He refused. Ah! If only she had offered him some schnapps!

Madame Babinot went back to her corner, stiff and dressed in black like an umbrella walking on its handle. Silent.

Babinot moved his armchair closer to the general, and in a low voice, "I didn't want to tell the real story in front of my wife—it's a worrisome one, you know, General, but…" he glanced over at "Maman" again. No problem—as deaf as she was mute. He could raise his voice. "The fly—that was made up. The truth is, I ran into two spies."

"Two spies!" said the general, jumping out of his chair. He didn't believe there were spies in his district.

"Hush! Not so loud… I was walking by the station and, voilà, two soldiers came up to me, two…officers. Bravo, I said to myself, let's see what these gentlemen want with me? Do you know what they asked? I bet you can't guess! The number of the regiment stationed here! But I didn't take the bait; I'm an old wily one, I knew right away who I was dealing with. Not just their accents but also…a smell. The smell of Boches, I can sense it from miles away. 'The regiment number?' I said. 'Come with me, and I'll give it to you.' And while I was talking, I gave them a look. Seeing that they were found out, they jumped on me and hit me with the butts of their pistols."

"Extraordinary," said the general. Nabucet winked, warning him that Babinot wouldn't be contradicted. And the general went on, "Poor Babinot, it seems you got quite a blow!"

"That's for sure."

"And the two men?" asked Moka.

"Gone, alas. I think they managed to jump on the train. I'm letting you know about this business, General. Let's run them down! Don't say anything to anyone. Silence! Not a word to anyone! The fly! The fly! So as not to threaten your actions, General, let's all say it was a fly. And those young fools will be—whipped," he finished, cracking his knuckles.

Nabucet personally thought this was pure theatrics, this way of coming to a party with a bandage on your eye and dispensing all these fantastical tales. "They'll be locked up, my friend, without a doubt. Patience! Patience! *Sufficit diei militia sua.*"

He bent down to the general and whispered in his ear, "What an odd story! I think he's a little off."

Steps in the corridor. Was it finally Monsignor? Was it the Faurels? Should he rush over? Nabucet listened: no, it was nothing. Cripure's steps.

He came in, as if bracing himself for an immediate rain of blows. Luckily he hadn't put down his cane, which he was holding out as if to a servant, along with his little hat. But there were no servants in sight, and he came forward, with the air of someone who isn't sure he's on the right floor.

"Isn't this—excuse me…"

"Good afternoon," said Nabucet, from across the room, turning his head.

"Who is that?" asked the general.

"Our philosopher, General."

"What a funny fellow!"

"He's a bit of an...odd one," murmured Nabucet in the general's ear.

"Someone already told me something like that..."

"He says he knows Sanskrit, and it's quite possible, but he knows scarcely any Greek."

"That's the most important thing," said the general.

"I don't say that to disparage him," Nabucet continued, "but it seems to me that Sanskrit is rather remote from all this."

"Especially in wartime," the general said.

No one came over to Cripure. He took off the goatskin himself, putting it on a chair with the little hat and the cane, and sat down as far as possible from the group.

He could tell they were talking about him. *So what? What do I care?*

He could have joined in with the chorus. What could they say that I'm not already well aware of? That he wasn't what you would call a model of elegance and worldly manners? True. That his awkwardness was proverbial? Certainly. He was clumsy, he knew, and as for his wit, it was always a step behind the others, just like Rousseau's. Like Rousseau too, he lived with an illiterate Thérèse; like him, he was a misanthrope, with a mania for persecution. And lastly, there was the abandoned bastard child. The big difference, besides genius, was that he was *submissive*. "Submissive!"

He lowered his head like a defendant in a criminal court. Nabucet would have made such a good prosecutor for the Republic!

Maybe they were talking about his legendary feet once again?

One day, well before the war, a circus with a giant had arrived in town. Well, the giant's shoes had been nothing in comparison with

Cripure's, as everyone could see. The manager of the circus had exhibited the giant's shoes in the window of the largest shoe store in town—precisely the one Cripure frequented.

When they brought in the shoes, the boot-maker turned up his nose. To the incredulous circus director, he said, "I've got even bigger ones than that!" And running to his workshop, he returned with Cripure's shoes, which Maïa had just that moment dropped off for repairs. The circus director had to admit he was beaten. He expressed interest in meeting this "phenomenon." Did he want to hire him? He had joked for a minute with the boot-maker, who had strongly advised him to hire Maïa as well, since they were a pair.

But when the circus manager had learned that the owner of those astonishing boots was a professor, and of philosophy! He'd simply shrugged and changed the subject.

For three whole days, the giant's shoes had stayed in the window, a monstrous display, which had no doubt succeeded in bringing more than one drifter to the circus. But it had also revealed, to those who weren't yet aware of his existence, that somewhere, in some part of town, there was a man who was very intelligent, a savant, whose feet were even bigger than the giant's.

During those three days, the boot-maker made more than one trip to his workshop to get Cripure's shoes, to show them to some client who wanted to see for himself. And so the shoes were passed from hand to hand. They measured them, weighed them, sized them up with their looks and their fingers, compared them to the giant's, with comments that mingled pity and mockery. The physiologists imagined that Cripure's infirmity, in forcing him to look inward, had made him into a philosopher, so that you could say he drew his intelligence from his feet. Others, pretending to be experts, scratched their chins and wondered what illness could cause such a sad deformity. Someone used the word "acromegaly"—they needed a pharmacist to explain it to them. A medical dictionary was consulted, and the pharmacist came to over the boot-maker's, radiating science. This mysterious malady came from a gland with apophasis, which caused it to function poorly. All the extremities: the feet, the hands, the tongue, and the other thing too, the pharmacist added with a malicious smile, can start to grow unpredictably. It wasn't a hereditary disease. You could become symptomatic at any age. He'd seen twenty-five-year-olds suddenly get it.

They were fascinated. Did Cripure already have this sickness when he married Toinette? Since then? Did he come down with it during? And they chuckled. Cripure knew all that.

Babinot maneuvered, slipped over to Cripure and touched his arm. Cripure jumped. "Hey!" he said. "And by the way, how's that eye?"

"Shh! The eye's not too bad. It's still stings a little, but anyway, we've got to do our part. I wanted to tell you . . . but this isn't a good place to talk. Come to the buffet for a moment, my friend."

Why not?

The buffet table was deserted, since Werner had decided to give up. They could send someone else in his place, or those women could serve themselves if that suited them. As for him, no. Not a chance. Bastards like that . . .

Babinot pointed to a couple of chairs.

"It's about that little incident earlier," he said, sitting down, "I wanted to ask you, my dear colleague . . . not to speak about it in front of my wife, you see. She's such a worrier! I had to tell her that a little fly got stuck in my eye . . ."

"Ah! Bah!" Cripure was astonished.

"So as not to frighten her, my friend. So I wanted to ask you—"

"Come now, it's understood!"

"Thanks. But there's something else. I had good reason to think there was more to this affair. Oh, a mystery that's easy to solve! I've figured it out. But you won't say anything to anyone, will you?"

"Since you ask me not to."

"Until the day you're asked to be a witness."

"Me?"

If he was counting on him for that . . . what did he want? To put his aggressors through a military trial? "What you're asking of me is very serious."

Babinot threw up his hands. "By God, of course it's serious! Certainly!"

"But don't count on me to testify."

"What! You astonish me, my dear Monsieur Merlin, you really shock me! You don't want me to think you're indifferent to the fact that German spies are walking among us and assaulting patriots!"

This was a glimmer of light. "That's what this is about!" cried Cripure, who was struggling hard to repress laughter. The expression he used to stifle it was such that Babinot no longer doubted the extreme impression the news had caused.

"It was two spies, I'm telling you. I now have undeniable proof. They've been marked out in the area. The general is aware of it. You know, my friend, what a great man the general is. He seems like he's come to pass an hour in company at this little party, and during that time, do you think he's not working? Don't be fooled! Runners have already gone out, my friend, those foolhardy boys will be identified everywhere. It only took one word!"

"Magnificent!"

"If you talk to him about it, make sure to point out, you know, that they were two officers."

Officers? Where had Babinot gotten that idea? Probably the same place he got the fly. "Officers?" said Cripure.

"Yes, yes, I'm sure."

"Bah?"

"I'm sure of it, my friend. Anyway, they always disguise themselves as officers. Everyone knows that."

"Ah! Bah!"

"But you know they had those little stripes like they wear now. You surely noticed them, didn't you?"

"I wouldn't swear to it."

"There...on their sleeves?"

"But they had backpacks!"

Babinot looked serious.

"Hmm. Are you quite sure?"

"I think so."

"Ah, you think so. So there's a doubt. That's it, that's it. I also wondered ... but no, they weren't carrying backpacks. They were two hearty fellows with blond hair and blue eyes, and pretty heavy steps. I can see them walking in front of me. No, my friend, now I'm sure, they weren't wearing backpacks. They were definitely officers."

"So be it," Cripure said.

"Remember it well."

"They might have been officers."

That devilish Cripure! He never said anything directly. He'd seen in a blur or not at all. Hadn't his pince-nez fallen?

"Didn't you lose your lenses? Excuse the question—but it's highly important."

He would go along with it—it was simpler. What did he care that they weren't officers? "You're right, Babinot, I remember everything now."

"So they were definitely officers?"

"Why yes."

"That's what I was telling you! I'm sure of it. But I wanted to check my memory against yours, you know. Yes, yes, yes, they were spies disguised as officers. They were waiting for me at the turn. But he who has the last laugh laughs loudest. We're cooking them up a little dish ... à la française! So," he finished, getting up, "you're in the know and you'll see what happens."

"Perfect!"

"Let's go back over to the others. They must be wondering what we're gossiping about! And along those lines, my friend, allow me to make a friendly ... suggestion, on a subject that has nothing to do with our business?"

"But of course, Monsieur."

"It's delicate, but ... too bad. Well then," he said, "well then, I was watching you just now ... the devil take it! Why on earth do you always keep to yourself like that? They say—I'm not offending you am I?"

"Oh, not at all!"

"They say ... it's difficult to say this ... they say you keep yourself apart, that you refuse... Come now! A little vigor! A little mingling! You mustn't stay aloof, if you'll allow me to say so, since that always creates an impression that upsets people. They won't understand, you know, they'll start to ask questions. Your speech last year won you a lot of support. You mustn't get discouraged. Mingle with us, my friend, mingle! Mingle!" And he abruptly interrupted himself and announced, "Oh, goodness! We've missed the bishop's arrival! And the Faurels!"

And it was true—at the center of the room, Monsignor stood and offered his ring for the gracious and humble Madame Faurel to kiss.

"It's irregular, it's very irregular," grumbled Babinot, leaving Cripure.

He went over to the little group of solemn new arrivals where Madame Faurel was smiling.

What a beautiful person! What a slender and supple body, with those long legs and shapely bust. What perfume she dispersed! Her face was pink as a young girl's, glistening with freshness. She looked not a day over thirty! What frantic joy in her blue, kohl-rimmed eyes! And her blond hair, her lips so red against her false teeth, and her sparkling necklace and rings! And her black satin dress! A queen.

Faurel was shaking hands.

Everywhere, people were excited. The brouhaha continued endlessly. Cripure thought he was at the theater, when the musicians tune their instruments before the curtain rises. Each one was testing his voice, his look. Alone, he stayed silent in the chair. Nabucet was holding forth, directing things, going from group to group, whispering in people's ears. Moka and Glâtre were bickering in a corner. The women were talking about chiffon, mourning outfits, sharing recipes. Mademoiselle Rabat, the headmistress of the middle school, had found a portrait of Descartes on the wall and was gushing:

"That dear René! I love that man, and with good reason!"

The prefect was talking about Bolsheviks with the academy inspector. "Besides, they're all fugitives from the law."

"What do they expect—Russia isn't ripe for revolution."

"They'll fill their pockets and then—poof! They'll disappear with the crown jewels."

"Do they even know what they want?"

Cripure cautiously approached the open window, and bent down. A little air!

He caught sight of a nearby classroom. It was barely six feet away— a little old man with a beard put a parcel down on a chair, took off his hat, then took out a fancy sword, which he held between his hands like a crucifix. The sword belonged to his son who'd been killed two months before, and they had just sent it back to him. "Gentlemen," he said, turning to his students, "my dear young friends, today I am asking for more than just your attention—I'm asking for your whole hearts..." his two big hands, passionately clutching the sword, trembled so much that the blade clacked in the sheath. The students, mute with awe, fixed their eyes on the man in black who clutched to his meager chest that cold and recently bloodied blade. He moved the hilt to his lips, as if ready to kiss it. "Gentlemen, my dear young friends, behold the sword of my murdered son..."

Cripure fled, returning to his chair.

The din died down—a solemn moment! Nabucet approached the hearth like a poet at a salon. He pulled a roll of paper from his pocket:

"Monsignor, General, Monsieur Prefect, Mesdames, Messieurs..." he bowed to Madame Faurel, "Madame..."

And with his lovely viola voice, he began his speech.

Cripure lowered his head, hiding his dark, angry look. What a comedy! And what comedians! It never crossed their minds to rip off their disguises, to stop dispensing the fables they had taken such pains to learn. *A red ribbon, for God's sake! What they needed wasn't ribbons or medals, but...* and he shook his head, a movement which fortunately no one saw, since the gesture would have been taken for disapproval of what Nabucet was saying. No, no ribbons. What they really deserved were some heads, and others arms or legs. Eh? What would that Madame Faurel look like with the head of her groomsman pinned to her breast by his hair? And Nabucet, with an arm through the buttonhole of his tailcoat? And so on! For the women in love, the beautiful Isoldes, they'd make splendid necklaces of the terrified eyes of their Tristans—say you'll never leave me darling, you're mine alone and I know how to keep you!—As for Monsieur Babinot, oh! That one there, he deserved a whole corpse to himself. Perhaps a general's? Not so easy to find these days. Perhaps a major then. The gift bestowed in a moving ceremony with great pomp on the parade ground, with the troops assembled for review. The corpse would be brought in on a cannon cart, a whole corpse, preferably one that had been gassed or strangled—since they were strangling themselves too!—in short, a corpse that looked exactly like what it was. In his clear, bugle voice, the general would make a solemn presentation to Babinot, who would hoist the decomposing thing onto his shoulders—one, two, three!— while the trumpets blew. That's what would be a glorious undertaking! That's what you could call decorating people! It wouldn't deceive anyone. Later, when you saw Babinot appear in the street with his decoration on his shoulders, you would know right away whom he had dealings with, and that this Monsieur had attained the highest rank in the hierarchy of honorees, that he was the supreme-superior-ace-knight-commander of Death. And those who'd only gotten a little torn ear, a small frozen foot, a tooth, to wear as brooches or hatpins, they'd have nothing to do but bow low. Small fry. And the hearts? The hearts would be—exclusively—for generals, to make pompoms for their caps, or rosettes for the lanyards on their swords, or when they were retired and suitably spoiled—trinkets.

A thunder of applause greeted Nabucet's speech. Madame Faurel rose, smiling.

"Bravo! Bravo!" cried everyone around the room. And Babinot

nasally dominated the tumult: "Bravo, bravo, I applaud!" And standing up, he turned his head this way and that to encourage reinforcements for his clapping, and when the applause finally died down and he had to sit again, he confided to his neighbor Madame Poche:

"That's what I call enlightenment! Good God, that Nabucet is a beautiful specimen. What style! What charm..."

"Hush!"

Nabucet turned to the general: "The rest is up to you." And bowing he handed over the precious box containing the precious object.

"So be it!" said the general, smiling with good cheer. "That's a pleasant duty to fulfill." And bending down to whisper in the bishop's ear, but in a stage whisper so everyone could hear him, "What does Monsignor think?"

"I certainly wouldn't hesitate," the bishop joked back, "with such a lovely penitent, General!"

The general got up.

"Dear Madame, I'll spare you more speeches. The art of rhetoric belongs to Monsignor and Monsieur Nabucet, who is far too modest," he said, as Nabucet bowed deeply. "My dear professor, you've left me with nothing to add to your gracious praises of Madame Faurel. So that only leaves..."

Speaking the traditional formula, he pinned the red ribbon to Madame Faurel's bodice.

"And now we find ourselves in an embarrassing situation Madame."

"How so, my dear General?"

"I'm afraid I must remind you that the ceremonial kiss is required. It is true that in this case, the duty is all on one side—yours, Madame. Remember only that war is as war does and allow me..."

"Oh, General! From one soldier to another, you know," cried Madame Faurel, throwing herself into the officer's arms.

The room went wild.

Once again, Babinot stood up and bashed his hands together. "Mag-ni-fi-cent! How magnificent!"

They heard two kisses smack on Madame Faurel's cheeks, then, rising over the tumult and making everyone quiet, the general's voice, that beautiful voice everyone admired on the fourteenth of July when he commanded "Swords out!" at the review on the parade ground, engaging and filling the whole room:

"You heard her! Spoken like a true Frenchwoman!"

The applause increased in series of tumults. The general's elegance was acclaimed. He'd known how to turn the compliment like a madrigal. Madrigal and general—two rhymes in a poem by Babinot.

"And with his grace? Did you see him with his grace?"

"Oh those two. They're always teasing each other."

"Father general and the cheery old bish'."

"We're not complaining! We're not complaining! If the bishop and the general are joking with each other, that means the sacred union is alive and well and France is strong."

A brouhaha. Joy and ease. They were all standing, crowding around the heroine, pressing in—trying to see who would be the first to congratulate her. She was laughing, shaking hands, embracing Madame Poche, her dear old friend, who went so far as to shed a tear. Babinot battled with voice and bandage. Cripure, at the back of the room, lowered his head and waited.

Everything flooded his ears and fluttered in front of his eyes. It was as if he could only see the world through a periscope. And it seemed like a reflection in the lens when he saw Faurel take Nabucet's arm, and it was as if through the depths of the water he heard: "You were perfect, old friend…"

The groups were linking and unlinking in fairy-like quadrilles. It was the general now who took grasped Nabucet's arm and said, "I've just put the last touches, my friend, on a little one-act which will go down very well with your Society for Dramatic Arts. It's an interlude. It takes place in Spain, neutral territory. War! War! It's beating down on our ears."

Madame Marchandeau had vanished, but not her husband, and Cripure realized all of a sudden that they were sitting next to each other.

"Hey!" he said. But it wasn't the moment to talk to him about the bikes ... and what's more ...

"How is your son?"

Beneath the white shirtfront, Monsieur Marchandeau's chest filled. "Well, I hope." At the same time, he passed a finger under the opening of his collar. "It's suffocating in here, don't you think?"

In short, the party had reached its peak.

The guests were coming and going, passing by the buffet to have a glass of champagne or a cup of hot chocolate, and going back to gossip by the fireside. Monsignor had hightailed it out of there, and the prefect too. The general would follow shortly.

Cripure let himself slump into the chair. He succumbed to his fascination with these unreal images. Where was truth? Why was this life rather than death? Indifference. He could hear snatches of talking, someone replying to Madame Poche, as if he had taken a vital interest in what she was saying, or as if it were of primordial importance to give the flabby old bitch that impression. Her ruined bust topped her wrecked thighs like a sac beneath the lace; little black eyes with bug-eaten lashes; her nose bone a spur like a chicken's wishbone; horse teeth, yellow on the bottom and green on top.

"I just came back from Bourges where I saw my cousin Édouard. Right now he's taken on some very interesting work to try and prevent the Boches from using their gas masks. He's found a way. The principle protective element in their masks is carbon. So Édouard searched for a way to make the carbon less porous, and to make it lose its ability to neutralize the body when it inhales the gas, which was making our gases lose their power to asphyxiate. What a beautiful discovery, don't you think? And won't it be neat to make all those Boches kaput! Right now they're in the process of applying Édouard's research to make our soldiers new masks. He replaced the cloth plug with a solid one, I don't know what kind, which presses or hangs away from the mouth at will. He also found a way—a famous one!—to neutralize the Boche gas before it reaches our trenches. To turn a wave of gas into nothing, he would have needed a thousand shells and special grenades with the neutralizing agent. The higher-ups replied to my cousin that the cost was excessive. Then, because I told him that my pee is cloudy and that I often see a bluish tint on the surface, he explained that it's part of a phenomenon of 'interference,' I think, but I'm not sure if that's the right word, and he gave me long and interesting explanations of this phenomenon which turns out to be the underlying principle for color photography..."

A LITTLE group of the faithful had gathered in Babinot's wake as he returned from the buffet, where he'd drunk a cup of hot milk. Like someone in an ecstasy of delight, Babinot advanced, his head high, inspired, the bandage shining like a banner, and with his arms he made the movements of a village fiddler leading a marriage procession. A flute would have suited him better—besides, they said he played one.

"Let's never forget this," he said, standing still so the little troupe could gather around him, "the secret to the gaiety of our heroic soldiers is that they stick to-ge-ther, it's that our brave boys don't have time for solitary contemplations. Excellent for moral hygiene, it seems! Well then, let's follow their example. Let's know how to come together, like today, and let's give our meetings a certain flexible discipline, very flexible..." And Babinot twice mimed a high jumper who catches himself on tiptoe. "The first rule," he said, lifting a finger: "let's not talk too much about the war. Without falsely ignoring the subject, let's talk a little, like we would in peacetime, of our affairs, about our daily lives, of simple pleasures, of the small joys life gives to everyone no matter what their circumstances. It's what I call the human-interest page, you see. A little human interest," he said, making a gesture with his hand as if he were seasoning a dish, "yes, a little imagination and everything will go well. The way to show confidence and inspire it is not to seem mesmerized by endless visions of war. Oh I know it! I'm aware of the difficulty! The fateful moment will come when we'll have to talk about it. But more than anything, don't change your attitude! Don't change your voice! Let's take it upon ourselves to stay very calm and unruffled," he went on, with gestures like a conductor. "Let's always say what we think. Never lies! But say it softly, with calm and almost playfulness."

He caught sight of Moka, who was waiting with his arms crossed over his stomach. "What does my young colleague want?"

"You wanted me to remind you to tell us a story, Monsieur Babinot," said Moka. And he rubbed his hands together.

"Which story, if you please?"

"I don't know, do I?" said Moka, rolling his eyes. "A funny story, no doubt?"

"Yes, yes, yes! Young man...funny stories! Ah, ah! We haven't missed out, thank God...later on," he said, with a dismissive wave, "I don't want to tire anyone out..."

The faithful shouted their encouragement.

"Should I really tell one now?" Babinot asked

"Yes, of course!" (When was it not the moment to tell a story?)

"So be it! Since you demand one..."

A general "Ah!" greeted his reply.

Babinot chose a chair close to Cripure and Madame Poche. Spreading the tails of his coat with his hands, he sat and said, "My young colleague reminded me of a promise...so be it!"

"Hush," murmured people around the room, "Monsieur Babinot's going to tell us a story." They approached with curious faces.

"What's going on?"

"Shhh, a story..."

Leaning back in his chair, Babinot clasped his big hairy hands over his belly, crossed his legs so that everyone could see his thick, blue wool socks, and smiled, but with only one side of his face. The bandage had slipped a little.

"Ladies and gentlemen, I'm going to tell you a story that is, in fact, funny."

A pause.

"It happened over there," he began, "on the other side of the Rhine, where the Boches live."

Moka snapped his fingers. "No way!"

"Yes, yes, with those ones. I didn't misspeak. My son was visiting Dusseldorf…you know it, I think?" he said, turning to Cripure.

Cripure had made a fabulous tour of Germany once upon a time—was it before or after he split from Toinette?—and come back salivating with admiration for the organizational genius, etc., of the Germans. "A wonderful town, don't you know?" he replied.

Babinot's goatee trembled.

"Nah!" he cried, jumping out of his chair. "Nah! My learned colleague, I take no part in your enthusiasm for that species over there. God forbid!" He proudly lifted his chin.

"But," Cripure babbled, "I didn't mean—"

"Nah! I'm telling you nah! We've got cities here that are a thousand, a hundred thousand times better than their stupid Dusseldorf!"

"As you say," said Cripure. "Yes, it's true, we do have cities that are a hundred thousand times better—"

Babinot was reassured. "Perfect, that's just perfect. A man like you, my dear colleague, making such a mistake as that!"

The faithful who had feared an outburst relaxed again.

"But, the story, Monsieur Babinot?" Moka asked.

"I'm getting there! Patience!"

Babinot resumed his comfortable position. "My son was staying in Dusseldorf. He was living with a family—you'll laugh—a typical German family, you know, the family of the honorable Herr Professor Schröder, ah, ah! An impressive family of Fritzes and Gretchens," he said, taking a little white metal box from his waistcoat pocket and fishing out a black licorice lozenge. He stuck it in his mouth and continued, "I was taking my son there, and by a singular coincidence, the day we arrived among those people was the Sedantag[12] holiday."

"Which is?" asked Madame Poche.

"Day of Sedan, Madame." Babinot whistled, winking his one good eye. "It's a big holiday for those fools over there! They celebrate our defeat in 1870. Their flags, their music, their fifes…"

"Ayayay!" said Moka.

"Since you're familiar with Germany," said Babinot, turning to

Cripure, "tell me, my dear colleague, have you ever been there on a day like that?"

"Goodness, no."

"Well then, good for you! Good for you!" Babinot repeated, tapping him twice on the knee. "It's a rough, rough ordeal for a good Frenchman. Those animals over there are filth personified. You'll see, I said to my son, they'll find some way to trouble us. During the meal, they'll talk about it. My son, being generous, imagined they wouldn't. He was wrong, gentlemen, he was wronger than wrong."

Babinot was quiet, and in the silence Cripure said, "Germans are clumsy pansies."

"Hear what he said!" cried Babinot, carried away with enthusiasm. "Clumsy pansies! That's great! That reminds me of another, even funnier story I'll tell you someday, remind me Monsieur Moka. Clumsy pansies! That's them to a T. A great way to put it. And the proof is that despite all our efforts to avoid the topic of that wretched Sedantag during the meal, well, he brought it up! Fat Professor Schröder told us matter-of-factly, 'In France you don't know how to celebrate your victories!' The clumsy pansy! But those Cossacks over there are neither refined, nor thoughtful, nor enlightened, eh! eh! I was embarrassed for him, ashamed. But listen. Can you guess what I said to him? '*Wir hatten zuviel!*' 'We have too many!' Ah, ah, ah! Too many? *Zuviel!* What do you say to that?"

"That," said Madame Poche, "that was neat!"

"Bull's-eye! What a hit!" said Moka. "Say, Monsieur Babinot, he must have had quite the look on his face?"

"That's your mistake: he took it in stride. Those fellows? Squashed as bedbugs, you know. It's from all the beatings."

"That authoritarian system, eh?" someone said.

"That's just it," Babinot replied. "And I've seen them up close, you know."

Glâtre observed that there was enough there to have caused a duel, and Babinot's eyes glowed. "It would have been the happiest day of my life."

No one thought to smile at this first-communion phrasing, not even Cripure. But had Cripure heard him? His thoughts seemed to be elsewhere as Babinot already began another: "Listen, another time..."

Cripure stopped listening.

Sitting behind Babinot, he studied that little bird-like head, round as a ball, covered in stray hairs which had once been red, which let the white skin of his scalp show through around the bandage like a peeled fruit. After two or three moments, his gaze seemed so indiscreet and dishonest, he had the impulse to get up and leave. It was like surprising someone in his sleep, like listening at a keyhole. It wasn't right to look at people's scalps that way. But this scalp held an irresistible fascination for Cripure, like a piece of evidence.

How much truer it was than a face! It seemed to him that all the reason left in Babinot, all the pure tenderness, had deserted the face— which for a long while now had been incapable of expressing anything but an inhuman passion for patriotism and war—and had taken refuge in that innocent scalp, and especially lower down, in the folds of his neck, which were very red while Babinot was delivering his speech, and which, at any other moment, would have inspired only Cripure's disgust and perhaps his amusement. But how far he was from laughing! Nothing Babinot said, nothing he was, lent itself to laughing anymore, since looking into his face had become nothing more than looking at a cardboard mask, but in his true, tender flesh that was starting to sag, to come unstuck and to hang from his jaws, to swell like the flesh of a corpse... Soon enough, anyway... but why soon? He could go on like this for a long while yet—maybe years, eternally, perhaps. *Yes, it was well said, eternally. How awful!* The strangest part was that Babinot believed he was his mask, that he would rather ignore the person, hidden like a riddle in the folds of his neck. Only the fake Babinot wanted to be seen. There was the Babinot who thundered against the Boches, the everyday heroic imbecile Babinot, and another, the real one, who cried silent tears for the closeness of his son to death and for his own fate. Perhaps there had to be the thundering Babinot before the other one could cry all his tears. *Oh God! God! And that whitewashed face with its dead black eyes that watches me with reproach!* In a corner, discreetly set apart by chance or choice—undoubtedly choice—sat Madame Babinot, immobile as a stele, all in black, already cold as if wrapped in her shroud. Before her time! Just barely, by a few shiverings of that paper face, could they tell it was still living. If there had ever been a mask there, it had fallen long ago. She no longer feared to show herself as she felt, in all honesty, like all those who die while still alive. When they killed her son, Babinot might change, but as for her—no. Awful. She was already skeletal. Awful! But what was there to say? He saw them asleep, both pressed against each other, searching for warmth with the knowledge, even in their deepest sleep, of that death—their son's! *No. Oh no! As the saying goes, we can't afford to pay so much for admission.*[13]

"It's a conspiracy," someone whispered in his ear.

Cripure jumped, stifling a cry. Moka was bent over his shoulder, smiling like an accomplice. "They did it on purpose."

"Did what on purpose?"

He put an index finger, straight as a drumstick, to his lips. "Come with me!" he said. "Shhh!"

Cripure got up carefully, trembling with fear—would he really be able to flee? But the story Babinot was telling must have been more interesting than the last one, since no one paid attention to him, and he followed Moka, who was slipping away on tiptoe, holding out his arms like an acrobat on his tightrope.

The door closed behind them without a sound.

"Not seen, not heard," said Moka. "Pfff! Come on."

"Where are you taking me?" Cripure asked, reaching for the hand Moka offered him. He let himself be pulled all the way down the hall. Moka ignored the question, but as he went he said softly, though there was no longer a reason to think they'd be overheard:

"They're encouraging Babinot to tell stories because, you understand—his son—"

"No!" Cripure stammered, catching his breath. Moka had to pull him forward.

"Yes! They've known since this morning. But he doesn't know yet."

"No!"

"But I'm telling you, yes. It's official. Only no one dares tell him. So they egg him on..."

They passed before the open door to the buffet. There, all by himself, his hat under his arm, the mayor was furtively, hastily, but seriously getting his fill of hot chocolate and brioches. He left the champagne for the others today. What he needed was something solid. And while he drank his hot chocolate, the mayor with his big sad-lion eyes, imagined those cold cuts that would have been so pleasant to nibble on with a little mustard, a hard-boiled egg, a little bit of lettuce. Alas! Cold cuts hadn't been included in the menu and Monsieur mayor would have to content himself with pastries. He took revenge with a second helping. All that his heavy paw could reach he engulfed, gobbled, his pinky in the air—sucking in his stomach—so as not to stain his handsome waistcoat. He was focused only on the refreshments, and if it weren't for his fancy ceremonial suit, he could have been taken for an errand boy some kindly client had let into the pantry.

"Hurry!" said Cripure, giving the mayor a rude glance.

Since not even the smallest pastry remained, he licked his lips, dried them with his handkerchief, brushed the crumbs off his pants, pulled on his gloves, and went out.

Moka and Cripure put a hand to their hats in the same moment.

"No time!" growled the mayor, and he went off with big strides.

Moka pushed Cripure into an alcove that smelled like a dusty cellar.

"What's this place you've dragged me into?

The green boxes, the plaster cast of the statue of the Republic—salute!—the dusty, ripped curtains, the disemboweled couch in the back, the silence!

"It's like a tomb!"

"Have a seat."

Once the door closed, Moka bent down and pulled a bottle of champagne and two cups from behind a hanging. He bowed deeply to Cripure, and, with a glass in each hand, he started dancing, placing the bottle on the ground. He crooned:

> "Drink again, drink to the dregs
> The wine that wakes the dead..."

He was dancing without the slightest sound—Cripure could barely see the furtive pattering of his steps. His long dark silhouette went back and forth across the pale window frame, the red crest flamed on his forehead like a will-o'-the-wisp, and the little bit of light left in the chamber tumbled into the glasses as they moved with the rhythm of the dance.

"Enough craziness," he said, stopping. "We're going to have a little glug glug. The important thing is that they don't hear the cork pop."

With a quick movement, he grabbed the bottle and uncorked it.

"My head is spinning," Cripure murmured.

"Atten-tion! The cups?"

Cripure hastily held out the glasses and Moka turned and filled them triumphantly. The cork had slipped into his hand without a sound—not a drop had been spilled. "Aren't I a well-prepared fellow?" he said, putting back the bottle. "I've got my little store, eh?"

"Good old Moka," said Cripure. He drank it in one gulp, then lowered his head and let the glass dangle from his hand.

Moka sat next to him on the couch.

How quiet it was! Even here, the silence was grimy.

"What an innocent," murmured Cripure. And Moka leaned closer, meeting his eyes.

"Would you come and see me someday?" he asked timidly. "Some Sunday?"

Cripure raised his eyes to the window. The rain was coming down, sideways and quick. "What do you do on Sundays?"

"I go to mass. Then, in the afternoon I have my stamps...with my stamps—but this is my idea—you won't tell anyone?"

"No."

"I stick them to my plates, you know. I...cover my plates with stamps. It's very pretty, with all the colors. You know what I mean?"

Oh Flaubert! thought Cripure. *Oh your tax collector, carving his table legs.*[14]

"Dear Moka, give me another drink."

They drank. Moka got up, walked around the room, worrying. His angular hand toying endlessly with the red forelock. He suddenly asked, "You haven't heard anything...about me?" Standing in front of his old teacher, he stuffed his hands in his pockets and fixed two suspicious eyes on Cripure. His lower lip slowly swallowed the upper one, reached almost to his nose..."You haven't heard anything?"

"Like what?"

"That I'm crazy?"

Cripure pretended to think about it. Finally he shook his head twice. "No."

"Ah?"

"No, nothing."

"Because," said Moka, sitting down (he bent as he spoke, elbows on his knees, his face tipped forward) "because I'm aware of myself...I think it must be apparent...You, you've never noticed anything?" he asked in what was almost a whisper.

"Nnn—no. Nothing at all."

"So that's all right! Something of that nature wouldn't have escaped your notice. That's all right," he continued happily. "But all the same, as a student of psychology, what do you think of this: from time to time I see a fly...it's very hard to explain. It usually goes by very quickly. A giant fly, not in the air, but crawling. It goes by like a flash, from up high on the left—vroom! Like this, and on a slant, this way," he said, motioning toward the ceiling with a quivering hand. "I noticed," he continued, "that it didn't change until I went to bed. In that case, the...fly passed under my nose, coming from the right. It runs like a spider from one side of the bed to the other. I barely have time to catch sight of it. Hang on! Hang on! You must be wondering why I care if the fly sometimes comes from the right and sometimes from the left. It's because I connect it to another phenomenon ... you see, a kind of threat weighs on me, almost all the time, and it's precisely the threat of a blow."

"An emotional shock? Are you expecting something bad?"

"No, not at all! A blow like from a fist. But," Moka continued, "that threat always comes from the left. It's from the left they watch me. That's why I have a tendency to run away to the right. Does that make sense?"

"Uh..."

"For example, I'll be at my desk, totally calm, in the middle of reading—head in the clouds—or maybe gluing my stamps, when I'll start to sense a kind of vertigo, to be forced, in spite of myself, to duck my head at the threat of a ... fear. I don't see, I don't know, what to attribute the phenomenon to, but I know I always duck toward the right."

"And what about the fly?"

"No, not in those cases. And another thing: in the street I start to have these ... these panics. I feel someone behind me. Someone is threatening me and the threat lodges here, look! in the scalp," said Moka, tapping his skull. "It makes my head feel sort of empty ... a ticklishness ... But I can't turn around, and I keep on going as if it's absolutely necessary ... The worst is when it happens in church ... so then..."

Moka got up, stuck his hands in his pockets, and walked around the room again.

The rain fell violently, battering the panes. Moka walked over to the window and lifted the curtain. Four o'clock. Noël rang the bell for all he was worth. Everywhere doors were slamming and students were running through the courtyard in the pouring rain. The gentlemen of the faculty put on their greatcoats and opened their umbrellas, bending their backs. Another day done! One less day, eh, thank goodness! But what were they doing here in this hole! They were drinking champagne stolen by Moka, the imp! That was also a beautiful thing.

The little old sword-kisser trotted across the courtyard with his prop under his arm. He almost dropped it all of a sudden, after moving too quickly to keep his good Sunday hat on his bald head in a gust of wind.

In the back of the alcove Cripure sat motionless, his head on his shoulder, his still-empty glass hanging from the end of his arm which was limply resting on the back of the couch. The bell stopped ringing. Not a sound. Moka let the curtain drop.

"I had a fiancée," he began, in a soft, trembling voice, "I had a fiancée and then what? She was only a typist, but so what if I wanted to marry her anyway? What harm could it do to them? Filthy bourgeois, you know, my mother and sister, real bigots. And then so righteous! Oh!"

He whistled between his teeth and cracked his knuckles. Cripure barely stirred.

"My father was dying of tuberculosis. He was always a bit shaky, and the war succeeded in decimating him. In short, he was fading. They very well could have sent him to a sanatorium, it wasn't the money that was missing, but fuck! They wouldn't admit he was tubercular. They said he was tired. You get the idea?"

"Perfectly."

"He was a good man, you know, my father, bighearted. In his day he must have also fallen in love. He knew what it was to ... But he was at the end of his rope, and, by God, I don't think he cared about getting better. All that," Moka went on, picking up the bottle and filling the glasses once again, "all that didn't prevent me from wanting to get married. He didn't say anything. He played like he knew nothing about it, which was a great delicacy on his part."

He interrupted himself to empty his glass. Cripure had already emptied his own.

"One evening," he continued—he balanced his glass on his hand as he walked—"one evening, as you can imagine, I stayed with my fiancée for a little longer than usual, and my mother and sister put me through a horrible scene. Yelling, tears, a real showcase, something for the ages . . . they were experts! 'A tutor doesn't marry a typist' and so on and so forth. All their dirty foolishness. I should tell you it was all happening on the first floor, in the dining room. When my father was in the room right above, and he was sleeping, you understand, the poor old man, he didn't sleep much. I of course tried to signal to my mother and sister that he could hear us, but it didn't help. Instead, it seemed to egg them on. And my mother yelled at the top of her lungs 'and while your father is on his deathbed!'"

He stopped, putting down his glass on the little pedestal that held up the statue of the Republic, and blew his nose. Cripure put his glass on the ground, and while Moka refolded his handkerchief and put it carefully back into his pocket, Cripure passed a hand across his forehead, rubbed his temples with his fingertips, readjusted his pince-nez.

"You understand," Moka went on, "how nasty they could be! Right away, I ran outside. I thought if I stayed, I would have killed them. I fled into the garden . . . a light was burning in my father's room. Had he heard? Yes or no? I didn't dare go upstairs. A word of it would have finished him off once and for all. And I'll say again that he was a good old man I really loved. Finally, I went up there. I've never told anyone this. He opened his eyes when he heard me coming. He was stretched out on the bed, very calm. He held out his hand . . . imagine the scene: we were both holding out our hands without saying a word. Downstairs, my mother and sister were putting away the dishes, the forks and spoons clinked as they fell back into the drawer, that I also remember. So for a moment my father squeezed my hand tighter, and you'll never guess what he said: 'My poor child, one quickly gets sick of one's wife!'"

In the little room, a silence came, like when the train stops suddenly in the countryside. Moka walked around the room for a long time, wiping his forehead.

The rain was easing up on the panes. The storm had passed.

"And then?"

"What do you mean, and then? Well, I went to the front. I was wounded. I came back. In the meantime my father had died and the girl...poof! She'd flown away...vanished...disappeared! My friend, they did that to me," he went on in a trembling voice, taking Cripure's hand.

But he immediately got back up. "I beg your pardon," he said with a childish smile. And once again, he refilled the glasses. "Do you believe in God or not?"

Cripure shrank into himself. He huddled on the couch and his big hands fidgeted with the goatskin. "Your...your question..."

A vague memory of the morning's scene with Étienne went through his mind. He lowered his head, to hide his eyes.

"When the answer is yes, it comes naturally," said Moka.

"Well then," said Cripure, his head still bowed, "well then it must be no."

"Must be?"

"Let's say it's no."

Moka took a few steps, still twirling his red forelock. "Glâtre also says no!" he murmured. And whirling around, "Listen: someone told me something about you, something astonishing. It seemed...someone told me that one day you were walking on the shore, with one of your friends...you were talking about poetry. And all of a sudden you cried out...that the most beautiful poem was the Ave Maria, and that...this is the most astonishing thing—that you started reciting the prayer as you walked out toward a little chapel built on the tip of a rock, which means you were walking into the sea, as if...and another time," Moka continued, gasping, "in front of someone who was telling you how he'd lost his faith, how he'd suffered, how he had to forget that suffering...you responded—wait," said Moka, putting his head in his hands, "I'm trying to remember the exact words... you replied that for you, the pain existed always, yes, it existed always, that's what you said. Is that true?"

"All that is too true," said Cripure, sighing.

"So?"

"So what?"

"So you were kidding me...you believe it, eh? So why don't you say so? I also know you don't eat meat on Fridays."

"That has nothing to do with it."

"How! How can that have nothing to do with it! It's a lovely piece of evidence, anyway. Go on, admit it . . . say: I believe in God?"

"The all powerful Father, creator of the earth and the heavens, and in Jesus Christ, his only son," Cripure railed. "No my dear Moka—alas! But that's enough philosophy! They tried to kill me."

"Huh?" said Moka, "What did you say?"

"They wanted to murder me."

Moka's lips started to tremble with a strange sound, as if they were chattering from cold. "But who did? Why?"

"You've uncovered a riddle there, a tough one! It would be too long, and too painful. I've thought sometimes that they were right without knowing it. That's enough about that."

And Cripure got up.

"Right? They were right?"

"I told you: that's enough!"

He grabbed Moka by his lapels, and said, in the style of Babinot, "I'm going to tell you a tragic story. It was one night in Paris, in eighteen . . ."

He remembered all of a sudden that it was in the year he had left Toinette and he quickly hid his eyes behind his hand. Then, in a labored voice, he went on with his tale. It was a spring evening and he was strolling down the boulevard Saint-Michel. It might have been nine. He was about to sit down on the terrace of a café when two shots rang out behind him. In the blink of an eye, the boulevard was deserted. A tiny little man, a skinny Chinese fellow, was running for his life down the middle of the road, chased by the police. From time to time, he'd turn and fire at them from the pocket of his jacket, batting the air and leaping like a furious cat. With his hand that wasn't firing, he was holding part of his pale gray jacket. His shoes, which were bright yellow, beat the air like mechanical birds. The police finally grabbed him and clubbed him almost in unison, laying him out at the foot of a tree, without a cry. Alas, he didn't have any cartridges left, but he wouldn't left go of his revolver. Two policemen were holding his shoulders, another one put his knee to the man's forehead, and a fourth was pulling his revolver out of his hand, repeating in a low voice, 'Give up your weapon, give it to me, let go...' But he kept on fighting them. So no doubt they started twisting his arm, since the poor man—the brave man—started squealing like a rat. And the weapon rolled on the ground. A policeman stuck it in his pocket. Since they were sure their victim was no longer dangerous, they stood him back up and started hitting him. Two policemen held him up by the shoulders since he was already unconscious and the blood was running down his face—the other two hit him with their fists and also kicked. An Inspector in plainclothes with a big round head and black hair repeated: 'Go on! Go on! He's dead meat!' In their hands the poor man became a bleeding wreck. His head bobbed right and left like a doll's. Maybe he was already dead."

Cripure took a breath and went on:

"They finally stopped hitting him and dragged him towards the station. His long black hair hanging over his forehead looked like it had been dipped in water. His pants had slipped off, showing his thin, ropey legs. And then a slender little man broke off from the crowd and skipped over to the sinister cortege. He was one of those nice little petty bourgeois from around here, some kind of bank employee or paper pusher somewhere. He was wearing a cheap black suit, with celluloid cuffs, a false pearl tie pin. But he had a straw hat and a cane, and he was already brandishing it..."

"I finally saw him catch right up to the little cortege, and the cane that went straight up in the air came down, yes, one strike, on the bleeding face of the dying man. There you have it," Cripure finished. There was a long silence.

Moka was trembling like a leaf. He babbled something indistinct, and Cripure thought he heard Moka say something about sadism.

"Sadism!" he cried out, angry. "I don't much like that way of rehabilitating the bourgeois with psychology, Monsieur Moka." Cripure let go of his lapels, and shrugged.

"What's more," he continued, "at that time, Nabucet certainly wasn't in Paris."

"What are you saying?"

"I'm saying," Cripure calmly went on, "I'm saying that Nabucet surely wasn't in Paris then. I know enough about his life to understand that the year in question, he must have been a boarding school supervisor somewhere in the provinces, studying for his certification. If he wasn't doing his military service. Besides, there wasn't the slightest resemblance between that lovely man and the darting little character with the straw hat. Why then, tell me, why, each time I think of that scene, do I imagine it was Nabucet I saw, brandishing that sinister cane? Eh? Why do you think?" And without waiting for Moka's reply: "The heart has its reasons," drawled Cripure, and with Moka still trembling, he continued, "If it's madness, it's not without reasons. Through a language without words and therefore without lies, Nabucet must have told me about that little cane of horror. At least it's clear I must have dreamed it. Let me finish, Moka my friend! So that for once I can speak, and tell you all. No, it's not words that will give you the key to Nabucet. The cipher that will let you crack the code has elements other than those in the dictionary! A language exists that speaks in skin and blood, through which the most secret of secrets are passed from one to another with fail-safe surety, revealing, in some ordinary gentleman, the anguished beating of a heart. And this way, all men can become brothers to me, I can recognize myself in all of them and love them. There are days when I'm so close to it, when the sharp feeling of common unhappiness among brothers disarms my hate. But people like Nabucet always knew how to bring it back even stronger!"

He went on like that for a while.

Of course, beyond this psychology, born from it, there had been great hours of idealism mixed with unconditional love, but his feeling was above all that man was abandoned in an agonized world. Since, in the end, he always found the same anguished beating of the heart in each person's chest, the same horror of death, not only for himself, but for his love—to be separated!—what else was there to do but hold out your arms, if not to a God that he no longer believed in (or thought he no longer believed in) than to a brother who was just as unhappy as you were? He'd tried a few times, discovering to his amazement that his own unhappiness diminished at the knowledge that he wasn't suffering alone, that he could share it with others. But they weren't the least bit interested! And yet more mysterious: though they could also sense it—to a greater or lesser degree—it didn't matter to them, they continued to act as though everything was normal, as if the secret were foreign to them. For the same reason Cripure thought of the mystery of this language and its infallible transmission, his instinctive conviction was that no one—from the dumbest idiot to the greatest genius—was entirely deaf to it. That painful beating of the heart, he was sure that everyone in the world felt its presence, guessed its meaning. But then, how could the cradle of that suffering produce so much hate, and not only hate but idiocy, how could it create not only the war, but also the platitudes of these gentlemen, especially Babinot, even though Babinot had a certain grandeur to his madness like the Clopper? Since they didn't know how to question these Punchinello's secrets they all wore around their necks like medals, how, how could they stand it, not to live, but to live like that? With that leaden anchor in the bottoms of their hearts, how could they be so dry and hard, sending their sons to the charnel house, their daughters to the brothel, renouncing their fathers, cursing at their wives who, at the same time, were manipulating them—an unending battle—chipping away at the wages of the maid who went out too much, was too "pretentious," all the while thinking about the progress of the fiscal year and the next funny film they'd go see at the Palace, if they could get free tickets? And then many other things, since this was only the surface level, and underneath was that suffering which Cripure wanted everyone to have in common, they had ideas, they wanted things. There was no hope. To love them? Ah, God no! To love them, that would mean Nabucet and the little Chinese man could join in the bottom of his heart in the same forgiveness. No, no, and no! Since he had to admit it: these idealist daydreams always lent themselves fatefully to forgiveness. Nabucet was forgiven, and his sinister little cane was redrawn as the instrument of divine anger or justice, an ominous sign of shared unhappiness, and therefore exempt from disdain and revenge.

"But once again, no! I don't want to forgive!"

And he walked heavily towards the door. Moka watched him leave without a word. Just before closing the door behind him, Cripure had a moment of hesitation and turned back.

"Excuse me," he said, vanishing from sight.

Having closed the door behind him, with care and an escapee's smile, he felt an attack of vertigo, like a blow, and lifting his hand to his forehead he leaned against the doorframe, with the look of a hunted man.

He stayed like that for a long time, then he let fall his arm and stared in front of him, fascinated, like someone who perceives a monster. Nothing there but the spacious opening of a stairwell, a wall, green and rotting, a skylight the rain had battered. Familiar surroundings. Familiar smells, too—of furniture polish and mold, a known silence, nothing out of the ordinary.

Suddenly the silence was troubled. Doors slammed, voices came to him, still far away. There was a burst—a loud racket of feet on wood like a dull drum roll. It was the others leaving, the party had ended, running along the muffled corridors like big rats, circling Babinot, who he heard whining, "Nah, nah, I told him, let's not unbuckle our armor!"

Cripure tore himself from the door, quickly going down the iron-rung staircase, his hand dragging along the railing. On his way! But it was only as a memory of himself, as if he were a character he'd once known and loved to whom he had given a task, a mission he hadn't dreamed of accomplishing except through a feeling of loyalty and honor, since love was dead.

"The spell is broken," he murmured. And, not really knowing why, "Crybaby!" he scolded himself, "crybaby!"

He passed by the concierge's lodge without seeing anything, passed through the door and the grate, finally found himself outside, astray, as if the view of the town had ceased to be recognizable. Where had he gotten to? What new discovery had he made in his sorrow? After pausing a long moment, he shook from head to toe, his jaw clenched, his eyelids trembling, and, moving his cane like a officer's sword, "advance!" he murmured, wrenching himself off the stone of the sidewalk. He lurched forward in one movement.

Never had his leaden feet been so agile, his face more open, his chin more thrust out, his eyes heavier, his lip more tremulous—never had his cane battered so furiously the air around his calves.

IF MOKA'S hobby was decorating plates with stamps, Glâtre's less innocent one was to cut out images from fashion catalogs that he picked up or sent for, and from magazines like *La Vie parisienne*, which the waiter in Café Machin saved for him from time to time. He glued the images into magnificently bound albums, bought on sight and for next to nothing at the auction house. They told him they came from a poor curate who had died not long before. There were at least twelve of them. But out of the ten he bought, barely four of them had been filled, since the curate had died a bit too soon. It must be said, in the curate's defense, that if he'd been struck by the same scrapbook disease Glâtre had, the subjects he'd chosen from newspapers and magazines had nothing in common with the ones Glâtre found so seductive. The lovely gold letters which adorned the luxurious bindings declared nothing more than *Picturesque Family Scenes*, *Military Themes*, and *Comics*—containing all the caricatures which the holy man had been able to get his hands on, in the course of however many solitary years which, apart from this little hobby, were entirely given over to worshipping God. Glâtre had patiently peeled off the pious priest's pictures to glue in his own, delighted with the irony that the gold titles were labeled as such, delighted also that he'd created a little profanation, since he didn't hesitate to spend whole hours looking for ways to glue his images into the most extravagantly erotic scenes possible. This was how he made up for the bitterness of never being able to set foot in the biggest Paris brothels (too expensive), which, along with his hope to smoke opium at least once, and his wish to assist at the closed trial for a sex crime (if possible: the rape of a young girl) constituted more or less the essential things he wanted in life.

Pausing in the middle of the staircase, his hat over his ear, busy rolling a cigarette, he was dreaming of the long chunk of scrapbooking he had to look forward to at home, when, hearing Moka, he turned:

"Hey! We looked for you everywhere. Where were you hiding out?"

"Oh, my friend, I beg you, leave me alone. Please!"

"Hey, hey, hey… here's something new. Monsieur is in a bad mood? What happened to you, princeling?"

"Leave me alone…"

"But," Glâtre cried, "you're not even being polite. Oh! Go on, friend, run along, go, trot! I'll tell you my impressions some other time. I hope it won't be too late."

Moka stopped.

"What impressions?"

"Go on, go on, don't be long."

"What were you going to say?"

"Go… it can wait until tomorrow. You'll be in a better mood then, I hope. Don't worry about it…"

"But come on, what's it about?"

"Your museum, my friend," Glâtre replied, joining him at the foot of the stairs. "This will interest you a little, I think?"

"My museum?"

"Come on. Where's your head? Yes. Your museum…"

"But, Glâtre, it's not my museum. It was your idea, you know. We should say your museum. Anyway, it's all the same!" Moka shrugged his shoulders, raised his eyebrows, cracked his knuckles. "What do you have to say to me about the museum? Hurry up, hurry up. This is no day to…"

"Some kind of fly bite you too?"

"Fly?"

"Ok, what is it, what's gotten into you? If you're in a rush, once again, run along. This can wait."

"No, tell me."

"Oh, careful now! I'll tell you if I want to. No, but my dear Moka, have a care for your manners with those who are thinking about what's best for you, who look after your soul…You're becoming disrespectful. Enough, enough, I forgive you. Listen, I've thought a lot about this: what's the point of this museum?"

"Oh, oh, oh!" scolded Moka. "Are you keeping me hanging here to ask questions like that? You're playing with me, my friend! Come on, we've talked for more than eight hours about the museum. The point is clear, it seems to me."

"Say it anyway."

"No."

"Ah! Well then, goodbye."

"But come now, Glâtre…"

"No, no, no, no." Glâtre advanced resolutely toward the door. Moka joined him.

"Come now, my friend, the point is to serve the country…do I really need to say it?"

"Ah!" said Glâtre. "In the end, you make up your mind. But that's exactly the question, my friend, that's just what the problem is." He stared Moka straight in the eye: "You can't see farther than the end of your nose. If I wasn't here to enlighten you, I don't know what would happen to you, my poor boy…you want to serve your country, but in what way? A war museum! Which is to say you want to encourage naive young people to enlist, meaning, Moka, to encourage them to die. Hush! Let's be quiet!" said Glâtre—and his two hands joined together like a preacher's—"Let us not speak of it, Moka. For the peace of your soul, I forbid you to work on this museum. I'll take care of it myself. It's a task fit for a miscreant like myself, nonbeliever and patriot. But you! I don't want you to have a single one of those young men's deaths on your conscience. You couldn't handle it, you'd go crazy…"

"Crazy?"

"Yes. Crazy. And so, Moka, God, what does he do with crazies in the afterlife? No, no, dear friend, for you, God comes before country. Don't forget that, you pious idiot!"

"God?"

"Yes, God. Don't you get it?"

"As if there was a God!" Moka cried. "Ah! ah ah ... no, dear friend, no, go peddle that to other people. Not to me!"

Glâtre's jaw dropped so far that his cigarette fell. He just barely caught it against his stomach, in a rain of sparks. "That's new ... very new ... what happened?"

"Leave me alone for God's sake!" Moka cried in a shrill voice. "Leave me alone in the name of God, or you'd better watch out!" He went into Noël's lodge, where, without a word to anyone, not even to poor George, stretched out in his chair, he untied his dog. He ran out, grumbling.

"What's with him?" Noël asked. "Is he sick or what?"

Glâtre relit his cigarette. "Dunno ... blind belief."

"Or maybe ... champagne?"

"Ah! Perhaps."

He might have had a few too many. And since he was never all that sensible ...

"No big deal," said Glâtre, throwing away his match. "Tomorrow's another day."

And he calmly went down the steps.

Ah! If he had to go through all that every time Moka lost his faith it would go on forever. One day yes, the next, no. He didn't know what Moka wanted. It would end badly—he'd really turn loony.

Five o'clock: the streets were coming to life a little. Soldiers were wandering around, Sammies, Italians, artillerymen with heavy gaiters, little Vietnamese with flat feet, shrill as parakeets, herculean Senegalese, shivering and wide-eyed, walking in pairs, linked together by their pinky fingers, Arabs employed at the powder factory, yellow as lemons, tubercular, half-crazed with nostalgia and proud to the point of throwing in your face the box of cigarettes you offered out of patriotism.

Glâtre was watching the women. On the whole he wasn't unhappy with his afternoon. Everything had been pleasant, and he'd eaten and drunk so much that there was no point in going to the pension for dinner. He always did that to save money. If he got hungry in the evening, he'd make himself a nice hot chocolate on his burner and that would be that.

That Moka! He was annoyed all the same. What a pity! They could have had a good laugh. Maybe it would be better tomorrow. Maybe Moka would still turn up his snout at him, like he had after that brothel business. He'd tried one day to invite him "au voyage" as a surprise—where there were so many lovely girls now, at least three times as many since the war began. The attempt had failed.

In front of him, a young woman who seemed poor was wandering about. She wore a long gray dress that fell all the way to her heels and a fitted, multicolored jacket. There were as many colors as there were pieces. Her little black straw hat was decorated with a green ribbon. She held a basket in her hand, and when she thought no one was looking, she gathered whatever she could find: little bits of wood, shoelace ends, paper. From time to time, she exchanged a few words with a passerby before retreating, loitering in front of store windows: candy stores, mainly, and dress shops. *There's Henriette making her rounds*, thought Glâtre. He wondered if he would approach her.

Why not? It wouldn't be the first time. She was dumb, and dirty, but no uglier than the next girl. He should really bring her home with him sometime. It would be even funnier because the poor little idiot, he knew, had a crush on Moka.

He went over to her: "Good evening, Mademoiselle Henriette."

"Oh! Good evening, sir," said the young woman, holding out her little round hand. He held it in his for a while.

"You're taking a walk?" she said.

"Yes. And yourself?"

"I'm looking in the stores. It's pretty isn't it? Oh! They're full of beautiful things. But all that's for the rich folks."

"You're not poor."

"Oh! But I am ... Mama is rich, but she's stingy. She doesn't do anything with it," said Henriette. "She's afraid of dying."

"Is she sick?"

"No."

He took her arm. "Would you like to walk a little with me?"

"Sure."

"You're sweet."

"Me? No. I have a bad temper, you know."

"Is it your mother who says that?"

"Papa too."

"They don't know what they're saying."

"They do. But they're sad."

"Why, you're wearing face powder," cried Glâtre.

"Oh! It's nothing." She quickly rubbed her cheeks.

"Coquette!"

"No, no, no, it's nothing."

"Do you want to sing?"

"A little love song?"

"Yes."

"Or a hymn?"

"I like love songs better."

"No. Better be the hymn."

In a frail little voice, a child's voice, she started to warble a hymn:

> "In heaven, heaven, heaven
> I'll go see her one day
> I'll see my mother Mary…"

"You started too high."

"Yes. I don't know how to sing."

"What did you eat today? Rice?"

"Oh, no! We don't eat rice in our house. Papa likes it too much."

"And what did you find in the streets?"

"Shoelace ends."

"No wood?"

"A little."

Glâtre bent down to Henriette's ear, so close that the end of his nose ruffled the young woman's pretty black hair. He whispered, "Someone told me you were getting married?"

"Oh!" she cried, beaming, "someone serious said that to you?"

"A priest."

"His confessor?"

"No."

"Do you know his confessor?"

"No."

"And my fiancé?"

"A little."

"He's very pious," she said. "He kisses the priest's ring, but he's shy. He holds back. And me, I don't know how to say it. That's too bad, isn't it? But if we got married, though... I know how to do everything, it's true, except for cooking. It seems like he doesn't know how to manage a budget? We'll go well together."

"Have you known him for a long time?"

"More than a year. Since the day he picked up my umbrella at church."

"What did he say?"

"Nothing."

"That's it?"

"He's shy. But it depends on the day. Sometimes he jumps. Like this!" and she did a little caper on the sidewalk. "And other times," she continued, "he talks! He talks! He gives me a headache."

"But then... where do you see him?"

"At his place," she said.

"His place?"

"I have a key. I go whenever I want. Usually in the evenings. Papa and Mama go out when it gets dark. That way, they don't need to burn the lamp. So I go out too."

"And where do they go?"

"For a walk. Picking up what they find."

"Wood?"

"All kinds of things."

"And your... fiancé, he's never kissed you or anything?"

"Oh no!"

His arm circled her waist. "Do you like it when people kiss you?"

"Oh, yes."

"Do you want to come over to my place?"

"Is it far?"

"It's very close by."

"I'd like to."

"He won't be jealous?"

"Why would he be? I don't love you."

"Ah? And you love him?"

"Oh, yes."

"And if he were to love someone else?"

"Doesn't matter to me."

"Hey! Wow! You must be some kind of angel."

"Why are you so mean?" she said.

He changed tactics. "And do your parents know about him?"

"They really want to marry me off. It would give me a living. They have no more to spend on me."

"But didn't you tell me they were rich?"

"Mama has fifteen houses."

"Mama? Not Papa?"

"Mama's the one in charge."

"And what would you do if you were rich?"

"Me? I'll never be rich, oh no!"

"And if you don't get married?"

"I'll go straight to a convent."

"Would you do the dishes?"

"I'm used to it."

He suddenly didn't want to walk with her anymore, and he removed his arm. "See you around."

"You're leaving?"

"Yes. I forgot an errand. We'll go to my place some other time."

"Yes."

"What will you do now?"

"I don't know. Go to church."

He abandoned her at the corner.

Henriette did in fact start out for the church. As she approached, she caught sight of Moka. He was pulling like crazy on the poor dog's leash.

The dog hobbled after him. *I know I'm going to do something stupid . . . I feel it growing!* Moka thought. He could very well promise to punish himself if he did something dumb, to deprive himself of lunch tomorrow, for example, but he knew he wouldn't keep his promise. He shivered, and gave the poor dog's leash a big tug. *Lord forgive me!*

It was true that once he had done something silly in church. Why? He wasn't angry, that day, he wasn't desperate, nothing out of the ordinary had come up, no one had made a mean comment. It was a day he hadn't thought about misbehaving. But he never thought about it! He did it without thinking.

He went into the church, knelt down, and hiding his face in his hands, he murmured, "God, if you exist, make my hat fly all the way up to the vault and make the chairs trot like little rabbits."

He looked for something more difficult.

God still didn't appear, so he went on: "God, if you exist, make the whole church collapse on me."

Dying was ok with him, if he died with proof that God was real.

Alas! Nothing came of it. Not a single grain of dust fell from the height of the vault.

Moka got up and walked around the church.

"If I started to sing some little song? To shout!"

He wanted to flee. He started toward the door. A little light filtered through the crack underneath and he looked at it with a racing heart. Suddenly he turned: "Arooo! Arooo! Arooo!" he cried at the top of his lungs, and the vaulted ceiling echoed and amplified his cries. Moka, standing still, listened and smiled. Nothing. Nothing came of that attempt either.

He shivered all of a sudden. A hand took hold of his.

"Henriette!"

"That's not very nice, what you just did," she said, leading him outside.

WITH A sure, almost silent movement, the prefectural limousine stopped at the gates of the Veterans' Hospital. Answering the horn, a door opened, and an office boy ran out. Recognizing the car, he hurried. Léo followed him out of the corner of his eye, an imperceptible smile hovering around his mouth—it was nice to see a viscount come running when he called.

The viscount, who had gotten himself the safest post he could, was elegant, even in uniform.

"Hello, Léo."

"Hello, Viscount."

Léo pretended not to see the viscount hold out a hand.

"Go tell the chief I'm waiting for him."

"Fine."

The viscount turned on his heel. Léo let him get as far as the door. When the viscount was about to vanish, he called him back:

"Viscount!"

The viscount hesitated a moment, then go a hold of himself and came back over to the car—this time at a walk. Léo held out a cigarette: "For your trouble."

The viscount's hand trembled so much that he almost dropped the cigarette. But once again, he controlled himself. He stuck the cigarette in his mouth, popped a match, and raised two calm eyes to Léo. "Need a light?"

Léo also had a fresh cigarette in his mouth. He shrugged, stuck his head through the window, and took a light.

"Thanks."

"No problem."

"Run along now."

The viscount left. Once again, Léo shrugged. He liked these low ways to get even, but today it wasn't fun.

The office boy had a standing order never to make Léo wait. He knocked on the chief's door.

"Come in!"

"The prefect's car is here, Monsieur Surgeon General."

"Again!" Disgruntled, Bacchiochi threw his pencil down on the table.

"It's urgent."

"Fine, fine, I'm going."

A secretary stood up: "Any orders, Surgeon General, sir?"

"I'll call."

"Very well, Surgeon General, sir."

The secretary fell back into the chair.

Bacchiochi went into the vestibule to get his cloak. Fat Bertaud was there, a two-striper who was looking at himself in the mirror. Bacchiochi looked around for his cloak. He didn't see it. Fat Bertaud turned red as a peony.

"My cloak?"

"Oh! Pardon me, pardon me, Monsieur Surgeon General. Pardon..."

"You've got it on, haven't you?"

"Pardon, pardon..."

And tangling himself in the felt sleeves, sick with shame, he did his best to get the unfortunate cloak off. How long had he been there in front of the mirror, admiring the effect of those handsome, sought-after stripes on his body?

"Paardon...paardon..."

"Disgusting!"

"Pardon me, Surgeon General, sir!"

"I'm waiting, Monsieur!"

Fat Bertaud finally handed the cloak back to Bacchiochi, who ripped it out of his hands. In the same instant, without even being able to say how it happened, fat Bertaud disappeared.

Bacchiochi smiled then, running as fast as he could to the car. *Bah! I did the same when I was younger.*

They drove for a while without saying anything, Bacchiochi in the backseat of the limousine.

"Everything went well, Léo?"

"Smooth as velvet."

"The girls?"

"They're over there. We'll pick up Kaminsky first. Then to the camp."

"He wants to bring his little Italian?"

"Yes."

"Not a good idea."

"He really wants to."

"Well then, there's nothing for it..."

Kaminsky was waiting out on the sidewalk in front of the boardinghouse. The car barely stopped. He got in and sat down next to Bacchiochi.

"A world of trouble to disentangle myself from Madame de Villaplane. She gets more and more prickly. We're going to the camp, right?"

"Straight there."

"Perfect."

Then, they would go to their cottage, the cottage Madame de Villaplane imagined was the site of so many orgies. It would be the last time for a while. Since Kaminsky was leaving, the cottage would be rented...

Kaminsky burst out laughing: "The provinces are really a funny sort of place. You know what we seem like? Like conspirators. And what's this really about? To go get our mistresses in peace. It takes a devil's worth of trouble, and so much cleverness, and the patience of Russian terrorists who want to blow up a cabinet minister's carriage."

"Speaking of bombs..." said Léo.

"Yes, yes, I know it. We're nothing but comedians, my dear Léo. I remember one time, in Poland, I put on a great comedy for them.

My father was rich and well regarded. He entertained a lot. Fat bourgeois husbands and their wives. Dinners, etc. Hilarious! They weren't worth any more than they are here, you know. One time, my father was traveling, so I was the one to host them."

"Why do you always say 'them,'" asked Léo, "since you are one?"

"It always comforts me a little."

Léo didn't say anything more. He drove slowly through the town, listening with one ear to what Kaminsky was saying, entertaining himself with a game: when people out strolling stepped into the road, he'd get as close to them as possible, almost without a sound. Then, he'd violently lean on the horn for the pleasure of seeing them jump as if they'd been shocked in the ass with a wire. Kaminsky continued:

"My guests were all gentlemen and ladies in their fifties, very respectable people—bankers, lawyers, magistrates. A few military types in dress uniform. I'd cooked them up one of those Russian dinner parties, you know, something to die for."

An able storyteller, he paused and waited for Bacchiochi to ask, "And so?"

"I rented, for a small fortune, the twenty most titillating prostitutes I could find. Gorgeous girls. The oldest one wasn't even nineteen. They ate separately, in the adjoining room. When the bourgeoisie had eaten, the double doors opened, and my young ladies appeared— totally naked."

"You did that?"

"Don't you think that's great? The old bourgeois wives went crazy with anger. What yells! What a scramble! They wanted to kill me, I think. As for the gentlemen, well, you would have thought they were the naked ones. They didn't know where to hide. They didn't dare look at each other, or at the girls, and certainly not at their wives. What a stampede to the cloakroom, the old women leading their husbands by the hand! Not a single one dared to stay. They all jumped ship. Extraordinary, no?"

"You've got guts, I'll say that."

"No, no, this isn't about guts. I simply wanted to know if a single one would stay. One who was comfortable with what he thought about love and women. But at the risk of shocking you, Léo, old friend, I have to say that over there, they aren't any more comfortable with themselves."

"You're exaggerating, my friend," said Bacchiochi. "All that's just stories...you don't know how to take life simply, the right side up."

"You're joking," said Kaminsky.

"No. You're a funny one, my dear friend. You're always splitting hairs. Oh, la, la! Do you know what I'm going to do?"

"No."

"Well, I'm going to settle down here. Yes, these three years I've lived here, I've loved it. I'm going to sell my house in Toulouse and buy one here. And then we'll see..."

"Politics?"

"Why not?" said Bacchiochi, surprised he guessed so well. "Don't you think there's work to be done in that quarter? After the war, they'll need new leaders. Well then, there's nothing stopping me, it seems, from running for office. Everyone knows me here. I've done favors for piles of people..."

Léo, hunched over the wheel, swerved abruptly, throwing the passengers against each other. The car skidded left, for about twenty yards. Léo finally got it back under control.

"Name of God!"

"Are you trying to kill us?" Kaminsky asked, smiling.

"Almost wiped out Cripure," Léo grumbled.

In the back of the car, the two men turned. Cripure, in the middle of the street, waved his arms, open-mouthed, his pince-nez lost once again.

"In plain sight," said Bacchiochi.

"Not around a bend. Of course, he would be on the wrong side."

"Not harmed?"

"Certainly not."

"Fine then," said Bacchiochi, "step on it!"

"Monsieur Surgeon General is in a hurry to get some love tonight," said Kaminsky. And he let himself fall limply into the backseat, adding, "as for me, I don't know..."

In the middle of the road: Cripure, the wind knocked out of him, his face turned to the sky, the goatskin covered all the way up to the collar with a huge splash of mud, seemed to be asking God to look out for him, begging to end his martyrdom, that he'd be struck down where he stood, or else find the strength for revenge.

His cane had gotten away from him and lay in the gutter—not only his cane, but also, alas!—the groceries he was carrying in his net bag. In spite of everything he'd managed to get the shopping done, taking his to-do list from the pocket of his vest at each stop, and deciphering it like a sheet of hieroglyphics, not trusting himself to read it right. And so of course the bag, full to bursting and beyond, had rolled on the ground, into the mud, all the contents ruined—the lovely round potatoes, the artichokes, the parsnips, the macaroni, everything, including the quart of grated cheese and the half measure of butter. Only the bottle of nice wine had escaped the disaster, since he hadn't been able to fit it in the bag, and so he'd stuck it in the pocket of his goatskin, the seal sticking out, looking, with its gold-foiled top, like the gold cap on a dress uniform sword. Ah! If only it were a real sword, not a fake one, but the real thing, a handsome and righteous sword, thin and well tempered and sharp!

Those who had witnessed the scene, the ones who had helped him back onto the sidewalk, helped him find his pince-nez, who found the scattered groceries, washed them in the fountain and put them back in the bag, who picked up his cane, dried it, and gave it back to him, would say later on that they'd never heard from the mouth of a man such a stream of oaths and profanity. So many crazy things, phrases that were absolutely incomprehensible to them, and, they would say: exaggerated. They weren't expecting him to be thrilled, of course, at having nearly gone under the wheels of a car, but really, it was something that happened to lots of people, and in the end, it hadn't happened! Enough fear. Besides that, what was the good of working yourself up into such a state of accusations, blaming the universe? Because it was the whole universe he blamed, not just the risky or clumsy driver, another proof of his bad faith, since the driver hadn't been clumsy, on the contrary it was he, Cripure, who had been in the wrong, in the middle of the road, against all traffic laws and what was simply good sense.

But he didn't want to see it that way! It wasn't worth discussing it in such absurd details that were certain to create only the wrong story. A light went on, an illumination. The shortsighted silliness of believing in a simple accident, finding the responsible parties, and punishing them, he'd leave to others! Would it have been *simple* too if he'd fallen off his bicycle and cracked his skull on the pavement? The filthy dunces had planned something. The driver, he hadn't premeditated anything, but ultimately, there was only one way to look at it: they, all of them, were nothing but instruments towards an absolute necessity—to see that he *vanished* from the universe. Twice today, he'd been given notice. Twice, he'd miraculously escaped death. How much longer could he count on this reprieve?

Standing on the sidewalk, he looked at his feet, waiting perhaps to see the earth open up so he could throw himself in . . . or was he looking, out of the corner of his eye, to see if everything really had been picked up and put back in the bag? They could have believed it . . . the bystanders were so convinced that they hurried to reassure him. But at the sound of their voices, he came out of his shock and started furiously insulting them.

In his angry delirium, he went after the witnesses of the scene and those obliging people who had lent him a hand. He wore a horrible scowl, sending them a look filled with hate. "Nothing but a bunch of assassins! Did you think to have my hide? Did you think I couldn't defend myself? Get your paws off me!"

He raised his cane, ready to bring it down on the first person who moved.

It was a shocking moment for everyone. Of course, there was no one who was truly intimidated by this threat, but all the same, everyone was seized with a mysterious unease.

"Let me through . . ."

They parted. And Cripure made his way through the little group, getting back on the road, resolved this time to stick up for himself and not let things go.

"Cowards!"

The unease gave way to disgust, and he went on his way through a volley of insults. He turned back around. He was going to see the principal.

"Poor man," said an older one who'd see the whole thing without saying a word. "He's off his rocker."

Someone answered that it wasn't the first time Cripure had thrown a tantrum like that.

"Yes," said the old man. "He thinks they've got it out for him. For a long time now he's been practicing with his pistol on the strand when he goes to his cottage."

"What! His pistol? Why?"

"Dunno. He likes it. And besides, yeah, he thinks he'd in danger since it started to go poorly for him. He thinks the revolution will come and he'll be killed first."

"By whom?"

"He said the workers will kill him. No one knows why. He has ideas like that. He thinks people see him as an . . . intellectual. And plus, there's a story about little dogs in there, go figure. Yes, the neighbors scolded him for feeding the little dogs but having no mercy for men. Something like that. And since then . . ."

"Since then he's been doing target practice?"

"Well," said the old man, "it's not so simple."

Cripure's shadow disappeared around the corner. The little group disbanded.

Since the day long ago when he'd run to the telegraph office to insult the judges who had rejected his thesis, he'd never known such fury. He went back through the streets as if in a dream, opened the school gates without seeing them, and scaled, as if in a huge hurry, the same too-large, too-loud staircase in between the oozing walls that he'd climbed down not long ago, with the haste of a hunted man. In black on a plaque of white enamel: *Principal's Office*.

He entered.

A somber entryway. At the end, a door was open, and in the office, Monsieur Marchandeau and his wife.

They hadn't heard him. Cripure felt like he had suddenly been transported to the hall of a theater. He held his breath, not daring to go further: panic. Now he wished he could run.

What would he say, if they noticed him?

The principal had his back to him. On Madame Marchandeau's face was a look of sorrow that reminded him of Toinette's expression during their last attempt at explanations: an air of distress, which he'd had no pity for, that same convulsive movement of the lips and in the throat, that little trembling.

Thank God he'd come upon them as they were finishing up. Madame Marchandeau retreated all the way to the back of the room and went home without a word. Cripure didn't yet dare reveal himself. A domestic squabble? He'd arrived at the end of one of those little . . . bourgeois ceremonies . . . and while their son . . .

The principal sat down at his desk and started writing, but he quickly ripped the paper and threw it into the wastebasket. He took another, but this time he didn't even try to write. He put down his pen, got up, took his wastebasket and dumped the contents into the stove. Still holding the wastebasket in his hand, he walked around the room.

Cripure finally steeled himself. He cleared his throat, knocked the floor with his cane, and entered the office with a heavy step like a drunk's stagger. His feet boomed on the rug and made some piece of glassware tremble in the room—one of the lamps poorly balanced on the piano, maybe, or a paperweight on the loose boards of the desk.

The principal looked at him without surprise. He stopped pacing around the office, forgetting to put his wastebasket back, and murmured, "Yes?"

"You understand," began Cripure, in a little wheezing voice, "isn't it so, Monsieur Principal, pardon me, you understand, but the door was open, and, don't you see, I thought that...you didn't hear me, isn't that so? It's that...excuse me if I'm inconveniencing you, but I need to make a complaint, you see..."

The principal didn't reply.

Cripure went on: "Monsieur Principal, I must protest against certain actions, you understand, which will be apparent to you..."

Still holding the wastebasket in his hand, he watched Cripure with a glazed, almost empty look.

"I've come to make a complaint," Cripure thundered, "a complaint, do you hear me, Monsieur?"

A vague smile appeared on Monsieur Marchandeau's face. *Oh!* thought Cripure, *he's making fun of me.*

"This is unacceptable!" he cried. "You dare to mock me! I'm going to..."

He was going to say that he'd go higher, that he'd find the academy inspector, or the rector, and why not a cabinet minister? The words wouldn't come. Monsieur Marchandeau put down the wastebasket and handed Cripure a letter.

Cripure made as if to refuse.

"Me?"

"Read it."

And the principal let out such a heavy sigh that Cripure interrupted his barely begun reading and looked at him. *What's happened to him, then?*

He read.

No, it wasn't an official notice. The mayor hadn't been here. No red ink. It was a personal letter, a short one.

"Wh...what! But that can't happen! But isn't it just...Wh... what!" Cripure yelled, letting his arms fall.

Monsieur Marchandeau didn't move. He stayed still where he was, a man of wax.

"And here I am..."

Complaining, crying as he had just done, in front of this man whose son was going to be shot!

"I beg you to forget..."

"You couldn't have guessed."

It was no longer a human voice.

"Forgive me."

The principal shrugged.

Cripure took another step, and, once again, the little glass object tinkled. How to hand the letter back to Marchandeau? The gesture would be so cruel, it would seem to imply such a refusal, a vile aban-donment...He put it on the desk. Then, his big arms rose and fell, flapping the goatskin. He opened his mouth, but didn't speak, lifted his pince-nez, put them back in place. Finally he sat, unmoving, head lowered, his hands grasping his pointy knees, his cane slung across his stomach.

"I'm leaving for Paris..." The principal rifled through a drawer, looking for money, no doubt, and papers. Cripure remembered what Faurel had told him that morning: not a single pardon. And Monsieur Marchandeau was going to try to sway Poincaré. *This is no time for weakness...*

"Oh! What a life," Cripure murmured, almost soundlessly. "Ah! The things we still have to see..."

The principal was bent over his desk, sorting papers and money into his wallet. He got up, closed the drawer, put the wallet back in his pocket, checked that he had a handkerchief.

"Do you have any money on you?" he asked Cripure.

Cripure scrambled to take out his wallet. "Money? Yes. How much?"

"A thousand or fifteen hundred."

"Yes, I have it. It's a pure coincidence, but I have that much." He handed it to the principal.

"It's because I may have to stay there for a few days," Monsieur Marchandeau explained, "maybe go all the way to the front, or, at least, very close to it . . . and I'm not sure if I have enough money on me. I should ask my wife, but . . ."

Did she not know? Cripure didn't dare ask, but the principal added: "I'd prefer not to see her again before I leave."

The maid came in, carrying a suitcase.

"Your suitcase, sir."

He looked at it.

"You're the one who chose that suitcase?"

"Yes, sir."

"Ah! Also . . . I was thinking . . . Fine. Put it down there."

The maid set it down and went out.

Why did she have to choose that one in particular? It was a little yellow leather bag that Pierre had used to carry his gear to the soccer field, to play center forward. The maid must have found his jersey, his cleats, his white shorts . . . all jumbled inside.

"His little soccer bag," he said. He bit his lips, lowered his head.

"Come, come, my friend. All's not lost."

Monsieur Marchandeau shook his head with closed eyes. He picked up the suitcase. "Walk with me to the station?" he asked.

They were about to walk out when someone knocked, opening the door without waiting for a response. Francis Montfort came through the entryway, his hair dangling in his eyes as usual, and books under his arm.

"What's this?" asked the principal.

He'd forgotten the note he'd left with the concierge for the young monitor.

"You called me in, Monsieur," said Montfort, coming forward and holding out a paper.

"Oh!" said the principal, remembering all of a sudden, "yes, that's true, but . . ."

And he looked at Cripure who was waiting, leaning on his cane, the string bag dangling from his arm. When he recognized Montfort, Cripure shivered. That morning's letter!

"I don't know," he said in response to the principal's look.

More silence.

Montfort waited. They'd asked him to come, it must be for a reason, mustn't it? And apparently he'd have to explain his role in what happened with the bikes, since Cripure was there? But more important—the poem.

The principal still said nothing. His suitcase in hand, he was looking at Montfort like you contemplate a ghost. To end the awkwardness, Cripure stepped forward: "Monsieur Montfort, it seems you've come at a bad time. The principal is . . ."

But he stopped. How could he explain, how could he make him understand?

"He asked to see me, Monsieur," said Montfort.

He started to explain. He had prepared his response. He resolved to take full responsibility for his actions, to say that he had read a defeatist poem in study hall, that his classmates had asked him for it, but he didn't mean that as an excuse. If the principal addressed him in Young Man, he'd respond in Grown Man. But the principal didn't ask him anything—and Cripure didn't have another word to say either. They both had a paralyzed air, and the scene dragged on.

Something new must have happened since he'd received that summons. The changed attitude of the two men, that suitcase the principal was holding . . . it flashed through Montfort. "Pierre!"

He said the name in one breath. His eyes met the principal's. There was his answer.

"Forgive me," he said, backing away to leave.

They didn't reply. They let him retreat. But they didn't immediately move on. They didn't go out themselves until Montfort's steps faded away on the staircase. The principal, who was trembling, couldn't right away get a hold of himself.

Once they were in the street, how much they hampered each other—Cripure, who couldn't keep up with Monsieur Marchandeau, and Marchandeau, who kept having to slow down so as not to abandon

Cripure! The cab could have saved the situation, but it was nowhere to be seen. Cripure hauled his horrible feet with a look of supplication on his face, and Monsieur Marchandeau was carried along in spite of himself, turning around constantly, opening his mouth to say something and shutting it again.

As they approached the station a vague rumor came to them, like a muted groaning whose cause they didn't understand, and Cripure, still on alert, pricked up his ears.

They went into the little square in front of the station. The shouts became distinct. Even if it was possible to recognize, from time to time an attempt at songs, a snatch of "The Internationale," it wasn't just singing but also cries, hissing, threats: "Death! Death to Poincaré!"

That call for death eclipsed everything else. Some mouths took it up with violence, stretching it out. Then, like a passing wind, the racket stopped, dispersed into the four corners of the sky. A chant got louder:

> "Goodbye life, goodbye love
> goodbye to all the pretty girls ... "

Cripure felt the principal's shoulder tremble under his hand. "Let's go on, my friend."

They walked a little further into the square.

On a bench, a man in his sixties sat with his wife. The man, a peasant, was wearing a big wool bonnet. He had put the collar of his raincoat up and he was smoking. The wife, who was tiny, sat enveloped in her big black shawl.

They sat unmoving, a bundle at their feet. "What's happening, then?" Cripure asked.

The man raised his head. The song continued, beyond the square, a dragging, savage chant:

> "It's not over, it's forever
> What a Godforsaken war
> It's at Verdun, it's on the plain
> Where we don't get up again ... "[15]

They could hear something else now—a metallic sound, like helmets being thrown down, and breaking mirrors.

"They've ripped apart the engine," the old peasant replied. "It's been going on since the beginning of the afternoon." He noticed Monsieur Marchandeau's suitcase. "Were you going to take the train?"

"Yes."

"We're in the same fix. We need to be in Orléans tomorrow. But there's no train."

"Are you sure? They told you that?" cried Monsieur Marchandeau. "Who was it?"

"They wouldn't let us through. Seems like everything's muddled."

"Are you sure?"

"Otherwise I'd be there," said the man. Then he added, "and after we walked four miles to get to the station. We started as soon as we got the summons." He stayed silent for a moment, then asked, "You too, you're going to see your son?"

Monsieur Marchandeau reached for Cripure's arm.

"Yes."

"He's wounded too?"

"Yes," Monsieur Marchandeau replied, letting his chin drop into his collar.

"We don't know what's wrong with ours. But if they sent the notice ... Pigs! After you've given him everything you had ... eh?"

The wife didn't say anything. She seemed not to hear anything. Huddled in her black shawl, she looked like a big, sleeping dog.

"Let's go on," said Cripure, pulling Monsieur Marchandeau's arm. "Let's keep going anyway! All is perhaps not lost. We've got to try!"

They went off.

"Good luck!" said the old peasant.

Couldn't things rely on more than chance?

Cripure's heart beat wildly. *A little noise in the evening around the trains for furloughed men*, Faurel had said. So that wasn't over then? And Amédée? Was he among them?

"Take my arm, my friend."

Was it to help the shaking one or to reassure himself?

The crowd swarmed in the square, and in front of the station, from the other side, came whistles, shouts: "Die, die!"

They fought a way through the crowd, up to the barricade in front of the empty courtyard, which a man crossed from time to time. Cripure towered over the angry mass, and his head was so far above them that those who came behind might have thought the crowd carried him on their shoulders in triumph. Monsieur Marchandeau had let go of his arm and was following, hampered by his suitcase, by his hat sliding down his forehead, and Cripure made a desperate effort to turn and urge him onward.

"A little group of officers, it looks like, standing under the overhang and watching, don't you think? The important thing..."

A shove from the crowd interrupted.

"The important thing is to get to them..."

He spoke with difficulty, already out of breath. People were pushing him, others, backing away, banged him right in the chest. It was a miracle he hadn't lost his pince-nez.

"Forward by God! Break through the barrier!" yelled a voice in his ear.

"Kill the pigs!"

Women's cries mixed in with the others, and the cries of children too. Cripure saw the barrier bend under the force of the crowd then spring back. They were still getting closer.

"Get back, get back!" the station guards endlessly repeated, their rifle butts ringing out against the ground.

"Let us through with our wives!"

"Get back!"

"Let us through!"

"Civilians, get back!"

But the crush continued, and even in the station itself, the chaos increased. "Kill the pigs! Kill them!"

Panic seized Cripure. He was whimpering, still clutching the grocery bag and his cane in his left hand, and searching in vain with his right for something to hold on to, like a man who wavers while walking the plank, sometimes putting a hand on a shoulder, sometimes a head, once right on the face of a poilu, who wasn't paying attention. The crowd was so dense that Cripure's little hat, which had slipped off, was trapped between the goatskin and a backpack, and it was a world of trouble to retrieve it. He looked around for a gap to escape through and couldn't find one. He was terrified that the order would come to clear the square, that he'd be thrown to the ground, trampled, crushed. They'd pull him up, bloody and covered in mud, half dead. What could he do on this nightmarish voyage? The cries deafened him. If he was hurt, who would take care of him? Someone stamped on his foot and he cried out in pain, but no one paid the slightest attention. What was a Cripure's cry here? Even the principal hadn't heard, carried away as he was by the currents of the mob.

It was the first time Cripure had gone unnoticed in a crowd. No one here thought to look at him and point a finger, to be shocked, to pity or mock him. And now, when he was so comic and pitiful in his feeble efforts to escape this angry crush a find a refuge somewhere. He didn't let go of the grocery bag or the cane and thought, in spite of his afflictions, of the bottle of nice wine, which threatened to shatter in his pocket at any moment.

"We can't take it anymore! End the war!"

"Peace! Peace!"

"Death to Ribot..."

The shouts were coming from the other side. Here, they took them up again, but it was mostly about breaking down the barrier, to get or force them to let the women and children accompany their husbands and fathers to the train. To which the station guards unvaryingly replied, "Get back! Civilians can't come through!"

"Break down the barrier!"

"Get back!"

And the stampede continued.

"That's a new one," murmured a soldier.

A hatless woman was pressed up against him: "Wait and see..."

He caught sight of a guard. "What's this all about?"

The man didn't respond. He was young and pale with strain under his helmet.

"Are you deaf?"

"Go through," said the train guard. "You … not your wife."

The wife clung tighter to her husband. "We'll see about that."

"No civilians allowed."

"Are you joking?"

The man looked right and left, as if to call in a witness. The young wife lowered her head to hide her eyes. She put her arm around the soldier.

"Lulu …"

"Do you realize? No, really, do you?"

"Get back!"

"Shut the hell up."

"Back!"

"Go ahead," yelled a deep voice behind him. At the same time, he got a blow to the back. "Walk! Pop that young one in the kisser and go on with your wife …"

A head taller than the crowd, waving his arms, he made signs to his comrades, lost in the crush. "We've gotta do like the Russians."

"These men are just asses," said someone else. "They're fighting among themselves."

"What's it to you …"

"Kill the pigs!"

The shout was taken up by dozens of voices. A sergeant intervened: "That's enough!" he said. "Haven't you finished yet? Get on the platform."

"With our wives?"

"No."

"So, no, we haven't. We're staying. We don't want to go. We resist."

The sergeant shrugged. "You're just making it harder for yourselves."

The crowd was still pushing.

"Can we go through or not?"

"No civilians."

The one who had threatened to punch the young guard's teeth out turned and stood on tiptoe, his hand on a comrade's shoulder.

He yelled, "You see now? The poilus don't count for nothing now, and the wives of poilus for nothing of nothing at all."

"What's he saying?"

"That poilus are nothing anymore..."

"He's chewing us out?"

The man cupped his hands like a megaphone. "They've forbidden your wives and your kids to wait with you on the platform. It's to intimidate you, don't let them do it!"

A mute murmur in reply. A voice cried, "Who?"

"The same ones who are sending you to get ground up like a bunch of sausages!"

"So we should go to jail?"

"Break down the barrier, break it down, break it down!"

What's more, it had started to rain, a gray rain, slanting and cold. In less than a minute, it was running down Cripure's face. The little felt hat was soaked.

He kept pushing forward, but he was so squashed that he couldn't even lift his pince-nez to dry the lenses. He could barely see. The shouts all around him made the noise of a squall. He put his hand on a shoulder. The man turned his head—he was completely disfigured.

The whole bottom half of his face, ripped off and put back together, was nothing more than a glob of red, grainy flesh. Like a sponge. The man's feverish eyes fixed on Cripure with anger, then softened. He said, with surprise, "Monsieur Merlin! You don't recognize me? Not surprising. I wasn't like this the last time you saw me." He added, "Matrod."

"No!" Cripure murmured. "No! It's not possible. You?"

The son of one of his tenants. Sure, they had told him the boy had been wounded, but... he leaned down. Easier that way to hear what Matrod was saying in all the chaos.

"It was a brick that did this...exploded...by a shell...and they sent me back and this is going to be the—" His words were drowned by the racket. Inside the station, there must be a brawl going on, the quality of the sounds had changed "—fifth time."

Cripure's hand squeezed Matrod's shoulder. He spoke some word of pity, something like "poor boy," but the other whirled around.

"What did you say?" This time, he yelled loud enough to be heard. "Are you kidding me? Men like you...you let us get killed." Picking up Cripure by the collar of his goatskin, as if ready to throw him to the ground, he looked him straight in the eye. "Fuck your pity, you understand?"

And, battering a way through the crowd with his shoulders, Matrod vanished, shouting, "We're not men anymore! We have no rights! They're all pigs! They're in it together! All of them, They're all piiiiigs!"

For a long time, among the other voices, Cripure could hear him, "...all traitors..."

The phrase *caught red-handed* came to him. Then, once again, he was being dragged, pulled from every side at once. A murmur ran through the crowd. From mouth to mouth people said the order had come to clear the square. But they wouldn't carry it out as usual would they? Open fire?

"They wouldn't have the guts..."

Cripure had made it to the barricade. He was touching the chest of a guard in a helmet, his jugular popping, totally still, his hands crossed over his rifle, his bayonet under his arm. "What are you doing here, eh?"

"Me? Are you talking to me?"

"Yes. You. What are you doing here?"

"I, I'm with..."

As a matter of fact, where was Monsieur Marchandeau? He saw him a few yards back, trying to get through to Cripure.

"I'm here with a friend."

"No civilians can pass."

"But..."

"Get back!"

The rifle butt smacked. A hand pressed to Cripure's vacillating chest.

"But really now..."

"Get back! Come on now. There's no reason for you to be here."

The principal finally caught up.

"Push through, my friend, push through," said Cripure.

Monsieur Marchandeau went up to the guard. "Let me through!"

"Back off!"

"You won't let me through?"

The guard shrugged. Was it his fault that...what could he do? Did they think it was fun for him to do this damned cop's job?

"There's nothing I can do."

"You could let me through."

"Get out of here!"

"Come now, my friend, I'm Monsieur Marchandeau."

"You could be the pope for all I care."

"But you're not listening! I'm Monsieur Marchandeau, principal of the lycée. I have to catch a train to Paris tonight."

"There is no train for civilians tonight."

"But no...come on now! I'll take any train! I have to be there tomorrow morning..."

"Go away, that's enough! There's no train for you. Move along!"

"No."

"For the love of God..."

"I'm going through anyway!" screamed Monsieur Marchandeau, grabbing the soldier's rifle. He'd let go of his suitcase, and wrapping both hands around the rifle, he repeated, "I want to see my son! I want to see my son!"

The man was losing ground. "Over here! In the name of God... over here! Stop him."

"I want to see my son!"

"But it's like I told you..."

"I want to see my son!"

His eyes popping out of his head, Monsieur Marchandeau was squeezing the rifle with both hands, crying, "I want to see my son! I want to see him!"

A sergeant raced over, wrapping his arms around Monsieur Marchandeau like a belt. "What's this all about?"

"Let go of me! I want to see my son! Let go of me!"

"Listen to me, Monsieur."

"Let me go!"

He fought desperately, but the sergeant, still using all his strength to hold him, said, "This is useless, Monsieur. There's no train, do you hear? I see why you're upset, but ... there's nothing we can do. There's no train—not for you, and not for anyone. What do you want us to do about it?"

Monsieur Marchandeau stopped fighting. The sergeant let go of him. The principal disappeared into another wave of the crowd.

A volley of whistles, unending yells: they greeted the arrival of reinforcements, called in haste from inside the station. The men raced in, and the crowd parted to let them through, covering them with insults.

"Bastards! You should be ashamed!"

"Sellouts!"

"This is a job for pigs, what you're doing. Do you know what we do to pigs?"

"We hang them!"

They passed by, weapons in their hands, not proud of it. A soldier boosted himself up on the shoulders of two comrades and, cupping his hands like a megaphone, he yelled at the top of his lungs, "Follow them! Follow them! Fall in behind them!"

The order was picked up all around them. There was total chaos in the square. Cripure found himself carried almost all the way to the overhang, where he grabbed a pole as a sailor in a storm grabs a mast. The barrier had broken, and the crowd invaded the station.

New banging rang out.

No doubt, the reinforcements weren't getting a warm welcome inside. Even so, the cries of hate were mixed with joyful shouts, exclaiming the new arrivals, then, an order, spontaneously yelled out: "Follow us! Follow us!"

Cripure let go of the pole. The square was clearing out. He looked around for Monsieur Marchandeau: gone. So he went off, making his way to a little bridge that overlooked the other side of the station.

In the endless rain, the lamps cast big yellow blobs of light onto the platform, while confused shadows appeared and disappeared in them, running from all sides, and the threatening racket came from their shouts, the crunching of their feet on the gravel, the shock of helmets thrown with hate against the train, the shattering of windows they were breaking with their feet.

"Death to Poincaré! Death to Ribot! Peace! Peace! We've had enough! End the war! Long live Russia!"

Cripure looked on.

"We'll crush them…"

Whose voice was that? Where did it come from, that voice strangled with anger, which didn't seem totally unknown to him, but which he couldn't identify right away, perhaps refusing to believe that such a meeting could be possible? Cripure turned around, slowly coming back to himself. All the blood in his veins froze. Nabucet. It was Nabucet! He was the one who had promised to crush them! Dear God. Through what horrible orifice had that sentiment come? Oh, the filthy snout!

"That's a lie!" cried Cripure, at the height of his fury. "Villain!" And his giant hand came down on Nabucet's "filthy snout."

The witnesses of the incident said later that it was more like a punch than a slap, or in any case, it wasn't an ordinary slap, but enough to knock out a bull. It was the first time Cripure had slapped anyone, but this slap made up for his whole past, it gathered together all the blows he'd stopped himself from doling out in the rest of his sad career. Nabucet was whirled around, and his hat rolled to the ground. He held his head in both hands, protecting his ears like a bad child who's about to get boxed.

Cripure panted like a worn-out horse. His pince-nez had jumped off and were resting on his chest. He quickly put them back on.

Nabucet gathered himself together. He stopped protecting his ears, revealing a squishy face—with one cheek white and the other crimson. What a blow! But Nabucet never lost his composure for long. Even in a situation like this one, he remained master of himself, calm, a man of the world, and he forced a smile.

Ah! This time he had him! An idea popped into his head and blew him away. What a great opportunity to push Cripure to ... *I'll challenge him to a duel!* What did he have to lose?

"You won't be surprised, I imagine," he said, "you won't be astonished, Monsieur, to receive a letter from me tomorrow morning..."

"What? A letter?"

"Such are the customary proceedings."

"Proceedings?" What new kind of conformism had Cripure stumbled into?

"I must write you a letter to inform you of my choice of seconds."

"Oh, oh!" Cripure shot back. "Oh! Monsieur! Enough pussyfooting around. Let's settle this here and now."

Nabucet gave him a pitying smile.

"That's not how it's done."

"Excuse me?"

"That's against the conventions."

"Ah! Enough. Let's settle this question on the field, I'm telling you. Why wait? Why all this pretense? Ah!"

Cripure heard himself give a couple of little gulps, "Ugh, ugh."

"A letter!" he murmured, returning Nabucet's look of pity.

Ah! If only he had his pistol in his pocket just then! And Nabucet had one too! They could go off together without a wait. The first lonely spot they came upon, and he'd settle the tab for that ... louse. The last time he'd practiced on the beach, it hadn't gone too badly.

Nabucet was still smiling, a cowardly, wicked smile that showed his false teeth.

"I should have considered," said Nabucet, "I should have known that in the matter of a duel, as in everything, following the rules would displease you."

"What?" thundered Cripure.

"Everyone knows you are—"

"Ah, by God, shut up. And I'll say it again, let's settle it on the turf. Let's be quick—name a time."

"What?"

"And a place!"

"Come on now, don't lose your head. Get a hold of yourself."

"Time and place, and I'll be there. You can count on me."

"Oh! But aren't you moving a little quickly on this? Are you so impatient to—"

"Kill you?"

"I was going to say: to die," corrected Nabucet coldly, his cloudy eye catching the light.

Cripure stared. He was frozen in place. "To die," he said so softly that Nabucet could barely hear him. "At your hands! Ah! That would be too awful," he cried, "something like that will never happen."

With a savage blink, Nabucet replied. "Perhaps..."

They looked at each other without moving, like two fighters sizing each other up. Then, with profound astonishment, they realized everything could still change. Maybe they didn't hate each other quite as much as they thought? It lasted maybe a second. And as soon as they spoke, the hate came back, much increased.

It was Nabucet who spoke first: "Name your seconds, and let's fight tomorrow at dawn. Your seconds can arrange it with my friend Babinot, who certainly will not refuse to aid my cause." With that, he saluted.

"My seconds?" babbled Cripure, confused.

Nabucet turned. "Well then? Two of your friends."

"Two of my friends?"

"He has no friends! He has no friends!" yelled Nabucet, walking away.

And Cripure, his arms hanging limply on the goatskin, his bag of groceries and his cane at his feet, watched open-mouthed as Nabucet left.

How he scampered!

Cripure was overcome.

Whom could he go to, whom to ask for help, for even a simple piece of advice? Nabucet was right—he had no one. No friend. The thought ripped him open. But still: *who could he go to, talk to?*

There must be a whole host of things he didn't know about, rules to follow, a dueling code to learn. Would he be reduced, like some ordinary adventurer who doesn't expect a duel in a strange city, to put his life in the hands of the nearest helmeted soldier or the Military Society, to beg two officers to assist him? Those men seemed to know what to do in affairs of honor. The rules of dueling wouldn't be unfamiliar to them. But officers! He made a huge effort to correct his thought that all officers must have been Toinette's lovers. *Oh, she's dead . . .*

In the station, the poilus seemed to have quieted. The engine was mysteriously reattached, and the men were boarding the train, which had not a single window left, and barely any seats. When the train started, a volley of whistles rang out. The men crouched in the car doors shouted, "We'll be back!"

One of them seized an officer's hand as he went by. To the officer's great surprise, he didn't relax his grip.

"Hey! What are you doing? Let go of me! Come on!"

The train picked up speed. The officer started to run.

"Let me go!"

"You don't want to come along?"

"You're crazy. Come on. Let me go!"

"Come with us, eh?" The man smiled.

The men were sticking their heads out all the doors. Some laughed, others cried out.

"Hold on tight!"

"Whatever you do, don't let go!"

"Hang on, in the name of God!"

"Oh the pig! He'll roll under the wheels."

"Get your foot on the running board, you big idiot!"

"Think about it! Then he'll have to come with us to the end of the line!"

The train picked up speed. On the platform, a station employee was whistling his head off. Deafened by shouts, the engineer heard nothing and the train kept going. The officer was running for his life now, his eyes popping out of his head, crazed with fear.

"The hell with it. Even if he lets go, he'll roll under the weight."

"Kill him!"

"But no... haul him on board."

The man finally let go of his prey, and a huge yell went up. Bouncing against the train, the officer spun around two or three times, rolled across the platform, and lay still.

The poilus leaned down to see better. One of them spat: "Shitbag!"

From the back of the station, men came running.

Cripure fled. They were animals, all of them! He hurried to leave the bridge, to go back into the town. No more shouts in the air. Nothing. The riot was over.[16] They'd been crushed. And as for him? A duel!

He stopped short at the edge of the sidewalk.

But whom could he ask? Where would he get advice?

A duel in the middle of a war. It was, of course, more than ridiculous. All things considered, it was quite revolting. He alone, among thousands, millions of men in battle, had found a way to embroil himself in this situation and to make it come to the dueling ground—he was resolved to do it!—such a strange event that it would undoubtedly become legendary. As time went on, they would talk about him as that madman who... and scorn, laughter, revulsion would cover his name for eternity. At least... at least he'd be dead. *Or the other one*, he quickly corrected himself. Unless the conditions of the duel might be so moderate that one, if not two, of the opponents could escape death. He thought about duels that were famous for the strictness of their conditions... Pushkin's... But whom could he ask?

Moka?

Not a bad idea. Upon reflection, it was even an excellent one. Moka was a pure soul. You could trust in Moka. Yes, Moka. He'd go see him right away, instead of stupidly standing there, frozen on the sidewalk. Could his other business wait? Did one ignore a duel? Since he had to fight, he would fight tomorrow morning, at dawn. Tomorrow morning, yes, everything would be settled. Finished.

And in any case, he thought, as he walked along, he wasn't as friendless as he had thought. After thinking about it for a few minutes, he could still find someone he could count on. How would he explain things to him, the . . . slap? Did seconds generally ask, before agreeing, for explanations of motives, for the start of the quarrel? That slap— how could he justify it? Certainly, it wasn't a premeditated blow—it was something that had come over him.

While he walked along the gray walls lining the street, so similar to the walls of a prison (which it was), he was disappointed once again that the cab was nowhere to be seen. He would have to walk. He forced himself to think of the questions he might be asked and to come up with answers. *Why did you slap Nabucet?* What could he say? Because Toinette is dead? Because once upon a time, I didn't dare fight the blond officer? Because, through Nabucet, I slapped a whole species of men I hate? Because, because. Would he dare tell them everything he was thinking, and argue that Nabucet had arranged the attempt on his life, the business of the bikes? All these reasons were good and bad, but none were relevant. The truth was made up of bits of all of them and also of many other pieces that remained murky to him, which he was afraid to examine. One thing was clear: he was the aggressor. He had trouble convincing himself of this. To be the aggressor was something new for him and, despite the evidence, he would have happily erased that fact. He would have to hope that the seconds didn't ask for such a long story. They weren't judges! He wasn't going to the courthouse, to hell with it! He was going to fight! The judgment of God . . .

With infinite trouble, he arrived at the little square where Moka lived. Curiously empty. Nothing. Not even a dog. Like the streets he'd just walked through—always before or after the thing happened, never during. A church in the middle—square stones, without the shadow of a sculpture or the hint of a smile. If you could imagine that cattle had once lived in something resembling a human society, and they'd had the idea, in their beef brains, to build a church suited to their idea of cattle, this shadowy façade would have been a won-derful example of bovine architecture, something for little cow-archaeologists to work away on. Two short towers, blank and angular, abrupt as a couple of commandments from the Decalogue, made a pretty good likeness of the stunted horns of the beast, and, between the towers, the low portico—it really was a portico—looked like nothing so much as a large, low forehead, bare, boxy, dark, and in front of it, a set of enormous pillars, the only roundness in all those sharp angles, which were obviously the hooves. The haunches stretched back, immense, formidable, taking up more than a third of the square, so still that the spectacle invited fear. Such was the beast. Decked out as if for market. Someone had hung flags everywhere, and the whole forehead was covered in a banner with a patriotic inscription. Besides, this cow, it hadn't been there so long. The old folks in town remembered a cemetery here instead. One fine day, the cow had arrived in the graveyard, and rummaged around in it, scratching the earth with its hooves, tossing up the dead. No more cemetery. But the dead got revenge—they'd quickly transformed the houses surrounding the square into tombs, and there they hid themselves under various disguises. You could ring their doorbells, but they never appeared without masks. They were generally very well dressed, and they even looked like the living, but a practiced eye could easily see past the surface: no doubt about it, these were the dead you were dealing with, and in spite of all the precautions with which they surrounded themselves, going so far as to decorate each other, fabricating "children" to better hide their plot, even becoming important downtown—some as teachers or doctors, others as bank employees or registry clerks, or even soldiers, going off to war, which was taking the joke a bit farther—they were still the bona fide dead, they were ghosts.

Cripure had got wind of it, being a little in on the secret, and besides, rather close to the Clopper who must live somewhere around here. And, without there being the slightest irony in it, this square—gray stone, dirt, sky, with its great, gray, snub-nosed façades and its gray premeditations, and on the gray roofs, mansard windows like watch posts—even so this square was what they called the heart of the town. Cattleton. Clopperville. Deathgrad. A heart of stone, a cow heart, a heart of death. Never had this truth been clearer to Cripure than today when he'd been confronted with the animal they had the nerve to call by other, nobler, names though it was, despite false labels, nothing but a will to negate. No. The cow always refused. The cow and its whole charming little family of prefectures and jails, of lycées and banquets, etc., the cow always said no, never yes. Cripure's eyes wandered for a long time as if he was trying to get deeper into the mysteries surrounding him. "Not a stone that doesn't cry out to be bombed!" he murmured, "And there are hearts heavy as bombs." He stopped, lost in thought. He thought with regret of the terrorists, whom he should have joined. Whom he hadn't joined.

But the heart of the unhappy hunchback, was it as heavy as a bomb? It didn't at all match the way she ran, jumping along in this desert, like the sole survivor of a wreck. She bounded forward, clop clop, then turned and bent quickly to the haggard cur, reluctant at the end of his leash.

No doubt he'd had enough, the dear little pup, of being pulled through the streets morning to night like a toy, when his unending curiosity made him want to run into every stream and doorway.

But with pretty words the damned hunchback pulled him after her and, still skipping along, she went on her endless way humming tunes from operettas.

Cripure shivered when he saw her turn towards him. The horrible hunchback! Why couldn't she stay in her hole! She came towards him in her too-large gown, tied at the waist with a rope. A funny way for a woman to dress, that gown that enveloped her from head to toe, and that she had chosen in blue, like, it occurred to him, the gowns people in prisons and hospitals wore. Horrible little hunchback! And yet it was true that she had eyes in the middle of her face and a pointy nose. Her head was covered with a blue-banded straw hat, and the big brim flopped down like blinders over her skeletal cheeks.

"Horrible crone! Hurry up and get out of sight!" he murmured, hiding in a doorway as she passed by, close enough to brush him. She hummed:

> "Turn! Turn! Let the waltz open arms
> She charms, she sweetens
> All the passionate hearts."

He followed her with his eyes.

"Damned wreck! I have no pity for you. Die!"

This unchristian oath didn't cause him the least bit of remorse. Perhaps a tiny bit of surprise.

But the hunchback wasn't the only one. There was also the old lady who had accosted him at the bookstore to explain her beliefs on reincarnation. As the old biddy explained that it was necessary to have faith in order to bear the sadness of life, he could only think of the widow who lived above the bookstore. Only two floors up. For fifteen years now, she'd lean out her window—waiting for what? "Well, well, what a strange insistence on living! Must dissolve, disappear," he murmured. And the little grocer on the corner, he'd almost forgotten, alone from now on since her husband was blown to bits by a shell, with only their half-witted little daughter? Four sous of pepper here, a nice head of lettuce there . . . until the end. And all the others, and behind that huge army of them, all the ladies who were still laughing, applicants about to enter forever into that world of ashes and darkness. And no one to save them! How horrible to see a girl of forty enter a movie theater, all alone, when she had hoped until that moment for a husband, for a family. No matter what, wherever she went, she would leave an empty room to return to an empty room, not once forgetting, before she left, to double lock the door—on emptiness—and to close her shutters—still emptiness! The next week they'd stare a little less when she entered the theater. Not much time before her novitiate would be accomplished.

Poor women! They'd believe they'd been disappointed, betrayed by life, and it would actually be by their own hands, their only crime would be not having the force to resist the decay of social rule—that was what was crushing them, not the will of God!

"And not the will of God, do you understand!" yelled Cripure at the top of his lungs, turning toward the church.

He raised his hand, and a fist was already closing, but he dropped it back down into formation—someone was appearing from the same direction in which the damned hunchback had faded away, the mayor in person, scraping along the walls, walking on tiptoe like someone who is about to sneak up and say *boo!* Refreshed, his heart and stomach full of chocolate, sandwiches, and little cakes, he'd lost his air of an errand runner and seemed no more or less lively than any other walker—someone out for a Sunday stroll, smoking a cigarette and thinking about nothing.

In front of the church, the mayor lifted his hat.

Run! Run to Moka's! Fight to the death! Disappear. Don't wait for the mayor to see him and speak to him—he must hum along, like the other one. Cripure veered away.

Only someone who'd been in the town for as long as he had, knowing every cranny, every shadow, every stone, who was capable of navigating blind like a mole in his mole hill, could have picked out Moka's house from among the others, on the first try. You had to be a local! They all looked the same, the same model, all built in the same ungenerous, withdrawn way, with their stingy windows, inviting as arrow-slits, the little fenced-in balconies, their doors with peepholes and little brass plaques like belt buckles, polished every morning by the housekeeper while Mr. Death goes to the National Bank to see if his interest income has gone up. And all the houses veiled, like a woman in mourning. He climbed the three stone steps. They all had steps going up to their doors, and some even put on naive airs, calling them terraces, as if Mr. Death hoped to deliver great speeches there, or receive a large number of honored guests, so great an effect that the little steps grabbed Cripure's attention, as if they expressed a long-held dream, reduced, as it was, to the level of a stoop. Speeches or grand parties had been out of the question for a long time, but Mr. Death refused to let go of the idea.

But his own houses were not so different, after all. When he bought them, it wasn't for their beauty. If he'd thought only of beauty, he'd never have taken the trouble to become their official owner. When he negotiated with the notary, Cripure had only thought, like everyone else, of the value they'd accrue. But since then, as much as he tried to deny it, a shadow of something was born in him, like a feeling for these houses, a sort of vague tenderness which pushed him from time to time to make the trip over here, just to see them. "Enough of that, enough, it's awful..."

Cripure had climbed up the three little steps and slowly his hand reached for the bell. Did he pull too hard, or was he dealing with an especially mischievous bell? Its ringing filled the whole house, which echoed like an empty box. And, at the same time, the beast behind him started its terrible roar. No doubt the cow was jealous that someone had gone to visit one of its subjects, and no doubt it had no other way to express its anger than to open its throat and howl. In its powerful bronze voice, a shout of death in reply to Cripure's disturbing the peace of this place, to his insolence, his nerve, in wanting a door to open.

The cow's voice quieted, and like a mocking little laugh the last echoes of the doorbell lingered in Cripure's ears, but the door still didn't open, no one came, and Cripure didn't move, his head bowed like a statue in his niche.

So the silence fell, returned, and from the interior of the house a loud voice came. Someone was singing his head off:

"Kiss-es, more kiss-es
Kiss-es always!"

It was Moka coming down his stairs—soon Cripure could hear his steps.

Seeing Cripure, Moka seemed so amazed that he stood for a full minute with his mouth open. "You!" he finally cried, opening the door wide, but forgetting to step aside to let Cripure in. "I'm dreaming! I must be dreaming," he murmured. At last he gathered his wits. "It's an exceptional honor! Come in my dear professor. Come inside! You find me so astonished to see you that I've forgotten my manners. Please forgive me," he said, stepping back. And very solemn, he made a bow to Cripure, who finally entered.

In his joy, Moka closed the door with a big kick, then, turning back to Cripure, he hopped and rubbed his hands. "Put down your things, my dear professor, make yourself comfortable."

He tried to help him take off his coat, to take the groceries, the cane, the little hat from his hands. Cripure didn't let him, putting everything down in a corner of the vestibule. But he didn't take off the goatskin.

"I came to see . . . I need to ask . . ."

"We'll get to it in just a minute!" Moka interrupted. He raised his hands as if to put them over Cripure's mouth to keep him from speaking. "Let's go up to my room first. It'll be easier for us to talk there. It will be more . . . intimate. This way. Come!"

They went upstairs, Moka offering his hand to his dear professor to help him with the painful ascension to the second floor where there was such a view! Oh!

"It's panoramic . . . you'll see."

Cripure panted. A panoramic view? Hm. A nice view of the cow, no doubt. From up high, they'd get a good look at its spine . . .

"Here we are." And Moka pushed open the door with his foot. Of course, he made another bow in stepping aside to let Cripure enter, and he straightened up, brusquely pushed back the red forelock, and, hurried, triumphant, he removed a pile of plates from the seat of an armchair and put them on the floor, crying, "Make yourself comfortable my dear professor! My goodness!"

Cripure was a wreck. You could see it in the way he dropped into the chair. So much walking, so much running around today! And that climb had finished him off.

"You did well to come by," said Moka, lifting another pile of dishes from the other chair, "I was about to go to work, you see. I didn't even take the time to change." He gestured to the flower in his buttonhole. And in a low voice, "So, you've reconsidered?"

Cripure didn't reply.

"For goodness sakes," Moka continued, "we couldn't part on that note!" He touched the end of his nose with his finger. "That was a joke, my dear professor."

Cripure still didn't answer. Maybe he hadn't even heard? Or had he fallen into one of his usual reveries? He looked around him in a stupor, with the amazed face of a sleeper who has woken up a thousand miles from his house, as if a carpet had transported him by magic. What, but what on earth was this astonishing room, with plates on the walls, and nothing but plates, like a hallucination? An iron bed, a table, two chairs, and the plates... the famous plates covered with stamps, arranged in perfect lines on every surface.

"Curious..." The word slipped out.

"Isn't it?" said Moka, delighted. Finally, an admirer, someone who understood! "And that, what do you think of that?"

"That" was a venetian paper lantern, an ordinary Bastille Day decoration, which hung in the middle of the room. An electric bulb was inside it. He lit it: a demonstration.

"It's a souvenir."

"Oh?"

"I brought it back from the last ball I went to with her..."

Silence. A silence full of sighs here and there, full of little gestures, hands fidgeting on knees, as if out of impatience, and finally Moka continued:

"Yes... as I said... it was a joke."

Cripure looked him in the eye.

"He exists," said Moka, with mischievous air.

"Who, my dear boy?"

"God, of course!"

"Oh, oh, oh!" Cripure exclaimed. "Him again! God again! No, no, no, no, no, my friend, listen to me. It's got nothing to do with that... character, you understand. Don't think that I came to..."

"Really?" And how Moka got these ideas! He would have bet his own head that Cripure, full of remorse, had only come to see him to say precisely that... to apologize for having said...

"Not at all," said Cripure, "not at all. I have something to ask you. A great favor."

"Anything, my dear professor."

"A very important favor."

"I repeat that..."

"Thank you, thank you my dear boy. Since we parted ways, which wasn't so long ago, something quite serious has come up, you understand, something...of first priority. Basically, I thought of you," he said, a smile at the corner of his lips, "in my hour of need, my dear Moka, you're the first person I thought of. To put it plainly, my friend, I have to fight. I have a duel on my hands, you see, and...I'm asking if you would be willing to agree to be my second. There."

"Ayayay!" yelled Moka, who hadn't waited for the end of Cripure's speech to jump out of his chair. "Ayayay!" he said again, pacing around in a circle without the slightest care for the piles of plates. "Oh my dear little God, what's happening here! And there I go trying to judge. Oyoyoy!" He waved his hands, bit his fingers, tapped his feet. "Oyoy..."

"There you have it," said Cripure, his hands on his knees, his forehead bent.

"A duel!"

"It can't be helped, my friend."

"Ayayay!"

"I'm asking you, you understand, to please, after the traditional rules, you understand, to take my interests to heart and...to help me find another second, since in this bitch of a town..." He scornfully shrugged his shoulders.

Moka came over to Cripure and very gently asked, "A real duel?"

"How can you ask!" cried Cripure. "A fight to the death!"

"Oh God, oh God, oh good God!" And Moka took his head in his hands and continued his frenzied dance around the room. "It can't be settled otherwise?"

"No."

"It has to happen this way?"

"Yes."

"Well then, my dear professor," said Moka, finally stopping his movements, "it's understood. I'll be your second."

Cripure fiercely shook Moka's trembling hands. "Thank you, thank you, my dear boy, thank you."

Now he had to tell him what happened, to say whom he was going to fight. But actually, to Cripure's astonishment, against all expectation, it was Moka and not he who said the despicable name.

"Nabucet?"

In a pale, whispering voice it was true, the questioning tone so perfectly mixed with discovery that it was impossible for Cripure to tell if Moka knew, was guessing, or had guessed from the beginning.

"Yes."

"Oh! Nabucet…"

And the two men looked away from each other. Moka did an about-face, lifting a hand to his mouth to bite his nails.

"…vidently."

"Right you are." Cripure spoke to Moka's back, hunched in that moment. The venetian lantern above Moka's head like a child's racket ball.

"Hehehehe!"

Was he laughing?

"What's so funny?"

"I…No," said Moka, turning around.

"Hm." Cripure frowned. "It's no laughing matter."

Moka really didn't find it funny either. He said so. Still biting his nails, he asked, "Because of the little Chinese man?"

Cripure couldn't remember right away what Moka was referring to.

"Come on, don't you remember!"

"What Chinese man?"

"The cane…the menacing little cane?"

"Ah! Yes, yes." But there had been a lot of other things. The affair of the bikes, the riot…everything, really.

"That…and then, in general," said Cripure. "I smacked him, you know, gave him a real whack, my friend! A whack…A first-class whack, world-class, that's the word. Ah, ha, ha, ha!" He started to laugh softly, his stomach moving so little you could barely see, then the heaves became bigger, then it wasn't only the stomach but the thighs, then the shoulders, until he was crazed with laughter, which Moka found contagious, doubling over, a hand on his spleen, sickened.

When they came to their senses they didn't dare look at each other right away—they were too ashamed.

"Let's get out of here, my friend," said Cripure.

"One moment." They turned their backs to each other, drying their tears of laughter.

"Wait," said Moka, putting his handkerchief back in his pocket. "Your other second, my dear professor, we'll find him at Madame de Villaplane's. But before we go, if you don't mind . . ."

And from under the eiderdown he pulled his little dog, who had been peacefully sleeping there in the warm.

"What am I going to do with him?"

Of course, bringing him was out of the question. Cripure didn't say anything. He looked at the plates one more time. They were starting to get on his nerves, those plates.

What to do with the dog? What to do with man's faithful little friend?

"Ah! Goodness me!"

Suspicious that Moka was trying to get out of it already, Cripure scowled. "What is it, my boy? Something stopping you? What is it?"

"No . . . a difficulty . . . about the puppy."

Ah! That was another matter. Ah! If it had to do with the puppy, he couldn't argue. "Ah! That's understandable. In truth, that's a delicate matter. Poor little fellow," said Cripure, rubbing the dog's head. He was thinking of his own. "What now?"

"I'm thinking about it," said Moka.

"You don't have anyone you could . . . It's clear as day! He can't just leave him all alone."

"No, there's no one."

"He's got such good eyes."

"Angelic," said Moka. "Oh, I have an idea!" Moka ran to the door, bent over the banister, and shouted, "Henriette!"

And turning to Cripure: "If she hasn't left, I'll leave him with her. You understand, she's got no place to go, poor girl, so sometimes she comes to see me, and she asks permission to stay in the parlor. She spends hours there, all alone, sitting in a corner. Henriette!"

"Yes!"

A door slammed.

"She's there," said Moka, winking at Cripure. "This'll all work out."

Cripure gave him an accomplice's smile.

"You understand," he started to say. But he was interrupted by Henriette's arrival.

She stayed in the doorway, not daring to enter despite Moka's encouragement, and she shook her head, plucking at her dress.

"Oh! What a little savage," said Moka. "And since you wouldn't like to come in Mademoiselle ... since you're so shy," he said, delighted to be tenderly scolding her in front of Cripure, who was tortured by the idea that he was nothing more or less than a specter to this pretty young girl, and so he stayed silent.

"Well then, my little Henriette," Moka continued, "see here—could we put this little fellow in your care?" he asked, pointing to the dog.

Cripure picked up the dog in his arms and held him out to her, smiling. Perhaps he'd seem less hostile that way?

"You don't want him anymore?" said Henriette, becoming very pale.

Moka wanted to play a game, no doubt for purposes of flirtation. The idea came to him to pretend he didn't want his dog.

"That's it, I don't want him anymore."

"Is that true?" said Henriette, in a tone she might have used to ask if it was true that he was going to cut off the dog's head.

"Very true. Do you want him?"

"Oh! I certainly do, but ..." And poor Henriette melted into tears.

"What's this!" said Moka, hurrying over to her. "What's the matter? Why are you crying all of a sudden?"

He took her hands, which she let him do, very tenderly. Cripure, embarrassed and also the intruder, or at least, one person too many—when was he not one person too many?—put the dog down on the chair and went over to the window, turning his back to the younger ones. What did she have to cry about, the little one? *I don't understand anything anymore ...*

Moka took his handkerchief out of his pocket and softly dried the tears that were flowing abundantly down Henriette's cheeks.

"Come now," he said, "what's wrong, why are you crying? Tell me."

"I...I...I," said Henriette, sobbing, "I understand that it's because..." Her tears fell even harder.

"What? What's this you understand?"

"You...You...You're...going to get married," she said.

Moka, taken aback, stopped drying Henriette's tears. "Why do you say that? What an idea!"

"Yes!"

"But no! It's not true, you understand! You well know it's not. Why do you say that?"

"Because you're giving away your dog."

She told a story, still crying, of how she'd seen it before. There was a man like that, whom she'd known, who also had a dog. He loved his dog very much, as much as Moka loved his own. Well, it didn't stop him from giving it up, yes, he simply got rid of it, as soon as he had a fiancée—Monsieur's fiancée didn't like animals. And so...and so...there you have it.

"But I'm telling you it's not true."

"Oh! Yes it is."

"Why so stubborn!"

"But I don't want a dog. The other man, he didn't give it to... to..." And her tears flowed once more.

"To whom? To you?"

"Yes."

"You loved him?"

"No," she said.

"Let's hurry!" said Cripure, tapping his finger on the windowsill, "let's move along, my dear Moka! It's getting late. If possible, let's speed things up a bit." What was this about? You didn't fight a duel every day. There were perhaps more important things in the world than the nonsense between these two...

"Oh, Lord!" groaned poor Moka. "Listen, Henriette—I swear in Christ's name...Wait."

He bent down to whisper in her ear. What was he saying? She stopped crying, suddenly radiant.

"Oh! Really?" she cried. "Oh, oh!"

"Run along now, go! Take the dog and run along."

She didn't need to be told twice. Taking the dog in her arms, she went down to the parlor.

"There, that's settled," said Moka, turning toward Cripure. "We can go."

"Ah! At last."

Henriette had disappeared. Passing by the parlor, Moka opened the door. Cripure caught sight of the young girl. She was sitting on a Louis XV armchair, holding the little dog in her lap, petting it with an ecstatic smile.

"And bring him to me tomorrow at school, at eight, ok?"

"Oh! Yes."

Stranger and stranger, Cripure thought to himself, remembering the horrible hunchback with her haggard little yellow dog. *Stranger and stranger!* Moka's house was etched in his memory between two women and two dogs, like two sentries on guard at the door. *Yes, these are mysteries. All that can't happen by chance. Funny set of signs…*

"Hurry, let's go!"

THERE was no more passionate collector of antique weaponry known to man than Monsieur Babinot. For years, he hadn't missed a single Wednesday expedition to the auction house, to look over what was on offer in the way of sabers, pikes, old rifles and pistols. He even owned a blunderbuss. He also had a drum, which he thought had once belonged to a brigadier in the Italian Army—even better if it might have been Arcole's drum!—and which probably came from a company of firefighters. No matter! The most beautiful piece in his collection wasn't a rifle or a drum, but a real suit of armor, placed upright at the bottom of his stairs. The curved helmet, which the iron man held between his gauntleted hands, received the incoming mail.

Monsieur Babinot owned such a profusion of weapons, and he liked so much to see them, that after decorating the walls of his living room, he had decorated the walls of several other rooms and the foyer. It gave his house the curious atmosphere of a museum or an antique store. But it was his pride and joy.

All the weapons shone with grease and cleanliness. The pickiest sergeant who passed by in review would not have been able to find, even with the aid of a magnifying glass, the slightest speck of rust. It went without saying that Monsieur Babinot, when he wasn't writing poems, spent most of his spare time taking apart his weapons, showing them off, putting them back together, checking their mechanisms, oiling them, searching, on his walls, for the spots where they would be displayed to best advantage like an amateur painter with his canvasses.

One time in particular, unable to stop himself, he'd dressed up in

318

the suit of armor and appeared in the middle of a dinner he was giving for some friends. People still talked about it. What he would have given to wear the suit to a ball! Unfortunately, it was too heavy, and however much he loved the Middle Ages, for a ball he wanted something more fitting, a musketeer's outfit for example, or, the ultimate joy!—a uniform from one of Napoleon's officers. Ah! To be able to recite one day, at a party, in that uniform, Victor Hugo's immortal lines:

> Onward! Call in the troops!
> And lancers, grenadiers in high twill gaiters,
> Dragoons that Rome could take for legionnaires...

His collection grew endlessly. If the auction house had nothing, he'd make a circuit of the antiques fair, making a point to visit the second-hand stalls. Those poor fellows understood so little that you could sometimes get magnificent pieces for the price of a heel of bread. He'd found poisoned arrows a sailor had brought back from Africa and sold, an Australian boomerang, a little Venetian dagger, a beauty, made more for the hand of a woman than a warlord. Monsieur Babinot used it to cut the pages of the *Revue des Deux Mondes*.

Like any true collector, Monsieur Babinot was a man plagued with want in the midst of a treasure trove. He was missing the unique artifact, the object of his dearest dreams, the unfindable rarity. He had told himself many times that this object wouldn't be found at the market, that these kinds of things didn't belong to private individuals, but this reasoning was powerless—and he invented a thousand arguments for why it wasn't crazy to believe that one day he'd put his hands on it.

History could give all the details of what happened in war, but it couldn't tell everything, for the simple reason that it couldn't know everything. In the course of numberless battles fought between the French and the Germans over the years, how many flags had they torn from each other! People knew approximately which ones and in what circumstances. Approximately: that approximately was where he based all his hopes.

It wasn't impossible that one day, a little kid from our side had taken the enemy flag, that he'd hidden that flag inside his jacket, and there... but there Monsieur Babinot, in order to keep hoping, had to undertake a violent conflict with himself. What would he have done, in the place of that little French boy? Duty demanded that he bring the flag to the colonel, so that the glory of the capture could shower the whole regiment. But modesty could also counsel silence, modesty or passion, both against the rules, of course, but how noble! There was also chance, fatality, like in railway accidents. And finally, finally, the war was over, the kid sent home with one leg fewer, an eye smashed in, bullets everywhere, his stomach hollowed, but a flower in his teeth and his trophy in his pouch. He lovingly guarded the trophy all his life, and upon his death he consigned it, weeping, to his children assembled around his deathbed, like the farmer in the fable. Disasters followed. The children, to whom the heroic father had left only this treasured flag but no fields to till, were reduced to the deepest poverty. Once the children scattered, the flag fell into the hands of some ignoramus who sold it. And that's how, one day, with luck on his side and God willing, Babinot would get his mitts on an Imperial standard. Ah! God willing, on that day, the larger-than-life copy of Detaille's *The Dream*, which occupied a whole panel, would move elsewhere. Or maybe not, he'd switch its placement, but it was there, in the spot now occupied by *The Dream*, that he'd put the eagle ripped from the hands of the Teutons, like you stick an owl, to protect against evil, over a door. What an impression that would make! People would talk, his house would become famous. He'd give a speech for the Society of Inscriptions and Fancy Calligraphy. Researchers and curious people would write to him. He'd give his life to piecing together the history of the trophy and publishing a monograph.

But since he hadn't yet gotten his hands on an imperial standard, it was once again the *Dream*, the armor, the sabers, the pikes and the stakes, the blunderbuss and the drum, which greeted Nabucet's eyes as soon as the maid ushered him into the foyer. Everything wrapped in the good smell of cooking and polish.

What a lovely contrast, what delightful opposition, what charming juxtaposition was created, in the middle of the pistols and pikes, this grand scene, that tomb-like armor, by the pink and white complexion of the little maid! Oh how these military trophies made her sweet, virgin's look more precious than ever, her forehead resplendent with innocence, that young breast he couldn't begin to imagine! What delicate hips, like one of Jean Goujon's sculptures, far superior to anything antique!

The little maid backed away fearfully, looked for a doorway to escape. The bearded villain! How she hated him! How he frightened her. How wicked he seemed!

"Hello, my child, hello! I hope Monsieur Babinot is home. Tell me my dear child?"

"Yes, Monsieur..."

How her voice shook!

Cute enough to nibble, he thought, taking off his raincoat with a disinterested air. *Delicious. A fearful porcelain look beneath smooth black hair. What white skin! Not sixteen yet, I'm sure of it...*

He handed her his raincoat and hat with a look that made her blush to the neck.

"Excuse me," he said in his most caressing voice. She took the garments without saying anything and hung them on the coat rack. "Thank you, my child. It doesn't offend you that I call you 'my child'? You're so young! You haven't been in town long, is that right?"

She nodded her head.

"There! You must be quite careful," murmured Nabucet, in a fake-scolding voice, waggling his finger under the little maid's nose. "Very, very careful! Town is the downfall of pretty girls."

She looked down and started twisting the strings of her apron. What an evil gentleman he was! He came nearer himself.

"Oh!"

"You don't ever go to the movies?"

"..."

"You never go out at all?"

"..."

He whispered in her ear, "Not a little boyfriend somewhere, eh? Pretty! A little sweetheart, who puts an arm around your waist like this...eh? Who touches..."

"Let go of me."

"Come, come, come! You didn't understand me at all. You can't be a prude, can you, with a little face like that, with eyes like that, eh? How is he, your little boyfriend? He's brown-haired, isn't he, a dark-haired one?"

The little maid backed away to the foot of the stairs.

"Oh you're a brat! Go on then, Mademoiselle. Show me in, since you scorn my advice. Let's go up!"

So he could pinch her ass as he followed her upstairs like the last time? She didn't move.

"Show me up."

She rushed away, ran straight up the stairs in one go, to the second floor where Babinot's office was, and knocked on the door as if there were a fire.

It was so quick that Nabucet barely had the chance to glimpse a bit of calf.

What a brat, he thought, *astonishing for a welfare child*. He asked himself where she'd learned to be so prickly? Not on the farm where she was brought up, that was for sure!

He prepared a death glare for the moment when they'd cross on the staircase, a look that would tell her she didn't need to put on airs with him, in her situation! What were the Babinots paying her? Thirty francs a month?

But the clever girl escaped him. As soon as Babinot opened the study door, she sprinted up to the third floor instead of going back down.

More weapons! They'd be hanging from the ceiling before too long. At the top of an assortment, pinned to red cloth, swords and sabers crossed over a pointed helmet, among a bunch of pistols. Here and there, portraits of Generals that *L'Illustration* had published, Scott's drawings—an alpine hunter kissing an Alsatian girl. Of course there were postcards from the front, pinned with little flags. And on the mantel, between two shiny shell casings, Joan of Arc and her standard beneath a glass dome. A military-issue revolver served as a paperweight for Babinot, whom Nabucet found in a policeman's cap and an old infantryman's cloak, worn like a bathrobe. A fresh bandage wrapped around his head. He was in slippers and holding, between his fat fingers, a cheap, shoddy fountain pen. A drop of ink escaped from the pen's tip and sank into the parquet.

Delighted that Nabucet had surprised him in costume, Babinot stuck the pen behind his ear and jokingly saluted.

"At ease, at ease!" Nabucet commanded, extending his elegant hand. And Babinot shook it for a long time, bursting into his nasal laugh.

"Did I do that salute nicely, my dear colleague?"

"To perfection."

"Good. Very good." He pulled Nabucet over to an armchair. "Do you mind if I keep my cap?" he asked. "I just catch cold so quickly."

"Make yourself comfortable, my dear fellow."

Babinot couldn't live without his soldier's cap, which he wished he could wear around town. He settled into an armchair. "What fortunate wind blows you this way?" He was decidedly delighted by this visit. He was already thinking of how he'd read Nabucet the poem he'd just finished, and he was quivering with impatience.

Nabucet crossed his legs, brusquely hiked his pants at the knee to avoid creases, and said in his honey voice, "Excuse me, I'm disturbing you in the middle of your work."

"I was composing, my dear colleague."

"A poem?"

"May I?" said Babinot, stretching a hand toward the table. But with a light touch, barely ruffling the cloak. Nabucet stopped him.

"One moment! Yes," he went on, softening the stroke of harshness, "let's read the poem in a bit, dear Babinot. Even in advance I'm sure that it's excellent. But it's important that I tell you right away why I'm here."

"It's a very short poem, you understand."

"In a bit, dear friend, in just a moment."

"Ah! Fine, fine," said Babinot, very put out. "No harm done. I'm listening." What the devil could be so important it deserved to go before he read one of his poems?

These men of letters are all the same, thought Nabucet. And he asked, "You haven't heard the news?"

"What's happening, then?"

"My dear Babinot, an astonishing quarrel has just sprung up, and in a moment I'll give you the details. *Rumpitur dum nimium tenditur funiculus*: a cord stretched too tight finally broke. Briefly, in a word that equals a hundred, I'm going to fight a duel, my dear friend." And he got up. But not as quickly as Babinot, who, at the word "duel," bounced out of his chair as if projected by a cannon.

"What on earth are you talking about?" he cried, lifting his arms to the ceiling. "A duel! What on earth are you talking about?"

"The truth."

"A duel!"

"With swords."

"A duel! A duel! And whom are you fighting in this duel?"

Nabucet's look expressed the regret of a man who is faced with a task he doesn't approve of, but which he can't leave unfinished. "It pains me to inform you," he said in a wet voice, "that my opponent is our esteemed colleague Monsieur Merlin."

All of a sudden, Babinot couldn't breathe. His mouth gaping, his arms still raised, the bandage slipping more than ever, he was the picture of amazement.

"Oh! It's too much," he finally cried, letting his arms fall. "Too much, it's too much." He repeated at least ten more times that it was too much, then, when he'd mastered the double shock of this double news—a duel, that was a huge deal, but a duel with Cripure, that was humongous!—he wanted to know why they had quarreled.

"Let's not get upset! Above all, let's keep our heads and sit down. Have a seat, dear Nabucet, have a seat and tell me everything."

Nabucet had let Babinot shout and scrabble around all by himself, without so much as wiggling his little finger. He'd teach them all how a man worthy of the name should behave during serious business. What's more, it was easy. He knew well that Cripure wouldn't fight. But hush! He wasn't dumb enough to mention that to Babinot, or to anyone.

"Why would we get upset?" he replied, smiling. "I truly don't see the reason." And with the greatest ease, as if there was nothing more to do than talk about, for example, which flowers would go best in a bouquet for a pretty woman, he took his seat in the chair.

"Let's take it *ab ovo*," he said, "And know that first of all, my friend, there was a bit of a ruckus tonight at the station." He told him what had happened, but made the mistake of pronouncing the word "riot."

"A riot, you say?"

"No, no, just a little bit of noise."

"But you said it was a riot."

Babinot's eye shone. Ah! How far he was from the idea of a duel! By what reckoning, good Lord, did a duel have more importance than a riot? His old, toothless mouth opened wide. It took his breath away. "I understand everything now!" he cried.

And he was off. Nabucet didn't hold back an impatient gesture. Already, in a voice that contained the gravest and most beautifully nasal notes he'd ever produced, he continued, ending on the highest sharps, "They're my two scoundrels! Goodness, those are my scoundrels. If there was a bit of a ruckus tonight at the station, what you called a riot, my friend, it must be because of those two rascals!"

And rubbing his finger under the bandaged eye, he said again that it was all clear to him now, and that it must be the two German spies who, in the devious way of Dame Germania, had attacked the army's morale.

"Oh! The Boches are clever little bastards."

"I agree, my friend, I agree."

"They know how to make trouble . . ."

"Yes, oh yes."

"But we're just as clever as they are—that goes without saying. The proof is abundant."

A story? Nabucet had escaped the poem only to fall into a story? The gods were harsh. He tried to nip it in the bud. "To get back to it," he began.

But Babinot interrupted. "Yes, yes! In a bit, my friend. In a bit. Let's finish the riot first."

Nothing to be done! *Since he wants the riot, I'll give him the riot. It's still the shortest way out.*

"Riot! That's still a strong word," he said. "A very strong word, certainly, for a few shouts, a little barricade, a few songs..."

"Ah! Ah! Some songs?"

"Garbled."

"No matter, my friend! They'll use anything to destroy us, even garbled songs. For idealistic fellows like ours, songs, even garbled ones, sometimes have a great effect," said Babinot, very sententious, and once again, he waggled his finger.

Nabucet had nothing to say against that. And Babinot continued, "the good side of the story is that with each blow, we tear away their mask. Bam! Patata! And their crafty constructions are in ruins. They're patient, but we're sly. The rooster, my friend, the little Gallic rooster. Much cleverer than their fat mascot, that black eagle!" He burst out laughing.

How long would this go on? Nabucet wondered. He'd like to know, since maybe he should be thinking about asking someone else to be his second, even though it was right up this one's alley! "Everything worked out, and in the end, our little soldiers went on their way."

"Goodness!" Babinot exclaimed. "I was sure from the start. A riot, you understand, my friend, think about it! It's impossible. A revolution? French soldiers mutinying? Fairy tales, my friend, the stuff of legend. If all that hadn't been fomented by those two rascals, I'm telling you, if it weren't for the grumbling of a couple hotheads. But nah, nah, all that is nothing. Fairy tales! Don't make me laugh."

And he laughed, not quite as loudly as he had earlier, but softly, like a man who's thinking of the very good hand he's about to play.

This little laugh went on for a while, then finally slowed and stopped. Babinot resumed his serious look, gravely harsh, and remembering the reason Nabucet had come to see him he went on, "Excuse this digression, my dear colleague, but in these circumstances, what touches France touches us all. Now that we've been reassured on the subject of the little disturbance, come, my friend, tell me—what happened between you and Merlin? A duel! Who would have ever thought I'd hear someone speak of a duel in this room!"

"And if I were to ask you to be my witness? If you're willing! If you're willing!" Nabucet hastened to add, as if he thought for a second that Babinot would say no.

"For the love of God!" cried Babinot, "For the love of God, I'm willing!" He got up and solemnly laid a hand on Nabucet's shoulder.

"My dear friend," he gravely said, "I couldn't bear not being your witness. We'll look back on this moment. Listen to me." And, his hand still resting on Nabucet's shoulder, he turned his one eye to the ceiling. "You are a man for whom I have the highest esteem. I have no need to ask you the reason for the fight, no! Between a man like Merlin and a man like you, my mind is already made up, you can have no doubt about it." He lifted his hand and raised it. "I've known you for a long time, my friend. I've seen you at work. I know, by God, how much you've always given to the right side. And what's more, dear friend, what's more"—he tapped Nabucet's shoulder three times to underscore the importance of what he was about to say—"it isn't merely your witness I'd like to be but your second."

And his hand didn't move.

Nabucet had listened to this speech, his head lowered with perfect attention. As soon as Babinot was finished, he got up and, without a word, took both of his hands. The sly dog! He knew exactly what he was doing! He knew what he wanted to do to that Cripure!

"We understand one another, don't we?" Nabucet said in a voice that was strangled with emotion.

Babinot squeezed his hand even harder. "For the sake of full disclosure, my friend," he continued more slowly, "I found this afternoon so touching."

It was Nabucet's turn to close his eyes. He inclined his head a little to the side, as he was so expert at doing, and in the same voice full of emotion, he said, "I brought my modest contribution to a great thing. Something I believe in with my whole heart." And he shook his head, opened his eyes, and sighed.

"You said the most important things in such a simple way," Babinot insisted. "But the Romans are your mentors. You can feel it, it comes across. Your prose has the feeling of antiquity."

"Horace, my friend. Horace is the best."

"So—measured! It was so, so on point. I was truly moved."

"Dear friend—"

They finally let go of each other's hands and, not without embarrassment, sat back down in their chairs. With an already-familiar gesture, Babinot rearranged his bandage, while Nabucet hiked up his pants. He looked for his handkerchief to dry a little tear—

He wiped it slowly, hoping that Babinot would notice, but the old bore didn't pay any mind, and Nabucet, putting his handkerchief in his pocket, found himself at the height of surprise, seeing Babinot suddenly scratch his head around the bandage, frowning with one whole side of his face, and crying "Ai, ai, ai! I wasn't thinking! Or rather, I remembered, but...oh! Ai, ai!"

"What is it?"

"I have a conflict..."

"Ai!" said Nabucet in his turn.

"It's just that, you understand, I don't want to set tongues wagging and have it spread around...Tsk, tsk, tsk...this is so tricky!"

He made another face and stopped scratching, placing his hands on his knees. "It's...it's...it's just that, really, when those two scoundrels assaulted me this afternoon...well..."

"Well?"

"What? You didn't hear? But he was there! Cripure was the first one to come and help me. He picked up my hat, he took me to the pharmacist. Ah! My God what a confusion this is, what a pickle!" And Babinot got up, took a few steps around the room, his hands behind his back, and planted himself in front of Nabucet to ask, "Do you think that would get in the way?"

Nabucet took his head in his hands and thought deeply.

"You don't think so?"

"Hold on, I'm thinking."

"Tsk, tsk, tsk . . . my God, what a mess. What was he doing there anyway?"

"Wait! One moment!"

Babinot waited, continuing to pace around the room tut-tutting and exclaiming endlessly. He had stopped scratching his head and had moved on to his ear.

"No," said Nabucet, finally uncovering his face, "it's not a conflict."

"You think so?" said Babinot. "They're not going to spread it around in town that . . ."

"Not at all! Not in the least. And here's why:"

Babinot was all ears.

"I haven't yet told you the reason for the quarrel. But when you know it, my dear friend, all of your scruples will fly away like bits of straw, I promise you." And he looked Babinot straight in the eye. "He was on the side of the riot, my friend."

Babinot took a step back. And in the same way he'd so recently reacted to the announcement that there was going to be a duel, he raised his arms to the sky and cried, "What are you saying! For the riot!"

"Alas."

"Him!"

"Come now," Nabucet cried, "one would think you'd never met him! I can't naysay certain qualities of his intelligence, one must be fair, but he's always had a rebellious streak."

He rubbed his hands while he spoke.

"Yes, yes," said Babinot, who had started scratching himself again. "I see, I see. He attacks everything, he wants to destroy everything, he doesn't believe in anything."

"He is to be pitied."

"Nonsense . . . to be pitied? This is no time for pity or leniency, my dear Nabucet. To be pitied," said Babinot again, warming himself, "a revolutionary? Ah! Certainly not. It's too much, that is," he said, turning purple. "A rioter, and a professor too. One of ours! And I had forgiven him everything after his speech last year at prize day. Do you remember?"

"A normal speech."

"He had us right in his palm."

Nabucet spread his hands.

"We were looking from a bridge down on what was happening in the station. The chaos was almost over. Our colleague Merlin was resting, leaning on the parapet. My friend—I went over, greeted him simply, some little word about how we'd prevail despite all that trouble, and do you know, but do you know—"

His hatred in that moment made him hideous. But Babinot saw only noble indignation.

"Well, he slapped me!"

Babinot was strangled with shock, and once again his mouth hung open.

"Do you hear me?" said Nabucet, after a silence.

The other nodded his head.

"Do you have any more scruples?"

Babinot had no more scruples, but neither did he have a voice. He mumbled something.

"What was that?"

"Scruples! You're joking, my dear Nabucet," he finally managed. He found his voice again and said, "We had to be sure that, with him, we were dealing with a defeatist in hiding, and more dangerous because of it. Since the Dreyfus affair, my friend, haven't we known that he hated the army? No time to lose! Name a second witness and let's go! I'm with you, my friend, until the very end. And since it may be that you haven't fenced in quite some time—I say, let's go down to the cellar and take a few passes to brush off the rust. I have my foils. And don't forget," he said, caressing his goatee, "that I was a pretty scrappy swordsman in my day. Come on!"

At madame de Villaplane's, Kaminsky and his friends were having tea. In the dining room, a big fire was burning in the grate. Its brightness would have been enough to illuminate the room, but the maid had followed Kaminsky's orders to the letter. Instead of the oil lamp that usually illuminated the sad pensioners' meals, he had told her to put candles everywhere. As for the rest, the chandelier hanging from the ceiling suited his purpose perfectly. It was an old chandelier, which must once have belonged to Turnier's father and held up its candles during grand gatherings. They had also put candles on the end tables, along the walls, on the mantelpiece. Splendid roses were scattered on the white table linen, among the cups, fruits, pastries, bottles. Around the table, the conversation was in full swing. Kaminsky had Simone at his right hand, more animated, happier than ever. Like she had just done at her father's house, she placed her famous "book" on the table in front of her, and glanced at it from time to time, caressing it, touching, under the cover, the silky banknotes. She had a crazy desire to wave them under everyone's noses, to tell them the whole story, bursting with laughter. But saying nothing was a more intense pleasure. Fat Bacchiochi was holding forth at the front of the room, scarfing pastries, and all the while surveying Marcelle, his mistress, just brought over from Kaminsky's cottage in the prefect's car, driven by Léo. She was smoking, her elbows on the table, two hands crossed under her chin. Next to Léo sat Francis Montfort, more disheveled, more uncombed, more bohemian than ever, not taking his eyes off Kaminsky. There was an empty seat left, as if they were still waiting for a guest. "Maybe a ghost," Kaminsky said, laughing. And then he'd started telling stories.

"When I was little and someone scolded me, I took revenge."

"Bravo!" said Simone.

The others laughed.

"Depending on the severity of the scolding, I stole a silver plate or a gold plate, or some piece of art—my father had a magnificent art collection—and I'd bury them in the garden."

There was a silence.

"Strange," said Marcelle. "And then you'd dig them up and sell them?"

"Not at all. I'd lost interest. They're still there."

"Was anyone ever accused in your place?" Francis asked.

"Yes. One time, they fired a maid. I also hurt my mother's animals."

"Cats?"

"No, go figure. My mother adored rabbits. But wait—my mother wasn't a farmer. She tamed the rabbits. There were always a dozen little rabbits trotting around the house. She would comb them, perfume them, spend hours petting them. From time to time, I'd hang one."

"How horrible!"

"I didn't say it wasn't horrible. And even so, listen to this, I always loved animals—dogs and cats of course, but also grass snakes, for example. Except rabbits."

"Kaminsky, my dear, you're vile," Simone cried. "I'm warning you that I won't hear any more of your dirty stories."

She got up. He ran after her, took her hand, and kissed it. "My darling! I'd like to have my way with you on a bed of roses..."

"Let go of my hand!"

"My turtledove, my little flame... grass snakes aren't disgusting animals at all. People give them a bad name."

"Otto! Once again..." she stomped her foot.

"My little soul... I mean, I don't want to offend you. I cross my heart. Pardon me dearest, I won't speak about snakes anymore, no, I won't say any more, but it's a pity, chickadee, my little heart, it's really too bad."

He accompanied his speech with all sorts of little bows and caresses which made the parody even funnier. It was a game they'd recently discovered. They called it playing Russian Novel. In the game he had to call her Nastassia and she called him Batuchka.

"Batuchka," she said, "don't you fear God?"

"Don't I fear God, Nastassia?" he replied in a trembling voice. "How can you say I don't fear God?" And violently beating his chest: "Nastassia, yes, it's the truth, I confess it publicly. I'm a sinner, my soul is a gutter, yes, it's true I have no fear of God. The proof Nastassia, my little soul, is that this damned grass snake..."

"Batuchka! If I hear you mention that snake one more time..."

"But Nastassia, since it's a confession?"

"Touché!" cried Simone, doing a pirouette. "Since it's a confession, go ahead my dear. I can't have anyone say I prevented you from confessing, which is to say, saving your soul. We're all ears," she said, sitting back down and copying the movements of an old woman—putting on her pince-nez, smoothing a fold out of her skirt.

"Kaminsky's confession," the Polish man declared, standing behind his chair, his two hands pressing into the back. "Hmmm..."

An ambiguous smile parted his full, oval face, pale in the candle-light.

"A general confession," he said, rolling his *r*'s more than ever, "would be too long of an undertaking. I'd have to tell you the story of the little maid, and about my brother I didn't want to take care of anymore, and a little bit about Madame de Villaplane. For the moment, let's stick to the story of the grass snake."

"In this country, remember, a snake in the grass means a lie," Simone interrupted.

"Let it be a lie then," he replied, unflappable. And he continued, "This snake was in some ways a companion. I'd whistle: she'd come when I called, stand up on the tip of her tail, curl herself around my arm. I'd feed her milk, of course, and it was a spectacle as exquisite as the meals of my little lady friend. She was full of delicacy. When I'd go out, I'd take her in my pocket. She'd sleep soundly there. One day—" Kaminsky gave such a well acted sigh that even Simone was uneasy. "Nastassia, little dear, must I say everything?"

"All the rest, Batuchka, my little dove. God is listening, which means you must get down on your knees before your brothers."

"What follows is harder to say than the rest. Well then, here it is—one day, a devilish idea came into my head. It wasn't more than a vague idea at the start, a fantasy. And then...there was, in our town, a very pious old woman. Her son had died while blaspheming. She believed he was damned. Every day, she'd spend hours at the church, praying for his soul—while my mother was petting her rabbits. So what did I do, Nastassia? What did I do? I went into the church. God forgive me! I took the little grass snake in my pocket, and I put it in the holy water by the door, that's what I did. Then, I hid behind a pillar, and I waited. In the whole church, there was no one but the little old woman and me. She praying and me waiting. It was a long wait! Finally, she decided to get up, she softly came toward the door and, just as she was about to dip her fingers in the holy water, right at that moment the little snake rose up. And what did the old woman do? She gave a terrible cry, you understand, just terrible! Me, I stayed hidden behind the pillar. I saw her run straight out of the church, as fast as she could. She never came back. She died a few years later without ever setting foot in it again, convinced that she and her son were both damned. It was the devil who told her, which is why people thought she had gone crazy. There. You all have the right to think I was lying. And I do as well," he said, sitting back down. "But you're not drinking! You've got no drinks," he cried, uncorking a bottle of champagne. And he refilled the glasses all around. "Ah, ah, ah! One would say my little story had an effect on you. I'm going to give you some advice," he said, glancing at Bacchiochi, "you must take things in a positive light and not put too much faith in..."

"To the Confabulators," said Marcelle.

"That's it! That's just the word I was waiting for. Bravo! All this is

a joke. It's literature. Enough about me, let's talk about other people."
He continued: "Boredom drove a poet crazy after he'd been showered
with glory. He believed that he was dead for a long time, and became
the custodian of his own museum. He displayed the fountain pen,
the portrait of the woman he loved . . . he was otherwise a very kind
young man. That's it, end of story."

"Another one," Simone asked.

"Fine. In an honorable family, in the countryside very close to
here, there was a young girl of thirteen. A vagabond rapes the girl.
What happens then? The father can't bear to look at his daughter.
No matter how much the mother begs him, he becomes cruel to the
girl. The more the father suffers, the meaner he is. The little girl becomes depressed. She doesn't play anymore. Lads run after her, laughing, wanting to know about it. She threw herself in a pond. There,
end of story. Another one?" asked Kaminsky.

"A different kind," said Marcelle.

"Good. The story of a whore who runs away from a brothel, and
the police drag her back by force."

"No . . ."

This time there were more voices protesting. Fat Bacchiochi found
that the Pole was overdoing it again. Kaminsky smiled, looking from
one to the next.

"Let's move on," he said. "This kind of account frightens you. Let's
move on to something else. Do you all know Monsieur Trémintin?"

"Yes," said Francis.

"And you Marcelle?"

"Yes."

"Simone surely knows him, even though she's not saying anything."

"Yes."

"And you, Léo, do you know him?"

Léo didn't answer.

"You're nodding off, eh?"

Léo's big fleshy lip rose. The cigarette butt was stuck to it, like a
mole. He closed his eyes almost completely, and gave a scornful shrug.
"Not me."

"Do you know that you could be taken for a general, if we didn't know you were just the prefect's chauffeur?"

Léo raised his heavy eyelids like nutshells, with their strange white lashes, revealing a stormy gray-blue eye.

Kaminsky insisted. "How did you get your white hair?"

The legend was that Léo's hair had lost its color in a single night, a dramatic night when one of his mistresses, a young girl of twenty-two, had committed suicide right before his eyes. They accused him of killing her and only getting away with it because he had friends in high places, in the police department itself. He was certainly mixed up in something. Besides the young woman's suicide, there were Léo's past troubles and some other matters that were mysteriously hushed up, all giving the story some credit, compounded by the fact that since the war started, he hadn't left the prefecture.

"Fool," he murmured.

"Ah! So you're awake! Tell me, then, is it true that they wanted to get you out, to make you go to the front? Something serious for once?"

Léo nodded his head.

"And who do you think had it out for you? Do you have any idea?"

"Yes. More than an idea. I know." His eyelids lowered, he bent over the table with his arms crossed, hunching his neck down towards his shoulders, which were enormous. Kaminsky looked at Léo's hands.

"You have ... strong hands," he said.

"Get on with your story," Léo shot back. This was getting to be more than enough. "Tell us about Trémintin."

"I'm not forgetting Trémintin. So everyone knows him then, except maybe Monsieur Bacchiochi?"

"What!" Bacchiochi cried, "why I've run into him more than a hundred times in your office, my friend."

"That's right. His office is next door to mine. He went there every day for thirty years."

"Went there?" said Simone. "Has he died?"

"No! Wait a minute. He's only coming a little less regularly. He's not dead. He's ... he's asleep."

"In his office?"

"In his papers, my dear Francis. His nose in his papers. Asleep. He lost track of time. It happened ten days ago. No one suspected that the division chief was sleeping. When he woke up, it was nine at night. He was surprised himself, very very surprised. He told me, 'It's strange, I don't recognize anything anymore. My boxes, all this . . . It doesn't look familiar.' He went out into the night, he went home . . . he thought he was about to die, and he couldn't shake the idea. Then he had dinner, then he went to bed and slept, and the next morning when he woke up, he still thought he was going to die. He could do nothing to shake the thought. The next morning, it happened again! Since then, he comes to his office every once in a while, shuts himself in, and paces back and forth. He wanders around town for hours, preferring the night. He wanders, he walks. He doesn't go out in anything but a dark suit, as if he were dressed for a funeral. I left him a little note to invite him to our little party . . ."

Bacchiochi suspected that Kaminsky was fooling with everyone, and he was a bit worried he'd be asked his professional opinion of this clinical case. Evidently, it wasn't in his purview, this situation. This one was really pathological. Not his area of expertise. Francis looked at the empty chair.

"Is that chair for him?"

"I admit that would be a good joke. But I doubt he's coming. I really doubt it. He didn't read my note. He doesn't read anything anymore. He doesn't talk to anyone. He . . . wanders."

"For ten days now?" asked Bacchiochi.

"Today is the tenth day. This morning, I saw his wife, imagine that. A strange character: skeletal. And do you know what she told me? Here's exactly what she said: 'Yesterday evening, last night really, he came into my room around two a.m. and he sat down on the side of my bed. There, without saying a word, he melted into sobs, and he said to me . . . but it's not what he said that matters, it's how he looked at me. He held his finger in my face like you do when you're scolding a child. He kept on, kept on, and I was afraid. He was wearing his coat, with his hat on his head and a white tie, and tears were running into his beard. Him! And do you know what he said to me? He said, *I love you.*'"

The only sound was the fire, crackling in the hearth. All the faces were turned towards Kaminsky, and no one was eating or drinking. All of a sudden, a piercing laugh rang out—it was Simone.

"For once, you didn't lie," she cried. "Your story is certainly true from one end to the other. That's how they are! That's how they are!" she repeated with fury. "And then? Finish it."

Kaminsky shrugged. "Madame Trémintin made a desperate little movement with her hands when she told me this. I understood that she intends to lock up her husband. There. The story is finished. Another one?"

"That's enough," said Simone.

"Why?"

"I hate them!" she cried.

"Everyone here hates them," he said.

"No one more than I do..."

"And so... what's to be done?"

"To choose... oneself."

He burst out laughing in turn—and kissed her hand.

In the street, loud steps like the strokes of a hammer. Kaminsky bent his ear.

"Monsieur Trémintin, maybe?" said Francis.

"You think? Those are soldiers' steps?" said Léo. "There's got to be more than one of them."

Kaminsky went over to the window, but instantly jumped back. "In God's name! I can't bear to see that. No, no, no!"

"What's gotten into him?" Marcelle murmured, hurrying over to the window in turn.

Kaminsky, pale, squeezed his hands into fists and stamped his foot. "Let them in!" he ordered in a sharp tone. "Let them rest! Let them have something to eat!"

"But who is it?" said Francis.

"You won't be opposed, I hope, if I let them come in? Just look at them! Practically corpses."

They all ran to the window: Marcelle, Francis, Léo, Simone, Bacchiochi.

"Prisoners!"

Three men came down the street—two Germans and a Frenchman.

"Horrible, it's horrible," murmured Kaminsky, letting himself fall into a chair. "I can't bear it. Prisoners! Horrible. Francis!"

"My dear Otto?"

"Go bring them in. No, no, I can't bear it! The sight of a prisoner has an effect on me like . . . guilt," he said, wiping a hand across his forehead. "Excuse me, I'm getting riled up, but I'm not in control of my nerves. Oh, it makes me crazy," he said, getting up and stomping his foot.

Simone put a hand on his shoulder. "Calm yourself."

"But there's nothing for it," Kaminsky began, sullen. "Don't you understand?"

"Today they're in luck."

The prisoners came up the street, bending their backs under an enormous load. The poilu followed them, his rifle in a bandolier.

"I'd really like to know what this is about," murmured Bacchiochi. "Excuse me!" he yelled. And the poilu raised his head. "Hey! A major here."

He saluted, weakly.

"Come here!"

"Hep, boys, hurry up," the poilu cried, "halt!"

The prisoners immediately stopped, letting their heavy load fall to their feet and sitting down behind it.

The soldier approached the window.

"What's the deal with your men?"

"Two who were taken in Morocco, Monsieur Major."

"In retaliation?"

"I wish!"

"Are you going far like that?"

"Another few miles at least. Except, here you see, they can't go on anymore, Monsieur Major, sir. They're mostly done for."

"So that's why you made them go on foot with their equipment on their backs? There were no cars where you're coming from, eh? Which bastard gave you the order... bring them here."

And Bacchiochi turned, he too, pale with anger. His fat little hands trembled. "There's no shortage of bastards..."

The prisoners came in, dragging their kits in their hands. They swayed in their boots.

"Leave the baggage in the hall!" said the poilu.

Kaminsky, leaning against the wall, watched them come in and trembled.

"Do they speak French?" asked Bacchiochi.

"Not a word."

"Look at those poor men! Let them sit down, by God! I can tell they're done for with just one glance. Late-stage tuberculosis. And they made them... Me too, Kaminsky, my friend, these things make me crazed too, because you see, it's not the first time. And all this because there are some sort of idiots somewhere. Bring the bottles. Make them something to eat, we'll take them in the car right away, eh Léo. Fuck your orders, you understand?" he said to the poilu. "This is on me. What are they putting in the bottles?"

"Hot tea," said Marcelle.

"That works."

"I'm putting together some cakes and some fruit."

"Good."

Kaminsky gave them money, many bills, which they took with indifference.

"It's not to the camp I'm taking them, but to the hospital. You tell that to your superiors, my good man."

"Very good, Monsieur Major."

"And if ever the bastard skrimshanker who gave you that dirty job falls under my watch, you can tell him I'll give him special attention, oh yes. Where is my cap? Are you ready, Léo? Quick, let's go. They should already be in bed."

For a long time after the prisoners left, they didn't speak. They didn't dare look at each other either. It was with discomfort that they came back to their places at the table.

The fire was dying, but no one thought to revive it.

"Much will be pardoned you," Simone finally said.

Kaminsky sent her a sharp look. That better not have been a joke!

"How do you mean, dear Simone?" He had stopped calling her Nastassia.

"As you yourself understand it: because you have loved greatly."

"Enough of that! I'm far from being a good man. As for forgiveness, the idea disgusts me."

"Is that true, dear Otto?"

"There is no shadow of that cowardice in me," he said, raising his eyes to his mistress with a look that was thoughtful and tender. "Did you see their faces?"

"And so, dear Otto, those men must hate their persecutors and get revenge?"

"Hate them and get revenge, yes."

"Yes?"

"Until death."

She took his hand and held it. "I love you for that as well," she said. "For that too, you will be pardoned."

He smiled. "Because I've hated often?"

"You said so."

"Well then, dearest Simone, for once at least, let me tell the whole truth. I will only receive a middling pardon, because I have only experienced middling love and middling hate." He looked into her eyes. "I never fully commit myself to anything."

She hesitated, then said, "Out of caution?"

"Alas, no," he replied. "By nature."

She gave a smile that was oddly complicit, and squeezed Kaminsky's hand more tightly in her own. "So there was a bit of theatrics in that affair?"

"What affair?"

"The business of the prisoners?"

He thought for a moment. "No," he said, "but it never lasts long."

She smiled again. "You wouldn't throw yourself into the sea for me, would you?"

"No, alas. I'm not crazy for the absolute like that Turnier, whose ghost hasn't decided to appear…"

Bit by bit, his voice returned to its normal tone. The usual Kaminsky came back.

"It's true that…I'm not Mercédès," said Simone, still with the same smile. "I won't abandon you."

Marcelle and Francis, embarrassed by this exchange, were happy with a direction that would let them reenter the discussion.

"Don't forget that they conspired against him," said Francis. "Mercédès was whisked away."

"What do you mean whisked away?" asked Marcelle, in a particularly sugary voice, implying that if she had been in Mercédès's place, she wouldn't have let it happen. She stubbed out her cigarette butt in her saucer and brought her hands together under her chin.

"Popped straight into a car and from the car onto a train," Kaminsky replied.

Marcelle replied, "That's the plot of a bad movie. Nowhere but in bad movies do families dare to whisk away young women in love like that." She gave a tiny shrug.

"Are you condemning Mercédès, Marcelle?"

"Yes."

"And you Simone?"

"You have to ask?"

"Our young student, do you condemn her too?"

Francis condemned her too. In his view, the two lovers should have run away together as soon as they realized their love. Anyway, they were to be pitied.

"Pity?"

"Yes, pity."

Kaminsky turned toward the empty chair.

"My friends, it was here that Turnier lived his last hours. It was this very armchair where he sat, biting his fists, I imagine, while he waited again for Mercédès, the second day. I propose, whatever your feelings about him and about Mercédès, we drink a toast to his memory, since we are all his comrades."

He lifted his glass first, holding it between his fingers, and the others followed.

"To unhappy lovers," he said, formal and grand.

"In that case," said Francis, "we must also drink to Monsieur Trémintin."

"To Monsieur Trémintin," said Kaminsky.

"And to Cripure…"

"To Cripure!"

They clinked their glasses.

After emptying his, Kaminsky, without sitting back down, continued:

"Do you know what I think? Well then," he said, "oh! Of course, I don't want to give a lecture, but in the general way, in the social structure, psychologically, well then, we find ourselves right smack in the middle of imperial Russia, my friends. Your Christian petty bourgeoisie, it's the bourgeoisie of Tolstoy. And your peasants are real serfs. Yes, I'm serious. Believe me," he went on, "the finest characters, in, for example, Chekhov—I've run into them here trait by trait, minus the samovar." He stopped, his tone closer to anger than irony, then went on:

"A great Russian writer devoted a whole book to the portrait of a man who spits in the curtains because he's bored."

"Oh!" Simone cried, "my father doesn't spit in the curtains. He's too busy stealing from other people for that. But as soon as he gets the chance, he writes anonymous letters and cuts up borrowed books."

"Not bad," said Kaminsky. He continued, "all the same, they're missing that streak of madness that possesses even Gogol's vilest characters, and which always stopped me from totally scorning those individuals. I understand Gogol and the others better since the Bolsheviks won. The revolution ripped off all the covers and brought everything to light. Hmm…Yes, this could be Minsk, or Rostov, or

Novgorod, or Yaroslav. You understand that we have our pick. The houses would be wooden instead of stone, and there would be domes with a few orthodox crosses. But you also have quite a few churches and quite a few convents. Yes, Minsk, that's to say…" And he stopped with his mouth wide open—Cripure and Moka were standing in the doorway.

"Fascinating! What you say is extremely relevant. And so, for you, the connection…" and Cripure closed his eyes, lifted his pince-nez, and passed his index finger slowly over each eyelid, without letting go of his cane all the while. "The similarity," he continued, "is so absolute…yes, yes." And he put his pince-nez back in place, murmuring, "their souls are dead." And he was quiet.

A bitter wrinkle curled his lip.

Everyone was standing.

"Monsieur Merlin!"

They hadn't seen him come in. He stayed there for a moment, and Moka, at his side in his nice suit, a white flower in his buttonhole, had the air of an impresario about to present his troupe's best number to the public. He didn't give Cripure his arm (impossible because of the grocery bag he was still carrying) but, in a delicate gesture, he took his elbow, and holding out his hat as if begging, the red forelock more vivid than ever on his chalky forehead, he smiled at each one in turn, as if to say that they hadn't seen anything yet, and that this was just the beginning.

"Excuse me," said Cripure.

"Excuse us," said Moka.

"We didn't dare to interrupt you. And what you were saying just then—it was a revelation for me, you understand…" He played with his pince-nez again.

"The business which brings us here," Moka said.

"Yes, yes, that will suffer no delays."

"And," said Moka, "there was no one to announce us. There you have it. We barged in."

"We're looking for a Monsieur Bourcier."

Kaminsky decided to leave the table. He went over to Cripure, his hand held out. "But come, you are welcome here. You are my guests, gentlemen." He looked inquiringly at Moka. "Monsieur?"

Moka bowed. "They call me Moka." No use pining after lost time!

"Monsieur Moka," said Kaminsky, "would you please accept... and you Monsieur Merlin...whatever the importance of the business that brings you here, you must certainly have a few minutes and wouldn't refuse to sit down with us? It's a farewell party..."

"A strange coincidence," muttered Cripure.

"Shall we accept?" said Moka.

"But come, my boy! An invitation made with such good will, isn't it? Let us sit. I...permit me only," he said turning to Kaminsky, "to put down these..."

He held up his cane and his grocery bag.

"Right away!" said Moka, taking them out of his hands.

He put them down on a side table, along with the little cloth hat that it had just occurred to Cripure to remove.

"Have a seat," said Kaminsky, pointing to the armchair that was still empty, since Monsieur Trémintin hadn't decided to turn up, and since Turnier's ghost had wisely remained invisible. "That seat has been waiting for you," he said, sending Simone a conspiratorial look.

"If I understood you right, you've lived in Russia?"

Moka pulled his sleeve. "Let's speak first about our business."

"In just a moment, my friend, just a moment..."

"Until the revolution," Kaminsky replied, filling two champagne glasses himself, and holding them out, "I was a Russian subject. I completed all my studies at Varsovie. I traveled widely in Russia, and for two years I lived in St. Petersburg."

He spoke standing up, a glass of champagne in his hand. Something in Cripure's look seemed to fixate on Kaminsky. He burst out laughing, in a way that made everyone jump. It was a short laugh, sharp, which stopped all of a sudden, as if chopped off. Cripure settled into his chair, sagging, his vague hands on the edge of the table, head slumped into his shoulders, as if he had fallen into one of his singular trances which sometimes lasted so long. Kaminsky looked around the table, a look full of questions to which the others replied with wide eyes, doubtfully biting their lips. Moka alone winked at Kaminsky, as if to say that Cripure's reverie wasn't important, that he knew all about it, that he knew what was going on under there, and that in any case it wasn't serious. Try as he might to communicate through gestures the reason they had come, it was impossible to guess what he wanted to say with his manner of holding out an arm or sticking his fist beneath one eye and pointing his index finger.

What was up with him? All his miming strangely resembled the gestures of children hooting during a game.

Cripure shook himself like a fat dog who's just woken, and got to his feet, saying, "Let us drink while we may!"

They all stood and clinked their glasses.

"Let us drink," said Cripure again, "for tomorrow may be too late. At last, Messieurs, and you, Mademoiselles, it is time I told you the reason for our visit. Tomorrow, we're fighting a duel," he said, raising his glass.

And Moka, who had been waiting only for this moment, got up and made a grand gesture, his glass in one hand and his hat, which had been on his lap, in the other. And as if he'd worried they would doubt what Cripure was saying, "It's the complete truth," Moka said. "We have a duel on our hands."

They looked at each other. A duel! It was unbelievable!

"A duel!"

"An affair of honor," said Cripure.

"A real duel?" asked Simone.

"Mademoiselle, how can you ask!" cried Cripure. "Of course it is. A duel . . . yes, a real duel."

Kaminsky himself was shocked. Which one of them had to fight? Since when it came down to it . . .

"But which one of you?" he asked. "Is it you, Monsieur Moka?"

Cripure waggled his finger. "By no means." And he pointed to himself. "It's on my honor."

The whole group was silent. Cripure broke the quiet to specify, "A duel with pistols."

"At twenty paces," said Moka. He was repeating what Cripure had told him on the way over. "I'm Monsieur Merlin's witness. And we came to find a second witness, Lucien Bourcier. And Monsieur Bourcier is a friend," he said, waving. "Do you know him?"

"Do you know him?" said Cripure.

"Do we know him?" asked Kaminsky, coming to, and discovering with joy the vaudevillian aspects of the situation. "Yes, we know him. He's the young man who arrived this morning, and who, it seems to me, hasn't gone out since." He clapped his hands. "Ernestine!"

Ernestine appeared.

"Monsieur?"

"Your new boarder, Ernestine?"

"He's in his room, sir."

"*Bono, bono,*" said Cripure.

"If you please," said Moka, "Would you please, Mademoiselle, tell him that he is needed below? It's on behalf of Monsieur Merlin... It's very important. Tell him... tell him it's about a... No, don't tell him anything. I'll go myself. The way, if you please?" He looked at Cripure and winked. "I'll have him convinced in two minutes."

"Second!" said Cripure, with a slow movement of his arms, "Do your duty!"

FOR THE whole day, Lucien Bourcier hadn't left the boardinghouse. He'd stayed in his room, sometimes pacing, sometimes lying down on his bed. At noon, he'd gone down to the dining room and found himself alone, Madame de Villaplane having decided to eat in her room. And once lunch was over, he'd gone back upstairs.

What else could he do? He'd learned to control his impatiences, large and small.

He was writing when Moka knocked.

"Come in!"

And stunned, he saw the tutor enter.

"How the devil..." said Lucien, getting up.

"Hush!" said Moka. "Excuse me, my friend. When you know what brings me here...ay!"

And mysteriously, he placed a finger to his lips.

"But how on earth did you find me here?"

"Very simple—Francis Montfort told me."

After all, Lucien hadn't sworn Francis to secrecy.

"You're here on behalf of my father?"

"No."

"Ah! Very well then."

He offered Moka a chair, but he refused. "No, no, my friend, it's not about sitting, it's not about...well, it's not a social visit. I came to ask you to do a great service, not for me, but for one of our mutual friends, a great friend."

"Tell me."

"You can't guess who?"

"Tell me!"

"Cripure!"

Moka held himself very straight in the middle of the room and spoke with an odd lack of gestures, his hands linked over his stomach, his hat under his arm. He looked straight into Lucien's eyes, which darkened at the mention of Cripure.

"What does he want with me?"

"He wants...that's to say...He has to fight a duel, you see!"

Moka lifted his arms and the hat fell to the floor. He picked it up.

"What do you mean?" said Lucien. "Is this a joke?" Cripure, fighting a duel? Had the poor old man gone crazy? "You can't be serious?"

"I didn't believe it either," Moka replied, "but alas..."

"A duel! Against whom?"

"Nabucet. He slapped him."

"Slapped? Why?"

"It was a...universal slap, Cripure told me. When it comes down to it, he hit him. At the train station. Oh, it's been building for a while, this business. For a long time, Cripure and Nabucet..."

"But come on, it's idiotic. It's completely stupid. We can't let them do this. It's...grotesque."

"He's asking if you'll be his second."

"Me?"

"With me. You won't refuse?"

"Of course not." Too bad, he'd delay his departure if it came to that, but he couldn't deny Cripure this service.

"Bravo. He's downstairs, you know."

"Cripure?"

"Yes, with a bunch of other people. Montfort. A certain Monsieur Kaminsky, two young girls..."

"What do all these people have to do with the duel?"

"Nothing...But they invited us to join their little party and we accepted."

"In what senseless world…"

They scrambled down the stairs as fast as they could.

Downstairs, around the table, they seemed to be occupied with other matters than the duel. Kaminsky, in finer form than ever, fiendishly excited by Cripure's presence, offered yet another toast, and Cripure, standing, held his glass towards Simone's.

Moka and Lucien's appearance didn't seem to bother them.

"Just as you were arriving, or perhaps a little before," Kaminsky was saying, "we were talking about Turnier. You're aware, of course, my dear sir, that this was where he lived."

"But how can you ask!" cried Cripure. "They should really put a marble plaque up, don't you think, to teach future generations how to die for a woman!" He burst into laughter. "Ah! Ha! Poor, poor man!"

"And so, in your opinion, he was a wronged man?"

"A very wronged man, Mademoiselle," replied Cripure, turning toward Simone.

"And Mercédès?"

"Mercédès?" Cripure dreamily replied, all traces of a smile vanishing from his lips, "oh! Mercédès—that's another thing."

"Should we also drink to Mercédès?" asked Kaminsky.

Cripure didn't answer the question. He murmured again, "Mercédès…"

He raised his head and everyone could see that his eyes were full of tears.

Kaminsky watched him out of the corner of his eye. Lucien, standing next to Moka, didn't dare come forward. The two young women exchanged a look. Cripure put back his glass without sipping it. He sat down.

"Mercédès refused," he said, in a sullen voice. "But why are we talking about Mercédès again? This morning already… Leave it! Let's forget it."

And he slumped brokenly into his chair.

Moka bounded over to him, bent down and whispered in his ear, "He accepts."

"Who?" said Cripure.

"Lucien."

"Ah! *Bono, bono.* With Faurel as a referee. That my friend, that's first-rate. Don't you think so?"

"That's how it's done."

Moka went over to Lucien, and Kaminsky went on, "Back to the subject of Mercédès..."

But at that instant, the door slammed open, and Madame de Villaplane appeared, pale with anger. All the faces turned towards this unexpected apparition.

She gasped.

"I find," she said in a snapping little voice, "that you have the audacity to condemn Mercédès without hearing her side." And doing her part for the general atmosphere of shock, she added, "I am Mercédès!"

Her words dropped into a solemn silence, and for a few moments, it seemed to everyone that the silence would continue for some time. Cripure, stooped in his chair, shot Madame de Villaplane a look of surprise, astonishment, and possible collusion, mixed to great effect. Kaminsky's laugh rang out.

"But come now, my dear Madame," he cried, "your name isn't Mercédès!"

"Fool!" Madame de Villaplane shouted, advancing on Kaminsky. She must have wanted to slap him with her fan, but she had to content herself with miming it. "Fool!" she said again, "That was my name before. But because he alone had the right to call me by that name, I changed it after his death."

And to their astonishment, the good little woman hid her face in her hands and burst into tears.

Kaminsky winked and, gesturing "no" with his finger, he touched it to his forehead.

"You think so?" murmured Cripure

The question made Kaminsky laugh. "Devil take me," he said,

approaching Madame de Villaplane, "but the old lady's still tempting." He rubbed the nape of her neck: "Go on my little dove..."

"Oh!" said Madame de Villaplane. And her little porcelain hand
smacked Kaminsky's oily cheek.

Cripure tugged Moka's sleeve. "Let's go, my friend, let's get out of
here... fly the coop, if you know what I mean! I think this..."

"You're right," said Moka, "I think this is just heating up."

"Do you think you're some kind of conquistador?" cried Madame
de Villaplane, glaring proudly at Kaminsky. "Brute!"

Moka quickly gathered up the bag of groceries, the cane, and the
little hat, and, with a thousand apologetic grimaces towards Lucien
and Francis, who had also stood up, ready to leave, he followed Cripure, who was already out the door.

Lucien called him back. "Don't leave yet, Monsieur...we have
some things to settle together."

"Ah, so we have," said Cripure, "that's true!"

He turned to Lucien. "Thank you, dear friend. It's very kind on
your part. Thank you."

"But of course."

"With Faurel arbitrating, right?" He thought if anyone could get
him out of this business it was Faurel. He didn't have great confidence
in Moka or Lucien, and thought that they wouldn't dare speak of his
handicap, while Faurel would be quite willing.

"But that goes without saying," said Moka.

"Excuse me," said Cripure, "but this isn't the place to talk. Moka
will explain everything to you... elsewhere."

And without another word, he fled.

Meanwhile, Madame de Villaplane went after Simone, whom she
had just called a hussy.

"I forbid you to call Simone that!"

Simone laughed, without apparent meanness. "Leave it, Otto, leave
it my dear."

"What?" said Kaminsky. "Go wait for me in my room, Simone, so I can have a moment alone with this...old loony."

He went over to the "old loony" who stood in the middle of the room, her hands open, her eyes burning, looking in front of her without seeming to see. Kaminsky approached as Simone disappeared, and this time, Madame de Villaplane gave no resistance to the caress he gave to her cheek, and she seemed to take no offense at his informal address: "You too would like very much to leave your world, but you can't. Come now, dear...you'll stay here with your precious memories..."

This time, Madame de Villaplane turned on her heel with the dexterity of someone possessed and ran out of the room. Moka barely had the time to glimpse her.

"This is going to be a big scene," said Kaminsky. "That's it! I bet you she's going to scream!"

Madame de Villaplane's voice did in fact ring out, more imperious, more pleading than ever. "Monsieur Kaminsky! Monsieur Kaminsky!" And since he didn't respond quickly enough to her demands, "Otto! Come quick, quick, quick!"

Abandoning Moka and Lucien, Otto sprinted up the stairs four at a time and went into Madame de Villaplane's room, slamming the door behind him. "One must say, where your manners are concerned..." he began.

But she didn't give him time to finish. She threw herself down at his feet and started to wail, with hot tears, "Take me away! Take me away! Take me away!"

He tried to push her back, to untangle his knees, which she'd wrapped in her arms.

"Stop crying."

"Don't leave me...Otto, if you leave without me, I'll die, I'm sure of it. Take me away! Take me away!"

"Stop your cries this instant!"

"Say you'll take me away."

"First stop shouting. And let go of me why don't you." He tore himself violently from Madame de Villaplane's grip, and she got up, no longer shouting, still wet with tears. They both hesitated for a moment.

"What do you want with me, when it comes down to it?" he said in an exasperated voice.

"He has to ask!" she said, brushing herself off, her hands falling back to his knees. "Haven't I told you a hundred times? Oh, Otto! Otto! You're cruel," she murmured.

He leaned forward, as if he had trouble hearing. "Cruel?"

"Oh! Yes." She cried like a little girl, almost without sound.

"But," he said, "it's you who've... don't make me be really cruel, dear Madame, no, don't go against me. You've put me in an impossible situation. Good sense..."

"Good sense! Good sense!" Madame de Villaplane interrupted with a bitter laugh, "Oh! Don't torment me with your good sense, I beg you." She lapsed back into a sharp, sarcastic voice. "Good sense? But do you know what you're saying... what it means, to me, your good sense? It means," she said in a sullen voice, "that if you leave without me, everything, for me, is finished. Do you understand?" She got up, approached Kaminsky, and repeated once more, "Do you understand?"

This time it wasn't comical anymore.

"Tell me!" she said.

Angry with himself for feeling so clumsy, and, in a way he hadn't predicted, so beaten, he replied, "That's not the question."

"Oh!"

Shock. Her eyes glazed, her mouth hanging open, she looked at him with scorn, leering. And her fury took over again, not the earlier howling fury but a mute fury. She began to speak almost without moving, with only a brief blink from time to time.

He stood before her.

"Heart of stone! I don't doubt it," she said, bringing her hands together, and from then on she spoke with her hands joined. "I can't take it anymore, how many times did I tell you? Is it true?"

"Yes."

"Brute! I can't go on living like this, and especially, oh, especially..."
She shivered.

"What?"

"I don't want to die like this."

In the space of a few seconds, she grew younger and older by turns, passion giving her eyes a juvenile gleam, a warm shine. But since she had spoken of death, it seemed to Kaminsky that her face was decomposing. The eyes aside, she became paler, and her teeth chattered.

"No, no, no," she said, shaking her head. And her voice, which was ordinarily so firm, wavered. But she got hold of herself. "No. Not this way. I don't want this."

He sighed.

"Listen."

"I'm listening," he said.

"I'm old in years, and I'm afraid of death. But I'm young at heart, younger than my body would lead you to believe. Do you understand?"

He understood. His gesture indicated that he understood perfectly. And even that he was not without compassion. But what else could he do besides hurt her?

"And I'm in love."

"Yes?"

He couldn't stop himself from smiling.

"With you," she said.

He didn't respond, not even with a look. Madame de Villaplane didn't consider herself beaten yet. She pushed him towards an armchair where he sat, she made sure, and continued, appearing very calm.

"I want to tell you everything. Everything."

He crossed his legs. This nonchalance didn't stop her.

Silence. She pulled back, waiting, perhaps, for him to speak first. But since he said nothing, she raised her head.

"Otto?"

"..."

"Dare to look me in the eye and listen. Say something! Look at me."

He looked at her.

"Good. You, you can hear and understand everything. You don't think it's ridiculous for a woman of sixty to be in love again. Once again," she said bitterly, "I'm telling you it's for the first time. If you knew my life! You, whose spirit is free and profound—"

"..."

"Yes, I'm sixty. But my body's no older than forty, it's true."

She suddenly stood.

"Do you want me to bare myself for you?" She glared at him.

"Come, calm down," he said.

"What was that?"

"Calm down, won't you? No hysterics. What an idea..."

"He doesn't want me! Oh," she cried, and leaning towards him, and putting a sharp little fist under Kaminsky's chin. "You act towards me, like they act... all those you pretend to scorn, to hate. You too, Otto, you're a contradiction of yourself. Cruel!" she gasped. "Think that in any case, I can't have more than a few years left to live, two, three, maybe five. If you refuse, I'll finish out my days here, in this... cellar, among these memories I hate, people I hate, a whole life I hate," cried Madame de Villaplane, losing all self-control. The tone of her voice climbed and finished on a horrible, sharp note.

"Unbearable," Kaminsky muttered.

"Unbearable, ah, yes! Yes, it's unbearable!"

He got up, wanting to take her hand just as he had taken Simone's a moment ago. She didn't let him.

"Those memories you send me back to!"

"But I think it's quite the opposite..."

"Ah, ah, ah! You knew I lied, especially when I pretended to be Mercédès? Yes, it was a lie. But that wasn't the biggest lie. That was when I told you about my prefect father and colonel grandfather."

"What? What? Your grandfather wasn't a colonel and your father wasn't a prefect?"

"Oh! The perceptive man! Yes, they were certainly all that. That wasn't where I lied."

"You're an abyss, dear Madame."

"And you, my dear Monsieur, you're nothing but a little paper-pusher, a pathetic psychologist, despite your grand airs. And again, a heart of stone. You call me dear Madame—will God permit it? Tell me, will you leave me here to die like this? Will you? Listen, I'm not finished..."

This clump of words, this mix of truth and lies, passion and reason, dazed Kaminsky. Just then, she had refused Kaminsky's hand, but now she took it in hers, raised it to her lips, and held it.

"Listen. I wasn't resigned, just the opposite, I was desperate. Nothing but death in sight. Until the day you showed up, there wasn't an hour where I didn't curse my life. But I loved you. I thought then that life could be worth it. But you refuse. Listen: I'll just be near you, I'll be your maid. What do you say? You can have all the mistresses you want. I'll be Simone's maid, without jealousy. But take me out of here. Rip me out of this tomb. Let me die in love. Speak, speak? You don't say anything! He says nothing!" She said, letting go of his hand. "He refuses! Oh despicable... murderer..."

And as her furious delirium took over, she twisted her hands, burst into sobs, while Kaminsky ran away.

THROUGH streets deserted as if after a plague, between unlit houses, Cripure darted, leaning heavily on his cane. Tired. He went along the walls so as to keep out of sight, since when it came to it, it would be easy for brigands to assault him, knock him down, rob him or— and was it so impossible?—murder him. Footsteps. He shivered. Someone walking down the middle of the road. Who? A man? Yes, something that resembled a man. A thief? The man passed very close to Cripure, his hat low over his eyes. It was Glâtre, also in a hurry, squeezing in his pocket the money that was ready, the exact sum he usually gave to the hostess at the brothel.

He passed and Cripure breathed a sigh of relief. All the same, it was a warning. Wasn't he more likely than others to fall prey to robbers? And wasn't the best defense of running away denied him also?

The cab, oh what luck!

Cripure rushed over to it—stopped at the edge of the sidewalk, and cried, "Stop! Coachman, stop!"

Old Père Yves bobbed his head and sat back in his seat.

"Well, Monsieur, very well."

"Ah!" said Cripure, climbing into the cab, "ah!" He threw in his cane and his grocery bag, and gripping the doorway with both hands, he pulled himself onto the seat, the springs groaning.

"On your way, coachman!"

Père Yves clicked his tongue and the cab gently set off.

Cripure let himself fall back into the cab as the wheels bounced over the badly paved streets, and he half closed his eyes. A lull. Sometimes, you got an unexpected break. It was pleasant to let himself be rocked in that old, creaking cab, with the upholstery trailing in ribbons. Père Yves, sitting up straight on his box, made little noises from time to time to keep Pompon going. The town was almost cheerful, like a town you are arriving in or just leaving. He stretched out, not very different, really, from who he would be tomorrow, afterwards. *But no, I can't think about that. I'll go tell Maïa everything.* That thought made him happy. He contented himself with it for a while.

The town disappeared, if it's possible to say that something so unreal could vanish, and with the jingling sound of bells, the cab left the town center.

How nice it would be to roll along like this for a while, rocked by Pompon's gentle trot, to go straight ahead without thinking about anything, to let the night come in, to drink in the moon, and to wake up tomorrow in a real dawn, reborn,

In deinem Tau gesund mich baden.

But to be reborn! Was everything really given once and for all, and must he finally believe in fate?

The cab pulled up in front of the low little house, which for the moment was silent and dark. Cripure got down as clumsily as he'd climbed up. After giving Père Yves the usual forty sous, he picked up his cane and grocery bag, and, making sure not to trip on the stone sidewalk, he went up to the door. The cab made a half turn, and while Cripure rang, listening for the sound of Maïa's clogs and the yapping of the little beasts, Père Yves's whip cracked the shadows, and the cab faded away to the sound of tinkling bells.

Maïa came running. Her steps clacked on the wood of the corridor and the little beasts yapped. "Come on, be quiet! Enough, Turlupin, enough Mireille! But the yapping only increased, the little beasts jumping against the door she carefully opened.

In her rough blue work apron, her arms red from being plunged in dishwater, she appeared. "Where were you, babe? Getting home so late—you should be shamed to show up at this hour…"

He went in, dragging his cane and his grocery bag, head lowered, looking at Maïa from under the brim of his crooked hat. The little dogs jumped for joy around him, and he cursed at them.

First things first, he had to get out of his dressy clothes, take off that tailcoat, the too-tight vest, to get back into his old hunting jacket and slippers. To breathe again, by God!

He put his bag down in the corridor, handed his hat and his cane to Maïa, took off his goatskin and went into the kitchen. All the while she was muttering stories that he didn't even listen to, gossip from the neighborhood maybe, or something about her stew, and she helped him out of his clothes and back into the old ragged pants, the black jacket, the velvet vest, the big slippers, and the red scarf. He still wasn't saying anything. But she didn't need him to respond in order to keep talking. It was often like that when he came home from town, especially in the evening. He didn't say a word, sometimes not responding for hours, even to questions. It depended on what he had seen on the way, or more often, what he had drunk. She didn't pay attention to it anymore.

She carefully folded the dressy clothes and put them back in place in the wardrobe. Cripure, arranging his muffler, sat on the edge of the bed. He bent his head, deeply absorbed, it seemed, in the contemplation of his slippers. Maïa set the table.

All four of the dogs slept around the stove.

"Maïa?" He thought he spoke very loudly, shouted even, but Maïa didn't move.

"Maïa?"

"What's going on? You're not coming down with something at this hour," she said, turning around. "Yer face looks like a wet cabbage. What's wrong with you?"

He lowered his head, and like a child admitting a mistake: "Maïa, I'm going to fight."

"What's that?"

"I'm going to fight a duel."

He said it with his chin trembling, close to tears, in a little pale, wavering voice. His fat hands hung between his knees and his forehead was lowered. He looked at the wench through his eyepiece, with an air of pleading.

"He's dreaming!" muttered Maïa.

"No. I'm not dreaming. I'm fighting tomorrow morning, at dawn."

It was obvious to him she hadn't yet understood—from the way she was looking at him, fists balled on her hips, eyebrows raised, and that dazed air, like a fat gossip at the washbasin who doesn't believe her ears! But soon, by tomorrow in any case, she'd understand perfectly when they brought him home on a stretcher.

"So I'm the one who's dreaming?" she said. He was going to fight? How? With who? And why did he need to fight? "Who's that you want to fight?"

He hesitated—the modesty of hate—to pronounce the name of his opponent. He tried twice before admitting in a whisper, "Nabucet."

She bent down, squinting her eyes, her fists still balled on her hips.

"Eh?" she said. "That cow pie? What'd he do to you?"

In spite of everything, a little smile slipped across Cripure's face, but so lightly, so sneakily, that it went unnoticed.

"To me?"

"Who then?"

He didn't dare reply. Too late, in any case, to turn back. But . . . it was stupid to have told this woman. What could she understand about the whole business? A duel, what would that even mean to her? Did she even know what a duel was? And could she understand the gist? *Dear God! I don't dare tell her I was the one who slapped the man . . .*

"I gave him a—" he made a gesture. She understood.

Cripure lowered his head, brought his hand back between his knees. Maïa's fists finally left her hips and her too-short arms lifted and flapped like flippers. He heard her breathing in and out. Cripure's lowered eyes could see nothing more than Maïa's feet in their wooden clogs, as if they were riveted to the floor.

"A whack?"

"Yes."

"Why on earth did you give him a whack?"

He made a vague gesture.

The ideas he gets, she thought, stunned, *are things no one will ever understand.* The whole time they were together, she'd lived as if under a threat.

"And how's it going to go?"

"With pistols," he said, still not raising his eyes.

And an instant later, he added, "at twenty paces."

This time her clogs moved.

What kind of a stupid business had he gotten himself into! A duel! She'd seen that before on the stage at fairs—handsome gentlemen in golden suits and wigs who slung their swords around while complimenting each other. But that was all stuff for the theater, not real life! And because of a slap! If she'd had to fight a duel every time she'd gotten slapped! She'd run into no small few who weren't satisfied, like Cripure, with insulting her. But it didn't frighten her! She'd always known how to defend herself. Him? He was trembling.

"You've got a yellow-belly attitude," she cried, finally letting her anger come out. "You're shaking to the tips of your butt-cheeks, and you want to play the little soldier. I wish he could see you, your Nabucet, he'd have a good laugh. If you had a little bell on the end of your nose, he'd hear it a mile off. Godforsaken old fool!"

Cripure got up, scowling. He was shaking, it was true, all over his big body.

"Enough, do you hear! Silence!"

"Sausage brain!"

They didn't move, staring face to face.

"I don't have to discuss it with you, Maïa. I'm merely informing you about something, and I would have done better to keep quiet."

She snickered. "You think I wouldn't of guessed?"

Busybody! he thought. She would have guessed, that was certain. She always guessed everything.

"Yes, you would have guessed . . ."

Maïa turned sarcastic, a mean light in her speckled eyes. "You want to be like those fancy gentlemen."

"Eh? Fancy gentlemen?"

"A little bit of prancing…"

"Enough!" he said, turning slowly around so he could flee. But he didn't make a step, and Maïa watched and smiled with scorn. *She sees that I'm afraid.*

This duel, which he'd fled before, sacrificing his dearest love to cowardice—Toinette!—here he was, after all these years, thrown back into it. But there was no longer the question of the officer. No. Fate had given him a worthy adversary, a miserable brown-noser. Oh!

"I'll…you'll see." He made a gesture with his right hand to his left, which clearly meant: I'll knock him out, I'll wipe the floor with him, I'll make him disappear.

"You?"

She gave him a sideways glance. It was possible, after all, that he would kill Nabucet. And then what, would he go to prison in the end?

"Why not me?"

He pulled himself up, enormous, formidable, more like an ape than ever. She backed away.

What frivolity! Where the devil had he read the quote that had meant so much to him in the past? "The frivolous takes advantage of man at random, and while he expresses his astonishment and wishes to return to himself, it seizes him and puts him in chains." Hm. Another literary memory. For how many years had he let himself be randomly seized and enchained? Frivolity, scorn all down the line. And this moment too, however great its importance, grossly wasted, like the rest, like the duel would be, no doubt, tomorrow morning. "I've nothing left but her, and she doesn't understand anything."

"What are you muttering?"

"Nothing."

"Nothing," Maïa sneered, "nothing?"

This whole story, she thought, was just as dumb as throwing yourself under a train, for example. And less than a year from retirement, when he had nothing left in sight but his little cottage, his books, hunting, since that was what he loved. And he was going to go fight a duel! But what about her? He hadn't thought of her? She must mean something to him still? He was certainly fond of his little dogs...

"For Christ's sake!"

Ah! Of course, you couldn't say that life with him had been all roses, and she wasn't just thinking of the insults, but of his phobias, his mood swings, the things she had to do for him endlessly. In spite of it all, they lived pretty companionably together, in comfort and ease, practically in fidelity, Basquin aside. But he could screw some-one else if he felt like it. That had nothing to do with what brought them together. And now he wanted to...

"Oh you idiot!"

"Again?"

He raised his hand, ready to slap her. He was on a roll with these slaps, today. She told him as much, adding that he could go ahead: at least he wouldn't have a second duel on his hands. There was only one person inclined to that, and that was plenty for him. One look at Cripure was enough to see that plainly.

"Trembling coward! No, you don't scare me one bit, not enough to shake a stick at."

He lowered his eyes and fled—Nabucet wouldn't be frightened either, he wasn't frightening, despite looking like a scarecrow.

HE WENT into his study and closed the door behind him. So she'd leave him alone. Alone. He didn't need anyone. He wanted to yell at her, "No one, do you understand me, Maïa!" But he satisfied himself with thinking it.

It was dark in the study. Dark and cold. But there was no question he'd open the glass door. He'd give up the heat of the stove tonight. All he had to do was light the lamp, and already that was no small matter.

Usually, it was Maïa who took on that task. Would he know how to do it? And the matches? Maybe on the corner of the mantel.

He found a box, but through clumsiness and his trembling, he didn't succeed right away in lighting a match. The strip was worn out. He finally managed it, and with the flame burning his fingers, he grabbed the lamp, lowered it, lifted the glass—a miracle! he didn't break it—and brought the match close. Saved! The light of his evenings, the dear light of innumerable past evenings and reveries, shone over his kingdom like a crown in the silence. He wiped his hands, greasy with oil, and examined the floor to make sure there were no sparks, that he didn't need to worry about fire, and reassured on that front, he looked around him and murmured, "Well then! Well then!"

Well then! It made sense anyway, even if it was unexpected! And so, in this moment when everything would be settled and the plot started to reach the climax, what did she find to say to him but *idiot . . .* trembling coward. She called him an idiot! She was probably right about that. *Yes, I was an idiot to think she could understand.*

What had he imagined, in the carriage? He'd go home, his heart burning with anger and bitterness. He'd admit everything to Maïa. She wouldn't say anything. She'd let him tell her everything—he'd finally tell her about Toinette!—and she'd keep listening without interrupting him, understanding every last word through a miracle of compassion and love. It would be an angelic scene, a divine moment, where they'd pardon each other and love one another with their fates finally realized. After that moment, nothing else would make him tremble. He'd no longer be a coward, death would no longer be terrible, he'd feel not only renewed, but cleansed, purified by this...he couldn't say either confession or admission, since he refused to think of himself as guilty whatever the cause...by this gift, that was the right word for it. All the time he was coming home, he hadn't stopped thinking about that, that he would tell Maïa everything, and that afterwards, come what may, he wouldn't care one way or the other. What man wouldn't want to tell all before tempting death? And that was what he should have done—instead he'd fallen into a household spat. Frivolity, once again, got the better of him. Idiot! He could say it a hundred times.

In the height of his sadness, while he was still young, some deaf part of him had held on to the hope that everything would begin again. He'd be dealt a new hand: he'd see the game better. "You live like you have a lifetime to learn," he murmured, letting himself slump into his chair. He looked at his books, his papers scattered on the table—another aspect of the disaster, the *Chrestomathy*.

It was, however, the moment to put the final period on that erudite work. Nabucet would take care of it tomorrow in a different way. But while he was waiting, wouldn't it be necessary—for the interest of science, perhaps!—to tell what had just happened between him and Maïa, and then to keep noting, hour by hour, even minute by minute, what was still happening, up until the last minute when, at twenty paces, someone would say, "Are you ready?"

No, he would not be ready. Yet he would say "yes" in a voice that forced itself not to tremble. That would be another lie, but the last. After that, it wouldn't matter if he lied or not. A bullet in his snout.

Finished. Settled. No one would speak of it again, not about him, not about his *Chrestomathy*.

So far, this work consisted of scraps where he'd written—in his small, delicate handwriting, elegant, spiritual, how different from his person—notes on bits of paper, calling cards, the backs of envelopes. There were a great many of these notes, gathered day by day and year by year. They made up a fat folder. He took these cherished bits out of a drawer, making the effort to put the books and papers cluttering his table on the mantelpiece, and in the shiny space of ink-stained wood, almost unrecognizable to him in its new nakedness, he dumped his sheaves and notes as if from now on he'd only think of this work, as if everything going on in the world, including the duel, would be suspended until the moment when he had succeeded not just in telling but in *saying*.

But the attempt went no further than dumping the papers on the table. That done, he surveyed them with a sort of hatred, as if the *Chrestomathy* too had betrayed him, and arms limp, eyes glazed, he didn't move.

It would have been more reasonable not only to renounce the project—and was this the time to do so, and did one make plans in front of a pistol?—but also to destroy the papers down to the slightest scrap, to burn every last one and drown the ashes. *You are dust and to dust you shall return.* Burn everything—that's what people did in these situations, through an ultimate discretion, a last, violent concern to drag everything with them into the purity of death, perhaps also a last revenge. A curious concern all the same with total self-effacement, like an animal who wants to confuse its trail, to make all traces down to its shadow disappear, haunted by this madness until the last breath, so it was no longer a matter of trails or traces since the path had been chosen, and in any case, everything would go forward with the ring of a blade that would flash in his eyes and which, in less than a second, would strike him down. A handsome system of contradictions: he should put it in the *Chrestomathy*.

And along those lines, if he didn't burn his papers, what would happen? In Maïa's furious hands, what would become of these little scraps of secrets? Sold at the auction like all the rest, he was sure of it, since she would sell everything in bulk, to the highest bidder, the most curious, the most repellent, even to his enemies. You could count on her to despoil the corpse, o dear companion in misfortune! Everything. She'd auction everything. He didn't have to be a prophet to imagine how things would go. Of course, all his books, all his papers, she'd trot them out in a pushcart or in Basquin's car, off to the fair! Two or three boards on trestles, an awning in case of rain, and that would be it! *Step right up! Come on over! Reading materials at a low price! Take your pick for twenty sous!* And since salesmanship made her hungry and thirsty, he could picture her quite well, standing behind her trestle table in the midst of breaking bread, her knife in one hand, her bread and lard in the other, and, in a corner, the bottle of cheap wine she'd drain in a few slugs without using a glass. That would be all for his books. It would always be the bread and butter for a few poor "intellectuals" and in particular the priests who were well off, but miserly. In his capacity of town librarian, Monsieur Babinot would ask for the privilege of getting the first look at the pile. The rest—the furniture, the bookcases no doubt, and surely his clothes—would go another direction, that of the auction house. He didn't have any illusions about that either. She'd send everything there, even his slippers, the goatskin, and his little straw hat. Nabucet would collect the enemy spoils to make a diorama!

But what else would he want? That Maïa herself would make a diorama or a museum? Dark madness. She would be right to sell everything. Or did he want to keep hoping that unknown admirers, forgotten friends...

These horrible scenarios fascinated him. Elbows propped on the table, he stayed unmoving as a block of stone until Maïa barged into the room. But then, he jumped. In a second, he was on his feet.

She appeared, hatted, costumed in her "lady" clothes, her good church dress, for Easter and Palm Sunday, a parasol in her hand, such as he had only seen her two or three times, on very special occasions— a first communion she had to go to, or a baptism—looking just as she had always dreamed she would look on that long-awaited day when he'd take her down to the courthouse.

A huge feathered hat, antique and wilted, hid her ruddy mug, like an unbalanced yoke on the most readable of foreheads. A white dress. A white blouse, ridiculously low-cut and sleeveless, squeezed that ample bosom like a straitjacket, giving a view of her skin, rough as a rasp and jiggling like an egg. In her haste and in her rage, Maïa had dressed herself clumsily, but she undoubtedly thought she looked beautiful and seductive. It was good enough for a long laugh.

"What's all this? Where are you going?"

He knew only too well, and he panicked in every crevice of himself.

Maïa fancily put on her gloves.

"Tell me!"

"You'll see about where I go. You'll see! If you think that cow pie of a Nabucet..."

It was too much. This time it was too much. For God's sake, the awfulness couldn't go that far. What right had this old hag...

"I'm my own person!" Cripure howled.

He meant that his death was his own, and that she had no business with it. But she replied, all the while putting on her gloves and trying to look at herself in the mirror, "We'll see about that soon enough. Your Nabucet? I'm going to give him a taste of his own medicine..."

A raft of horrors followed. She knew all about that bastard pighead of a Nabucet, with his honey manners and his habit of groping the girls. With two of her good smacks, for starters, everything would be sorted out. He could take a big whiff of that stew and see how he liked it. Had there ever been such a...

"And what's more," she said, "I'm putting on gloves, you know, cause I don't want to dirty my hands. I'm better than him, even if I am a whore."

"Maïa!"

"There's no Maïa-ing me."

"You're not going, Maïa."

"Who's going to stop me?"

"I am."

He came forward. The blouse, badly hooked, bunched over the camisole and the skin of her neck made a big red roll under the gray hairs she'd haphazardly combed up.

"You will not go," he said, letting his hand fall heavily on Maïa's neck. She bent her head. Her hat fell over her eyes, but not for long. Cripure ripped off the good hat and threw it into the middle of the kitchen.

"There!"

Crazed with anger, she turned, trying to scratch his face, going for the eyes. He bent his head, pressing his forehead under Maïa's chin, bracing his legs against the table while his arms fell slowly on the wench's back, tearing her blouse and joining in a powerful grip behind her waist. As big and fat as she was, he had her well pinned. She couldn't escape.

"You're not going."

In its flight, the handsome feathered hat had bumped the green glass of the hanging lamp, pushing the lamp into a dangerous pendulum swing. They stopped struggling, without letting go of their prey, eyes fixed on the lamp, waiting to see it crash to the ground. But except for dust, nothing fell. For an instant, Cripure had the feeling that it wasn't the lamp swaying, but the floor, and that he wasn't in his familiar study, but in the cabin of a ship in a big swell. But soon everything was calm. The sea became flat again, the rocking of the lamp lessened and then stopped. He held on tighter to Maïa.

"You will not go," he murmured, almost in a whisper. "You're staying here."

"I will too."

She tried to hit him, to knee him in the stomach. Furious that she couldn't scratch him, she tried to stamp on his painful toes with her the heel of her clog. "Dirty cow foot! Lemme go!"

"No."

"Cuckold!"

For less than a second, he relaxed his grip, but he grabbed her again and squeezed even tighter. "What does that matter?" her murmured, his teeth clenched. "What does that matter? You're not going in any case. This's my affair. Mine alone."

"You're choking me."

"Say you won't go."

"I will..."

"I—I made my will," he said, astonished to hear himself say those words. "Everything will go to you."

In the same instant the words tumbled out of his mouth, he realized with horror that it was useless to fight any longer since Maïa had stopped struggling. He could let go of her, sure that from now on she'd no longer try to leave. He did, in fact, let go of her and saw her turn around the room as if blind, her back bent, her arms dangling in front of her like someone groping for sight. He wondered anxiously if perhaps in his fury he had hurt her, and he looked at his hands. Maïa finally found a chair and slumped into it. Her face hidden in her arms, she started to groan.

"What'd you say! What'd you say!"

"What did I say?"

He was—already—prepared to rescind whatever idea, and ready to play the innocent. *Pleading not guilty, that's my strength!* But he well knew what made her groan. *She made me deliver that blow.*

Hadn't she called him a cuckold? What was that about? Basquin? But it wasn't Basquin she'd been thinking of.

"Maïa!"

"What'd you say!"

It was horrible, shocking, to see this fat whore with her hair hanging down, her blouse in shreds, shrinking into her armchair as if she'd been burned, as if the blow Cripure had dealt touched something more than herself, something fundamental, inviolate, perhaps even sacred. "Oh, oh, oh!" he moaned in turn.

Of course, when it came to baseness he considered himself well educated. For a moment, he'd thought, with a kind of awful delight, that he'd struck home, that he'd proved once more the horror of man's hideous moral decay. He'd been dizzy at the thought that it didn't matter to Maïa if he died, and in this way that so resembled a killing, as long as the sous went to her, that money he'd watched with such jealous care, making a thousand plans to use it for his escape and his freedom, and which would in fact go to giving Maïa a dowry which she'd squander away with Basquin the moment they got engaged. All those thoughts passed through his soul and pierced his heart in the moment Maïa had torn herself away from him and run to the chair like someone wounded. Yes! He'd hit her squarely, but through an accident he hadn't foreseen, and he hadn't struck the spot he'd aimed for. Seeing and hearing Maïa, he felt something like the horror of a man who fires at a wall and suddenly hears the cries of someone he didn't know was sitting behind it who has been caught by the bullet.

The worst thing was that Maïa didn't stop. She seemed to be in the grips of an exclusively physical sorrow, like a wild toothache or a liver malfunction. It was strange to see how much the sorrow seemed to come from her body—in all her big bulk, not a bit seemed to be at rest.

He didn't dare approach. The idea of even touching her in that moment inspired an insurmountable horror. And finally since she didn't stop, he turned his back to her and covered his ears.

His two pointed hands opened, climbed, in the gesture of a soldier turning himself in, slipped slowly down his cheeks, and with the grimace of someone hearing nails on a chalkboard, his two index fingers stuffed themselves into his ears. Everything then seemed to rumble like a flood—it was the blood beating hard in his head.

A BURNING smell, a snuffling of gas in the kitchen. Maïa stopped moaning. "My lentils!"

She jumped out of her chair and rushed to her stove. Cripure, who still had his fingers stuffed in his ears, his head facing the window, didn't see or hear anything. For a long time, he stayed in that ridiculous, grimacing pose, until his attention was finally caught by the smell of burned lentils and he turned, realizing he was alone. So he took his long fingers out of his ears, letting his arms fall slowly back against his body, catching himself in a gesture of shock.

Perfect. The lentils had burned. Thanks to this fact, he found himself alone, rescued. Perfect! Perfect! But he didn't know what to do with himself, almost like an interrupted dreamer whose dream has vanished without leaving something else to contemplate, except, like someone capsized, the emptiness left inside him that may be eternal.

Maïa went back and forth in the kitchen like she had every day for so many years. A noise of dishes, the bang of a poker against something iron, the rumbling of water boiling in a pot, all those familiar reassuring noises, as if that life of objects expressed some guarantee that he wouldn't die, as if everything that frightened him was just some flimsy construction of his spirit.

Dumbly, he took shelter in this thought: despite everything, they would eat soon.

Soon. But in the meantime?

An idea! He went back to his desk, bent down, rummaged in the cubbyholes by the chimney, where he kept his dictionaries. With care, he grabbed a volume of his old *Littré*, which he put on the table. His fingers flipped ably through the pages. He adjusted his pince-nez, pursed his lips, and with a familiar movement, groped behind him for a chair, without taking his eyes off the dictionary.

Everything happened as if he were behind his lectern at the lycée, as if he were preparing to read his students a page chosen from some philosopher.

"Let's see, let's see," he murmured, turning the pages, "let's take a little look: ductile, ductility, ductilometer, due...ah! here we are: 'duel (du-el), *n.* individual combat between two men. "*She loves in this duel his want of experience.*" —Corneille, *Le Cid.*' Let's go on. See a little more. Judicial duel. *Judicial duel*—no entry. Moving on. *Philippe le Bel*...no. All that's useless. Let's take another look. Hmm... *duel with pistols and swords.* No question about the swords. *Duel to first blow*... Ah, what might that mean?"

He bent over the dictionary and, passing his finger below the lines to keep his eye on them, he read on, ignoring the beating of his heart: "*duel to first blow: a duel which must end with the first injury, even minor, of one of the combatants.*" He read the entry again. "*Even minor,*" he murmured, raising his head. There was a chance he wouldn't be killed, that it would all end with a minor wound and stop there? A bullet in the arm maybe or the leg, at worst in the shoulder? If he ignored all the rules of dueling, he'd remember this one!

"Hmm...hmm..." he said, looking at the ceiling, drumming on the dictionary, "if I escape..."

If he escaped—one chance in a thousand—well then, he'd marry Maïa!

This time, he didn't tap on the dictionary but gave it a good whack with the flat of his hand, as if he were concluding a trial. *I'll marry her!* She certainly deserved it, especially after everything that had just happened, and the way he'd seen her racked with sorrow on the chair. *I've been a bastard*...He'd buy her a nice outfit to replace the one he'd torn, he'd bring her to the town hall in front of everyone. It would be a great triumph for her, and at least then he wouldn't have to think about making a will if another duel came along or whatever it was that finally…Yes, he would marry her. Why not? He had no other way of showing his appreciation for so many years of good care, good food…etc.

He closed his eyes, thinking of her groans from a moment ago. How horrible they were! He'd marry her, but he wouldn't tell her about it just yet, he'd wait until tomorrow, after the duel, if he lived. A duel to first blow: a duel that must stop after the first injury, even minor, to one of the combatants…

He vowed: if he didn't die, he would bring a new Madame Merlin into the world. It would go like this: he'd hire Père Yves's cab, recommend that the man rent a top hat somewhere for the occasion. Ask him to tie a pretty ribbon on the handle of his whip, to pamper Pompon nicely, and if possible, to put little decorations on her mane and tail. A little brushing of the seats and everything would go splendidly. At the stroke of ten one morning, they'd get in the carriage, he and Maïa, and on their way, on their way to a new life! Tsk, tsk, Pompon! The whip would clack, Maïa would carry herself with pride in the back of the cab, her parasol open and slung carelessly over one shoulder. She'd ask him not to go too quickly, that they take their time, since she wanted to be seen, and also because the marriage was a special moment and she wanted her money's worth. He could see it as if it were already happening. He could hear Maïa: "You'd say he's got a fire under his ass, that Pompon. What's the rush? The town hall's not going anywhere." And he'd lower his little straw hat over his eyes and press the whole of his large back into the seat, saying nothing.

This time, scorn would reign, completely inseparable from parody. What an idea! Maïa playing, at his side, what was once Toinette's role on that luminous wedding day of long ago. Toinette in white with her veil and crown of orange blossoms, turned to Maïa, his new fiancée, soon to be his legitimate bride by virtue of a "yes" spoken in front of a scarf. "Will you take, to be your lawfully wedded wife…" It would cause a good laugh in town, they'd talk about it for a long time! What a defeat. Look at him now, they'd say, that champion of anarchy, that impossible enemy of society. Look at him now, getting down on his knees for mercy, burning what he adored, adoring what he burned. *Submitting!* They'd say lots of other things too. But so what … After the yes, they'd gorge somewhere no doubt, perhaps by the sea? "Son of a bitch!" he muttered to himself. It didn't matter. They'd bring the witnesses. Who would they be? Basquin, of course. And the others? The first to arrive, it didn't make a damned bit of difference. On the contrary, the more wretched they were the better it would be. The guests shouldn't clash with their symphony, the carriage's squeaking wheels setting the scene. He should choose witnesses that were as dusty as the seats themselves. The real stroke of genius would be to lay his hands on a few vagabonds, those old beggars in clogs the police harassed, and for whom a good feast would be the luck of a lifetime. It would be something to see them all coming back together. Would they sing? Perhaps …

In this reverie he almost forgot the duel, pushed for the moment to the far horizon of his consciousness, not without some images of slow and silent cabs, full of the wounded and dying, but enveloped in a fog so that it wasn't yet the moment to unload them. It didn't make him less convinced that all these fancies of marriage and feasts with vagabonds (the only kind of man, in addition to mercenaries, that he'd ever been able to love) were nothing, in the end, but a way to deny or stave off the duel. In promising to marry Maïa, he was making a bargain with the gods, like a peasant or a good wife would take a grievance to a saint. So as not to be in the carriage where the mortally wounded rolled, he promised to be in the cab where Maïa would be displayed as a fiancée, and he in the role of future husband. "Maïa's hand if I'm not killed!" Was that enough of a price? Who would be fooled? The gods, Maïa, or himself? Everyone. When it came down to it, it was a farce, which would really take place one day, if he escaped the duel, outside of his imagination, in what they called "the concrete." And continuing to dream of this farce, he realized that if one of Maïa's witnesses had to be Basquin, his could be no other than the Clopper, in person.

Again! The Clopper again! Him! To the devil with the Clopper and all his complacent musings about this character of night and grime, so little a character and barely a person, barely a cheap mirror, as false, as frozen and fragile as glass. That he dreamed of him as a witness to his marriage, or as the coachman, having taken Père Yves's place on the day of the ceremony, or that he'd fasten, on that black mummy, Monsieur mayor's scarf... enough! Enough! Enough scaring himself for fun, wallowing in the shadows.

Since, in the end, what did it matter! It wasn't him, Merlin-Cripure, who was the Clopper. The Clopper was, in spite of everything, a person of his own. Another "other." It was clear as day—a funny thing to say when you thought about that man—it was clear as day that it wasn't the Clopper who would fight tomorrow at twenty paces. The hour when the voice of one of the seconds would pronounce the fatal "one, two, three—fire!" it would be high time for the Clopper to return to his cave or his garret, full of shadows, to sleep on his mattress of straw.

Maïa opened the door. "Eat."

And understanding that he hadn't heard, she repeated louder, but without impatience, "Come eat."

He raised his head. His look grasped that there were traces of tears on the wench's face. He frowned in a reproving way, more annoyed than compassionate. "Eat?"

She backed away without answering.

Cripure got up. In fact, he had to eat, even if she had nothing to offer him but burned lentils. An absurd saying, about certain soldiers—obviously Napoleon's—who fought better on an empty stomach came back and irritated him. What idiocy! Who came up with such ridiculous garbage? And to think he had remembered it. He would eat, eat well, even, drink well, and sleep well, so as to be at his best on the field. Which general was it—these historical anecdotes kept coming to him—who slept so well the nights before battle? Turenne or Condé? Probably Condé. *Turenne was a trembler like me.*

You tremble, carcass...[17] Not ruling out that he was fair and square a...Oh! I'm not demanding so much of myself...spirit even? Irony about myself? Oh! Charming. I could continue, argue, for example, that this whole story is such buffoonery that I wouldn't give up my spot for a cannonball, etc. Easy. This is tired thinking. Good sense would be to go eat.

He decided to push the door he'd been standing in front of since a moment ago, and go into the kitchen where everything seemed so calm and orderly, so much like other days that he doubted it was true he was going to fight a duel, as if that whole novel, including the domestic spat, the battle with Maïa, the groans and all that, were nothing but a pure imaginative invention, a dream, or simply the beginnings of madness. Was it possible that he had made it all up, a not-inconceivable hypothesis, which would seem to correspond with Maïa's composure, if, at any rate, he couldn't see her face?

Where was that feathered hat he'd torn from her and catapulted into the middle of the kitchen, that lace blouse that was so ridiculous, that sumptuous white dress, in short that splendid bride's outfit she'd emerged in just a little while ago with the furious air of a bourgeois mother? There was no trace of any of it. Instead of those marvels, Maïa was wearing her ordinary clothes, her big black skirt, her jacket, clogs and apron, and, as usual, she went about her cooking. No, truly, there was nothing to raise an eyebrow at. Even the smell of burned lentils had vanished. He'd taken a big sniff of the air, searching for a trace of that acrid smell, and it had been in vain. He breathed only the fresh perfume of the night beginning, the smell of the garden—wet earth, grasses and leaves, which came through the window like a flood.

And in the rectangle of that kitchen window, what an overwhelming profusion of stars, which—through what new consideration?—seemed virginal to him. And what depth brought towards the sky this reverent gesture of his arms? In the frame of the window, the night was crystal, pure and noble between the leaves of trees. Maïa saw him approach the window and once again hold out his hand to the night, a gesture that was incomprehensible and foolish to her—did he want to know if it was raining? As for rain, they'd had quite enough of that. He stayed on his feet in front of the window, unfortunately too short to kneel in, and suddenly, as they did every evening around this time, the young, grave, and moving chorus of Russian soldiers lifted their voices, slow and muted at first, which bit by bit filled the night.

"And if you said you're sorry?"

She snuck a look at him with her head lowered, measuring the effect of her words. She was completely limp in her chair, like a woman overcome with weariness at the end of a day when eating will be just another chore.

The spoon Cripure was lifting to his mouth stopped moving. But try as he might to catch Maïa's look, his eyes met only her lowered forehead, the wench's disordered gray mane. She dropped her head as if she were absorbed in searching for something that had fallen into her soup. A fly?

"You could say something to him," she went on, timid. "You could send him a little note?"

The spoon at the level of his mustache still didn't move. Was Maïa going to say something else?

Still without lifting her head she in fact said, "You don't want that?"

No answer. Cripure's mouth did open eventually. But it was for the spoon. *She's crazy . . .* He resented her for reminding him of that shameful and secret temptation.

"Apologize? Never!"

"Whyever not, kitty cat? It would be over . . ."

If she persisted, he'd start to get angry. Already his hand was trembling, even though he wanted to seem calm, resolved, unshakable. And in order to seem all those things, what else could he do but eat his soup as usual?

"You won't say something?"

"Leave me alone."

She didn't press him. Nothing for it. But not playing at bravado, not even thinking to, she didn't begin to eat her soup. Immobile, her arms resting on the table and her forehead bent over her plate.

Outside, the Russian soldiers were still singing, but their songs had gotten louder, and Cripure listened, as if those splendid and incomprehensible songs were, for him, more than songs, as if they contained some mysterious reference to the drama of his life and death.

Of course, they probably knew nothing about him, they were singing for themselves. But to believe that was another unworthy thought. They were singing for everyone, and though they trilled for his death and his burial, they were also singing for life.

"Life!" murmured Cripure. And one after another, he downed two big glasses of wine. "Listen, Maïa!"

She still didn't move, seeming not to hear anything. What a pity! It was so beautiful. And with the warmth of the wine aiding him, he turned an ecstatic face toward the window. "Cripure salutes you!" he cried, raising his glass. He emptied it in one gulp. "To the health of living men!"

Maïa didn't even raise her head. He put down his glass. She still didn't move. He fixed a heavy gaze on her and perceived that tears were falling one by one into the wench's soup, fat tears that hit the soup with little splashes.

It was the first time he'd seen Maïa cry. They'd lived together for a number of years, and never, at least in front of him, had she shed a tear. Once the initial moment of surprise had passed, he scowled and carefully considered this old woman whose eyes he couldn't see, eyes that were shedding tears for him. Maïa's tears! No, no, and no!

"No!" The fury that took hold of him at first seemed to come out of nowhere. For once it was an overwhelming emotion that left no room for spectators. A second time, with building violence, he repeated, "No!" And he was shocked to feel the same desire return: to hit her. *If she doesn't stop this instant, I'll slap her.*

He pushed his plate away. But on the table, his tapping hand didn't reach for the bottle anymore. She made a vague gesture of threat and supplication.

"Maïa!" What did that cry carry—tenderness or anger? "Maïa! I don't want you to..." He said, "to cry." But he thought *to love me.*

For a moment, his relief at having stopped himself in time hid the horror of that thought, but an instant later, the truth eviscerated him. Ah! If it were Toinette asking him to make his apologies! He would have done it posthaste. For the love of Toinette, what wouldn't he have done! He would have left with her, laughing in their stupid faces. But this Maïa!

"For the love of God!"

She finally looked up. But whether it was cowardice on Cripure's part or something else, he turned his eyes away.

"Just look at him, mouthing off at a moment like this," murmured Maïa in a faraway voice.

This way of speaking about him without addressing him was strangely touching, and in a gentle voice, he said, "It's not worth crying over..."

"So why do you..."

"It's not worth it, I say!" Cripure interrupted. "Ah, ah, ah, ah! It's no use. No use," he finished with a sigh. He jerked his head. "Listen!" he said, his forefinger raised.

He looked towards the window—the singing went on in the depths of the night.

"Do you understand?"

"I don't give a hoot about those howlers over there," cried Maïa, getting angry. "You can't even figure out what they're bawling."

He smiled anyway. He understood.

She finally stopped crying, dried her tears the way children do, rubbing her eyes with her fists. And paying no more attention to him, thrusting herself forward, which was her way of showing resolve, she drank down her soup while he poured himself glass after glass of wine. But he could drink and even get sloshed for all she cared! He could do whatever he felt like, and fight that cow pie of a Nabucet tomorrow morning, that was his problem! Was that all he'd found to say to her when she started to cry, which, in her language, she didn't call crying but braying?

He had not a kind word—"leave me alone"—and he'd started cursing. What was she to him then? Nothing but a servant? Fine then, since she was nothing but a servant, she'd act like a servant. And her soup drunk, she changed the plates, bringing not the lentils, which she'd thrown out, but a cassoulet she'd set aside, one of those canned cassoulets she always kept on hand in case something went wrong. It only needed twenty minutes warming in a double boiler to be ready, and besides, he adored it.

She could see the way he helped himself. Had she let him, he would have doubtless taken the whole thing, even though the can held more than would have satisfied four hearty eaters. But him! He didn't hide his glee.

"Oh! A cassoulet!"

Those were the only words he spoke until the end of the meal.

Everything was repaired, it seemed, with the arrival of this well-timed cassoulet. He ate unsparingly, happy, with obvious pleasure, and outside the singers could keep on singing, nothing in Cripure's face betrayed that he was listening to them again, that he was aware of Maïa's presence, of her recent tears and the anger that had seized him.

Did he know why her tears had upset him so much? Did he know that he had to fight tomorrow? He recovered a little piece of fat and drowned his cassoulet in a big slug of red wine, calling for his coffee and his finger of rum. Maïa served him without saying anything. Afterwards, as usual, she started on the dishes while he leaned both elbows on the table, falling into a reverie. Or perhaps into the simple heaviness of men who are stuffed.

Holding onto her bad mood, which was really a cover for something deeper in another part of herself, Maïa calmly did the dishes, with excessive care. To break her boss's dishes! God forbid! Good maid that she was, she would do anything to avoid such a calamity. And it was also on this disastrous day that the kitchen would be more orderly than ever, everything in place in perfect neatness.

If it hadn't been so late, if this business had come up in the morning instead of at night, she knew very well what she would have done! Her dishes organized, her table wiped, and her sweeping done, she would have polished her brass, that's what! The handles of the stove to start, then the pots, then the doorknobs. And the silver. With a bit of chamois too, like they did in those great mansions. And if all that wasn't enough to show him who she was, once the knives and the spoons were nicely put away, she'd wash the floor.

Kneeling on the ground, dunking her rag again and again into the bucket, it would be obvious what she was capable of and whether or not she knew how to tackle her work. A servant! He wouldn't have stayed there, dozing off in his chair. He would've fled to his study, amongst his papers since he wasn't comfortable anywhere else, leaving her free to work.

But there could be no question about it. It was getting late, and despite all the good reasons in the world—night wasn't the time to start washing a kitchen. So once her dishes were done, she started to undress for bed. What else could she do?

But here too, she was treated like a servant. He didn't notice that she was undressing, not showing the slightest interest in coming to bed too, and passing, next to her, this night that might well be his last. While Maïa got under the sheets, he shook himself out of his lethargy with difficulty, moving toward the glass door. He entered his study, where the lamp was still lit. So many things to do before this encounter! It had just occurred to him that one didn't expose oneself to death like this without at least taking care of certain papers.

As for a will, he had none. Despite the specter of death, which was always present in him, he'd never dared to write that document of capital importance, through which one's assets and money were given to another. Maybe he feared, through some superstition, that the act would bring a faster death. But there was no time left to avoid it. The hour had come to apply himself, to write what he must call his last wishes in a firm, clear hand, in precise terms, so that no one could doubt the soundness of his mind. As much of it as possible written on official letterhead. He couldn't find any, which astonished him, as he always had some saved in case he had to write to his supervisors.

He looked everywhere in the drawers, rifling through his papers for a long time, and despairing of the cause, made do with a sheet of writing paper which was fairly appropriate, even if a whole piece had been yellowed by exposure to the air and the corners were bent. But too bad. He had no choice. Now for an envelope. The envelope was as essential as the rest. What would they think of a will abandoned on the table like a receipt or some scrap? He took an envelope, and forcing himself not to tremble, he wanted to write on it the ritual words that seemed so funny to him at that moment: *This is my will*. He finally wrote them, in large handwriting, practically the size of a sergeant-major's, and placing the envelope at the ready on a pile of books, he grabbed his sheet of paper. But the words didn't come. There must be laws here as there were elsewhere, as there were for the duel, rules he was ignorant of, a whole way of proceeding which, if one didn't strictly conform to it, would render his acts null and void. Maybe, maybe! There was a set of rules in all this clutter. But to find it! No, it was better to open the drawer, taking out the titles and the cash, to make a bundle of it all, and tomorrow, before going over there, to give it to Maïa. That's what he must do. As for the rest, the money regularly deposited at the bank, the houses, Maïa would make arrangements. Nothing to hand over but the bills and once again he didn't know how to go about it. Would that he were already dead!

He opened the drawer. It wasn't any kind of secret, just a drawer that was a little more hidden than the others, larger, which he'd had lined with iron, for fear of fire, a little strongbox. He alone had the key and Maïa never had permission to see what went on in that drawer. She kept an eye on it anyway, and knew within almost a penny what it must contain. Cripure didn't suspect anything. The drawer, when it opened, made practically no noise, barely a tiny squeaking, and with a smile reserved for looking at his "spoils," forgetting why this evening more than another—and for what reason—he'd just opened the drawer, Cripure stared at his little hoard.

Everything in the house could be in disorder—papers scattered everywhere, the books stuffed willy-nilly into little crevices and bookcases—but the money drawer was the image of domestic order.

In the right-hand corner were the bonds he hadn't yet deposited at the bank, for reasons of his own, and a mass of bills, carefully stacked, as carefully as if they'd been organized by the cashier of the Bank of France himself. The only difference was that Cripure had noted the serial numbers of his bills in a ledger, a precaution the cashier would have doubtless considered useless, but one that held a primordial importance for Cripure. A moleskin portfolio held his business papers: bank statements, papers related to the houses, gains from businesses, letters from tenants, taxes, and finally, in the back of the drawer, more hidden than the rest from indiscreet eyes, a twill bag, stuffed with gold Louis.

It was for others, this idiocy, this credulity to spend their gold on war bonds, like the foolish good men they were, like poor dolts who let themselves be fooled and fleeced like sheep! He'd limited himself, since he'd been unable to do otherwise, since that also had been demanded of him, to dragging himself through the rural municipalities of the province to give presentations and encourage people to subscribe. But to let himself be stripped of that gold, his only recourse, his only defense! He'd never considered it for a second. God be thanked, the gold was always there, far more valuable than the bonds and the bank notes. And it wasn't that he was a filthy miser at all, but for more mysterious and poignant reasons, in the pile of his riches, it was the little sack of gold he touched. It was heavy, as if, instead of gold, it contained the earth, heavy and plump, tied at the top with a simple shoelace, which he set about untying. A long, painful process, but one that made him forget everything else. The lace untied, he grabbed a newspaper that was lying around on his table, opened it and put it on his lap; then he gently tipped out the entire contents of the little bag with great care so that Maïa didn't hear the gold clinking. Then he shook it to make sure it was empty. Under the gaslight, the gold glimmered, and with a gesture he couldn't resist, he thoughtfully plunged his heavy hand into the pile.

Though he knew perfectly well what sum the pile of gold represented, he had to resist the temptation to count the coins one by one. That game was familiar to him. Often, in the evening, when Maïa was sleeping in the kitchen, he gave in to it, not without, he had to admit, base feelings of greed—at least it wasn't only with those sentiments, but also with the emotion of an adventurer contemplating a stolen treasure and laughing at his new accomplishments. To leave! To roam the seas! Didn't he have the means right there? That problem so many men considered, of flight to a foreign country, of escaping not only death, but the baseness of his world, didn't he hold the key in his fingers? The miserable ones! They never saw more than money! But in his case, didn't he have enough to flee? There was still time. The duel and all the rest—goodbye! He could go finish out his life on some Pacific island somewhere, barely more alone than he was today, and surely more honest. They could go on saying that he'd been afraid, that he'd fled like a rabbit from Nabucet's pistol, as he'd fled before from the blond officer's sword—what did it matter! It wasn't only his life he thought of saving.

The gold kept flowing through his fingers with clear, laughing clinks, like a temptress's voice which whispers a barely audible call, murmuring softly in his ear her corrupting and reasonable words. Flee! Pack a suitcase and flee! Take the morning train to Paris. There would be plenty of time, in Paris, to get himself a passport. They wouldn't refuse him. A cripple, almost an old man! They might be all too happy to get rid of him—all things considered, he was one more mouth to feed.

Maïa was snoring. Her reassuring animal groans came to him from the kitchen. He carefully lifted the papers for the *Chrestomathy*, put the little pile of gold on the table in front of him, and put the bag in his pocket. Soon, if he decided to leave, he'd put the coins back in. But for the moment the gold was fine there, surrounded by papers, well in sight.

Leaving wasn't perhaps as difficult as they seemed to believe, and it was in truth the only way to prove himself, to finally be comfortable in his skin. Flee, at least break from a rotten world, since he didn't have the force to make another!

What time was it? He looked at his watch, left on the table out of habit. It pointed to ten. Surely it was later. If it were only ten, he would still have heard the chorus of Russian soldiers. It had been a long time since he'd heard anything, since the soldiers had gone to bed. The watch must have stopped. He raised it to his ear—no more tick-tock than in a stone.

It even occurred to him not to rewind it. He stared at it with a bitter little frown, and put it back on the table saying, "fine, if you don't want to work, don't work!" And he rubbed his temples with the tips of his fingers and pushed his pince-nez back into place: his tic.

He must be stupid to think of checking his watch at a time like this! He didn't need a watch to know...

He searched without success for the flavor of that night in his youth when happiness had rushed within him unannounced. On that night he had truly failed to foresee what would happen. If later on everything had blackened and tarnished, at least his beginnings had been noble. He thought back to it as perhaps he'd never done since that moment, freer to think of it now that Toinette was dead. As opposed to what people might have thought, and what they maybe still believed, he hadn't strategized about anything, he hadn't courted her—he'd wanted nothing, hoped for nothing, hadn't schemed to get Toinette's hand. The bourgeois follies didn't begin until later, after their marriage, but for long months he'd been content to love Toinette without saying anything. A lover! A husband! Him? The women who would put up with him—he'd always known where to find them and at what price. But for a woman to love him—that was impossible, he'd vowed to himself never to believe it, he'd told himself a thousand times. But on that night, it hadn't been necessary for Toinette to tell him a thousand times that she loved him for him to immediately believe. It wasn't necessary for her to say it even once. Perhaps, no, he was certain, she hadn't even said the words "I love you." But without needing either one or the other to say the words, they'd known all of a sudden that they loved each other and that they were meant for each other forever. How had that happened? What looks? What movements? What speech? Suddenly they'd found one another on the far side of the abyss, not knowing anything about how they'd crossed over.

It was a night much like this one, a soft night. When he'd walked her home. And after that, he'd gone back to his place. Crushed with happiness, but freed, he'd begun to twirl around his room, and towards morning, he sat on his window ledge, his hands on his knees.

In the depths of the night, long clouds ran across the sky in strange metallic colors; the air held a smell of hay. Everything had been etched in him, down to the tiniest details that now returned in abundance.

Why he should think about this night above all other nights, when Toinette was dead and he was on the eve of getting killed, was another mystery he didn't seek to unravel. In remembering his love, he was in the truth of it, as he had been in its truth when he discovered it and when he made his vow. Everything else had been nothing but lies, madness, tarnish, and contradiction.

That night, how full the hours had been, and what perfection there was in everything, inside and outside of him! There were no words for it. His most perfect hour, his dearest memory, these were things which yet came back to him in the shape of a cloud, a smell of hay, the steps of a workman who was going to the work. This night there was no smell of hay, and the high clouds running over the neighborhood were barely visible. But suddenly there were steps which made him recoil like he had burned himself—not the steps of a worker at dawn joyfully announcing the end of such nocturnal perfection, but those well-known steps, heavy and threatening, the steps of the Clopper in the flesh.

ONCE MORE, the Clopper, with his herald cane and his hobnail boots: clop! Clop! Clop! And his ritual of standing under the pink gaslight, prolonged, this evening beyond measure, as if to finally weary Cripure's fascination. Never before had the Clopper stayed for so long in this spot, and God knows, his usual pauses were long. Long, but of the same length. Cripure had something to feel uneasy about, that the usual clockwork was disturbed. This surely wasn't normal. What could he be planning? *Something against me? That man is ridiculous!* But it was easier for Cripure to mock the clopper than to hush the beating of his heart. And those beats became wild, his heart jumped into his throat when he suddenly saw something he'd never seen before—a second shadow appearing by the first.

Truth be told, the second shadow didn't appear right next to the Clopper; it came into view at least twenty paces from him, at the edge of the lighted space, and it seemed to Cripure that this second shadow was accompanied by a little dog.

Not possible, not to be believed, that the damned hunchback with her operatic airs had left her garret and decided to walk in the night, which must so frighten her. But the skipping shadow and the little dog! No doubt that it was the little dog, yellow and thin, the horrible cherished fido, the whole heart of that cursed hunchback. Dragging her heart on a leash in the form of a little dog, yellow and haggard . . .

The Clopper turned around slowly like a pivot. Cripure didn't see his feet stir, only a slow mechanical turning, like a mannequin in the window of a candy store, and he understood that the Clopper never once looked away from the movements of the hunchback and her little companion.

This one performed a sort of dance, always at the edge of the lamplight. The hand holding the leash stretched up, the little fido stood up straight, dancing on the tips of its paws in silence.

Nothing. Not the slightest sound, not even the sliding of feet, not even the smallest growl from this show-mongrel. And the dance went on, all around the edge of the lighted path, the Clopper turning in place to follow the hunchback's movements.

Shaking behind his blinds, Cripure forgot all about the duel, the gold left on the table, his decision to leave. The hunchback's dance fascinated him at least as much as it fascinated the Clopper himself. And in order to see better without being seen, he left the window and ran to turn down his lamp. Then, tiptoeing back to his post, he silently pushed back the shutter, leaned out, and looked. The hunchback was still dancing. He told himself she wouldn't stop until she reached her point of origin, completing once the total (and perhaps magical) encircling of the Clopper. And in fact that was how it happened. Returning to the spot where she'd appeared, she suddenly stopped dancing, and almost beside herself, she grabbed her pup, crushed it into her arms and embraced it. So the Clopper was decided.

He who was ordinarily so slow, whose steps battered the stones with such a heavy weight, suddenly became agile. With a single bound, he launched himself, and the little hunchback, still squeezing her dear little dog in her arms, took flight. Cripure saw her gesture—tying up her skirt for ease of running and throwing a lively look over her shoulder. The two shadows disappeared, pursuing each other into the night.

A sound of iron steps rang out, reminding Cripure of the steps of the police pursuing the little Chinese man, but instead of gunshots and the sinister cries of the unfortunate man, it was a little laugh he heard from the depths of the night. Surely it wasn't the Clopper laughing, it was the little hunchback. And hunchback though she was, old, ugly, and in love with only her haggard little dog in all the world, her laugh rang out into the night, a young, mocking laugh, feminine, a laugh which he had to admit—dear God!—was not so different from the way Toinette's laugh had been when Toinette still laughed. It was the devilish laugh of a woman in love who flees but encourages, and the laugh echoed into the night, piercing, cruel, overwhelming, so overwhelming that the Clopper himself must have been shocked into stillness, since you could no longer hear his steps. Somewhere on the edge of a sidewalk, he must be listening to that laugh, interrupted in his pursuit by that call and doubtless dreaming, letting the little hunchback run for all her might. There was a moment of silence, but from the depths of that silence a clatter of steps suddenly erupted: clop, clop, clop! And the pursuit began again.

She could laugh, and flee, and tease him, and squeeze the little yellow dog in her wasted arms, he wouldn't give up! And Cripure found a sort of comfort and happiness in hearing the iron steps battering the pavements of the night. *Courage! Courage!* He murmured, as if to brace himself. And his face pressed up next to the window, his body bent, gripping with two hands for support, he searched through the shadows, listening as hard as he could. The steps grew nearer. The little hunchback—gritting her teeth, no doubt, he imagined—reappeared in the circle of light, galloping, out of breath. The Clopper followed her closely, brandishing his cane, as long ago the skinny little man had brandished his before bringing it down on the dead man's bloody face! But Cripure guessed, without knowing quite how, that this brandished cane wasn't a threat. Even in this movement, there was something soft and innocent he couldn't describe, and in fact, at the moment when the Clopper got close enough to the hunchback to grab her or strike her, the cane fell out of his hands. Cripure understood that it wasn't entirely an accident. The cane hadn't slipped from the Clopper, he'd thrown it away. He placed his fat, deformed hand on the hunchback's shoulder with the gentleness of an angel. They looked at each other under the gaslight. That flight could have been nothing more than a childish game, since now that the Clopper had finally reached the hunchback, he was so tender. And she knew it. Not the slightest fear in her, not the slightest suspicion that she was afraid of whatever it was. She let the Clopper tenderly put a hand on her shoulder, not far from her hump, both of them absorbed in a silent and profound dialogue. *They must be looking into each other's eyes.* But everything changed once again, the hunchback tore herself away with a bat of the Clopper's hand, and still holding that sad little dog in her arms, she ran away like she had a moment ago. He didn't think to pick up his cane; he only thought of catching up to her. Cripure saw that he set off with a leap, as agile and fearless as a young man of twenty. The hunchback was his equal in agility. Despite being hampered by her cherished little dog, she ran like a young girl, and this time, instead of running toward the shadows at the other end of the street, she ran straight toward Cripure, ready, it seemed to him, to ask him for help and protection. He hid himself, pulled back, covered himself as best he could, and waited, his heart pounding. The iron steps filled the night. No doubt dizzy with excitement, the Clopper ran with all his might on the hunchback's tail, holding out his arms in a gesture that was both pleading and menacing, desperate. Almost beneath Cripure's window he caught her, but far enough away that Cripure could sometimes see only two shadows. She stopped, turned towards him, still holding the yellow dog to her chest, and once again he approached her gently, since she had given up running. He took something out of his pocket and offered it to her. She hesitated, shaking her head, but she held out her hand all the same, and the Clopper, making a deep bow, handed her the object after first holding it up to his lips. She looked at it for a long time. In her turn, she raised the object to her lips, ready to kiss it, when suddenly a little laugh rang out, as before, no longer joyous but terrible and crackling. The little object she held so close to her lips went flying into the shadows. It fell to the sidewalk with a tinkling of money. Then, for the third time, she fled, holding the little dog in her arms.

He no longer thought to run after her. He remained standing there for a moment longer, while the hunchback's laugh echoed still and was lost in the night. Then Cripure heard the heavy, troubled steps of the Clopper who went off the same way.

Cripure stayed for a long time, leaning out his window, facing out at the night in which there was nothing left to trouble him. From the kitchen he could still hear Maïa's snoring. The hunchback and the Clopper never disturbed her one bit! He finally turned: night inside, night outside. He groped for his matches and lit the lamp. Once more, the gold Louis sparkled on the table, but Cripure barely looked at them. That was his hoard sure enough! What had the Clopper grasped in his hand? What had he kissed with such emotion? What was that object the hunchback in turn had brought to her lips and then rejected, tossed with such a heartrending laugh? To go out was quite an adventure for Cripure. Besides the fear of running in to the Clopper, since he knew he was gone, there was that of being killed by some evildoer hiding behind a patch of the wall—going out, that meant unbarring the door, pulling up the chain, opening the padlock, undoing the double bolt. He was barely capable of it. That task wasn't his, but Maïa's. He would have to take care of it in silence, like a thief, and surely he wouldn't succeed. That left the window. It was low enough that he might be able to step through it. And once again, so that no one could surprise him in such an unusual act, he approached the lamp, not putting it out all the way, but shading it. Then, in that feeble glow, he went to the window. Not impossible at all, with a bit of courage and a lot of luck. He wouldn't fall. But the hoard? Was it really wise to leave it alone with the window open to thieves? "Bah! Bah!" And he stepped through the window. Once he sat himself on the sill, which was not without difficulty, all that he had left was to slide down, and his long legs, his huge feet would reach the sidewalk all on their own. He didn't dare decide yet, despite having accomplished most of the job. Would getting back inside be as easy? And if someone attacked him? "You enormous coward, what was he holding in his hand?" he murmured to himself. And without further hesitation, he slipped to the ground.

How changed everything was! How abandoned he felt, despite touching his own house with his hand! He hadn't expected that, or that his squeamishness would go so far as to make him think he was risking his life in this little nocturnal jaunt. That might be what he thought, but it wouldn't stop him. Tearing himself away from the house in one movement, letting go of the windowsill as someone else might let go the edge of a ship's deck to plunge into the sea, he bent down, moving toward the sidewalk, advancing as quickly as he could toward the place where just moments ago the scene had unraveled. While he walked, he held his eyes fixed on the ground. It wasn't at all convenient to be searching the night for that mysterious little object. Perhaps it was simply crazy, since the night was dark, the gaslight was far away and feeble, and Cripure's eyes were bad. If he had lost his pince-nez in that moment, there would have been no mayor to come and take his hand and rescue him. But he still looked, understanding that despite the duel and all the rest, he wouldn't be able to sleep until he found it.

The night was cool, and he shivered. His monstrous slippers, more like socks, resized by Maïa, made a little whispering on the stones, like a mute parody of the galloping iron steps he'd heard earlier. Here and there, Cripure stopped and crouched, bent over, his pince-nez held between his thumb and forefinger. It couldn't be far, that thing. Whatever force the hunchback had used to throw it wouldn't be more than twenty or so feet from where the scene had taken place. With a little patience, he'd know.

He finally noticed something shining in the middle of the road. He thought at first that it was just a piece of glass, so impossible had the recovery this mysterious object seemed. A simple piece of glass! He thought at first it wasn't worth going to take a look. The object, piece of glass or not, glowed, and glowed alone in the shadows, touched by the last rays of the gas lamp, proof that the hunchback had thrown it pretty far. Who would have suspected that there was still so much force in those old skeletal arms? But who would have suspected that

Cripure still had so much suppleness in his big, rusty body either? He'd barely noticed the little glittering object, when, despite all the precautions he'd given himself, he rushed over, as if it threatened to fly away, as if there wasn't a moment to lose in trapping it. And like a child smacks a net over a butterfly perched on a wall, Cripure's heavy hand came down on the shiny object and closed over it. *I have it, I have it!* And without even looking at that much-coveted object, but feeling its flat and pointy form, grasping it in his hand and smiling in the depths of himself and of the night, he went back to his window, puffing a little on his way.

He didn't even open his hand to climb back in, a more difficult operation than getting out, but he achieved it not only without falling but without ripping his clothes, without bruising himself.

The night-light created the effect of an everlasting fire on an altar, and, in that weak glow, the little pile of gold was barely gleaming, like embers dying in the ashes. He turned up the flame. The gold glittered, sending out its sparks. Cripure went forward, opening his hand under the lamp—a schoolboy's medal, shaped like a star.

For a moment, he was ashamed of his gesture, which seemed, through some godforsaken means, like a parody, but he raised the little schoolboy's star to his lips. The cold metal, which was neither gold nor silver, but probably nickel, stayed frozen to his mouth, as it had been to the Clopper's—the same motion the hunchback had refused. But this furtive kiss, voluntary or not, he took it back. And the little star fell back into his hand, suddenly losing all its charm.

A little nickel-plated star! A schoolboy medal! He was tempted to repeat the hunchback's gesture, to throw the ridiculous star as far as he could forever. For the second time, the little tinkling of a moment ago would ring out in the night, for the second and last time.

"They made a fool of me..."

But he didn't throw away the star, though he had approached the window with that intention. He held it in his hand for a moment longer, then dreamily put it on the table, murmuring, "Who knows?"

"Who knows?" he went on. And this time, the words spurting out of his mouth made him perceive the silence more deeply. Nothing, not a murmur, not a breath, not a creak of wood. Maïa had even stopped snoring. Her sleep must be peaceful and wholesome, with that light breathing he so envied, he whose sleep was more and more often filled with nightmares. Why not go to sleep as well! Why not mark the end of this night of mistakes by stretching out as usual next to Maïa, since there was a Maïa!

Wasn't that common sense? He started to feel that particular tiredness which he'd so often felt during his nights of debauchery in Paris, that little fever and that numbing of all the senses, making him think he was moving through clouds, a cloud himself. He passed a hand across his forehead as if to chase away a fly. His head hurt. It was definitely time to go to sleep. Perhaps he only had a few hours before the fatal moment . . .

The time? No point in looking at his watch. He knew it had stopped. What was it, a moment earlier . . .

"Yes, it's true. But so?"

And he listened.

Tick-tock, tick-tock, tick-tock. Was that really what it was? "That's astonishing . . ." He picked up the watch, lifting it to his ear: nothing. "I'm not . . . all the same . . ." He pressed the watch to his ear a second time . . . still nothing.

"That's so . . ."

It couldn't be the alarm clock either, and for a reason! Maïa insisted that the ticking of the alarm clock prevented her from sleeping and in the evening she took care to put that object further away, placing it on the sill of the garden window. She'd done that a little while ago, without thinking that today, an alarm . . .

But then, what was this godforsaken tick-tock?

He heard it as clearly as if he were carrying the watch it came from in his waistcoat pocket. But he didn't have a watch in his pocket, he knew that perfectly well.

"So what? What is it? In the end, how wonderful . . ."

He was standing in front of his desk. The little star glittered next to the treasure. What was the connection? The little star had nothing to do with the tick-tock. Besides that it had come from the same madness. The wine he'd drunk perhaps? The wine? "It isn't the wine," he murmured again, daring to lift his eyes to Toinette's portrait, with the little watch pinned to her bodice. His arms opened like those of a man who abandons himself and gives up, his lips spasming, his chin and shoulders trembling.

"Oh Lord!" He begged Toinette and took her as a witness. The tick-tock still in his ears. And Toinette's smile, that adorable smile, seemed inquiring. "Do you want to? Do you want to start over? The watch is already ticking . . ."

He let himself fall into a chair.

If he started to believe, or to make himself believe, that the watch pinned to Toinette's breast had started to tick all by itself, that would mean he'd gone crazy. It was fine to play with ghosts when he had ten glasses of Anjou in his blood, but at a moment like this! He'd lost track of which parts were theater and which were real. That sort of ticking or nibbling was the worms chewing the wood somewhere, maybe even Toinette's frame itself.

"I'm losing my mind," he groaned. "You know well that I don't believe . . ."

Do you want to?

He looked away, searching in the shadows. For what?

"Oh Lord!"

His big red muffler unraveled and hung down along his arms. Head lowered, his hands on his knees, he didn't move, pleading for mercy. "Oh Lord!" he cried for the third time. And he brushed himself off, shook his head like a man getting out of the water. "But you're dead!"

The little tick-tock still went on insistently. But Cripure no longer dared to look at the portrait.

"Damn it to hell! I'll settle this for myself!"

Clenching his teeth, his forehead striped with a fat crease, shaking from head to toe, he got up, stood on a chair and took down the portrait. He held it up to his ear. But he dropped it right away, falling off of the chair where he'd perched. Hastily, he propped the portrait on the chair with little "ee, ee, ee" cries of sacred terror, and he fled into the kitchen.

MONSIEUR Marchandeau, finally escaped from the crowd, had taken refuge in the square. It was there that night came upon him, sitting on the same bench where the peasant and his wife had disappeared, his suitcase at his feet as their bundle had been. He'd gotten up finally, and since then he'd been wandering, passing from one street to the next, night against the night, with a stammering but relentless stride. How could he reappear before his wife, how could he tell her?

Like everybody else, Monsieur Marchandeau had often perused, with a hand that was sometimes distracted, those war tabloids offering to the world such a list of horrors it was unbelievable that anyone could bear to look. In those tabloids, some of which would pay any price for interesting documents, he'd stumbled upon photos of an execution: a spy put before a firing squad. The man, his head lowered, his hands tied, a last cigarette on his lips, marched between his executioners, and Monsieur Marchandeau noticed that there was always one who smiled. It was as if there couldn't be an execution without that smile! Which one would be smiling in just a few hours?

Then came the actual execution: the man, blindfolded on his knees before the post. And then, finally, the line of soldiers in front of the corpse.

He'd looked at these pictures, not without emotion, but with the feeling that these things didn't directly concern him, that these horrors took place in a universe that wasn't connected to his own, his peaceful one where he'd never be shot, nor anyone he knew. Now...

It had happened to him as to so many others, a crisis he wasn't prepared for: he was at the theater, comfortably seated in an orchestra seat, and now someone was asking harshly for him to get out of his chair, to shuffle onto the stage, dragging his wife and son with him. He hadn't expected that. Naively, until August 2, 1914, he'd taken life for a fairy tale. Today they were asking, whip in hand, that he take an active role in the spectacle, without even asking if he'd *at least* learned some of his lines, if he knew what made up the scene as a whole and for whom this gala was being staged. But he didn't know anything. He only saw that it wasn't about the play anymore at all, that the comedy was turning into a drama—a real drama—that the bullet was a real bullet, the sword was really covered in blood, the corpse was really dead.

They were shooting spies—so be it! But nobody told him they also shot protesters, or that there were any. They'd led him to believe that everything was going wonderfully, and that the thousands of young men thrown into the manure joyously accepted their deaths. He let himself be fooled without thinking for a second that the murdering machine could turn against him and his son. He'd let it happen, he'd consented. He was complicit—alas!—with that smile which in a few hours would walk with Pierre to the stake, complicit with the prayers a tender chaplain would make sure to say over his son so that all the rules would be satisfied and the dead attended.

Night was rolling its fat clouds full of spray over the town and the principal walked. He'd wanted so badly to fool himself. He understood now that in addition to the sorrow of losing his son, snatched from him in such a dishonorable way, another misfortune would be added which would complete his ruin—Claire would never forgive him. She'd stop loving him, and maybe she'd even hate him. He'd betrayed both of them. That was why he was so sure of Claire's disgusted look. *She'll never forgive me and she's right.*

A bitter doubt pierced him: that of having been enormously wronged, of having let himself be dragged, like an innocent, into an ambush at the hands of practiced crooks, of having agreed to gamble, blindfolded, everything he had in the world. And with the card they gave him, which was worse than the others, he discovered that the whole game was rigged.

When he went home, Claire's look would perhaps still contain only sadness, and not yet hate. But hate would come, and despite all that, they would stay together. In a devastating moment of clarity he understood that she would never leave him, he wouldn't leave either, and they would continue to live side by side with this sorrow in common. Was it possible? Maybe not, but it was certain.

He went back to the station once again.

Everything was silent. The courtyard seemed to have grown in the night. Gaslights trembled in the shadows around the courtyard, but the station itself had no lights burning, not even the usual light of the clock. The trees around the square came out of the night like fat torches dunked in ashes.

He approached the square with little steps. *Where was it?*

He wanted to find the exact spot where he'd pushed up close to the barricade. Understanding that the search was in vain, he shrugged and went off, shivering in the dampness of the night.

What to do? But what could he do?

His hand lifted mechanically to the knob of a door—the waiting room.

He turned the knob and pushed, taking care, in passing through, to hold the door with his fingertips. He knew that door! For years he'd been coming there, in the evening, to buy his favorite newspaper, *Le Temps*, at the bookstore. But the door escaped from him and slammed shut in a gust of wind, groaned, shook, with a long trembling of the glass, and the echo reverberated in the empty room. It was lit by an oil lamp. In the center of the room, a stove was rumbling, stuffed to the gills. The custodian must have filled it with too much coal before he left. The whole inside of the stove was red, and the top part white. The pipe too, was white. But there was no one to benefit from this heat, not a vagabond, not one soldier. The peasant and his wife must have found a cottage nearby, or had they already gone home? Monsieur Marchandeau was frozen—he put his suitcase down and held his hands out to the fire. He stayed like that for a long moment, totally still.

"It's my fault…"

Hadn't he prodded Pierre with encouragements? Hadn't he sent him to his death like you show someone the door, pushing both their shoulders? *Yes, someone you hate, not a son you love. I should have…* what? Given him money and helped him to desert? Pierre wasn't a deserter, he was a rebel. He wouldn't have wanted his money. What he had done, he had chosen to do. "Poor child, poor sucker!" murmured Monsieur Marchandeau, who had never taught his son anything except what was taught and whose opinion of heroism was only respect tinged with suspicion.

He moved away from the fire. The heat was so intense that he couldn't stand it anymore, and the suitcase had started to buckle. He picked it up, put it on a bench and sat down. "My God!"

Too late. Finding a car? Running to Paris? It was crazy to even think of it. Where could he find gas? And the passbooks? No matter what, now he'd be too late. *What was Claire doing?* It had seemed to him a little while ago when he passed in front of the lycée that there was a light in her window, but he could have been wrong. He might know all the buildings by heart, but it was difficult, in total darkness, to say… The light could have come from a monitor's room, bent over his Latin translations. *That must have been it.* He passed a hand across his forehead: an ill feeling. The heat was making him uncomfortable. He didn't move right away, overcome by fatigue. He waited, as if in the face of his son's death and his wife's sorrow his own suffering had to reclaim its rights. His ears thundered and rang, as if full of water. He didn't cry, but a low whimper came from deep in his chest, like the barbaric wail he'd once heard in criminal court from a mother listening to the verdict that condemned her son to death.

He got up, took his suitcase and went out. The door banged behind him, creaking and trembling, multiplying the echo of its shaking panes into the night. The cold grabbed him, and he shivered for a long time, lifting the collar of his overcoat with a mechanical gesture.

What to do? What could he do? He climbed on to the little bridge where Cripure had witnessed the scene of the riot and slapped Nabucet. Two lights burned, the signal lights, scattered in the night. Others, closer to the platform. The debris from broken glass, benches, helmets the men had thrown down had all been cleared, and the rain had finished the tidying. There wasn't a sound—nothing but the tender puff of the wind over the roofs and in the treetops. He could have taken the station for an abandoned one in a dead city. He sighed, shivered, and went on.

Streets. Everywhere, the windows closed, the iron gates pulled down as if by hateful hands, and stretching out further and further in front of him, roses poisoned by the night. The suitcase weighed like lead on his fingers wrapping the handle. What would he say to Claire? How would he say it?

He walked.

Dawn would break soon; they'd come upon him loitering in the streets, soaked, covered in dirt, stumbling like a drunk. He wanted to know what time it was, and took out his watch as he approached a gaslight. The yellow light wrapped his long black shadow, and he bent over the watch held out in the palm of his hand: one a.m.

In his cell, Pierre must be pacing, if they hadn't put him in irons. What would his thoughts be? Would Pierre have forgiven him? "It's true, you're right. But your mother, my little one, your mother isn't guilty of anything. Why didn't you write to her?" He shook his head, bit his lips, made, with his arms, a vague gesture. Behind him, an iron shade, shining like a mirror. His grotesque shadow repeated the gesture. "Why?"

A clock sounded a quick toll. His watch hadn't deceived him. He wavered—an idea of the hour and fate—and tearing himself from the lamppost with a shaky step, leaving the little corner of light, he went back into the shadows, moving on, scraping along the walls.

The dogs, kings of the night, wandered in little groups of threes and fours, without a cry, rummaging in the garbage bins, scratching with their paws in the piles of trash outside the doors. A bin fell loudly and the dogs fled.

On a street corner, a gust of wind took off his hat. He ran after it. The hat rolled, bouncing. He grabbed it finally and brushed it off on his thigh. A coughing fit sized him, bending him toward the sidewalk.

From time to time, he stopped, slowly shrugging his shoulders. The suitcase became heavier and heavier, viciously battering his calves.

He stopped sharply, looking down at a thing—living or dead?— at his feet which he'd almost stepped on: a man's hand, open on the stone of the sidewalk; a small hand, fairly delicate, with a wedding band on the ring finger. A hand, yes, the hand of a drunk, no doubt, who was digesting his wine there . . . the hand, in fact, came out of a sleeve, and the sleeve belonged also to something indistinct, but which could be a body, forming a black stain against the wall like a scorch mark with two points—the knees. A drunk or a . . . corpse? He bent down.

The man was sleeping, his face hidden under a hat. A drunk.

Monsieur Marchandeau backed away, circling the streets. Then remorse took hold, and he retraced his steps. He couldn't leave the man lying like that without helping him, at least without offering. That would be . . . he searched for the word: inhuman. Yes, inhuman.

His shoulders gave a little shudder as he approached the shadow stretched out on the ground.

The man hadn't moved. At the base of the wall, the black shadow remained. Only the open hand on the stone formed a relatively bright splotch.

He shook the man: "Hello . . . sir?"

The man made a small movement with his arms.

"Did you hear me?" And the principal gently lifted the hat covering the sleeper's face. "Wake up. You'll catch your death if you sleep out here."

The wind picked up, scattering a fine mist of water into the air.

"Eh?" said the man, waking up, "what's all this?"

"Are you sick?"

"Me?" He sat up.

"Sick? No...I'm not sick. Why? Why did you wake me?"

"To save you..."

Monsieur Marchandeau knew a place where, if it was just for one night, a vagabond or a drunk would be better off than on a sidewalk. The fire must still be burning in the heater at the station.

"Why don't you go over there?"

"Where?"

"To the waiting room?"

There was no response.

"There's a fire over there. Do you understand me?"

"Yes."

"Ah! Can I help you with something?" The man, pressing his hands into the ground, looked like a legless cripple.

"Thank you. No." He brought his hands together and raised his head. Monsieur Marchandeau could finally make out his bearded face. A glimmer of madness was shining in his eyes. The man murmured, "My son!" and he lowered his head.

Under his hand, Monsieur Marchandeau felt the heaving of his shoulders like a violent shock. The man let his hands hang down between his legs, stretched straight out on the sidewalk, the toes of his shoes in the air.

"I asked, I had asked Monsieur Point for an evening off so I could go with Étienne to the barracks, and..." But sobs choked him, and his hand batted the air in front of his face. "Can't tell you! I can't tell you!"

Monsieur Marchandeau knelt and put an arm around his shoulders.

"I got drunk!" The wind blew white hair soaked with drizzle across the unhappy man's forehead. "I couldn't get myself to go over there. They've already killed one of mine. They'll kill this one too. I drank because I couldn't make myself go to meet him. I...I wouldn't have been able to speak to him. This morning, I understood that he wanted to tell me...something. And me...I wanted to tell him...something. I couldn't do it. I couldn't do it!" he went on, sobbing harder. And he pushed the principal away. "You must leave me...leave me. Leave me alone!" he cried, getting up.

Monsieur Marchandeau stepped back. The man pressed his shoulder to the wall, continuing to groan, "I couldn't do it . . ."

From the depths of the night, a dull sound, like the faraway drumroll of a tambour. Monsieur Couturier stopped whimpering. He came back to the principal. "Do you hear them?"

Steps, mixed with the clinking of weapons.

They retreated together, hiding in a doorway.

"A deployment!"

The sound of steps came closer, and soon the company appeared at the end of the street. Nothing but feet and the clink of bayonets. Not a word. They moved forward in a block. One, two, one, two. Under the light of a lamp, the helmets, the weapons gleamed. Who was first—Monsieur Marchandeau or Monsieur Couturier—to take the other man's hand? Who, when the company had passed, was the first to let go? Monsieur Marchandeau suddenly found himself alone. Monsieur Couturier was retreating, his steps dragging on the pavement.

The principal set off again. It was definitely time to go home. But he could barely go on. From time to time, he had to stop and cough. The fits were so intense that he had to put down his suitcase.

Finally, he reached the lycée.

Under the gaslight, the golden points of the gate shone weakly, like the moving reflections of oil lamps on calm water—or like those bayonets the group of artillerymen had silently brandished, already prepared for the task.

Monsieur Marchandeau, planted before the gate, realized that it was closed, and went around back, as he and his wife did when they came from the theater, not wanting to disturb Noël. He went down a street even darker than the others, where a door opened on to the gardens, close to the kitchen. The vents gave off a nauseating smell of cabbages. He took a ring of keys from his pocket, finding the one he needed by touch, then opened the door.

Silence. A heavy sleep weighed on the institution, confusing humans with stones. He crossed the garden on tiptoe, passing silently behind Noël's lodge. He looked like a bad soldier who'd jumped over the wall, or an unfaithful husband coming back from his mistress's house. At the bottom of the grand staircase, his finger pressed the switch mechanically, and the light that sprang up blinded him.

He went up.

One hand still holding his suitcase, he gripped the greasy banister with the other, climbing step by step. He stopped once again and coughed.

I've caught something bad.

The coughing fit became violent. *Noël will hear* . . . but no one came. His coughs woke nothing but noisy echoes from the walls. No door slammed, no steps approached. Nothing but the silence, moist and heavy, the light, the greenish staircase, the black banister.

He wiped his brow with his handkerchief, taking the time to put it carefully back in his pocket, and picking up his suitcase at last, he kept climbing.

And if she's sleeping? Will I have to wake her?

He hadn't thought of that either.

CLAIRE wasn't sleeping. After her husband left, she'd thrown herself fully clothed on the bed, and since then she hadn't moved—the world, the universe around her, had become a fragile edifice, ready to unravel at her slightest gesture. It was already too much to breathe, to feel the blood battering her temples, to know that her eyes (to see what, by God?) were open. But she didn't dare close them. Not for fear of the dark—was it possible to be plunged into a night deeper than the one she already inhabited? But because the slightest movement, that of reaching her hand for the switch, would unshackle everything she was trying so hard to hold back—the cries, the wild gestures of grief, the folly of tears. She didn't want any of it. The best thing was to clench her jaw for as long as she needed to ... to reassure. But what? Who? She didn't want to ask. The same way she'd stopped all her movements, she'd stopped that mute will of her body to leap up, mastered it like you tame a beast. This too was the way she silenced all her thoughts, breaking them up as quickly as they appeared—and they kept coming—concentrating only on her desire to wait and to be nothing while she waited. That could go on for a while, perhaps beyond her strength, until the moment a telegram arrived from "Papa." The word "Papa" almost jeopardized everything. In thinking that word, she was on the point of surrendering and letting herself be conquered. And it took no less than all of her determination to resist. But a moment later, she could keep going.

Her grief was almost without connection to its object. It was something automatic, which, if it came out of nowhere, wasn't less likely to stay once it came, mysteriously oblivious of its source.

The maid had come in. She had announced that dinner was served. That, too, had almost jeopardized everything. At the simple sight of the maid, Claire sat straight up, ready to yell, and her mouth had opened wide, round, to the amazement of the maid, who was used to a calm mistress, always even-tempered, master of herself. But Claire pulled out of the misstep once again, finding the courage to act out waking with a start, illness, a migraine, and she let the maid off work until the morning. No question of eating. The maid gone, she'd immediately fallen back into her lethargy, which she wished was more total and more real. Long hours rolled by. For a long time now, nothing and no one had come to disturb her. As if from the depths of a sickness, she heard without impatience or resignation the ordinary sounds of the school—the bell the concierge rang, the clogs of the boarders on their way to the dining hall, the fanfare of tin-glazed plates on marble tables, then the return to study hall, then again the clogs climbing back to the dormitory, then nothing, nothing but the silence, the whiplash of wind in the night, nothing but the electric light that made a gilt frame sparkle in the corner in front of her, nothing but the waiting, which tomorrow she might have to conceal. Would she be capable? Better not think of it yet. First she had to exhaust the night—her pain sufficient to each minute.

She sat up, her eyes wide open. What could that be but a key…

"You!"

She jumped off the end of the bed with the unique and muffled sound of two heels sinking into a carpet.

"What a state you're in!" A murmur he barely heard. "But what's happened?"

"No train for civilians…"

It looked like he'd rolled in every gutter in town. His mud-stained overcoat stuck to his shoulders like a towel. He didn't let go of his suitcase, didn't move, lowered his head, a long black silhouette against the gray-blue of the door. A hunted man, reaching his last gasp after a desperate race, who has only the strength to press his shoulder against the door his pursuers will soon be battering. This crazy idea flashed through her mind. Standing in front of the bed, as still as her husband, she jumped at a muted thud, which she took for the bang of someone stumbling on the staircase. But it was the suitcase he finally dropped, letting go of the handle with his swollen fingers. It fell and opened, all its contents rolling on the floor—the nightshirt, the toiletries, the papers. He didn't even move his head, but his red hand, still marked with white traces where the handle had been, climbed tremblingly to his mouth, as if blasted by harsh and successive shocks. And well before it reached that height, Monsieur Marchandeau was torn from the door in the grip of another coughing fit. He took a few steps, bent in half, and collapsed onto a chair.

Claire rushed over to him as if to stop him from falling, and once the fit had passed, she wrapped an arm around his shoulders and bent down so as to better understand what he was trying to say. He couldn't breathe. She understood all the same that he was talking about a stove heated until it was white.

"A stove?"

"In the waiting room . . ."

He made a gesture with his hand like someone choking. She started to undress him and he let her do it like a passive child.

The quick transition from the cold night to this warm room had stunned Monsieur Marchandeau. He let his head fall like a man close to sleep or to fainting.

She held up his head with her hand while still undressing him. Valor in that moment consisted of doing very simple things and doing them well. She'd have plenty of time to break down later. The daze she'd plunged into at her husband's return dispersed little by little, like a swelling disappears, and the blood that had been blocked in her veins started to flow again, to give her body back all its desirable flexibility and force. She existed only in the tension of her gaze—she felt her eyes pulling from the back of their sockets, the skin of her temples stretching—and down to the smallest and tensest fibers of her being, moving all her person to the thing that needed doing. It wasn't exaltation but presence, an attention brought to her task, a will, but one that was involuntary. She had become a sort of taut and crystalline character, entirely made up of her actions, gifted with a wonderful and barbaric ability to see herself acting, thinking, and suffering. This state would last for as long as the task was unfinished. Perhaps. Then would the crystal self break? Still it wasn't clear: she hoped she would control it even after. She astonished herself with the accuracy, the economy and the patience of her movements, as if a double inside of her was acting on her behalf. Her interior distress barely passed into her fingers, and full of goodness and love, forgetting herself, she found a way to smile when she needed to at this deathly face.

The buttons resisted. Once she got his blazer and vest off, she still had to remove the rest, the most difficult parts, and she kneeled down to untie his shoes. They were knotted like those of a child. She untied one with her teeth. He let her do it, with a limp passivity that multiplied the difficulties of her task. She, all the while, was thinking of a thousand immediate things—bringing him to the bath, rubbing him with alcohol, making a hot water bottle, putting him to bed, making him swallow a hot drink. The maid could have helped her with all these things. Nothing would have been simpler than to leave him for a moment and go wake the maid. She didn't want to do it, not because she was hesitant to let a maid see the unhappiness that was striking them both—and in what guise! But precisely because this sorrow was something that pertained to both of them and to no one else, she would have refused anyone who offered to help her in that moment. Pain, no less than love, couldn't be shared, and if anything could help her then, it was the thought that this task to finish was hers alone.

"Can you stand?"

He tried, but immediately fell back into his chair, with a limp movement, and he shook his head. She wasn't sure she could get him in the bath.

"Wait..." She squatted. "Put your arm around my neck."

He obeyed clumsily, groping like a blind man. His arm finally reached around his wife's neck. She steadied him by taking his hand.

"Stand up."

They got up together.

This time he stayed standing, Claire supporting him almost completely on her shoulder where he rested his head.

"You're going to go to bed and sleep."

"Yes."

It was an almost imperceptible "yes" that lingered in Claire's ear like the word of a defeated man giving up on himself.

With little dragging steps they approached the bed. Claire, with one hand, pulled back the covers, touched the sheets. They were cold. Too bad.

"Can you do it by yourself?"

"I'll try."

He'd spoken more distinctly. At the same time, he put one knee on the edge of the bed, and with a push on his hips from Claire, he stretched out in a single movement, heaving a sigh as deep and howling as a scream. Then he stuck his hands under the covers and was still. He looked for Claire's eyes, and his mouth hardened into a child's frown. He groaned, "Can you believe it! Can you believe it!"

And he burst into sobs.

Claire didn't succumb even a little bit to the contagion of tears, which any other circumstance would have surely produced. But in her state of extreme tension, she experienced something that was more like the opposite of contagion, neither repulsion nor condemnation, but a narrow consciousness of total impossibility, as painful in other ways as its opposite. And then, there was something else.

A sobbing man is a relatively rare spectacle, something Monsieur Marchandeau had given her little occasion to see. The few times she'd seen him cry—at the death of his father, when Pierre was sent to the front—Monsieur Marchandeau had stayed on his feet and fought his tears. She remembered a man bent under his sorrow but hiding his face in his hands, instead of this time, when the tears leaked out of his eyelids, his hands like strangers, unmoving on the whiteness of the sheet. It looked like the hands didn't know the eyes were crying. Some kind of immortal curiosity glued that woman in place before this man who cried, lying on his back without resisting. The tears were having trouble finding a path, visibly soaking the depression of the eye before seeming to flow back down, shining like oil in the bushy beard. How could he cry like that without her lifting even a hand? From the depths of his chest came the same low, muted moan as had come in the waiting room, like a cry of agony. She put a hand on his forehead but he didn't seem to feel the touch. From nearby and faraway at the same time, Claire felt a lurch of pity. She removed her hand, tucked him in, brought the sheet right up to his chin, and disappeared on tiptoe. No, she wouldn't break down right away. There was something else to do. She quickly returned with a flask and a napkin, and made her husband sit up. She rubbed him down, dosing him with a tincture of iodine, as she'd done for Pierre one evening when he'd come home from the stadium with a bad case of pneumonia after a soccer rematch. A devastating memory, which she pushed away with all her might, but which rooted itself in her, coming back with savage insistence at each gesture she made that was so similar to those earlier ones. She disappeared a second time, not to the bathroom, but to the kitchen, boiled water, made a broth and some grog. He wisely drank the grog and stretched out again, making a little gesture of refusal with his hand, as if he were demanding to finally be left in peace. But he was happy that she sat by his bed and took his hand. A sort of vague smile wandered for an instant over his face, but only an instant, a few seconds at most. Claire, still silent, her husband's burning hand in her own, looked at him crying and thought *he's going to cry himself to sleep like a little child.*

That was, in fact, how he slept. The sobs quieted, the whimpering tapered off, becoming, in the first moment of sleep, nothing more than a murmur of chagrin, a soft complaint, a slackening, which would soon stop. With precautions that reminded her of the times when Pierre, as a very little boy, had demanded his mother's presence and her hand before "going to the moon," she freed her fingers, removing them from the feverish, moist grip of the sleeper. He sighed, turned his head slightly as if conscious of this abandonment, and his lips sketched a frown that gave his sleep a curiously disdainful quality. The whimper came back for an instant, like a protestation or a reproach, then nothing more—a strange and overwhelming dispersal into sleep, absence. She got up.

More and more she felt her eyes pressing in their sockets and her temples hurting. She passed a hand over her forehead, felt her jaw tighten, her teeth clench, and her whole body jerk into an arch. She wanted to cry out, to run away somewhere from the blood that was beating violently in her head. Her steady hand seized the switch to turn out the light. The vertigo passed. Once again she mastered herself, entirely sure of what she was doing, confident that she would achieve what she had to accomplish.

She went out on tiptoe, listening one more time for the sleeper's breathing before softly closing the door. As far as she could tell, he slept peacefully. She could only hope he'd sleep for a long time, the time it would take her...

But no, not to the doctor's right away she thought, dressing in haste.

Despairing was cowardice. Why hadn't it occurred to him to find Faurel? If anyone could still do something, it was Faurel. She scribbled a note, went into the maid's room without a sound, and put the note on her night table. Then she went down the stairs, out through the little door her husband had made use of in returning, and half running, half walking, she went toward the deputy's house. Who could say? Perhaps he could telegraph, call, prevent...

FAUREL had been shocked to the point of indignation when he learned about the challenge to a duel. Not only was it stupid and cruel but also grotesque, and from the first instant, he'd resolved to do everything he could to stop things from going any further. Between Nabucet and that poor, crazy Cripure, anything could happen! At worst, surely, a murder in cold blood. Cripure, feverish and transported by sorrow, was capable of not waiting for the moment of the duel to grab a weapon and bring down Nabucet. Not at all impossible. And Faurel, who didn't lack a certain imagination, had sadly shuddered at the thought of Cripure's arrest, of the trial, of his years in a penal colony. Was it really a stretch of the imagination to envision these somber possibilities? Faurel didn't think so. He thought he knew Cripure well enough to believe him capable of killing Nabucet outside of the laws of the duel. And as for Nabucet... Eh, as usual Nabucet had the starring role. His position was strong, and it truly seemed difficult to reach a settlement. He was the wronged party. He was the one who'd gotten slapped, a slap that was apparently so gratuitous. One had to admit, that in this business Cripure had shown himself in the worse light, as a man incapable of mastering an angry impulse, someone completely in the clutches of hate. The result of all that was that Nabucet had every advantage, including the choice of weapons. Poor Cripure! What a mess he'd gotten himself into! And would his whole fate play itself out over that slap? To make things worse, who had Nabucet picked for seconds? That Babinot who was nothing but a hothead and Captain Plaire whom Faurel didn't know, but who didn't give the impression of having a great penchant for reconciliation. And Cripure, whom had he picked? Young Lucien Bourcier who never said anything and Moka! Cripure could have at least come to him. When everything was finished and the problem figured out, Faurel promised himself he would give Cripure a friendly reproach for not thinking of him in such a scrape. He would so willingly have been of service. But Cripure hadn't thought of him, or maybe, once again, his sad imagination had judged Faurel to be an enemy, ready to wrong him. Faurel wouldn't dream of being offended. He only thought one thing: since they'd chosen him as the arbiter, there was a little bit of hope.

The most irritating one wasn't that idiot Babinot. When it came down to it, he could tell him what to do, and Babinot couldn't be happier than to obey a staff officer. The most annoying one was Captain Plaire. Where the devil had they dug up that stubborn fool who kept repeating in various ways: "I only look to the laws of honor, gentlemen. Nothing but the laws . . ."

And what a stern attitude!

Nabucet himself wouldn't have recognized his even-tempered guest, this morning's instructor, in this swashbuckler. And it was true that Captain Plaire was not at all the petty bourgeois who'd dreamed of a secluded house and an easy maid. What happened had transformed him. You would have thought he was the one who had to fight.

And would they never get to the bottom of it?

"You know," Captain Plaire explained, "in the past witnesses were called seconds, and they too fought—they weren't confined, as they are today, to a simple diplomatic function." This took place at the Café Machin, where they'd met for an initial contact, a preliminary exchange of views. Moka was in charge of organizing the meeting at the café. But Captain Plaire had begun by making rather unpleasant observations that this wasn't how it was done, that the witnesses weren't supposed to meet in cafés. The gravity of a conflict over a question of honor had to be maintained, and under the circumstances, the hostess of the café, the fat blond woman who was still at her cash register, the one Cripure had compared, that morning, to a hen on her roost, had given them a private room to use, an empty room, a room no one set foot in, a room for events. But it wasn't a room decorated by Nabucet, like the one where Madame Faurel had received the Legion of Honor a few hours earlier, and where Babinot, unaware as he still was of his son's death, had told such good stories. Dust took the place of rugs and of ornament in general. It was so bad no one had dared to sit down, even though there were chairs around a table. A long monologue from Captain Plaire had begun as soon as they entered the room. The mission of a witness, he'd said, is not one to be accepted lightly, and he knew what he was about. He'd been a witness in thirteen duels and this one would be the fourteenth. He could also say without fanfare that he was quite familiar with affairs of honor, and he asked these gentlemen to trust his long experience. Undoubtedly none of them had yet undertaken the formidable honor of being selected for such a task, and the normal procedure, without being totally unknown, was perhaps not very familiar. And then he'd thought it prudent to tell them in so many words how things would happen. The first question for debate was obviously to decide whether there were grounds for a duel or if, on the contrary, they should consider from the beginning the possibility of a settlement. But, in the present situation, there wasn't a shadow of a doubt. The offense done to Nabucet was so flagrant that the duel was absolutely necessary, and not a fake duel, not one of those shameful comedies so many people engaged in (Captain Plaire, warming to his subject, became, if not eloquent, at least profuse), but a serious combat. A slap, that required an absolute reparation, and there was nothing but a duel to the death which would give it. Babinot, listening to the captain, approved it all with nods of the head and conniving little smiles, cries of "Wait! Wait!" if anyone looked like they were about to speak. He was delighted with what he heard, and enchanted that a captain was saying it. And the captain went on. The choice of weapons belonged to his client and his client had chosen swords. But the combatants shouldn't be familiar with the weapons, in the interest of justice and equal chances. Some duelists in fact preferred lighter weapons and others heavier ones. They would give them ones neither had used. The captain would take care of everything. That was it. Of course there were plenty of things to say about the duel in general and stories to tell, which Monsieur Babinot could have made good use of, but this wasn't the moment and anyway all was clear as could be. An elementary case. A slap: a duel. No need to beat around the bush—they had to fight at dawn. All that was left was to choose the field, to inform the combatants, to rent the vehicles, and to ensure the indispensable presence of a doctor. There was no time to lose.

The others listened to this monologue in the deepest silence. Lucien stayed very calm. As for poor Moka, he was distressed. As much as he'd spoken of the duel with Cripure himself, the thing hadn't appeared to be all that serious. He hadn't believed it. The idea that Cripure could fight a duel was so crazy, that even considered as a reality, Moka hadn't been able to believe it. For once, he'd lacked imagination. But Captain Plaire's speech had made up for that. From the first words of the speech, he'd started to realize that it wasn't all fun and games anymore, and his old teacher would be forced into a meeting on the field, ayayayay oh oh! And with swords! If only they'd chosen pistols! But nothing to be done, and nothing to be said. Nabucet had his choice of weapons and they were all stuck with it. That left Faurel. He might know how to settle this. He was used to diplomacy, and he wasn't a cutthroat like that terrible captain. But they'd had all the trouble in the world in bringing the captain around to Faurel's house. What good was it? he'd said. Why did they need a referee? Once again, the case was extremely simple. Were the four of them so green that they needed help appropriately overseeing this affair? If he'd had the Chateauvillard Code in hand, he could have proved to them, with supporting quotations, that only in the case of a disagreement among the witnesses, when, for example, they couldn't come to a consensus on the start of the quarrel, or on the reciprocal roles the combatants had taken in it—in sum, when it wasn't possible to determine with certainty which side was in the wrong—and only if all the witnesses were agreed, would it be useful to have recourse to an arbiter, a person of influence in title or reputation. But that wasn't the case. This affair was the simplest of all the ones he'd been involved in, all of which *let it be noted, gentlemen,* had been settled on the field. And doubtless he would have held to that uncompromising position if Babinot hadn't observed that Nabucet himself wouldn't be opposed to this arbitration, that he'd take it as a surety. Besides, there was no way, no fear that this arbitration could go against the wishes of his client. The facts were the facts. A slap was a slap. They would not risk heading toward a settlement. This speech didn't have a great impact, but everyone stuck to their positions, Cripure's seconds insisting on the question of pistols, and Captain Plaire refusing to entertain them. In the end he'd decided that they should indeed have recourse to Faurel's mediation. He didn't say, but he thought it was astonishing that Nabucet hadn't asked Faurel to be his second. But that was another question that was none of his business. And whatever he believed, it was decided they would go to Faurel's, who had a higher rank than Captain Plaire, eh, since he was an officer of the state.

But, it had been more than a half hour at Faurel's, comfortably seated in the great parlor, and they were still stuck on the same points. Faurel had ordered liqueurs brought in by a young, pretty chambermaid whom the captain hadn't even noticed. God knew how striking, under any other circumstances, he would have found that charming face. But he was focused on the duel and kept repeating: "My only concern is for the laws of honor, gentlemen, nothing but the laws of honor."

And Babinot kept pushing it.

Moka twisted his red forelock, crossed and uncrossed his legs, cracked his knuckles, sending pleading looks to Faurel, to Lucien, even to Babinot, who smiled, winked, and pushed his bandage, which alas was looking like a rag, back into place. It was no longer, it must be said, the sparkling white bandage that had made such an impression on the grand assembly when he'd appeared at the party that afternoon. It looked like the dressing had been dragged through the dust, rolled in soot.

"If you knew what this man was to us," said Faurel, "you'd try to help us avoid this absurd thing..." He wanted to say "that is a duel," but he didn't want to offend the captain.

"But again," said the captain, "did Monsieur Merlin slap Monsieur Nabucet?"

Out of patience, Faurel replied, "But that's obvious. There's no denying that, my dear captain. But when you know him..." He would have liked to add, "and when you know Nabucet," but that was impossible. "A man as worthy as Merlin!"

Lucien didn't say anything. This silence seemed strange to Faurel. It didn't seem that Lucien was very enthusiastic about the cause he had agreed to support.

Faurel asked, "What are your thoughts, Lieutenant?"

"In my opinion," Lucien replied, "it's useless to try to explain what qualities make Monsieur Merlin worthy. That's not the question. The slap is flagrant. It would be more productive, the way I see it, to focus on the medical side of the question. Captain, we've already spoken this evening in various ways of our client's infirmity. Note that he didn't mention this himself and has agreed to fight. I even think that he will be very... unhappy if we prevent him. But it's up to us, Monsieur... Moka, Faurel, and me—to take it upon ourselves to insist on this particular side of the question—disability—and we ask you if, under these conditions, you insist on thinking that a fight, especially with swords, is always unavoidable. I insist on this point: that, perhaps overstepping our rights as seconds, it is us who propose the form of a settlement, it being well understood that our client wants to fight."

"A question of pure humanity," said Faurel.

"Or, at least, of pistols," said Moka.

"There's no chance of pistols!" cried the captain, waving his hands. He'd listened to this speech with impatience. "My client has the pick of weapons. He picked swords, and it's with swords they will fight."

"But he can't stand up!" groaned the unhappy Moka.

"Well, too bad for him. He'll be killed," said the captain.

When one has to deal with idiocy...Faurel thought. *And with meanness*, he thought, imagining Nabucet.

"Poor Cripure," he muttered.

"But, come now, gentlemen, come now," cried Captain Plaire, lifting his arms to the ceiling, "according to you, your client is in part a man of genius, and in part a very weak man, perhaps even—"

"Captain!" cried Babinot.

"Well now what?"

"See here, captain, we don't want to wrong ourselves by speaking ill of the opponent."

"I agree! I agree," said the captain, "but when all the devils point that way, he slapped someone, and he has to fight!" Wasn't that obvious?

Faurel was warming up: "It's not a question of genius," he said rather roughly, "but when it comes down to it, Monsieur Merlin is not an ordinary man. You must be aware, my dear captain, that he's not only the author of a remarkable work on the philosopher Turnier, but he's also published a few other volumes, including one on *The Wisdom of the Medes*, which had their moment of fame—Merlin is a scholar. A Sanskritist. And don't forget either that he's brought us new insight into Greek tragedy. As for the rest," Faurel continued, seeing the Captain's wide eyes, "as for the rest, see here!"

He went over to a cabinet, which he opened forcefully and rummaged through the papers. All the while, he kept talking as he went about this task.

"Gentlemen, I was his student back in the day, and if my memory serves, I should be able to find, in these papers, an old photo and maybe more than one. I'd be pleased if you would take a look at them, my dear captain. Be assured," Faurel said, to flatter him, "that I perfectly understand your point of view, which is that of a man of honor and a soldier, and that of a friend, too. But we"—and he continued to rifle feverishly through the papers—"but we have ours too. Permit me to say that Monsieur Merlin represents, in our eyes, the noblest thing we have in the world: the Spirit incarnate, if you'll allow me to use such a grand word. We don't think of Monsieur Merlin as a man of genius, captain, but, as we said, he's a worthy man. With looks that are deceiving, and through a life of infinite sorrows," (despite himself, Faurel fell back into eloquence) "infinite sorrows," he continued, thinking of Toinette, "and whatever people might want to think—excuse me, Monsieur Babinot—of the bad example of behavior he has given us, this man, you understand, is a master to us. In a certain way, he represents the best that our civilization has to offer, even if it's an intelligence that denies itself, but that's perhaps where its grandeur lies. We have for him, and for what he represents, an infinite respect, and it would be a terrible thing… Hang on!" he cried, "look, here's the photo! It's that man there you'd like to see fighting with a sword!"

He threw the photo on the table. The captain picked it up. It was one of those photos from the end of the school year, taken in the June sunlight, already announcing the next vacation. The aged Cripure—he already seemed old, thought the photo was taken twenty years before—was standing next to his students, head bare, without his goatskin. His hands were in his pockets and his shoulders slumped, scowling, seeming to reproach the circumstance that had dragged him there among those idiots in a gesture that was supposedly friendly. The shoulders slumped, the knees bent, and the clumsy photographer had pressed the shutter at the moment when the sun caught the lenses of the pince-nez and made them flash. As for his legendary feet, they seemed even more enormous in the photograph. They looked like two pediments riveted to the ground, and it seemed like the astonishing statue that rose from them could never be torn away. Captain Plaire had never seen anything like it. It was comical and horrific at once. Besides, even Cripure's face, as the photo showed it, and in spite of the flashing pince-nez, had nothing of the duelist in it. It was more like the face of an ordinary petty bourgeois, not warlike, sick, bored, a sad face like many in Europe, which had so shocked him when he came back from Indochina.

"Wait! Wait! Wait!" murmured Captain Plaire.

"Here," said Faurel, "I've got a few more." He threw four or five more photos onto the table, pulling them from the bottom of a box.

"May I?" said the captain, picking up the photos which he examined one by one with a profound attention and increasing astonishment. "Oh! But," he said, "so it's true? I thought, you see, in looking at the first photo, that those big feet...well, I thought it was a mistake of the cameraman's, you see. But no, it's the same in all these. There's no mistake, none at all. Wait! Wait!" He didn't stop looking at the photos with an air of surprise and anger. "What's all this, eh?"

Nabucet hadn't told him the whole story when he had come, Babinot at his side, to find him at the mess hall where he was finishing dinner. Nabucet had presented Cripure as a sort of troublemaker, a giant "rather badly put together," a dangerous personality, a notorious subversive, unhappy with himself and others, someone bitter who needed to be taught a lesson. But he hadn't mentioned his feet, he hadn't said anything at all about what this shocking photo revealed at first glance, even to someone like Captain Plaire. And once again the captain murmured, "Wait, wait, wait."

He put the photos down on the table and, crossing his arms behind his back, he took a few steps around the room.

"I repeat," said Faurel again, "that our shared duty is to prevent this encounter...I see that the captain is changing his mind," he said, smiling.

The captain didn't reply. He reflected and remembered.

How sly memory is, he thought. The little incident he was remembering was one he hadn't thought of since childhood. He did the math: now, I'm fifty-eight. This must have happened when I was thirteen, and Nabucet was ten. It's been exactly forty-five years. One day, during Carnival, they'd worn disguises, a whole band of kids, adorned with trinkets stolen from their mothers. The game was to guess the person under the costume. But, on the street corner, towards the end of the day, Plaire had met Nabucet, whom he'd recognized right away under his mask, and he'd run happily over to Nabucet, shouting, "There he is, Nabucet, I see you, that's it!" And poor Plaire had gotten, in return, a massive whack on the hand from a cane. The captain could see the scene, and felt his astonishment as if it were yesterday. Of all the children playing the game, only Nabucet had thought to arm himself with a cane, to make use of his mask to hit people. "Wait, wait, wait."

"Are you convinced?" asked Faurel.

The captain stopped pacing and sat down in his chair, saying, "Gentlemen, it's not a question, in fact, of making Monsieur Merlin fight with swords. I find this document," he said, pointing to a photo, "absolutely convincing. I regret that I wasn't better informed of Monsieur Merlin's physical state. I owe you an apology," he said, addressing himself to Faurel, Moka, and Lucien.

"Ah! Permit me, permit me," cried Babinot.

"To do what, Monsieur?" said the captain, ready with a sharp word.

"Permit me, my dear captain. On the contrary, we explained to you that he was disabled. I was the first to say so."

The captain looked at Babinot severely. "It wasn't completely clear to me," he said.

"Are you still holding out for swords, Monsieur Babinot?" asked Faurel.

"Ah," Babinot replied, "I will second the captain's opinion."

Discipline is the primary force of armies, thought Lucien.

"Seeing that he hasn't spoken of pistols as of now," said Moka, who was thinking aloud.

"Be reassured, Monsieur," the captain replied. "The duel will not take place."

"Ah!" cried Moka happily.

"Ah!" said Faurel.

"I say: bravo," said Babinot, clapping his hands. And once more he snuffled his nose (his trumpet) and repeated, "I say again and again: bravo!"

Only Lucien remained impassive. The captain turned to Babinot. "You understand, Monsieur, the real state of the question?"

"My dear captain it doesn't seem impossible to me . . ."

"That he can fight a duel with swords?"

"Ayayayay!"

"Devil take it!" cried Babinot, "it never seemed possible to me, in fact . . ."

"That's good." The captain cut him off briskly and rudely, "I know now what to think."

Before he'd seen the photographs of Cripure, the captain had believed that everything they told him about the opponent's handicap was exaggerated, and that they wanted to use that to force Nabucet give up the idea of swords and agree to fight with pistols, which he wanted to avoid at all costs. He'd been so insistent about his wish to fight with swords, he'd so emphatically repeated to the captain that in no way was he to accept pistols, that Plaire, far from thinking there was another goal behind it, had innocently believed that it was the others who wished to fool him and that they demanded pistols because pistols would give Cripure an enormous advantage. Things had been presented to him in such a way that he thought he was fighting step-by-step to get them to conform to what his client had legitimately demanded. But as soon as he'd seen that astonishing photograph, things looked radically different. He was starting to understand what Nabucet meant when he'd talked about teaching that individual a lesson. In the captain's vocabulary, teaching someone a lesson meant something very precise and not very far removed from what was commonly called giving an enemy what he deserved. And of course, with honor at stake, the captain would have been in agreement. But he understood now that what Nabucet meant to say was infinitely subtler than that. As for Nabucet, he knew perfectly well Cripure couldn't fight a duel with swords if he'd wanted to, and that he'd be faced with the dilemma of either a cowardly refusal of the combat or accepting it—knowing full well he'd be killed.

In a word, Plaire had been deceived.

"Allow me one more remark, my dear captain," said Babinot.

The captain allowed it, with rather bad grace.

"See here," said Babinot, bringing his hands together so that the fingers touched at the tips, "see here, let's try to understand one another: you think that Monsieur Nabucet committed in sum, an...abuse when he demanded swords and refused pistols knowing full well—let us understand—that Monsieur Merlin is crippled. Is that right?"

"Yes."

"Fine," continued Babinot. "But," he said, getting up, and his hands disappearing beneath the tails of his coat, "so much the better! But in that case, cripples would make a nice game, it seems, of administering slaps to the healthy, imagining that..."

They didn't let him finish. A general cry of reproof met these words.

"Merlin certainly never made that low calculation," said Faurel.

"Ah! Permit me!"

"Not at all! Not at all!"

"He slapped him in spite of himself," said Moka.

"A slap doesn't happen like that," said Babinot. He knew it. He'd found out very recently what had to be done to provoke a slap (or a blow from a belt). His hand touched the bandage.

"If you'd said that to me before," said the captain.

"Before what? Before the photo?"

"Yes." And also before he'd remembered the cane. But that he didn't say. He finished, "I might perhaps had believed it. But it's too late."

"Ah! Fine, fine!" said Babinot, "since you're all in agreement. You too, I understand, Lieutenant?"

Lucien, holding his knee between linked hands, bent forward. "I think that Monsieur Merlin won't accept a form of settlement."

There was a silence.

"But Nabucet won't either!" said Babinot.

"That's less important."

Moka saw that everything was in jeopardy and became somber.

"You believe that Monsieur Merlin doesn't want a settlement?"

"I didn't say he wouldn't want it."

"Unfortunately, I think I understand you," said Faurel.

The captain intervened: "Eh, well, I understand it poorly. There's no other way to get out of this, it seems to me. It's either the settlement or the combat. And if your client refuses, Lieutenant..."

"You see, Captain, he can neither accept nor refuse."

"Yet it's he who must offer his apologies," said Babinot.

"In principle," said Faurel, "Seen... from the outside, he's completely in the wrong. But he won't apologize."

"He's arrogant," said Babinot.

"I don't think it has so much to do with his pride," replied Lucien. I don't think it will do us any good to discuss his psychology either. The fact is that the situation presents no way out for him. All we can do is to prepare a contract and submit it to him, that's it."

These commonsense words momentarily put an end to the debate. Moka claimed the honor of serving as a secretary. He had beautiful penmanship, and he was proud of it. They seated him at a table.

Moka, Babinot, and the captain engaged in a new and endless debate about the terms. Lucien lost interest. He took Faurel aside and in a low voice, said, "In my opinion, he won't even read that paper."

"You think?"

"It's more or less certain ... as soon as he knows it's about a settlement..."

Faurel gave it some thought.

"I fear that you're right. But so, in that case ..." and he let his arms fall, discouraged. *Poor Cripure!*

They moved even further away so that they could talk more easily. The others forgot them anyway, entirely absorbed in their task. From time to time a concept—apologies, honor, intention to offend—rose above the noise of their conversation.

"You understand," said Lucien, "Cripure is above all to be pitied in this: we can't help him. We can do nothing for him, as he can do nothing for us."

"Exactly."

"We can, at most, prevent him from the duel. He won't be at all grateful. I predict that his fury will turn on us."

It was likely—the deputy could believe it. Cripure would think they had betrayed him. But was that a reason ...

"I didn't say it was."

"Do you know ... I love that man."

"And me? Do you think I don't love him?" replied Lucien. "My poor Cripure! He initiated me, you understand. He was my master in the noblest sense of the word. I adored him and I cursed him. Then, I understood him. I don't want to say: justified him."

The others were still talking behind them. They sat down.

"Are there things you can't forgive him for?"

The reply was slow to come.

"No . . . I think that *everything* can be forgiven him. Cripure will disappear. He has a right to all our pity. And then, it will be over."

Faurel found that Lucien was quite hard.

The latter continued, "I discovered that what Cripure taught was contempt."

Faurel had never thought of Cripure through that lens, but he agreed that what Lucien said was revealing. He added, "Yes. But at the same time, he was very attached to what he was condemning."

An insight.

"And I thought," Lucien continued, "that contempt was the same as grandeur. I even believed that all great intelligence was by nature contemptuous. I don't like to remember those days at all."

Faurel asked himself about the value of that life, of the heroism in contemplating the absurdity in it. "And besides," he said, "the meaning of this life—"

"The question isn't to find out the meaning of this life," interrupted Lucien. "The only question is to find out what we can make of it."

"Do you believe in mankind?"

Cripure's phrase. Lucien thought he could hear him. Without trying to, Faurel had mimicked the old master's tone of voice, as it amused him to do when he'd been Cripure's student. How many times had Cripure spoken in class of that idiotic belief in a so-called man, capable of so-called conquests . . .

"You can put it that way if you want to," Lucien replied.

"Why did you agree to be his second?" Faurel asked.

"Out of friendship."

"But you just said . . ."

"That he deserved all our pity. I should have added: all our friendship too. I made my choice, but that doesn't mean I abandoned my friendships. Cripure stands for the inverse of what I want. Is that a reason not to help him in extremis? We're not executioners."

"We?"

"Well ... I'm going too far." He wasn't going to set about explaining these kinds of things to this staff officer? He'd chattered on too much. He got up. "Perhaps we should involve ourselves a little in this document?"

"One moment," said Faurel, obliging him to sit back down. "You use words that frighten me—Cripure will disappear, help him in extremis. What are you really thinking? You're speaking in the abstract, aren't you, when you say disappear? You're taking Cripure as a symbol?"

"I'm thinking also of the individual that he is."

"Oh! You mean to say that he'll take ..."

"What else could he do, otherwise?" Lucien replied briskly. He added, "It's why I ask myself if we're doing the right thing, if, not good sense but goodness wouldn't have been to let him have his duel."

The others, in their corner, did battle with the pen and their voices around the table.

"Then, and you can think what you like about this, I realized that after all, Nabucet is less certain than the other solution."

"Out of goodness, that too?"

"I told you you could think what you like."

His coldness seemed more put on than involuntary to Faurel, and he didn't reply.

"Listen," Faurel went on, putting his hand on Lucien's shoulder, "between you and me, we have in common this man we both love—"

Lucien cut him off. "It's not about knowing if one should live or die, love or hate. It's about knowing: in the name of what?"

And their conversation ended there.

The others, once they'd got something in motion, started to be shocked at the absence of Faurel and Lucien. Moka, putting down his pen, stuck his long, bird-like neck out towards them. "Let's have a reading! A reading! Tell us what you think!"

He'd become jovial again. This time, his luck had come through. The document had been written in such a way that it didn't seem possible to him that Cripure would refuse to sign. They'd completed the overwhelming tour de force of passing off the "universal slap," which had escaped Cripure against his will and which was certainly given without the intention of offending Nabucet. But Nabucet too, had to make a sort of apology. That was Captain Plaire's undertaking. "You get yours to sign, and I'll take care of my side," he'd said to Moka. And Babinot had fallen in line.

Moka, standing, gave a solemn reading of the text. When he had finished, he placed the document on the table. "What say you, dear sirs?"

"Nabucet will never sign that," said Faurel.

"Oh," replied the captain, "I'll take care of it. If it's only a signature you need, you can count on me!"

"So be it, gentlemen," said Faurel, "you've done a great piece of work. Your mission for tonight is accomplished. It's time for some refreshments, don't you think? It seems our little reunion has gone rather late, and I thought it would be good to have a little cold supper prepared. Let us move into the dining room. My car will take you home."

CLAIRE fought to at least spare herself the folly of placing too much hope in a man she didn't even know, who would perhaps listen with only one ear, bored, or even hostile, since really he was a staff officer and complicit. But perhaps not. Everything she'd heard rumored about him, all she'd been able to guess from the rare times she'd seen him in public, like a few hours ago at that ridiculous party where they'd decorated his wife, came back to her memory; her courage returned, and she thought that her excursion would be undoubtedly well received, that in any case Faurel couldn't be a bad man.

At the edge of town, practically almost in the countryside, the avenue that lead to the Faurels' forked off a roundabout, and the deputy's chateau rose behind it, defended by bars, as if there were crocodiles ready to bite. Of course, it wasn't a chateau except in name, since there was nothing in the way of architecture. It was a bourgeois house, larger and more pretentious than the others, surrounded by far-stretching lawns and gardens, a façade in pure 1900s style, as serene as its era. At the sight of that façade, one could guess that the man who built it had been a bigwig. The chateau was in fact the work of Madame Faurel's father, the Count of Trinquaille, a great hunter, huge eater, big smoker, big drinker, owner of tons of property, and huge dandy, prodigious fucker of women, fat and crass in everything, loving the fatness and the crassness. This fat descendant of a large, crass family had taken a liking to this little town, and for a widow here, and since, strangely, he didn't own anything in town, he'd built (with money stolen from his farmers) this chateau, which seemed to have been built for a Monsieur Prudhomme. And yet, the chateau took on a feudal aspect at night, as if the count had influenced his architects without knowing it. But perhaps it was also that Monsieur Prudhomme, feudal himself, liked feudal castles, as he liked to walk on the skins of lions other people had killed. And still the straight eaves flanked the building with its pointed roofs, high in the air, spiked with arrows on weather vanes and lightning rods straight as pikes, like the lances and standards of fantastical knights who jousted on the roofs, perhaps against the town or against the clouds. The weather vanes creaked like the clanking of armor. One of them stood out in black against a shred of pink sky and seemed to lead the cortege.

Claire rang the bell, realizing sharply that this moment would engrave itself forever in her memory, that she'd always remember, until the end of her life, the tinkling of the bell in the night. Dogs barked in response to her ring, and someone came, a man in clogs who held a lantern and a guard dog on a leash.

Above the grate, a lamp shone, lighting the deserted drive, and the avenue leading to the chateau looked entirely pink and white under the ashy foliage of lindens. She had to negotiate with the concierge through the grate, to say that it was about something urgent.

But the concierge wanted to discuss it. A rather late visit by a woman ... hmm. And his boss wasn't expecting anyone. Was it perhaps an old mistress, with a revolver up her sleeve? That wasn't unheard of.

"Monsieur Deputy is very occupied at the moment," he said.

He didn't think those gentlemen had finished their discussion yet, and he wasn't totally sure the deputy would be in shape to receive anyone. But in the end, he went to ask. He tied up his dog, opened the grate, and Claire finally entered the park. He left her there.

The wooden clogs slipped on the too-fine sand of the drive, and the man, still holding his lantern, walked slowly towards the chateau where she could make out the lighted rectangle of a window. The night smelled of earth and wet wood. The dogs weren't barking anymore, but in the back of their kennels, they growled softly without stopping, making a savage accompaniment to the light sound of a breeze in the branches, brought to the town on the faraway rising tide.

After a cruel wait, at last the man in clogs returned. She heard his monotonous and indifferent steps at the end of the drive; she saw his lantern, which he still held out at the end of his arm. She could go in! The deputy would see her that very moment.

She followed him.

The man took off his clogs, and they went into the immense vestibule. He opened a door, showed her into an elegant little parlor, and she'd barely sat down when Faurel appeared.

She trembled and stood up, seized with panic, her sight clouding with the blood that rushed to her head. She wasn't going to be able to say a word... How could she speak of Pierre to this elegant man, so visibly different from his surroundings?

Yet she spoke, and as she spoke, in a calm voice, raising her eyes to Faurel from time to time to ensure that he was understanding, the deputy became somber. He changed his seat to be nearer to her, as if to hear her better, but really it was so that he could better hide his eyes. He'd understood. It was too late. And time enough for a hundred interventions wouldn't have helped at all. She didn't know them!

He asked, "When did you receive the letter?"

"This evening. The five o'clock post."

"Do you have it on you?"

She took the letter out of her bag and handed it to him.

"Dated the day before yesterday," he said, handing it back to her. And he was quiet. Claire put the letter back in her bag.

"Yes, the day before yesterday."

And announcing the execution for tomorrow morning, he thought.

"My husband wanted to leave for Paris, but..."

"I know. There was a riot at the station this evening. There were no more trains for civilians."

"Only you can tell me you tell me if there's still something to be done."

Claire's voice was almost natural, like her gestures. Nothing betrayed her distress. There was an almost perfect symmetry in her, a coherence of herself with her sorrow. Faurel felt it and he was afraid. He was less fearful of saying what had to be said than he was of the connection created between himself and this woman—a connection absolutely without lies. He couldn't fool her, even if he wanted to. By everything she was in that moment, she forced him to resemble her, so that she drew him, in spite of himself, into a country of cruel truth, absolute, where he wasn't sure that he would escape suffocation.

She was waiting for his response. He couldn't find the words, at once racked and complicit before this woman who was also a judge. He wished she hadn't come. That cowardly desire—he justified it with his own sorrow. Wasn't it some sort of injustice that she'd chosen him to bear this burden? He felt a moment of hate towards her, as if she were no longer a wife and a mother full of grief but a pain in him, like a wound in his flesh he should have had the right to resist. The moment passed. He discovered something else, a strange necessity of the circumstances, by virtue of which her presence here was legitimate, maybe even necessary. Two human beings, couldn't they find each other this way and see into the depths of each other through their connection to the most extreme sadness?

He finally dared to raise his head. She hadn't moved, hands crossed over her bag.

"If I were a doctor, and if you'd called me to the bedside of a sick person, would you ask me to tell you the truth?"

She said yes, with her lips and her nod.

"Yes?"

"Yes."

He didn't say anything else. She'd understood. Her eyes closed. She turned pale all at once, that supernatural pallor of women after giving birth. He saw before his eyes that transformation of her face, turning toward an absolutely pure beauty that was almost transparent—the face she must have in the moment of love, and surely the one she would have in death. As for his own face, he felt it hardening, tightening at the top of his cheeks, grimacing. Claire closed her hands over her bag once again and her fingers linked. He bent towards her, ready to catch the fainting body in his arms. But she fought with all her might, as if swimming from the depths of the water to the light of day, not for love of the light, but because, above sorrow, there was still something to reach. This horror must be overcome—the horrible revelation that not only can children die, but they can be delivered to the executioners.

She wanted to get up, and didn't succeed right away. She felt a weight of lead all over her body, a heavy disturbance, and when she finally stood, it seemed that everything was in chaos around her. Out of instinct, she reached for something to lean on, found the back of the chair, put her hand on it. Faurel had also stood up, feeling the same grimace on his face. She heard him offer a bit of port and she refused, stammered.

"Thank you."

"How can I assist you?"

She refused again.

"Thank you. You have been..."

The word wouldn't come. He bowed his head. And Claire took a step towards the door.

"It would be very easy to have you driven home."

"I think not," she said.

"My car is at the ready, in fact, we just..."

"No. I prefer to walk home."

"Are you able?"

"Yes."

"Are you sure?"

"Yes, thank you. Completely sure."

They went out, walked through the garden without saying a word. She walked next to him with a firm step. His was less so. He opened the gate and backed away, searching for a gesture, a word. Which one?

AFTER Madame Marchandeau left, Faurel didn't return to his guests right away. As much to collect himself as to escape questions he was neither willing nor able to answer. He went back to the little parlor, sat in his armchair, tossed away the cigarette he'd taken from his case without lighting it, and put his head in his hands.

It was too much horror, too much blood, too much grief. For what reason? Once again he was confused, lost himself in his thoughts and pushed them away.

Poor woman! And it's only just begun!

Soon, when her son was officially reported "missing,"[18] the torment would take a different form. She and her husband would have to pretend to share with their friends the hope that their son could return one day—not all the "missing" were dead. They had to keep on hoping for as long as they had no proof of death—it wasn't possible to avoid. One of the wounded, the Germans had picked him up, they were taking care of him in Germany, but he was forbidden to write. People would cite a thousand cases like that, instructing them to have patience. Hadn't they seen soldiers rattled, losing their memory in the middle of a battle? Sure, there were papers, the identification tags, but, so the good Samaritans would say, didn't they know that for certain missions, the soldiers weren't allowed to wear anything that would reveal their identity? Once again they *had* to keep on hoping.

To all that, they would have to respond without betraying themselves. Would it be possible? It would show so little on their faces, but in the back of their eyes, would there be a dead son, executed? Would the others be wracked with that rotten compassion for long?

Wasn't it a thousand times better to tell the truth at once than to let them all guess? At least silence would make a shield around them and they could suffer in peace. They wouldn't need to alienate anyone, people would flee of their own accord. *Enough!* The deputy sighed once more, rubbing his hands over his face.

In any case, that's what people would end up doing. Here, their easy compassion would be denied that element which elsewhere made it so correct. They only had to look! That grief, they'd suspect it wasn't real when enough time passed so that it wasn't possible—they'd say, reasonable!—to wonder if her son was still alive, they'd see that Madame Marchandeau didn't dress in black, that not only did she refuse to wear mourning clothes, but that she also kept away deliberately—they were sure—from remembrance societies and commemorative ceremonies, solemn masses for the rest of dead soldiers' souls. *At least*, he thought getting up, *they weren't for their torment!*

He decided to go back to his guests, and composing his face with a smile, he pushed open the door.

Babinot, his hands crossed over his belly, nodded his head, vanquished by the emotions of the day. The discussion of the duel, the little meal which Faurel had served, had finished off his energy. But all the same he still chattered, in a voice that, admittedly, was mushier and more nasal than ever, and he often interrupted himself to yawn.

Moka had stopped listening to Babinot a long time ago. He was burning with impatience to go tell Cripure about the happy outcome of the negotiations, and found that they'd been keeping him here for a long while. As for Lucien, he was calmly smoking. His mission here was done. He'd given Cripure the last bit of help he could give him, and he was happy to think it had been a service of friendship.

"I must say," said Babinot, turning toward the captain, "he was one of those fat boys with chubby pink cheeks, you know, that dame Germania is so good at producing. My son went to study for a year in Dusseldorf; the following year, it was the son of Herr Professor

Schröder who came to stay with us. A real prewar Boche, you understand!" and he winked his one eye with a disdainful air.

"Isn't it time we should..." Moka tried to say.

What mortal purgatory must his good master be in! Why didn't Faurel give the sign to go? He'd just sat down and seemed to be thinking of something else entirely.

Babinot started in again, "and besides, heavy and clumsy...yes, yes, my dear Captain. And the proof was that little Angèle that my son's going to marry, well then..."

"He wanted to steal her from him?" asked the captain.

Really? They were going to talk about women?

"Nah, nah, not at all."

"Ah?"

"Nah, my dear captain. Not for anything! But that's not what the story is about. He found himself, my... Boche, having to accompany this little Angèle into town one day. She's wily, that one! Eh, do you know what he offered her?"

"I can't imagine..."

"To carry her purse! Her evening bag! Ah, ah, ah!" cried Babinot, giving himself a big slap on the knee, "that's a good one, don't you think? That fits the bill? Her little purse!" wheezed Babinot.

He rocked dangerously in his chair, waving his arms around him, the bandage mostly unraveled and ready to fall.

"He was exaggerating," said the captain. "But she, the young lady, what did she say to all that?"

"She?"

There was a moment of silence.

"Well, she gave it to him!"

And immediately the laughter returned, Ah! Ah! Hee! Hee! The clever little one!

"She's a clever one! They arrived like that at the house, and he was carrying the purse like a packet of cakes, with his fingertips, practically right under his nose. Ah, ah, ah! But that's it, that's comedy." Babinot changed his tone. "We weren't thinking yet of the tragedy... we found it funny, comical. He was just the way we imagined the

Germans before August 2, 1914, in our criminal blindness..." He put his head in his hands. "Oh! When I think about it! When I think that I had one of those men under my roof, at my table! Oh! He was a sergeant, you know. And here, proof of premeditation: he said to me, in his heavy Germanic accent, 'We zhall have de var, Monsieur Papinot, we zhall have de var!' Oh! When I think about it! But we were trusting, as honest as gold. Often, I tell myself that my son and that Kurt could find each other face to face in a battle."

"Not likely," said Faurel, getting up. Finally, he'd had enough.

"Not impossible," Babinot countered, "not impossible at all. And if that came about..." he winked.

They went out toward the car where Corbin was waiting, wild with anger at Faurel and the others who were making him stay up all night after a day of traveling, as if he were a simple taxi driver. The deputy, his father, was going a bit too far. There were days when he too easily forgot the things one owes to a bastard son, where Faurel, taking his role as a staff officer too seriously, was confused and didn't see anything more in Corbin but an ordinary soldier like the others. He'd make him pay dearly for it when the time came. As for the others, if he'd listened only to what his little heart desired, he'd have played a trick on them. To teach them something about how to live, he'd bring them as far out as possible into the countryside, five or six hours from the town, and there, he would pretend the car broke down. Playing the innocent, he would say that he'd taken the wrong road. Since there would be no one at hand to help them, the others would be obliged to go home on foot, in the night, while he, heroic soldier and faithful servant, would pretend he couldn't leave the car and would sleep in it until the following morning. Then he'd go home half an hour later, when he was sure they couldn't hear him. He'd been rolling these agreeable thoughts around in his head all evening, weighing the pros and cons, and he'd finally arrived at the conclusion that it was better to act as he was supposed to toward these gentlemen, the seconds, and to make his father, the real and only one responsible, in debt to him for a few hundred francs. Even the passion for revenge didn't make Corbin lose his head for long. Having reached this conclusion, his anger lessened. And so he seemed infinitely amiable, and even subservient, going so far as to open the doors, which he never usually did, at least when he hadn't calculated in advance how much drinking money he would make.

"If you please, gentlemen," said Faurel.

Corbin hurried to open the gates. It really wasn't worth it to wake the concierge for so little. And the men climbed into the car, Babinot first. He sat himself in the back, letting his entire weight sink into the seat, dead tired. Captain Plaire sat next to him. Lucien and Moka sat facing them. Corbin turned the crank. The motor rumbled. He climbed in and took the wheel.

"Safe trip!" said Faurel.

They wished him good night and the car went off.

"Oh!" cried Babinot, continuing his interrupted story, "I don't want my son to kill him right away. No. I want him to say his bit first, and before he kills him, to..." Babinot made a gesture of ripping something. "Exactly. To disfigure him!"

No one responded.

"Where are we going?" said Corbin after a moment.

Who would respond first?

"No one knows?"

"Monsieur Babinot seems very tired," said Moka, who couldn't take anymore either. "We should perhaps go to his place first?"

Lucien agreed. But Captain Plaire had another idea.

"Would it seem inconvenient to you all to stop by Monsieur Nabucet's house first?" he asked.

"Not at all," said Babinot. But he was lying.

This demand seemed odd to Lucien. Tomorrow would be soon enough to reconcile Nabucet with their negotiations. But he didn't say anything.

"Well then," said the captain, "if our chauffeur agrees..."

"Oh!" Corbin replied, "what's it to me if I turn the wheel one way or the other..."

There was a silence in the car following this observation. *That young man's got a funny attitude*, thought the captain.

The glow of the headlights cut into deserted streets like a knife. Corbin drove as fast as he could, trying to impress his "clients" with speed.

The captain tried to recognize the location, but it was no use. They were going too fast, the night was too dark. Finally he recognized the convent wall he'd walked along with Nabucet that morning. They were getting close.

Unbelievable. The little car trip hadn't lasted more than five minutes. It must be that the town was not, in fact, very big. And five minutes had been enough for Monsieur Babinot to fall asleep. He wasn't snoring yet, but, hands crossed over his stomach, he let his head drop onto his shoulder. Poor Monsieur Babinot! He wasn't used to staying up late.

"Here it is," said Corbin.

He slowed down. The car stopped in front of Nabucet's door.

"One moment," said the captain, getting out. "Would you please use your...what do you call it? Horn?"

"Horn, yes," said Corbin, leaning on the horn.

Now that was a good idea! If it was about playing Nabucet a little serenade, all right.

"That's enough," said the captain. "They'll think it's the last judgment."

"Very well."

"I don't see any lights. I'm going to ring the bell. Is Monsieur Babinot really asleep?"

"I believe so," said Moka.

"We've got to wake him up. I'm going to need him to be there, and you too, gentlemen, if you please."

"Us?" said Lucien.

"Just for a moment."

"Should we get out?" said Moka.

"That would be preferable."

Babinot slept with closed fists. Now he was snoring.

"Monsieur Babinot!" said the captain, putting his hand through the door. He shook his shoulder. "Monsieur Babinot, please!"

There was no response except even louder snoring.

"Monsieur Babinot!"

What glorious dream had Babinot plunged into?

"Alert! Alert!" he suddenly cried, jumping out of his seat so fast that his head hit the roof of the car. That bang on the head must have made him remember his rascals, since he added, "Where are they? Where are they?"

Corbin turned in his seat. He shrugged, lit a cigarette. "Nuts!"

"What is it?" asked Babinot, coming back to himself a little. "Where are we?"

"In the middle of the countryside," said Corbin.

"Countryside? How can we be in the countryside? We're in the countryside?"

"Our mission isn't finished, Monsieur Babinot," said the captain. "We have a word to say to Monsieur Nabucet. That's his door!"

"Oh!" cried Babinot, "that's right! I must have dozed off in the car?"

"That's it."

Lucien and Moka got out.

"Should I get out too?" said Babinot.

"But you most of all," the captain replied.

Only Corbin didn't move. The captain approached Nabucet's house, where all seemed to be sleeping. Not a light. He rang. Ferocious barking replied.

"Watch out. He has a terrifying dog."

"His guard dog," said Babinot. "I know it."

"Do you know if he's leashed?" asked Moka. He was scared silly. Anything but guard dogs!

"No, he's not on a leash."

Moka trembled. "Ring louder!"

The captain rang again. Corbin, seeing that they weren't getting anywhere, took it upon himself to sound the horn. It was worse than the first time. The racket became unbearable. The furious howling of the dog, the horn, the bell that Plaire kept on ringing, persuaded that Nabucet didn't want to open up, made a hullaballoo of all the devils.

Finally, two shades clicked open. Corbin stopped honking, the captain stopped pulling on the bell, and even the dog himself, leaping behind the gate like a wild beast, quieted his growls.

"What is it?" said a voice that they didn't recognize as Nabucet's, which gave Moka the horrible thought that they had the wrong house. "What is it?"

It was old Anna.

"We want to see Monsieur Nabucet," said the captain.

"Oh!"

"We want to see him right away."

"Oh! But who's there?"

"It's Captain Plaire speaking, Anna."

"Give her my name too," said Babinot, pressing the captain's elbow. "She knows me. That'll soften her." He didn't have the energy to shout himself.

"It's Captain Plaire and Monsieur Babinot."

"Oh!" Anna's voice rose. "Oh! Monsieur Babinot too!"

"And two other friends. Hurry, Anna. Go wake Monsieur Nabucet. We have something very urgent to say to him."

"I'm going, I'm going."

"Couldn't she have tied up the dog first?" Moka asked. He thought the dog was going to manage to jump over the gate, as he had been trying to do since he first heard them.

Widows were lighting up in the house. In front of the gate, they said nothing else. Corbin was smoking, his head on his crossed arms, leaning against the wheel.

Finally a light went on in the vestibule. And not only in the vestibule, but also outside, in front of the doorway a globe of light suspended like an antique lantern suddenly flashed. The front of the house looked chalky under the harsh light that washed over them. The sound of a key. The door opened, and Nabucet himself appeared on the threshold, wrapped in a magnificent dressing gown with braided fastenings.

"Here, Pluto," he commanded in his sharpest voice. They saw the dog approach his master and sit right at his master's feet. "Go inside, and try to stay calm."

Moka let out a big sigh.

Nabucet approached with a quick step across the garden path, the sand crunching under his leather slippers. He opened the gate. "I'm overcome, gentlemen, that you took the trouble of coming so far in the middle of the night. Please come in, I pray you. He sent a worried look toward Lucien and Moka. Was it normal for the *other one's* seconds to visit his opponent? It seemed irregular to him.

He opened the gate wide.

Captain Plaire and Babinot went in, took a few steps into the garden, then the captain stopped and said, "Now that I think about it, perhaps it's not worth going inside. What do you think, Monsieur Babinot?"

"My God," said Babinot, "I don't understand."

"What do you mean by that, Paul?" asked Nabucet. "You don't want to come in?"

"No," replied the captain.

At the same time, he took the written agreement they'd so laboriously worked on at Faurel's out of his pocket.

"Here," he said, "is a little piece of paper that we all wrote together, and we're all in agreement. But this document is deficient. The duel will not take place, Nabucet. You were very careful not to tell me who your opponent was, you bastard! And now," he said, advancing, "now you'll have to square with me!"

And holding the agreement up to Nabucet's face, he swiped his nose with it.

"There! I'm the one you'll fight. Tomorrow. Tomorrow morning, two of my officer friends will be at the disposal of your seconds, and since you like swords so much, as the offended party, I hope you'll choose swords again, you pig! Go. Go inside so I don't have to see your filthy snout anymore. And hurry up," shouted the captain, running after Nabucet with his hand raised.

Nabucet, frozen with surprise and terror, incapable of a gesture or a word, floundering, gave an animal cry, a sort of rabbit's scream . . .

"Coward!" shouted the captain.

Suddenly Nabucet screeched, "It's an ambush!" And he ran into the house as fast as he could, covering his ears with his hands. "Help! Help!"

The captain, hands on his hips, watched him run. "What a stinking little fool," he muttered.

And the door slammed, the light went out. The only light left came from the lamps on the road.

"Quick, quick," cried Moka, "he'll set his dog on us!"

They all got back into the car.

Corbin watched the scene without moving. He spat his cigarette butt out the door and drove off.

Silence. And the car rolled past the walls of the convent once again.

"And now?" said Corbin after some time.

He received the order to drop off Babinot.

That one wasn't sleeping, but worse: he'd been stupefied into silence. He still hadn't been able to understand what he'd just seen. And Moka wasn't very far from the same state as Babinot.

"All in a day's work," said Corbin.

The captain didn't answer. No one did. And the car rolled on in the night. They dumped Babinot at his door as if he were a drunk. He even staggered, and Moka had, of course, to ring the bell for him. When Babinot returned to his wife, who had waited up for him, Moka got back in the car.

"Whose turn is it?"

They dropped off the captain first. And finally, it was agreed that they'd take Lucien to Madame de Villaplane's. Then Moka would go to Cripure's house. But the plans were complicated once more.

They found that the boardinghouse was in a state of extraordinary uproar. Lights were burning in all the windows, and the door to the street was wide open. Lucien had barely set foot in the foyer when he heard the noise of steps, of calls.

Moka and Corbin joined him.

By all appearances, something strange was going on in the house. They called out. But someone was coming down the stairs as fast as

possible, and they found themselves nose to nose with Kaminsky—
Kaminsky in his pajamas, uncombed, his face gray with fear, and a
wicked gleam of joy in his eyes.

"Do you have a car?"

He'd heard them coming.

"Yes," said Corbin.

"Good. So we can bring her. Don't move..."

He was going back upstairs.

"Hey! You, sir, who I don't even know..."

"Yes," said Kaminsky, turning around.

And Corbin replied, "I'm the driver, you understand."

Kaminsky approached, conciliatory, and he spoke to Moka. "Please,
Monsieur Moka," he said, "could you ask your friend if he'd be kind
enough to drive Madame de Villaplane to the hospital?"

"That depends on what's wrong," said Corbin. He wasn't going to
get himself mixed up in some dirty business.

"Stuffed with sleeping pills," said Kaminsky, in a hurry to go back
to the sick woman.

"Is it serious?" said Corbin.

"Oh! Seven or eight packets...the stupid bitch!" he muttered,
clenching his teeth... And he added, "You'll stay, won't you? You'll
let us use the car? Monsieur Moka, would you be so kind as to alert
the police?"

Simone called from upstairs, "Otto! Otto! Come quick!"

Lucien looked on in wonder.

CRIPURE was sleeping.

Having abandoned Toinette's portrait on a chair, he'd taken refuge in the kitchen. A single thought: to lie down next to Maïa, to forget, to sleep if it was possible. He'd undressed in haste, his teeth chattering, and slipped into bed. Maïa had barely moved, sighed, and he'd stayed immobile next to her, not hoping to sleep, yet sleep had come like a blow.

In the study, the lamp burned on.

He dreamed. The Clopper had disappeared for a long time, perhaps he was even dead. No one saw him anymore. At night, no one heard his dragging step, no one heard the stones ring with the sound of his cane's iron tip. Cripure found himself seated in a large empty room, all alone, but on the side he heard voices, what was undoubtedly Babinot's voice, since it was so nasal. In any case, it wasn't at the school. "And why, gentlemen, for what reeeason does he drag his foot?" asked Babinot's voice. "Oh! I am at school," said Cripure to himself. And, in fact, he only had to turn his head to see Babinot before him, at his lectern, and all around Babinot about thirty little Cloppers, perched on their desks like toads with golden eyes. "Why, messieurs, whyyy does he drag his foot?" repeated Babinot, a finger raised. "Because," he repeated, leaning forward, "go on, gentlemen, go on, come now!"

"Because he jumped out the window!" the choir of little cloppers said in chorus.

"Ah! Ah! Ah! Ah!" sang Babinot, to the tune of "Cadet Rousselle," doing a pirouette, "he jumped!

"Ah! Ah! Ah! Ah! he jumped!
And his little foot he bumped ..."

And all the little cloppers started singing with him. Then there were no little cloppers. Even Babinot disappeared. Cripure found himself sitting on the terrace of a café, the Café Machin; he asked the waiter, "But, in the end, why did he jump?"

"It was when the husband came back," the waiter replied. "It happened two thousand years ago, two thousand years, two thousand years, that that river is exactly two thousand meters wide." Cripure wasn't, in fact, seated at the Café Machin anymore, but instead by a river so wide he couldn't see the other bank. The waters were yellow, muddy, and the trees planted on the banks looked like rifles. Cripure fished with a line, his head hidden under a straw hat, which oddly had the form of the police hats Maïa folded out of the newspaper, even his favorite newspaper *L'Oeuvre*. It wasn't a fish Cripure was after. Something precious, he didn't know what it was, had fallen into the water, and it was this something he was trying to reel in at the end of his rod. A boat appeared in the middle of the river, a sort of fishing boat with a blue sail, and, on the back of the ship, Nabucet's horrible face. But only for a moment, since the ship was suddenly engulfed by the river, leaving an ironic ripple. The sail detached and flew. It lifted, raced in one long streak up to the heavens like a Bastille Day firework, sticking like a golden spike, becoming a star. And from that new star, like an aeronaut from his parachute, like a spider on the end of his thread, the Clopper solemnly sank. No more river. The black street, and the Clopper with his star in his hair, which became the street lamp. "Attention," continued a commentator, "a terrible drama is about to unfold." *So*, thought Cripure, *he isn't dead yet?* And he hid behind his window shade.

The Clopper was there under the gaslight as usual, his chin in his hand. Cripure took his revolver and sighted: bang, bang ... The Clopper didn't even turn his head. "Impossible," murmured Cripure. Bang, bang, bang ... Three rounds. Bang. The last one. The magazine was empty, and the Clopper hadn't moved.

He finally did, he took a step, and with a gesture that shocked Cripure, he twirled something around his head ... not his cane. What was it? A sword! Under the light of the gas lamp, the pure blade glittered, twirled so nimbly in the Clopper's hands, so quickly it seemed to be a wheel, like those at the fair, for the raffle. Cripure jumped so much in waking that Maïa opened her eyes.

"What's wrong with you?" she said.

"Nothing, a nightmare," Cripure replied in a muffled voice. He searched under his pillow for a handkerchief to wipe his forehead.

That it was possible to sleep so long, to forget, even a few hours before death, and dream of the Clopper and ... *What a dream!* he thought, how he handled his sword! Maïa went back to sleep, but he understood that he wouldn't sleep again until the eternal rest they wrote about in the inscriptions on gravestones—and they wouldn't neglect to mention it on his own—and with great care not to wake Maïa, he got up, looking curiously around him and shivering.

The fire had gone out in the stove a long time ago. Everything seemed sad, sordid, freezing. He got dressed, asking himself if he wouldn't go back to bed, missing the warmth. He wrapped the goatskin around him. With that over his shoulders, he could stay on his feet. What a dear old goatskin it was! He suddenly felt a rush of Prudhommesque[19] sentimentality for that goatskin which enveloped him from head to toe, filling him with soft and tender warmth. *Enough!* And so he realized the light was burning in his study.

What? What light? He didn't remember right away that he'd left the lamp lit, and when it came back to him, he let out a big sigh, as if the fault in his memory were proof that he wasn't completely lucid, that something was starting to unravel in his skull. He walked toward it anyway, his look turning to Maïa. As he pushed open the door, the light came into the kitchen, climbing slowly, like the only illuminated spoke of an invisible wheel, brightening first a hand hanging over the bed, then the rest of the arm, discovering the shoulder, and then the face still thick with sleep. Cripure didn't move. His own hand froze on the doorknob, and he watched the sleeper for a long time. He could barely hear her breathing. He let go of the door, but didn't go into his study right away. He went back over to the bed as softly as he could and bent down, almost kneeling, and pressed his lips to that fat hand, abandoned in that moment and so innocent. He murmured twice, "good old hand... good old hand," and placed a kiss on it. Then, his chin trembling, ready to sob, surprised at the gesture he had performed, and wondering if there wasn't a bit of theater in it—for the benefit of whom?—he finally went into his study.

Strange how empty this study was, emptier than ever before. That was undoubtedly because the lamp had stayed lit for so long while he wasn't there.

It was very lucky, all things considered, that he'd woken up so early! They would come to get him in good time, and there were so many things to do! Shave. Wash. Which meant taking a shower. Get dressed. Not, of course, in the clothes he wore every day to that zoo, but groomed, back in his dressy clothes. Would there be time? And that hussy Maïa—hey, why call her a hussy?—who was sleeping with closed fists, she'd certainly made a fine fuss last night, but not for a moment did it occur to her that everything had to be got ready for the ceremony. He felt a new anger at her. Was it all the same to him to show up on the field with his shoes unpolished, his beard uncombed, in old clothes, so that they could make fun of him one last time before he was finally expedited to the worms?

Calm down! Calm down! It was perhaps still very early, three or at most four in the morning. *Just wait.*

He didn't even seem to see the gold, though he thought distractedly that he would have to put it back in its bag, and the bag in its usual place in the drawer. There was no question anymore of using the gold to flee. Did one leave, did one run away? The gold would go quietly back into its drawer where it would pass into Maïa's hands. For the moment, it was fine on the table. He could see it. Soon, he'd put it in the bag. Soon. There was no rush.

With the same great care, he opened another drawer and this time removed not gold but a revolver. In his massive hand that little black object seemed extraordinarily useless: a toy. He looked at it for a long time, checked the safety, and slowly raising the weapon, a finger on the trigger, he sighted the doorknob and noticed with pride that his hand wasn't trembling.

It was trembling. And so much that he was in danger of dropping the gun—he relived his dream, the Clopper still and impenetrable at first, under the gaslight, then, the exhausted magazine, that sort of dance with the sword which had freed the phantom... "a prophetic dream! a prophecy!" Cripure repeated. And the blood went out of his face. "A dream of warning! Oh what a fool I am. It's with swords they'll want to fight..." He sat up, one hand pressing his heart, the other still on his revolver, in the grandiose pose of the dying man, of the judge who asks for someone's head, and brandishes the final evidence under the noses of the jurors—the murder weapon. "With swords!" He sank into his chair like an ice cube melting instantly in water. The ice broke, banged the table, his head buried in his folded arms, his hair mixing with the hair of the goatskin. His elbow plunged into the middle of the gold, forgotten on the table, and the little hoard crumbled like a pile of sand, the coins bouncing, surrounding him like a marvelous rain of sparks, rolling at his feet and into the corners of the study. The gun tumbled to the ground. He didn't even notice. "With swords!" The idea that they could demand swords hadn't occurred to him, proof of his idiocy. "Me? Me? Me, fight with swords?" It was their right—wasn't he the offending party? They had the choice of weapons. And all the pleas in the world, all the medical attestations and expertise proving that he was crippled, and whatever he might think in his suffering, wouldn't stop them from taking him for a coward. He wept with rage.

The bell rang in the corridor. A discreet little ring, to start with, a single, light sound, as if the morning visitor feared as much as desired to wake the sleepers. But this shy ring was followed by a real blast, filling the whole house, and Cripure raised his head, his heart failing him, doubting still, or wanting to doubt.

Already! They were here already! It wasn't light yet and they were already there, like executioners, the car undoubtedly stopped in front of the door with the swords in it! He was paralyzed, incapable not only of getting up to open the door, but of even drying his tears. It was the idea that they would find him in this shameful state that brought him back to himself, to the use of his legs. But then, realizing the gold pieces were scattered around him, rolling all over the floor, he wanted to pick them up. Another ring of the bell sounded. He hesitated, looked toward the door. But he couldn't open it yet. Quick, quick, bending down everywhere, like he'd done the day before in the corridor when he picked up Amédée's scattered letters, he searched for his gold Louis.

A call came from the kitchen. It was Maïa waking up. She woke roughly, torn from some delicious dream. In the depths of her sleep, the tinkling of gold rolling on the ground, the clanging of the bell in the corridor, had been transfigured into the lovely sound of wedding bells. She dreamed that Cripure had finally decided to marry her, and that the ceremony unfolded under the eyes of the celebrating town. And the bells were ringing all over. Alas, it wasn't true! She'd barely woken when she understood, remembered everything, and this was the very morning that Cripure had to fight a duel, the moment they had come for him. She jumped out of bed crying, "Ah! My God!" and seeing there was a light in the study, ran to it.

She went in wearing her nightgown, puffy with sleep, her eyes still half closed, uncombed, horrible—just at the moment when Cripure, having finally gathered up his scattered gold pieces, threw the bag with both hands into the back of the drawer.

"Open up! Hey, open up!" the shout came from outside.

It was Moka's voice, impatient but joyful, the strong voice which had sung so well:

Kiss-es, more kiss-es,
Kiss-es, always!

Was that really the voice of a man coming to take another to his death?

"Open up!"

Cripure, still holding the bag of gold with both hands, looked toward the door like a man frozen in place.

"Go open the door, Maïa," he said in a shaky voice.

"Like this? In this getup?"

"Cover yourself with something!"

She put on a dressing gown and ran to open the door. The operation was long and noisy. Cripure, still unmoving, the gold in his hands, heard the chain banging against the wood, then the click of the bolts, and finally the key grating in the lock and the mechanism turning with the dry click of a rifle loading.

"God in heaven!" murmured Cripure, throwing the gold into the drawer. "Is it Moka alone? Great God!"

Moka was alone.

Not noticing Maïa's bizarre outfit, Cripure's even stranger accessory, or his dreamy air, not even remarking on the mess which had taken over the room—it wasn't about that!—Moka entered with a pirouette. He took off his hat with a generous sweep, saluted like a musketeer, straightened up, and shook his head, the little red forelock flaming on his milky brow.

The handsome tuxedo was rumpled and undoubtedly dirtied beyond repair, looking as if it had been rained on for months, and the pretty polished shoes, the heeled loafers he was so proud of, they were now horribly scuffed and covered in mud. What a race he'd had to run—from the boardinghouse to the police, from the police station to the hospital, where Madame de Villaplane was dying at that very moment, from the hospital here, which he'd had to do on foot, since Corbin had refused his services. His placket shirtfront was buckling, the badly stitched buttons looked like they were ready to pop off his vest, and his tie was no longer very straight. There was still something hanging in Moka's buttonhole, something that looked quite a lot like the head of an onion that had gone to seed, a sort of yellowish tumor that was scorched in places, which not so long ago had been a splendid and fragrant rose! Dressed like that, with his pale face and drawn features, his blue eyes widened by fatigue, Moka looked a bit like a reveler who's lost his heroine and knocked on the wrong door. For the illusion to be complete, he only needed a couple of paper streamers around his neck, some confetti in his hair, and a kazoo. But it wasn't a kazoo Moka held between his fingers—it was a sheet of paper he unfolded as soon as he entered, which he brandished with an air of triumph.

"Sign it!" he cried. "Put your scribble on there, my dear professor, and all will be settled forever—sign it! Sign it!"

Cripure didn't move.

"And he'll be free of this mess?" Maïa asked.

"Free, Madame. Yes, free! A little scribble, I'm telling you, and—"

He couldn't say anything more. Maïa had thrown her arms around his neck with such force that Moka almost fell over backwards. He dropped the paper, which flew around the room and softly settled on the floor.

"Oh!" cried Maïa, squeezing Moka enough to choke him, "you've saved our lives! Benefactor! Benefactor!" shouted the unfortunate wench, who, in her emotion, stumbled upon a word she hadn't used since childhood, when she'd learned it from her mother who must have heard it from a priest. "Benefactor! How can we thank you?"

And tears ran from Maïa's eyes while she smacked big childish kisses on Moka's pale cheeks.

He patted her back. "Come! Come!"

But all the while mumbling unintelligible words, she gripped him convulsively against her wandering breast.

Cripure lowered his head.

He didn't look at the curious couple, simply waiting for this to pass, and in fact it was over after a minute.

Maïa lifted her head. Moka stopped patting her back. She sniffled, turned to Cripure, "Your hanky?"

Since he didn't have one and since it would take too long to go looking in a dresser, she dried her eyes and her nose with the sleeve of her bathrobe, and feeling calmer, she asked, "Where'd it get to, your bit of paper?"

Moka was busy looking for exactly that. Cripure still didn't move, a curious witness, spectator of a scene where in fact the drama was all his own. He took his chin in his hand and watched Moka with profound attention. Moka picked up the paper and looked for a place on the desk where he could put it. It wasn't at all easy. The papers for the *Chrestomathy* were still all over the desktop, and, from the first glance, Moka had realized that these things had to do with his professor's manuscript, an object for which he had the deepest, the most sincere respect. Wasn't it a great thing for him to be brought here to see what no one could see, to contemplate the very papers where his master set down his thoughts? Hadn't he wished a thousand times to be involved in this unknown life, this life of the mind and the soul, which was embodied for him by Cripure? Hadn't he dreamed that Cripure wasn't really the professor everyone knew, the odd character they saw wandering so sadly through the streets, but a real poet, whose genius would only be revealed after his death? Surely all those little bits of paper he saw were the fragments of that genius poem Cripure had dedicated his life to. He didn't dare touch them. What if, through his mistake, something from the poem was scattered or lost, or even scrambled? It would have given him a feeling of endless remorse. No, it wasn't for a Moka to do anything that might displace a single comma in such a work!

Moka stopped moving. He still held his paper in his hand, his look moving from the table to Cripure's eyes and back. Cripure finally understood.

"Oh! That's all it is?" said Cripure in the voice of a man who is already resigned, perhaps already indifferent, and who thinks that the best thing after all is to obediently play out the game. "Is that all it is, my dear Moka? One moment."

He made a space, as if ready to toss everything away, to brush all the bits of paper away with the back of his hand, and yet not doing anything of the kind, on the contrary, taking care not to mix them up, he stacked them on the edge of the desk.

"Good," said Moka with a knowing smile, "that's your manuscript isn't it?"

Cripure whirled around all at once. "Manuscript?"

What did he mean to say? What! Your manuscript? So he knew?

But had he said *a* manuscript? Had Cripure been stupid enough to let slip a word about his *Chrestomathy*? Or was the other one thinking of some new *Wisdom of the Medes*?

"That's got nothing to do with it!"

"Oh! Excuse me," said Moka, "truly my dear professor, please pardon me, I ... I had no intention, none at all of ..."

"Let it be, let it be!"

Moka wasn't offended. He thought it completely natural that he would be rebuffed on the question of the manuscript. Of course, it was none of his business and Cripure was right.

He put the agreement on the table. "Voilà!"

With the flat of his hand, he unfolded the paper, but as if he wanted to caress it at the same time. He was so happy with this outcome!

"Here you go," he repeated. "A little scribble my dear professor. Nothing but a little signature at the bottom of this document."

He could barely stop himself from a burst of laughter, and in the bottom of his honest heart, he was shocked his dear professor didn't give him the signal to laugh, that he didn't show his joy. Devil take it! Didn't he have there something worth dancing about, even if he was crippled? Shouldn't they fall into each other's arms? But Cripure didn't show the slightest intention in the world of falling into Moka's arms. He'd returned to his silence and his stillness. Approaching the window, he leaned his shoulder against the frame, pretending to look outside—not as before, as a spectator of the scene, but indifferently, like a man getting bored behind a curtain.

His old face, or the bit Moka could see, since the way Cripure lowered his head left the profile only partly visible—a bit of forehead, the end of the nose, but not the eyes and chin, hidden in the goat-skin—this old face then, as far as he could tell, expressed nothing but an intense and perhaps suspicious meditation. In the end, Moka started to get worried. His look, which had become serious, searched out Maïa's. She was standing there, her arms hanging, her hair loose, the bathrobe open over her nightgown, her two worried eyes fixed on her man.

Catching Moka's look as he stood in front of the desk, his hand on the document, posed in his ceremonial garb, creating a passing resemblance to a lecturer frozen with nerves, Maïa responded with a bitter frown.

"Well then, you little fox!" she said, with a tone so harsh that Moka saw the whole of her large body tremble like a statue made of gelatin suddenly rocked by the passing of a car. And that trembling seemed to expand, to reach the other statue, Cripure, which also moved, but slowly. Cripure turned in place and his head lifted from the collar of goat hairs as if powered by a very gentle spring, and finally they saw his eyes, two dry eyes, hard, which seemed to have just changed color, to have shifted from blue to black.

What was he about to do? They weren't sure right away. In fact, Cripure looked at them for a long time, one after the other, then he shook his head from right to left, his mouth opening, his finger lifting slowly into the air.

"No," he said.

Moka gaped with astonishment. His hand still rested on the paper.

It was Maïa who responded. "What'd you mumble, just then? You don't wanna sign?"

He crossed his arms and let them fall again pained to have to refuse a prayer. "I said no."

"No what?"

"I won't ... I won't sign it."

"You ..." She didn't say anything more, choked with anger, red not only in the face but also her neck, and once more Moka saw her tremble from head to toe.

He intervened in his turn.

"My dear professor, come now! Please listen to me ... I beg you, listen! Don't take this decision lightly ... you must ... I would like ... My God, but what are you saying!"

He tangled up his words, unable to find any more. It was so unexpected. What was happening here? Cripure refusing to sign!

"Oh!" cried Moka.

And playing to the drama he hid his face in his hands and murmured a prayer, "All powerful God, our father! Have mercy! Have mercy! Save him in spite of himself!"

Cripure let his head drop back into his fur collar, and when Moka had finished his prayer he could see nothing of his dear professor but the tip of his nose and a little bit of his forehead. Cripure looked oddly like a child someone has scolded, who bows his head under the onslaught. But he also looked like he was thinking: *talk as much as you want.*

Maïa took a step. From her angry air, Moka feared the worst. With a gesture, he tried to appease her.

"This agreement," he continued, "puts you in a very honorable light. I don't see what reason... So then, in refusing to sign, you put yourself in a bad way... and so they..."

But understanding that his words had no impact, he turned towards Maïa with a look that clearly said *what should we do? It's your turn, give it a go!*

Maïa didn't have to think twice.

"What's all this nonsense," she cried in a screeching voice, taking another step towards Cripure. "You will sign!"

A little strangled laugh, which could also be an angry groan, replied to this order.

"Going once..."

"No."

"Going twice?"

"No."

"Going three times..."

"No."

And as it had a moment ago, Cripure's head rose from his necklace of goat hairs and his look turned towards Maïa. Was one of those horrible and brutal scenes from the day before going to start up again, and this time in front of a witness, the pale ghost with the red forelock, the man with the stamps, Moka the fly? In his floury face, Moka's vast eyes widened like saucers, eyes that could not believe what they saw, and his mouth opened, looking like it was ready to scream.

Maïa raised her hand, a round, short hand, but fat, powerful, thickening at the end of that red wrist, solid and flat as a stake, the exact hand on which Cripure, not so long ago, had placed a furtive kiss.

Was the blow going to fall?

Moka wanted to shout something, to stop that hand. But the wench waited another instant, wanting to give Cripure one last chance.

"Are you so sure you're not signing?"

He repeated, "No, never."

Maïa's hand fell, but into emptiness. He'd dodged the blow, slipping away suddenly like an agile dancer, while Maïa, carried by her force, tried not to break her head open on the floor like someone toppling.

"Bastard!"

"I beg you! I entreat you!" cried Moka, placing himself between the two of them, his arms held out to keep them at a distance. "Come now! Calm down! Let's not make a scene, come now! We've got to explain things calmly…calm…calm…" And saying those words, his large hands beat the air three times.

Cripure looked at him with an expression that said, *This has nothing to do with me, I'm not the one who started this…*

"Come now, Madame," said Moka.

She was trying to push him, wanting to get to Cripure and give him a whack.

"Don't get yourself mixed up in all this," she said.

"Calm down! See here—be quiet!" he said, feeling like he was still in study hall, facing a mob of schoolboys.

And once Maïa quieted, letting go of her belligerent intentions, Moka started twisting his red forelock, murmuring, "What should we do now?"

It was Cripure himself who responded to that question, in a clear, energetic voice: "What should we do? But I'll tell you! It's very simple!

You'll see ... I'll take care of it myself!" he said, crossing to the desk, his hand out, ready to grab the document.

"He's going to tear it up!" cried Maïa.

"No," Moka replied, hurrying over in turn, and covering the document with his hand. You're not going to do that, no, my dear professor. No! I'm begging you," he said, bending down in supplication. "You must not..."

Cripure didn't seem to understand then and there what Moka was asking him, but his hand which had been ready to seize the paper rested on the edge of the table, and the other wandered vaguely around a pocket, searching, without finding, the opening it could slip into.

If he'd really wanted to, he could have gotten rid of the document. Nothing simpler. Moka wasn't defending it very well. It would have been enough to forcefully bat away his hand. It was only Moka's look, he thought, which stopped him.

"Why?" Cripure finally asked.

"Wh...why? You have to ask! He asks why!" he said, looking at Maïa.

"Will you sign?" the wench shouted.

"Ah!" said Cripure, turning around, but still leaning on the table. "You again! It's unbearable," he said. And softly, "Go..."

"What?"

"Go away..."

"Me?" she said, a hand on her heart.

"Yes."

The nerve! Who did he think...did he really imagine...did he really think she would go? "Oh, and this isn't my own house?"

"Leave us."

"For what? No, I'm not leaving."

"But go, go on, that's enough! I, I'm telling you, I have something to say to this gentleman in private."

Moka frowned. This gentleman? What was that supposed to mean? Cripure was really upset. Wisely, Moka stopped covering the agreement. He folded it and put it in his pocket—this way Cripure wouldn't think of destroying it anymore.

"More stupidity," said Maïa.

"Get!"

"You'll sign?"

Pushed to the limit, he replied, "We'll see."

"You call me, you hear?" she said to Moka. "I won't be far, just there in my kitchen."

"Ah! No," said Cripure, finally letting go of the table, "no! Not in the kitchen. I don't want you to listen, to hear..."

"Listen? What d'you take me for?"

She stormed out, furious, slamming the door, and ran to the end of the garden, in her bathrobe, with the idea of shutting herself in the cellar.

What idea was he still keeping in the back of his mind?

AFTER Maïa left, Cripure started to pace around his study with sagging steps, as if he were lame in both feet. Hands deep in his pockets, the goatskin down to his slippers, with only his little head, round and short, emerging, he didn't say a word, and soon Moka uncomfortably cleared his throat and fidgeted. He didn't dare sit down or start pacing like Cripure. A delicate position! And what's more, he couldn't stand still. He would have happily paced a few steps, but then he would've been next to Cripure, or going the opposite direction, those were his choices. He thought about it. What a spectacle! That would be really...what? Comical? I walk, you walk. I meet you, you greet me...oh excuse me! I stepped on you. Did I hurt you? Absurd ideas. Moka's ideas. What a delicate situation!

Cripure seemed to have completely forgotten Moka's presence. Even the way he cleared his throat, which he began again, a little louder, couldn't succeed in getting his old professor's attention. For a long time yet, he paced around his study, his head bent, his look abstracted.

In the end it became...oppressive. This wasn't what Cripure would call speaking one on one with someone—this, clearly, wasn't why he'd sent Maïa away?

"Ahem, ahem!" Moka coughed again.

But Cripure's large shadow continued to pass back and forth in front of him, in silence. Moka started to get scared. Still standing in front of the desk, he started to tremble. Was all this actually real? Had he not, as they said in novels, fallen prey to a dream? This happened to him so often! He must be sleeping, dreaming. A nightmare

463

weighed on him and he'd arrived at the moment in the dream when the intensity of the horror brought the quick unraveling of waking, deliverance! He wanted to speak but as always in dreams his paralyzed throat was incapable of making the slightest sound, not even the little coughs with which he'd so recently hoped to interrupt that ghost's hallucinatory stroll, to crack the spell, to break the enchantment or the curse which held him prisoner. But the phantom didn't change his course. He still passed back and forth, huge and slow, before Moka's eyes. *What's happening to me?* Moka wondered. Once again his hands joined and crossed over his face. He prayed. It went on for a long time. But when he'd stopped praying and lifted his hands from his eyes, the ghost was still pacing, pacing, it seemed since eternity and for eternity. Following the random pattern of his steps, the glow of the lamp struck Cripure's pince-nez, the lenses shining with a fast reflection, uniform and pink, giving Moka the very painful impression that Cripure's eyes were lit from within, in the manner of those grotesque heads that peasants sometimes sculpted from hollowed-out beets to amuse themselves, putting a candle on the inside, with two large notches for eyes. To Moka's great relief, this phenomenon soon stopped. The lamp started to smoke. Cripure hadn't known how to set it up correctly, and Maïa probably hadn't thought of refilling it in a long time. As the store of gas ran out, the little glow weakened, diminishing more and more without either of them paying any attention; soon there was nothing left beneath the green shade but a little red crown around the wick of the lamp like a ring, a trembling glow, and a thread of blackish smoke from it, which expanded as it rose and filled the room with an acrid smell, a stink of burned bone. The ghost of Cripure became even more ghostly, caught between two glowings—the ending of the lamp and the rising day.

For once, the shutters weren't closed. Cripure had forgotten to shut them that night, after his journey to get the star, as he'd forgotten to put out the lamp, and so the first rays were able to enter into this hole where they never penetrated. It seemed like the whole thing was planned, that it wasn't by chance that Cripure's lamp completed its life at the very moment when the sun, a still waterlogged sun, it was true, beat back the shadows moment by moment with an explosive force of triumph, appearing here, where, it seemed to Moka, there was nothing for it to do. Cripure was better in the shadows. He found himself more at ease there, more at home. The way Cripure fled from the window made Moka understand that the arrival of day offended and hurt this ghost-like man, that he would have preferred from the bottom of his heart to be able to stay as still as possible with his lamp, meditating on himself and the nothingness of life. Cripure gave the dying lamp a pathetic glance, and when the light went out, after two or three sputterings, with a little noise that sounded a bit like a glug-glug, he lifted his arms, a discouraged gesture, and his bitter lip folded. But he still didn't say anything. He barely paused in his pacing for a moment, looking very different from the way he'd appeared until then. The golden light of the lamp had transformed that fat, heavy silhouette with a sort of warm, romantic sheen, which the cold light of day, barely risen, tore away with sudden harshness. The hairs of the goatskin, which had shone, under the gas lamp, with many varied shades from white to blue and red, suddenly became a uniform color—gray and dirty. His face, too, looked gray, and Moka could no longer see the lenses of his pince-nez sometimes catching the lamp and gleaming like beacons. No, the lenses themselves were tarnished. Everything, the person and the objects, seemed to have suddenly become cold, and in his goatskin, Cripure looked to Moka like a monstrous animal coming out of the water where a cruel hand had thrust it and submerged it for a long time. Or perhaps like some poor fellow, walking a hundred steps on the platform of a station, waiting for his train and shivering with cold.

Moka's heart was beating as fast as it could, and this time, without bringing his hands to his eyes, he contented himself with closing them, saying another prayer: *Lord! Deliver us! If all this is a dream, well then, Lord, wake us up!* And pressing the force of action into that prayer, he decided, without even considering it, to leave the table and move towards the ghost.

Then he would see!

Ghosts, apparitions, and, well, flies, never let themselves get caught between your fingers. All the examples of similar happenings went like that. Ghosts and apparitions in general vanished as soon as you made some brave gesture toward them. And if the great bear-like body that wouldn't stop going back and forth was a ghost, at the first real gesture he would disappear, go back where he'd come from, back into shadow and obscurity.

So Moka went towards him, holding out a shaking hand, large and bony, whose knuckles he so expertly cracked, and at the moment Cripure passed by him for the hundredth time, Moka fearfully put that hand on his shoulder.

The ghost, if it was a ghost, materialized immediately—a new trick, perhaps? In any case, it wasn't empty air at all that Moka's hand encountered but, under the hair of the goatskin, cold and slippery as scales, something hard and resistant, Cripure's very real body that so encumbered him. In response to that pressure, however light, Cripure came to himself, emerging as from the depths of a dream. His little round head made a wounded movement and bent towards his shoulder, and in the dirty gray light, still so weak in the rising day, Moka could make out, behind the lenses of his pince-nez, a morbid look, drowning in reproach.

"You betrayed me," murmured Cripure in a little voice, after quite an effort, as if the slightest speech was beyond him for the moment, or as if he thought there was no use in speaking anymore.

Then Moka was decidedly unsure of everything—neither what he was seeing, nor what he was hearing. Him! Betray Cripure!

"Me?" he said, but so softly, pressing his two hands against the sagging front of his shirt.

And he took a step back.

"You, you exactly," replied Cripure, in a voice that wasn't that of anger or even reproach. Moka searched for the word—it was an educating tone. *He's informing me, that's all.*

"Betrayed?"

"To a man."

"Never!" stammered the unhappy Moka. "How could an idea like that come into your head? I ask myself," he said, with some strain, "I who have always defended you, I who, for you, I..."

"Ah, ha, ha!"

This bitter laugh spared Moka the trouble of saying he would have thrown himself into the fire for Cripure.

"You don't believe me?"

Cripure took his time. He started walking, then stopped and looked Moka in the eye. "No."

He refused friendship too!

"Lord!" groaned Moka, "come to our aid! Make him understand that I love him!"

The way he joined his hands over his face made Cripure think he was crying.

"It's about time," Cripure murmured. "What difference does it make to you?" He'd spoken with passion this time, and anger had broken out in his big blue eyes.

"What do you mean?" said Moka, uncovering his face.

"If I die?"

Moka turned his eyes away, unable to bear Cripure's look. How could he respond to a question like that! How could he be indifferent to anyone's death? He thought to reply that friendship...no. Since he didn't want to use that word, then admiration? Not that either. Awe? Even more wrong, and respect too. And yet! "Something in you—"

"Yes?" said Cripure.

"Something in you," Moka continued, overcoming his emotion, "something says that we...that I...that men like me can't consent to..."

"To what?"

"To what you said a moment ago."

"Oh! Me, I call things by their names: this was about death, my death, isn't that right? And you act like a little thing means that we... that I...that men like...So what is that little something, my dear Moka?"

Moka wanted to say: a sorrow. He murmured, "a soul."

This time Cripure burst into a loud, careless laugh. As much as the goatskin would permit, he raised his arms to the sky in a gesture of stupefaction.

"Are you toying with me? Look at me," he said. "Do you think I don't know where I stand on that front? A soul?" Cripure repeated. "I will tell you," he went on, after a moment of silence, "I believed for a long time in a certain smile of the gods. But that's been finished since... for years. Yes, my dear Moka. I don't believe in anything, I don't want anything more." He paused. "I can't bear anything more. It's a dead man you've been trying to save," he said with effort. And he finished through clenched teeth, "If this is a joke, it's a bitter one."

He's crazed with sorrow, thought Moka, unable to say a word. And anyway, Cripure didn't leave him time.

He became animated: "You've simply pitied me," he went on, grabbing Moka by the lapels of his vest. "Admit it! You wanted to save my carcass, eh? Ah, ah! Is that it? Tell me!"

"My dear professor!"

"Tell me! Admit it!"

He didn't let go of Moka. He bent towards him and their faces nearly touched.

"That wasn't necessary," said Moka.

"Not necessary?"

"Why the bloodshed?"

"But in God's blighted name, this has nothing to do with anyone but me, do you understand! Only me! You wanted to save my life and in that way you have betrayed me. Life!" he continued, overcome, looking Moka straight in the eyes. "The hell with life, do you understand?"

He shook Moka and the last traces of the rose unraveled at their feet.

"Do you understand?"

"Yes," stammered Moka.

"Ah, all the same!" said Cripure, letting him go.

They didn't say anything more for a long moment, then, in a low voice, Cripure continued: "Soon, everything will be settled."

"But everything is settled, my dear professor. All that's left is your signature."

"That's not what I was thinking of," said Cripure.

"What was it then?"

"That's my business."

This brusque response sharply offended Moka. Cripure perceived it and apologized. "I'm a bit harsh, is that it? I'm aware of it. What do you want from me?" he said, shrugging his shoulders, "I ... at the point where I am!"

Moka took his hand. It was such a clumsy gesture that Cripure didn't immediately understand what Moka wanted from him, and with a look, he searched for what Moka must have found on his sleeve where there were no stains or wandering flies.

"My dear professor," said Moka, raising supplicating eyes toward Cripure, "promise me that you won't do that?"

Cripure frowned, but he didn't remove his hand.

"What are you thinking about?" asked Cripure.

"The same thing you are," Moka replied. He squeezed Cripure's hand more tightly.

"Ah, truly?"

"You won't do that?"

"What does it matter, Moka?"

"No!"

"What does it matter! Come now," said Cripure, roughly pulling back his hand "come now! Let's be done with this. The comedy has gone on long enough, Monsieur Moka, it's time to move on to serious things. Where is your paper? Come, I'll sign it! All that has no importance. But hurry up, hurry up, Monsieur Moka. The paper right away!" continued Cripure, agitated once again. "Take advantage of my good humor, since I feel it won't be difficult to go back on my decision and refuse to sign. I can feel it! The paper, Monsieur Moka. Ah! There it is," cried Cripure, "there's the famous paper of liberation," he cried, seeing Moka skip over to the desk and put the agreement down on it, keeping it nicely flattened, erasing the folds with the palm of his hand and raising towards Cripure eyes full of goodness and hope. Was Cripure saved, beyond a doubt?

Perhaps. He rushed over to the desk with such recklessness, made such an ugly grimace bending over the paper, that Moka was completely annoyed, like Étienne had been the day before, witnessing Cripure's cries about the bicycles.

"Where?"

With his pointer finger, Moka indicated the spot where Cripure had to sign.

The pen splashed, scraping into the inkwell. He made a blot, of course, and grumbled. Then, in one movement, he angrily swiped the pen across the paper, swiftly putting a tall sharp signature on the bottom of the document, which he underlined with a long, dark mark ending in a rain of little stains the pen flicked and spit. He stood up in the same gesture and threw the pen far away from himself, and it bounced off the wall, falling to the floor and sticking there like a knife. Cripure panted.

All this was very surprising to Moka, watching out of the corner of his eye. Cripure slumped into a chair, took his head in his hands and groaned. Moka grabbed a blotter, dried the fresh ink and put the sheet of paper in his pocket as he retreated. *Strange*, he thought.

Cripure wasn't the quietest crier in the world, and his groans were nothing if not badly stifled cries of anger, as Moka understood when Cripure uncovered his face and stood up, shouting, "Fooled! Fooled again!"

"Come now!"

"Like an ambush in a corner of the woods!"

"Me?" said Moka, touching his chest with his finger.

Cripure didn't seem to see.

"You pitied me, but it's the other one's life you've saved. I would have brought him down, yes. That's to say…"

It was the opposite. It was the other one who would have "brought down" Cripure. Three times in the same day, they'd taken away his death. He continued, "First of all, we must consider the question of pistols. You will point out to me that in asking that question, I lose all recourse to the formula of the arrangement, and that I was forced to duel with swords...and if I refused the arrangement, I'd once again be forced to duel with swords, and that—"

"But it's no longer a question of fighting!"

"What then is it a question of, Monsieur Moka? Of locking me up?"

"Jesus Christ!"

"But if they want to put me in with the crazies, everyone will say that's the proof I'm right," he cried.

"Jesus Christ almighty!"

"I would think it's a...unique case in the annals of dueling."

"Come, come, come!"

"See here, would I be dishonored in choosing the pistol? Tell me the truth," said Cripure, opening his hands.

"But everything is finished!"

Cripure gestured toward his feet.

"Me, fight with swords! It's like making someone with no legs into a swordsman." Fury overcame him. "Madness, madness," he cried, "but all the exits are hidden. Ah! Man's justice is good. Settled, my friend. The augers will have a good laugh. What did I decide to undertake?" he groaned. "I didn't know how to undertake anything, and it's too late. Everything is wasted, everything ruined. Oh," he said, turning to Moka, "it's not you I blame."

His gesture meant that since Moka was too little a character for anyone to worry about him and his role in such an affair, what was most likely then was that he'd been duped too, and by extension...

Cripure said it from across the room, "They fooled you too."

Moka wanted to protest.

"Excuse me, my boy, a thousand excuses," Cripure interrupted, banging his fingertip on the desk as he did in class to keep silence, "you saw nothing but clear skies. It was so easy. So easy! That Faurel, whose presence at least got this whole business started..."

"Faurel now?"

"The chief traitor."

"Him?"

"You won't defend him will you?"

"But if you had heard him..."

"Enough, Monsieur Moka. That's enough. An explanation can never erase what's been done. But as for that Faurel..." And he made a gesture of aiming a revolver.

Moka was furious. "No!"

"Absolutely," said Cripure. "To the end."

Moka lowered his head while Cripure continued: "He stole my death from me. Try hard to understand—the task was complete, wasn't it? I barely had to get mixed up in it. While as it stands now... But not before bringing him down," he cried, shivering, "ah, in God's name, no!" and his hand waved in the empty air.

A vague simile floated on Moka's lips as he raised his head. And to his great surprise, Cripure heard him say in a sweet voice, "You won't do either of those things."

"Ah?"

"No."

Moka shook his head, seeming to listen to some interior voice.

"No, my dear professor, you won't kill yourself, and you won't kill Faurel either."

"Ah?"

"No. Not a chance."

"Ah? And why is that?"

"Because... I don't believe you," said Moka.

"Well now!" said Cripure... they looked each other in the eyes, and Moka still smiled. A smile darted over Cripure's face too.

"Do you know what I think?" said Moka.

"I'm listening."

"Well then... I don't think you believe it either."

"Oh really?"

"Yes, yes. It's comedy. Admit it. You wanted to frighten me?"

He came toward the desk, bending towards Cripure, who was still standing on the other side.

"Admit it?"

"Perhaps," said Cripure.

Moka raised his pointer finger in a gesture of affectionate scolding. "It's not very nice of you to say *perhaps*. Come, tell me yes?"

"Well fine then," said Cripure, "yes."

"Hurrah!" cried Moka, seized with a crazy excess of joy. "Everything's settled. Hurrah!"

His success went to his head. He started clapping and, as he usually did when happiness filled him, he danced. Then he took Cripure's two hands and squeezed them for a long time.

"You won't hold it against me?"

"Hold what?"

"What I just said about comedy? You're not angry with me?"

His voice was low, barely perceptible.

"No," said Cripure, "not at all, come now." And he looked away.

"It was when you threw the pen away, you know, after signing!"

"Yes."

"That seemed funny to me."

He still held Cripure's hands.

"Well I must say," Cripure smiled, "that you're a hell of a good fellow." He burst out laughing, "Ah, ah!" and he squeezed his hands. "You, don't you know, that's to say, with you, one never suspects. Ah! By God, I take back what I said a moment ago: you, you're not fooled."

Now it was Cripure who didn't let go of Moka's hands. "It's priceless, all the same! There's some good in this sublunary sphere. Isn't it so, dear boy? Oh it's too much, too much . . ."

Someone was singing in the neighborhood, some early riser—they couldn't tell if it was the voice of a man or a woman. In any case it was someone who saw this new day as a day of happiness. And that too was annoying in that moment, as annoying as the song itself, a stupid refrain, some "Paimpolaise"[20] or other. Tired stuff.

"Shh ... shh," said Cripure, "can this go on for much longer?"

Moka looked through the glass door. He stammered, "Isn't that ..." He didn't dare finish his sentence and blushed, as if Cripure had guessed his thought. And in fact Cripure asked: "Maïa?"

"One might think ..."

They listened: Maïa was the one belting.

Finding that she was really putting herself down, obeying Cripure's orders and letting herself be treated like a servant once again, Maïa, shivering with cold in her cellar, made her resolution. Since he threw her out of her house, he must really be messing with her, wasn't that true? Well then, tit for tat: she'd mess with him as well as she could too, and let him know it. He was afraid she'd be listening at the door? Well then! She'd make it clear as day she wasn't listening. She'd sing.

Her mind made up, she climbed out of the cellar and once she got to the garden she sang the first song that came into her head: the "Paimpolaise." That's what they'd first heard, thinking someone was singing in the street. Now, she was singing in the kitchen as she emptied the ashes from her stove to make a fire and prepare the coffee. *Oh yeah? Fight or don't fight, old man, sign or don't sign, that's your business!*

474

Cripure knocked softly on the glass. She saw who was bending down.

"Maïa..."

She looked at the air and belted louder than ever:

"It takes more than greenhorns
To fight the English fleet..."

Behind Cripure, Moka appeared—the white face of a clown. But that one didn't say anything, his lips didn't even budge, he contented himself with looking hurriedly back and forth between them with wide eyes.

Tap, tap, tap.

It was Cripure once again.

"Maïa!"

Keep going! Maïa thought. Reaching the end of her song, she started over:

"Leaving behind the flowering trees
When the Bretons go off to sea..."

Like the day before, when she twisted so sorrowfully in the armchair, he could have simply covered his ears. Even without doing that, he could have ignored her. What was it that forced him to pay attention to Maïa? Nothing. Really nothing at all. Did one give consideration to a whore? Why then was he so exasperated, why did Maïa's absurd song come and disrupt everything, why did it seem to him that in order to go any further he absolutely must make her be quiet?

He wrenched open the door and burst into the kitchen. Moka planted himself in the doorway—it was already plenty to have to bear witness to that scene without becoming an actor in it.

Cripure lifted his pince-nez and scowled.

"That's quite enough!" he said.

She doubled her enthusiasm, and without looking at him, she sang at the top of her lungs:

"With all due respect to Saint Yves,
There's no color in his skies
As blue as the Paimpolaise's eyes..."

He grabbed her by the sleeve of her robe.

"Did you hear me?"

"Hey! What're you doing there?"

"What does this mean?"

"What does what mean?"

"You're singing, at a moment like this?"

"And why can't I be singing?" she said. "I can sing if I want!"

Nothing for it. She would have the last word.

"Painful," said Cripure, lowering his head.

"Everybody's got their own problems, isn't that right?" she replied, plunging a bit of newspaper into the stove and setting it on fire.

"Pre-cise-ly."

He played with his pince-nez.

Moka, for the past few moments, had been making a great effort to get Maïa's attention. Difficult. Since she was very busy with Cripure, she constantly had her back to him, and Moka wasn't even totally sure she had perceived his presence. In desperation for the cause, he whistled: "Huuuuit!"

She understood. Cripure undoubtedly did too, but he had the prudence not to turn around, and Moka could signal to Maïa at his leisure.

He winked, not once, but an innumerable quantity of times, with incredible speed, as if he wanted to get a little fly (a real one this time) out from under his eyelid. At the same time, he maneuvered his arm to point at Cripure in such a way that Maïa wasn't totally convinced at first that this whole mime show wasn't designed to get her riled up against her man. Since she was prudent too, she kept quiet, but seeing that she didn't understand him, Moka stopped pointing to Cripure and waved his hands in a grand gesture of starting over. *No, no, no it's not what you think!* And standing on tiptoe, his hands cupped around his mouth, he prepared to whisper something. Alas! It was impossible. He could speak very softly, but Cripure would still hear him. So Moka uncovered his face, and without the slightest whisper, his lips moved, articulating: *He signed it!* And to be better understood, he made a gesture of writing, of scribbling something at the bottom of a page. And pointing to Cripure once again, *him* . . . yes, yes his lips silently said, and he smilingly winked three times, nodding his head back and forth. If that wasn't enough!

It was. Maïa hid her laughing face. She was scared silly she would burst out laughing right under Cripure's nose, and to keep him in the dark she busied herself around her stove.

Then she turned all at once and let go of her poker.

"Kiss me," she cried, in a burst of joy and tenderness. She threw her arms around his neck. "You lucky old madman," she said, "I had my doubts, I had my doubts . . ."

A great explosion of tears followed. But the effect they produced was the opposite of what she'd counted on. Cripure became cold. He didn't push her away, but he didn't respond to her embrace. This time, they were tears of joy that she wiped. She took on a sort of beauty, almost like total honesty.

"Ah," sneered Cripure, "you doubted . . ." He neglected to mention that he too had doubted something of the sort. "What did you doubt?" he said.

"Eh? That you'd sign . . . since you didn't want to?"

"Tsk . . . tsk . . ."

"Huh?"

"Oh! You know me well."

She didn't know how to say that she loved him well too. But her eyes spoke for her. Could he see that? Was that the reason he turned away once more? In any case, the tender scene was over, and Cripure was grateful to Moka for the way he made prolonging it impossible by declaring theatrically with a handsome bow, but this time no pirouette, that his mission was over.

"I've played my part, my dear professor. It's time for me to retire. Farewell," he said, looking for his hat out of the corner of his eye.

"What!" cried Maïa. "He's leaving!"

Cripure sulked. What! Of course Moka had to leave. She wasn't thinking of taking him in as a lodger? To replace Amédée, perhaps, in the attic?

"Like that, without a drop?" she said.

"Madame—" said Moka.

"I wouldn't like to see that," interrupted Maïa. "Without having anything? We'll drink something, of course, what'd you say kitty cat?" She looked at Cripure.

He didn't say no. He didn't say yes either.

"No time," said Moka.

"This won't take long."

"Another time, another time!"

"It won't take two minutes."

"Impossible, a thousand apologies," he said, with a new bow, and grabbing his hat which he spied on Cripure's sofa, he got ready to go out, saying, "Another time, another time, Madame, I promise."

She grabbed him by the sleeve and brought him back into the middle of the kitchen by force.

"When I've got an idea in my head..."

"Hmm..." said Cripure.

"Sit down there," she said, pushing him hard into a chair. "Yesterday evening he brought back a nice bottle of wine...where's it got to? Don't go, don't go, come on now!"

Moka wasn't thinking of leaving anymore. Worn out, looking uncomfortable, he thought that he still had to change before he continued his service. And then he also would have liked to go into a church, to pray, to give serious thanks to God, as he should for the happy resolution of the affair.

"Where's it got to?" Maïa grumbled, looking for her bottle. "Where'd you tuck it away, Saint Pack Rat?"

Cripure, standing in the kitchen doorway, his hands in the pockets of the goatskin, didn't reply.

"I'm talkin' to you..."

"I don't know, Maïa."

They'd forgotten that bottle, in all the ruckus, and Cripure himself hadn't thought of it again, even though he'd bought it with the thought that the moment he got to empty it would be a good one. But where the devil had he stuck it? It wasn't in the pocket of his goatskin anymore, that much he knew.

"In the bag?"

It was next to the bag, in the corridor where he'd left it when he came home. Maïa found it there. She carried it over, disappeared into her pantry, took three glasses and returned with it all in her arms, the corkscrew between her teeth.

Moka hurried to help her. He ripped off the wax, and pushed the corkscrew in, holding the bottle between his thighs.

"Pop, there it is!"

And he filled the three glasses on the edge of the table.

"Let's clink," she said.

Cripure took a step. How morose he looked! He reached out a hand with indifference and took a glass.

"What's this about?" said Maïa. "That's a funny face to see at a moment like this. Come on! It's not the time. Seeing as everything's finished eh? So, off with it, to happiness. Cheers!"

He jumped. "So be it!" he said.

And he clinked. Then, he raised the glass to his lips, but before he touched it, he cried:

"To Nabucet's health! Drink, drink, to the health of my opponent..."

And he sang, like in *Carmen*:

"*de mon adver-sai ... ai ... re ...*"

"What's gotten into you?"

Maïa looked like she would choke on her glass.

"Me?" he said. "I'm laughing. We must laugh a bit, you see. It's you who asked for it! Ah! Ha, ha!" He drank his glass in one gulp and put it back on the table with a gesture of brandishing a sword. Moka and Maïa looked at him. In a false, weak, and very dishonest voice, he sang again:

"Cripure-a-dor en ga...a...a...ar...de
Cripur-e-ador!
Cripur-e-ador..."

At the same time he did what he could to actually get himself into the en garde position and make a go of it with his feet, which gave him the look of a fat dancing bear.

"Oui, songe bien, oui, songe en combatant..."

Maïa turned red with anger. Putting down her glass, which she hadn't emptied:

"Are you done yet?"

"What, Maïa?"

"Are you done joking around?"

"Oh! You were too! But it's *Carmen*," Cripure replied, "*Carmen, ma Carmen adorée*... Nietzsche was crazy about that music, my boy," he said, turning to Moka, "The heyday of music, he called it. And... hmm! He said too—but this is something else entirely—that man must love his fate. But that's a joke."

Maïa was reassured that he'd stopped playing at soldiering and taken a calm tone of voice, the one he usually used when he talked with people about things she didn't understand. She emptied her glass.

"You must rest a little, my dear professor," said Moka.

"That's just what I'll do," Cripure replied. And he sat down for starters. There was a moment of silence. Then, Cripure's little voice made itself heard once more:

"I'm grateful to you, of course, for... for your friendly assistance and... honesty. I won't discuss anymore your admiration for the success of Monsieur Nabucet. What good would it do! What good would it do!" he continued in a desperate voice, reaching out his arms, his eyes looking up to the ceiling. "I'll also spare you my recounting of the story from *my side*, a sinister comedy, you see, in which I was taken for a fool. What would be the point of speaking about it? Ah, ah! Success is success." He went quiet and lowered his head, his two big hands resting on his knees, with a childish frown on his lips. "Leave it, let it pass, let it drop!" he cried, standing up and closing his eyes.

In death, he'll have that face, thought Moka.

Cripure raised his two open hands in a gesture of refusal, his lips softened, and he said, still keeping his eyes closed, "Indifference is the wise man's umbrella, as solitude is his refuge . . . I think I'll retire, isn't that right . . . yes—"

"Don't listen to that," interrupted Maïa. "All that, that's for the picture show."

"Shush!" said Cripure, "shush!"

They reached the door.

On the doorstep, Cripure held Moka's hands in his own for a long time, then he bent down to whisper in his ear so that Maïa wouldn't hear him. "You have made me sign my disgrace," he said.

And without waiting for a response, he pushed Moka outside with the tip of his finger.

Day was rising. It was the hour when quite often, after a night of insomnia, Cripure would dress in haste, putting on an old brimmed hat, grabbing his rifle, and whistling for Mireille, who bounded with joy, he'd go out for a walk in the fields.

That was where he did his best hunting.

How many times had he returned from those morning walks holding a handsome rabbit by its ears, or a hare, or once even a fox! They'd had the pelt tanned. Maïa still had it in her wardrobe, next to Cripure's dressy clothes.

While he hunted, she made the coffee, cleaned the house, and he would return to breakfast with a light heart, happier to confront the day of chaos, the dirty mob of his students, the dirty snouts of those gentlemen.

How many times!

He left that morning as he had done so often, but he didn't whistle for Mireille, he didn't take his rifle, he didn't even think to put on his hat.

In slippers, his head bare, wrapped from head to toe in his cherished goatskin, he went down to the road with his tightrope walker's step. Standing at the door Maïa called to him.

"Where're you off to?"

He returned slowly, pretending to be listening.

"Where're you off to?" Maïa repeated.

Cripure raised an arm, seeming to point toward the countryside.

"Good," she said.

And she went back inside, unleashing the little beasts. There was no point in keeping them chained up now the night was over. They pranced. She let them out in the garden a bit then brought them back inside.

"There, that's done," she said, sitting down to grind her coffee. And she yawned. They'd woken her up too early.

"Sweet Jesus!"

She yawned once more, stuck a hand in her mane, and holding the coffee grinder between her thighs, she turned the handle.

That was all fairy tales, la-di-dahs. But he was like that, a funny one. One fart out the rump, one out the ear. Always. A little walk wouldn't do him any harm. When he came back he could swallow a nice cup of coffee and on the stroke of eight he could go off, take up that little job of his.

The coffee ground, she put the grinder on the table, yawned once more, cried "sweet Jesus!" once more. Then she lit the burner to boil water and wash her coffee pot.

The little dogs were making a lot of noise in the kitchen. Mireille, understanding that her master had left, howled plaintively, miffed and jealous.

"Hush, hush!" Maïa scolded.

But Mireille kept howling, so Maïa shut her in Cripure's study with all the others.

That was what she usually did when he wasn't there. In the study there was nothing for them to break, instead of in the garden, where they ravaged everything.

"Well!" she cried, glancing into the study before closing the door. "Well, isn't it pretty in there . . . he's moved everything around. What a mess!"

She promised herself she'd tidy up that . . . cave in a bit. He'd thrown books on the floor, he'd taken down . . . Her portrait . . . goodness! And that table, it looked totally different. There wasn't a single book on it, nothing but papers. All the books that had been cluttering it up the day before were piled on the mantel, and threatening to tumble to the floor. And what was that, now? A gold Louis? She picked it up. And that, under the table? A kid's medal, and then . . . a revolver? "He must have had one crazy night last night, my goodness!" she exclaimed. She'd better clean all that up in a bit. There must be other Louis hiding in the corners.

This time she closed the door with purpose and shouted to the little dogs, "Hush! Hush!"

Calmly she went on with her task.

Day was rising from the mist. The weather would be good. So much the better. She could put out her laundry as soon as the first rays appeared. Everything would be dry for the evening.

That was a close one for him, wasn't it!

Bah! No use thinking about it since it was finished.

With a corner of a rag she dampened under the tap, she wiped her eyes, her nose, and a little of her cheeks. A couple swipes with the comb and her toilette was complete.

She fixed the coffee, slowly, in her expert way. The little dogs fussed in the study. She opened the door for them and they bounded over to her. She mashed their scraps, still preparing her coffee all the while. The burned lentils, which she'd rescued from the trash, made them a feast, along with some dishwater and bread. Mireille was consoled. Now Maïa only had to get the coffee cups ready for breakfast and cut the bread for the toast. She put everything on the table and waited.

It was fully light when he returned. She recognized his steps, and the door opened. He stopped in the middle of his study and froze.

He looked at the floor.

Maïa, sitting at the table, was buttering the toast.

"Did you get a nice walk?" she asked.

He didn't answer. He was still looking at the ground, and Maïa, curious, craned her neck. Suddenly he stepped back. With one hand, he steadied himself on the wall. He called, in a strangling voice, "Maïa! Maïa!"

"What is it, babe?"

But he could only repeat, "Maïa! Maïa!"

His whole big body was trembling.

"Look!" he finally said.

And Maïa, following the finger Cripure stuck out, looked into the room. The floor was dotted everywhere with little bits of paper, chewed up as if by rats. The open door had blown them. *The little dogs*, she said to herself. *He's gonna yell now!*

He turned his head, but not towards her.

"It's the little dogs," said Maïa.

He made a sign. Did that mean he had understood? She thought she heard him mutter something between his teeth.

"What?" she asked.

"You shut them up in here?"

"Well yeah, of course."

He shook his head, looking left, right.

"They've gobbled up the *Chrestomathy*!"

"Eh?"

He was quiet. Why bother to repeat it! But he said, "I left some papers on the table, you see, Maïa. The little dogs knocked them off, played with them, and ... there you have it. There you have it!" he said.

He bit his lips. His hands hung down on the goatskin, curiously useless, robotic. He repeated, "There you have it!"

Maïa thought about it.

"Don't be silly, my little bear!" she cried. "I'll just do a sweep with my broom and there'll be no more mess. What? What're you laughing about?"

Was he really laughing? He knelt down. To pick up all those little scraps of confetti? *What silliness!* she thought.

"Wait, hang on, I'm coming. Wait till I've buttered this toast."

He was still crouching by the table, as if he hadn't heard or didn't want to hear. What was he looking for? He didn't pick up the papers or even the gold Louis. His hand reached out. To what? The little star or the ...

"Don't do that!"

The shot fired, dull and short. The body tried to straighten, then slumped, knocking over in its fall the chair where the portrait of Toinette had been resting. It fell in a clatter of broken glass.

"Oh! That fool!"

Cripure's thighs flexed then relaxed, his head rolled toward his shoulder. The room was full of blue smoke, like smoke from tobacco.

"What'd you do! What'd you do that for?" Maïa shouted, holding her face in her hands. Her knees hit the floor in the same moment, and she bent down, taking Cripure's head in her arms. "What'd you do! What'd you do!" she repeated, thinking at the same time that if Cripure wasn't killed with one shot, if he wasn't dead yet, he must be able to hear. Didn't she know that the ears didn't give up until long after the eyes? "What'd you do that for, bear?" Maïa said again, so softly, and she added: "my darling…" shocked to hear herself call him that for the first time, and feeling her sorrow grow sharply at the words.

With a large trembling hand, she felt Cripure's chest, pulling away the goatskin, searching beneath the barely stained shirt for the wound. There was barely a little hole, barely a bit of blood. "My God, but what'd you do that for?"

As if in response, Cripure started to moan, perhaps already gurgling. *He's not dead!* She got up with a jerk, stepping around this big motionless body, looking, in that perpetual goatskin, like a giant wild boar finally beaten. She grabbed him under the arms, Cripure's head dangling in her hold, and gathering all her strength, she dragged him, wanting to bring him to the sofa where she could lay him out and put a cushion under his head. But how heavy he was! Not only was he heavy, but there was something in that weight like a secret resistance. It would be easier, she didn't doubt, to pull a man who was up to his neck in quicksand. Never had Cripure's legs been so long, and his ball-and-chain feet so *contrary* in their black slippers. Cripure's legs didn't seem to weigh on the ground, but to stick there, and after a few minutes of trying, Maïa had to pause to catch her breath, with Cripure's shoulders resting on her arched thighs and his head on the crease of her blue apron. One of the slippers had fallen off en route and lay on the floor with a strangely animated inanimate look—like a stuffed and mounted animal, not far from the revolver, not far from the little schoolboy's star which was still glowing under the table, amongst the little bits of paper from the *Chrestomathy*, the last few pieces of forgotten gold, and the wreckage of the glass—a last symbol which succeeded in giving meaning to all the chaos.

"I've got to do this!" Maïa said to herself. And pursing her lips, tipping her head back and closing her eyes with effort, she pulled him further, still hoping she'd be able to slide him onto the sofa. But her strength let her down once more, and she had to make do with bringing him next to the couch and letting him softly back down to the floor. Then, like a moving man, she wiped her forehead with her bare arm and took a cushion from the sofa and slipped it under Cripure's head. He was still groaning.

The little beasts were running around the room, their tails between their legs, making low whimpering cries. *I'll never get it done by myself.* Mireille softly licked the open hand of her master. In response to her pitiful cries, the three other little beasts joined in at once. The racket became deafening.

"Dirty beasts," cried Maïa, kicking them away viciously with her feet. "Carrion! You're the ones to blame..."

The little beasts resisted. They didn't want to give way. Mireille didn't move.

Maïa took Cripure's cane and hit them with big swings, pushing them out toward the garden. The dogs howled. When she tried to shoo Mireille, the dog fought back. She turned to Maïa, growled, showing her teeth.

"You!" said Maïa.

And she picked up the dog in her arms. Mireille squirmed, trying to bite. Maïa, with a firm hand, grabbed her muzzle and, at a run, carried her to the garden, where she dumped her like a bundle of rags. Poor Mireille rolled on the ground, but jumped back on her feet right away. Maïa had just enough time to close the door. Already the little dogs were pressing themselves against it, scratching with their paws and howling.

"Filthy beasts," Maïa said again. "It's your fault."

If they hadn't torn up the papers, none of this would have happened, she was sure of it. So what could possibly be in those papers there? He'd always told her they were his "ideas" he was writing down, but people didn't kill themselves over "ideas."

She came back to Cripure's side. The dogs still howled. With a sharp push, she opened the shutters and called for help.

The response seemed like it was waiting for Maïa's call. Like in well-constructed plays, in dramas with good stagecraft, the new actors seemed ready to come on stage as if they'd been waiting for a long time behind some piece of scenery, perhaps even with impatience. The smell of blood, the passion to witness death—were they so strong? She had barely opened the door when they invaded the room, men, women, children, some shocked into silence, others crying already or rushing, all looking to Maïa for an explanation, and bending down, shoving each other to get a better view. Cripure had defended his door so well for so many years, with so much hostility, that for them it was a significant revenge, even like a victory. To the excitement of the bloody drama was added an almost equally strong curiosity to know what that strange man's house was like. And eyes wandered from the dying man, lying at the foot of his sofa, to the blackened walls, the dusty books, the mess on the table.

"What've we got to do? What've we got to do?" Maïa said.

A big devil with a birdlike head pushed through the crowd and came over.

"Let me do it," he said. "I was a nurse at the front."

He bent over Cripure and gently opened the goatskin, the vest, which he unbuttoned entirely, the shirt, and he asked for scissors.

Maïa didn't have them. Not there. Not at hand. She panicked but finally found some anyway, in the bottom of her workbasket, that same basket as the day before, which had rolled all over the floor at almost the same hour.

"Hey! Here they are."

The man took the scissors without a word. A large cut in the shirt revealed the tiny wound where a little stain of blood had leaked, barely larger than a hundred-sou coin, Maïa thought, a blackish stain that didn't really seem like blood, which resembled a bruise on Cripure's white flesh, the pale, greasy flesh of an old woman.

The curious approached. They bent down, looked on without saying anything.

"Better wash it. With alcohol," said the nurse.

"Rum?"

"No, of course not, with pure alcohol. With ninety proof alcohol."

"But I don't have any, I don't have any!"

"Ok, with boiled water."

With boiled water... how long would she have to wait for it, and during that time...

"But look at him, just look at him," she said, bending down. She took his hand: "My little cat?"

Cripure's eyes weren't totally closed. Between his lids there was a little space like a bluish slit. But the contortion of his face, that twisted mouth, the absence of his pince-nez...

"You can't hear me?"

No response.

"He can't hear me! Oh my God, he can't hear me!" She stuck both hands in her mane and rubbed her head.

"Go boil some water," said the nurse, putting a hand on her shoulder.

She went into the kitchen and found that there was boiled water ready, left over, since the coffee was finished. She'd forgotten about it. She brought the water. The man dipped the end of a napkin and washed Cripure's wound.

Basquin came in.

He'd been getting ready to go down to the camp as he did every morning, dreaming up new commercial possibilities, when a neighbor had come running up to him in the street to tell him the news: Merlin had just put a bullet in himself.

He'd jumped. "God's good name! As long as he didn't miss!"

It didn't seem like it.

He came closer, bending down over Cripure. His big dirty hand wandered for a moment over the face of the dying man. With his thumb, he lifted an eyelid, looked for the already glassy stare, and made a face.

"Done for!" he muttered. And turning to Maïa who waited next to him. "He doesn't look good. He shot straight, didn't he!"

Maïa didn't reply, but her round eyes examined Basquin with such contempt, that he became uneasy, and stammered:

"How did this happen?"

He felt that this was the better thing to say, and Maïa seemed to soften.

"But everything was settled," she cried in despair. "I don't know why he did that!"

What was settled? Basquin wasn't up on that. "Settled, eh?"

"Oh! This isn't the time," Maïa replied. "Look at him! Just look at him!"

"I see him," said Basquin. "But people who do things like this sometimes leave notes. He didn't write a little letter or something?"

"How should I know?"

"Let me see..."

He looked at the table, the mantelpiece, and found nothing but an envelope on which was written: Last will and testament. But the envelope was empty. And it was an old envelope anyway. That had nothing to do with...

"Nothing," he said. "So this came on all of a sudden, like that?"

"Me, I don't know. It was all finished," she said. "They'd signed and everything. Then there he goes out to take a walk in the fields and me, I'm warming the coffee. Well, then he came back. He looks, he says nothing. The little dogs they messed everything around in his study and chewed up his bits of paper. He sees that, he gets down... who'd have thought..."

She shook her head, stuck her lip out to keep from crying and went on: "Why was that revolver left under the table anyway? Whatever he did in there last night, nobody'll ever know. He was still there, then he got down, he grabs the gun... I didn't even have the time to see it." This time the lip stuck out further, and the tears spurted. "Without saying a word to me," she said.

"People who've decided that, they never say so beforehand," said Basquin.

The sententious and cold tone of this remark roused Maïa's anger against him. "You'd do better to shut your evil trap and help me. He's not dead, you hear. You'd do better to go find a doctor, maybe, since no one's doing anything," she added, turning to the crowd for help.

They drew back, offended. Someone left to find a doctor.

"That's right," said Basquin, "give him some air. Can't you see you're crowding him?"

Cripure was still moaning. It was a low groan, like a feverish child asleep in the depths of his cradle.

"It's not the doctor you need," said Basquin, "it's—"

What was he going to say? She'd just seen the joy on his hideous face. He hadn't been able to hide it!

"It's the surgeon."

And in the superior tone that was natural to him, with the pretension of a know-it-all, typical of ignorance and stupidity, he reached his hand toward Cripure and added, "That man needs to be operated on immediately."

To himself he said, *he won't wake up. Nothing but a little chloroform and . . .*

"Op . . . operate!" cried Maïa, "op . . ."

An operation, that meant death, that was certain. And for the second time she fell to her knees at Cripure's side, and took his hand, and held it to her face.

"Monsieur is right," said the nurse, who, moved with pity for Maïa, gently pulled her away, trying to get her to understand that she mustn't let him see that.

"You understand . . . for his sake. If he can see, if he can hear you . . ."

She rubbed her eyes and stood up, sniffling. He mustn't die like that all the same. Was he going to go like that, and they wouldn't have the time to explain themselves, to patch up what they'd said yesterday? It was hard to part like that, still angry . . .

"Let me take his pulse," said the nurse.

Taking Cripure's hand out of Maïa's, he pressed his wrist.

"And the doctor who hasn't come..."

"Don't worry, Madame, the doctor is less useful to us at the moment than, say, some kind of vehicle."

"That's what I said," Basquin chimed in, without having said anything like that, but he didn't shrug his shoulders less because of it—a gesture of global scorn for everyone present, without exception, all the poor chumps who couldn't think of anything.

"A car to take him to the hospital."

"But where?"

"Oh! But Madame... that won't be difficult. Aren't there hospitals everywhere? At the lycée for example. Bacchiochi will surely agree to operate..."

Basquin thought it over. All this, it could be good, it could be bad. Mustn't get carried away. If the dough was smuggled away, if that other sausage-brain hadn't made a will, or if he'd made one, but not in Maïa's favor—for someone else, he couldn't guess who, some kid like that Amédée—he'd have to stay sharp and keep his eyes open! He'd got to find out first if there was anything done to get back the sous. After that, he would see. In life, you had to know how to react. And if Maïa was left without a sou, she could see to herself. Jokes aside, she surely didn't think he was going to marry her for her beauty? The annoying part was that people could make up stories, since that other idiot hadn't even taken the precaution of writing a little scrap of a note saying that he killed himself and why. So that he'd give someone the idea that it was Maïa who killed him, and they wouldn't fail to add that he, Basquin, had pushed her to do it, and then you had a conspiracy on your hands! And all that just for the fleece!

He poked Maïa with an elbow, winking his eye.

"Come this way, you," he whispered in her ear, taking her over to the kitchen. "Close the door... softly. You've got to pay attention," he said to her, his voice low. "You've got to be on your guard."

He took care to say "you" and not "we." His tone emphasized his intentions.

Her arms dangling at her sides, she looked at him without understanding.

"What're you babbling about?"

"Listen ... be reasonable ..."

"What's it you're trying to say, get to it," she replied, with a violent jerk of her shoulders. He wouldn't have the balls, at this moment, to talk to her about the dough? What was he thinking? That she'd already stuck it in some drawer somewhere, tucked away most of it?

"Ok, what, talk!"

"Don't get upset, Maïa, when someone's trying to do you a big favor. He fired a shot from his revolver, eh?"

She squinted her eyes. What was he getting at? He told her:

"Be careful: they could say you did it."

"Me!" she had screamed it.

"Don't howl so loud," Basquin replied, shooting a suspicious glance toward the glass door. You were the only one in the house when it happened, eh? So be careful. That's enough," he finished, "now you've been warned."

For a long moment no words passed Maïa's lips, even though from the contractions of her throat, the twitches agitating her cheeks, the way she lifted a hand to her mouth like someone strangling, it was clear that she wanted to say something. Finally: "Oh, the bastard!" she cried.

Basquin turned. He'd already taken a step towards the study, judging that Maïa had been adequately warned.

"Me?"

"You deserve ..."

"Don't howl like that, come on ... They'll think we're plotting God knows what. Do you think they're so stupid?" he asked, pointing with his hand, to the shadows of the curious. "They know."

"What do they know?"

"That we're sleeping together," he whispered in her ear.

She almost replied that it wouldn't happen again. Yes, they knew. And so what? Her shoulders jerked again like a huge hiccup.

"You have the balls to talk about that now, while ... while ..."

He smiled a wicked smile, of a hunted man who's just managed to escape, seeing that she didn't dare to pronounce Cripure's name in front of him. That she didn't dare? No, she was unable. Furious at the thought that everything was undoubtedly lost to him, both the woman and the money, he didn't hesitate anymore, saying with a smirk, "If you're going to get sentimental about it…"

"Get the hell out of here!"

She said it in a low voice, but it wasn't the fear of being overheard that made her quiet. Basquin recognized that tone of fury and hate. That voice didn't come from the throat but from the depths of her being.

He approached her slowly. In the mahogany of her face, her eyes creased, becoming little slits.

"What did you say? Repeat it."

He spoke in almost a whisper too. She cranked out the syllables: "Get the hell out."

Ah! If only the others hadn't been there, behind that door! He bared his teeth, slowly.

"No."

"Bastard! You come here, I know exactly why. Keeping an eye on the dough, eh? You're pretty happy with what's happened. Are you happy? Say it then!"

She was scarlet with fury, with hate, with helplessness to throw him out the door. If she hadn't been the prisoner of all those people in there…oh, yes. He could have said whatever he pleased, and she would have sent him begging, and how fast!

She repeated, "Get out of my house, right now."

He turned his back to her, seeming to look for something on a placard and continued to talk to her:

"Listen…be reasonable. Listen to me."

She was steady as a milestone, right in the middle of the kitchen, confused to hear him speak that way still, in a calm voice, and since it wasn't possible to put him outside by force, it wasn't possible to shout, she listened.

"Shame on you. Now it's been too long that we've been all on our own in the kitchen. I'm telling you they know. Well then…we've been looking for medicine. Tincture of iodine. Ok? Fine. As for what I said a moment ago—think about it. There was only you and him.

In the study, everything's messed around. They'll say you two had a fight. From there to saying you were the one who killed him is easy. Are you listening to me?"

She'd had to approach him to hear—he'd lowered his voice gradually as he spoke. Had she understood? Was she finally convinced that what he was saying was good sense? She'd done a good job of crying in front of Cripure, and for the moment she could tell Basquin in every tone of voice to get the hell out of her house, but had she understood, yes or no?

It seemed she had. Her anger hadn't come back, it couldn't, but all the same, a gleam was there. She saw the case . . .

"Do you hear me?"

"Yes."

"This is serious. And not only for you. For me too. They'll say I'm the one who put it in your head."

Right away, Basquin regretted saying that. Even to Maïa, that wasn't the thing to say. He mustn't be so stupid as to stick that thought in people's heads. What? What did she look at him like that for?

There we are, she thought, *he's afraid for his own skin above all. Oh that . . .*

How well she knew him! With another jerk of anger, she replied, "I don't care three fucks about what they'll say."

He turned his head slowly, and his eyes uncrinkled, opened wide, and then his eyelids lowered, almost closing.

"Not me," he said, "that would seem too . . . too . . ."

Was she hearing or did she imagine herself to hear him saying that this would seem too real? She understood in any case that he'd thought about it, that he'd dreamed of this murder, finding no doubt that Cripure was taking too long getting to his final rest. But there: the task was done. And now he was afraid.

"Carrion! Me, I don't even know how to use a . . . a . . ."

She meant that she didn't know how to shoot a revolver. He interrupted her harshly:

"It's not about that. This isn't the time to discuss it. If you've understood, that's all I need."

She had understood. She'd understood many things today. Her head had never worked so hard. She thought about the harshness of the tie connecting her and Basquin—she who had always thought herself so free, who'd thought that kind of connection was so easy to break. But they weren't simply lovers: they were accomplices, caught, one in the other, forced, both of them, to play out the comedy in a moment when Maïa wanted to sink wholly into her sorrow. But there was nothing for it. She would have to deal with this. Despite love and grief, she'd have to watch herself and play a role.

"That's disgusting."

"It's not about that, once again. Have you understood?"

"Yes." She was devastated.

"Good. So, pull yourself together. And now let's go back. What we're doing here isn't very wise. Too bad, it's done." And pushing the glass door, "Go find some iodine," he said to a boy. "We've looked everywhere; it's not in the house."

The boy left at a run, pushing aside the gawkers gathered in the room and in front of the door.

Maïa crouched down beside Cripure. She took his hand; he was still groaning. Outside people were talking. They probably thought they couldn't be heard. A few among them were remembering the commotion the day before when Léo's car had almost crushed Cripure and his grocery bag had fallen on the ground. He certainly wasn't an ordinary man. He had some reason for destroying himself, he must have been thinking about it for a long time. It was books, maybe, that had made him lose it.

"Do you remember yesterday, what a mean look he had?"

"He wanted to kill all of us. If I didn't know him, I'd think he was crazy sometimes."

"Leave him alone, eh," said a woman. "He's not crazy at all, no, he's a man of ideas. I'm sure of it! But he's had troubles. You don't have the whole picture," she said.

Another one who'd heard about Toinette!

"Is he dead?"

"Why no! Come on!"

"Where'd he get himself?"

"In the head."

"No. In the heart."

"If it's in the heart, he's done for. If it's the head, he could pull through."

"He might not want to."

"Oh!"

"He was funny, too. Always humming all alone, like a maniac."

"He had too many ideas in his head."

"But there was something else going on, a big something else! They said he had to fight a duel?"

Maïa straightened up all of a sudden, letting go of Cripure's hand and, shoving aside the closest neighbors, she rushed toward the door, crying: "Aren't you done yet? Won't you go on and shut your traps, you band of filthy gossipers? This isn't right at all! Wouldn't this be better at your place, you fakers?"

They went silent, lowering their heads. Someone tried a reply, wanting Maïa to understand that they hadn't meant anything mean.

"You'd better be quiet!" Maïa shot back.

And she quieted herself, sharply changing her expression as she listened. Was she mistaken? A cab was arriving at a slow pace. The hoofbeats made a joyful clattering in the stony mud, and the harness jangled.

"Père Yves! It's Père Yves!"

She'd recognized the bells on the carriage.

Bursting back into the room like a gust of wind, she untied her apron while walking and threw it on the ground, where it seemed to complete the chaos, and arranging her hair with a wipe of her thumb: "Off with you!" she said. "We're going to take him to the hospital."

Père Yves was in fact arriving, a man of his word, sitting straight up on the seat of his cab, with Pompon's little trot. He slowed his horse to a walk and very slowly entered the crowd gathered around Cripure's door.

"What's going on?" he asked, from the height of his seat.

"They'll tell you."

He leaned back, pulled on the reins, saying "Whoa!" to Pompon, who stopped. Then he got down heavily, and asked again, "What's going on?"

Instead of answering, they let him inside.

He must have thought that Cripure was already dead, since as soon as he saw him he took off his hat and sketched the sign of the cross, perhaps looking for the cross and the boxwood branch in holy water. Cripure's groans had become so feeble that Père Yves hadn't heard him.

Maïa stopped the coachman's gesture.

"Are you deaf? Listen a little," she said.

"What's wrong with him?"

"Something that needs a ride."

"Ah?" said Père Yves.

What had happened in that house? It looked like they'd had a fight. There were things all over the floor; a chair knocked over, a slipper, papers, an apron, and even gold Louis!

"Why, what's all this?" he said.

"Don't worry about that. He's got to get to the hospital and that's all there is to it."

"In my cab?"

"How else do you think?"

Père Yves measured Cripure with his eye. That big body would never fit in the cab. Sitting, yes. But stretched out?"

"That's not going to work," he said.

"What?" said Maïa. "It's got to happen no matter how he does it."

Basquin intervened: "Don't fret—we've got to put a chair between the benches and pillows underneath him. We'll walk alongside. We've only got to go a little ways."

So it was done. Between the benches of the cab, Basquin, helped by Maïa, put two chairs facing each other with cushions and pillows piled on them. They put some under the awning too, so that Cripure's head would rest easy, and when it was ready, Basquin called for strong men. Several presented themselves. He chose four.

Maïa stepped away to make space. The men came carrying Cripure, so heavy their knees were bending. Maïa read in their eyes a fear of dropping him and perhaps that misfortune would have befallen them if others hadn't rushed to help the first ones as they approached the carriage and got ready to slide Cripure inside.

With six, lifting him took their full strength. Basquin got up on the running board and directed the maneuver. They brought it off, not without bumps. Cripure was still groaning.

The men panted, drying their hands by squeezing one in the other, and passing their fingers under their collars. Some task, wasn't it! Maïa closed her door.

"Where're we going?" said Père Yves.

"To the military hospital at the lycée."

They started on their way.

Père Yves, his whip wrapped around his neck, walked in front, leading Pompon by his bridle. He looked out for bumps, and to avoid them, he took the cab on a thousand little detours. From time to time, he turned around to make sure that everything was in order, looking once again in front of him, gesturing widely with his hands as soon as he saw a car coming the other way.

Maïa was walking next to the cab, her head bare, with big strides, keeping watch over the blanket which was slipping and putting it back in place. On the other side, Basquin walked, tormented by his desire for a cigarette. But even so, he didn't dare light one up just then. And he walked with his head down.

Behind them, a little flock followed.

IT WASN'T quite eight o'clock. An instant of freshness in the sky, barely delivered from nocturnal shadows, a minute of hesitation when the scale seemed to have no reason to tip one way instead of the other. It seemed that this new day that advanced, still wrapped in the last threads of dreams, would not and could not be anything but the fruit of human will. If the day dawned, it was because they consented. But, once again, perhaps they could desire the opposite. Each person appeared free to stick his or her finger in the mechanism, and looking at the faces of the people about in the streets, one would have thought each person was thinking only about this problem.

Throughout the night, the town had perhaps gently decided to give humans the gift of a general holiday. Or maybe they were the ones who, in the midst of their dreams of Cloppers, had thought of it, and who remembered it still, all the while smoking their first cigarette and hastening toward the office or the store, others toward the barracks—and from the barracks to death. It was like a secret they would all have in common, had any of them believed it, which seemed to carry them in that brief, cardinal instant, and gave even the most beaten-down of them something in their steps that resembled joy.

Shutters banged against walls, in front of stores the heavy iron gates rose, grinding at the end of poles. A car rolled by, a wheelbarrow—a bicycle's bell rang out in an empty street as if it were under a dome. All those sounds weren't very convincing yet—just appearances, a way to prolong suspense before the great happiness that was promised and due.

To the sky full of wisps of clouds the day before, and so recently full of night, the meadows and the earth gave back their brotherly reflection, of flowers, of waters, of silence. There was still in the west something like fat red carnations or roses, which the wind dragged toward the crevasses of snow.

This joyful chaos where all seemed to take flight, where nothing held its weight, where everything breathed in lightness for one more moment, suddenly came into sharp order: the mayor appeared. The wheel of the world found its rut, it could turn.

The mayor had barely walked a few paces in the street, with his bouncing step and fat stomach, which seemed ready to push everything out of the way; he had barely handed out two or three notices—and he was on his way to see Babinot, who was still sleeping—when other familiar characters came out, like jesters who were only waiting for the signal: Glâtre, bundled up, his eyes still swollen from sleep, unwashed, unshaved, dirty, late, with piles of IOUs still in his pockets. He was in a bad mood, as he always was the day after a "night with the ladies." Watch out!

From afar, Moka followed him, sometimes walking sometimes running, seeming to hop along, puffing, "hou! hou!," which the other one didn't hear or pretended not to hear. Every twenty feet, Moka would pull up his garter, and go on feeling better.

Poor Moka! He looked like an exhumed corpse. What torments he had been through since he'd left Cripure! He was only on his feet by a miracle, and he looked more comical than ever in the astonishing costume he'd thrown on in haste over his tuxedo jacket, decidedly ruined and only fit for selling to the thrift shop. Going back to his place and asleep on his feet, he'd changed clothes as if he were dreaming, and the result was out of this world. On this winter day, he wore a boater hat that bounced on his pointy head, his long legs were lost in some kind of golf culottes, and over his thin shoulders he'd thrown an old jacket which was torn everywhere: such was his great fatigue and deep uneasiness. No tie. Barely a collar. It was that in getting dressed he'd been thinking about other things: running over to the church, kneeling before the altar, praying with his whole heart, with his whole mind, with his fists squeezed tight, for his dear professor. He'd gone there. But there, a new fact had come up: God had spoken to him, he was sure it was Him, and reminded Moka of that bizarre scene where Cripure had made such unjust and bloody threats against Faurel. With a leap, Moka had run out of the church, knocking over a chair on his way, totally out of breath, panting with the fear of being too late. How could he have forgotten?

Of course, in the moment Cripure had spoken of bringing Faurel down as the chief traitor, Moka hadn't believed he would do it, and he'd even said so. And yet—it was night, it was trouble, he'd doubtless been wrong...Yes, it was quite possible he would do it! How could he have left Cripure all this free time to surprise Faurel in his sleep? He'd made straight for the deputy's house, learning that Faurel had gone out just a moment ago, in his car, with Corbin.

Reassured, Moka had gone on his way toward the lycée, still running, still tugging his garter back up. And now Glâtre had appeared on the horizon and Moka was shouting "hou! hou!" but in vain.

The unhappy little hunchback was also outside. With her dog. Moka crossed her path, giving her a sign—why? She didn't respond, passed by him singing:

> "L'amour est enfant de Bohème
> Il n'a jamais jamais connu de loi . . ."

and disappeared down the street.

The gentlemen of the faculty climbed toward the lycée with their precious folders stuffed with declensions under their elbows and a little bit of their breakfasts lingering in their beards. The little old man wasn't carrying his sword, but he was smiling all the same. The clockwork went without a hitch. No one was missing, not even the company of German prisoners going to work and stomping the pavement heavily, or the group of soldiers who had drilled their formations right by Cripure's house. Everything was happening as it had the day before, and as it would happen the following day. In the square, in front of the lycée, the schoolboys had started a game of soccer, and the ball flew right, left, straight up in the air with big kicks and cries, while beside them a company of recruits turned out, turned about, and pivoted under the vociferous orders of a little sergeant. Right-left! Half turn: right! Company, halt! The morning air filled with all these cries, of the slap of boots in the mud, the whack of the ball falling into puddles, yells from one side or the other about whether it was a corner kick, and on the other if these sons of whores would ever learn how to march in a way that didn't make them look like a bunch of scarecrows.

The most contradictory news was already flying around town. For some, the duel had actually taken place, but opinions were divided about the choice of arms. Some held out for pistols, but others had seen swords. There was one who claimed to have heard gunshots at dawn. They knew where the fight had taken place. Those who thought that Cripure and Nabucet had fought in a clearing in the woods were nothing but liars. The duel hadn't happened in a wood, but by the sea, Cripure had wanted it that way. Only the knowledgeable would guess why he had demanded it. Goodness! He'd wanted to end his life in the very spot where Turnier had finished his own—at that cross stuck in the cliff to mark the place he'd thrown himself into the sea. And so, through the ages the two philosophers would be comrades in death as they had been in sorrow, if you removed the question of God. Since you couldn't forget, of course, that Cripure was an atheist, a fierce enemy of men and of religion. Was, had been. The rumor, in fact, which Glâtre caught bits and pieces of as soon as he stepped out his door, proclaimed that Cripure had been fatally wounded in the duel. The theory of suicide in general had few adherents. It was easier to imagine the reasons for a duel than for a suicide, though after all, "for someone so off his rocker..."

The little flock had grown considerably en route. When it arrived at the square in front of the lycée, a long triangular column had formed behind the carriage where Cripure was laid out. Sympathizers, the simply curious, gawkers, hangers-on came at every moment to accost the crowd and jostle others aside, wanting to get close to the carriage to see Cripure's agonized face. A sort of thick buzzing emanated from the crowd. Père Yves, with his ever-measured steps, led Pompon by the bridle. Maïa, red-faced and disheveled, her face running with tears, did her best to beat back those who were to eager to see someone else's death, rediscovering all her fierceness, her genius for insults. Basquin lowered his head, like someone thinking hard. The crowd behind the carriage was so big that people feared a demonstration, and the police were hastily alerted, sending two black angels, two policemen on motorcycles, who led the cortege.

At the sight of this strange procession, the schoolboys stopped playing with their ball. A last kick lost itself in the middle of the crowd, bouncing against the carriage. Many of them froze in place upon learning that it was Cripure they were dragging like a corpse, and you could have asked those boys whose idea it was to loosen the bolts on the bikes. They ran away, seized with panic, hiding themselves in the school. Their joke had worked too well!

The little sergeant, more interested than annoyed by the invasion, commanded his men to be at ease as they parted, and still headed by the policemen, the cortege slowly came forward. The sky had turned somber. The pretty pink clouds were decidedly absent. Once again, everything covered itself over in gray, and suddenly, rising over the buzzing of the crowd and all the mixed noises of the town, the enormous voice of the cow rang out. The heavy bells, at the top of square towers, banged as if to break everything, ringing into the sullen sky. The cow must have smelled something, sniffed out somewhere the odor of death, and it saluted its prey. The cortege advanced like a parade, step by step, wrapped in the sound of bells, grave and dark as a punishment, to which was added, all of a sudden, that thin and hurried sound of the bell Noël was ringing. It was time! Time to go to class and recite. Monsieur Bourcier appeared before the gates of the lycée as he did every morning to hunt down the latecomers. But what was happening? What was this troupe, seemingly headed for the school? He went over, asking questions. "Merlin," they replied. It was Monsieur Merlin, also called Cripure, who'd gone and shot himself. What! His philosophy professor! He stretched himself up on the tips of his toes, searching between the heads and the backs to see if it really was Merlin, so-called Cripure, whom they were driving in this strange manner. He saw just a little bit of the goatskin and there was no more room for doubt. And the whole town on the heels of a professor who'd killed himself! And in what condition! Flanked by that woman who only ever seemed like a fishmonger's wife, thrown like a drunk into that old carriage, dilapidated and dirty, with wheels that screeched enough to make you tear out your teeth. And all this at the gates of the school, with the principal ill, very ill (the doctor, who'd come that morning, reserved his diagnosis). It was a moment of amazement for Monsieur Bourcier.

New events were happening at each moment, not by accident, but brought on by a daily fate, by the simple necessity of work and habit. A car arrived, pretending to take no notice of the crowd, making it open a passage. The horn rang out furiously, raising protests full of anger. Of course the car had to stop. Then they saw Faurel get out, followed immediately by Corbin. They wanted to part the crowd to approach the carriage. Faurel, very agitated, asked right and left: "Is it true? Is it my friend Merlin who's killed himself?" But the explanations he received were contradictory. He was still trying to press forward, to stand on tiptoe to see better. Corbin didn't say a word. And the carriage still went forward. Moka arrived at a run. He was already in tears. He didn't even pay attention to Henriette, who was also there, with the poor dog who'd been placed in her care the day before. "My dear professor! My dear professor!" cried Moka, throwing himself into the crowd, his arms held before him. And as if by a miracle, the crowd opened for him. They saw him beside Maïa before long, standing on the step, dominating the spectacle with his tall and thin silhouette, and turning to the inside of the cab, his white face running with tears. "Ah! My dear professor! And I'm the one who didn't believe you!"

The crowd was still growing larger. They saw Francis Montfort arrive, his hair blowing in the wind, then Kaminsky, Simone, and Léo, getting out of the car that would have taken them to the station. Simone, in traveling clothes, was still holding her precious "book" under her arm. Kaminsky, with a curious smile on his face, turned toward the cab where Cripure was lying. Was it true he had killed himself, that he'd "given up the world," like Villaplane had the day before? But they weren't yet saying he was dead. And the carriage continued its slow progress toward the lycée, the low, thin jingle of harness bells sometimes rising over the murmur of the crowd. At that moment, the square was dark with people, and still more were coming. But suddenly—not men, but dogs were running over. The four little beasts Maïa had forgotten in the garden had found a way to escape, and the crowd saw them hurrying, tails between their legs, Mireille at the front, followed by Petit-Crû and Turlupin. Fat Judas followed as best he could, rolling and tripping in the gutter and courageously going on his way. "His little dogs! Here come his little dogs!" The cry spread through the crowd, which the little dogs entered with fury. People got out of the way as best they could, fearing their bites, taken with a vague superstitious terror. Did the arrival of the little dogs mean that everything was finished? There was a moment of panic and pushing, then they saw pretty Mireille jumping and groaning around the carriage, soon followed by the others. Moka got down, grabbed Mireille by the collar, put her up next to Cripure. She stretched out next to her master and groaned softly. There were only a hundred feet left to cross before they reached the lycée when the carriage sharply halted. Moka made signs to Bacchiochi, who was coming closer. "Let him through! Let the doctor through!" cried Moka. The crowd opened, and on the other side of the carriage, from the other step, rose the fat silhouette of Bacchiochi. He bent down and stayed there for a moment. Then he straightened up, taking off his cap. The deepest silence followed. One by one, hats were removed from heads. Women crossed themselves. At the order of the little sergeant, the soldiers saluted. Maïa's sobs rang out in the silence, mixed with the whimpers of the little dogs. Moka cried too, and prayed. Faurel, who'd succeeded in getting closer, thought of his conversation with Lucien the day before and glanced around for him. But it had already been more than an hour since the ship weighed anchor.

TRANSLATOR'S ACKNOWLEDGMENTS

WHILE I was working on the translation, I was extremely grateful for the chance to visit Saint-Brieuc to meet scholars and artists who maintain Louis Guilloux's legacy in his hometown. Thank you Roland Fichet, Annie Lucas, Yannick Pelletier, and Yann Le Guiet for sharing your research and your impressions of the text and its setting with me. I'm also grateful to Arnaud Flici for his expert help with Louis Guilloux's archives at the Saint-Brieuc municipal library.

Thank you to my friends and fellow translators who offered suggestions on all or part of this translation along the way, especially Paol Keineg, David Wingrave, Elisa Gonzalez, Liz Wood, Chantal Clarke, Toby Lloyd, Susan Bernofsky, and her workshop at the Bread Loaf Translators' Conference. And finally, thank you to Alice Kaplan, whose generosity, mentorship, and excellent edits have been an enormous help throughout this project.

NOTES

1 Russian soldiers fought on the French front during World War I, but their presence in Saint-Brieuc (and in the novel) is somewhat mysterious. In 1917, Russian soldiers who were openly sympathetic to the Soviets were removed from the front to avoid sparking more rebellions in the French army after the mutinies. There could have been Russian soldiers passing through Saint-Brieuc that year, but it's also possible that Guilloux included them to make a connection to Dostoevsky and the Russian Revolution. Guilloux was a great admirer of Dostoevsky and wrote about his work in his letters and notebooks.

2 The name Clopper comes from the French "cloporte," a derogatory nickname for a building's caretaker or concierge. Cloporte also means woodlouse or pill bug—insects that live under bark and curl into a ball when touched.

3 The phrase may refer to La Fontaine's fable of the dog and the wolf. The dog gets plenty of food and affection and tries to sell the wolf on his well-kept life. The wolf is convinced, until he sees the mark on the dog's neck left by his collar. Then he refuses to give up his freedom.

4 Enemy aliens were held in the prison in Saint-Brieuc during the war. There were also several internment camps for civilian prisoners—one called Jouget in an old factory to the west of Saint-Brieuc, in Plérin, and one in Saint-Ilan. German and Austro-Hungarian soldiers and civilians were imprisoned for the duration of the war, along with other foreigners who were considered a danger to national security.

5 The philosopher Nabucet mentions is Baruch Spinoza, who characterized sadness as a diminishment of the self.

6   Romain Rolland's *Au-dessus de la mêlée* (*Above the Battle*) was published in 1914 in *Le Journal de Genève*. He was an anti-nationalist writer whose pacifism would have angered Nabucet.

7   In the allied press, "Maximalist" was a term for political movements associated with the Bolsheviks. A radical wing of the Russian socialist-revolutionary party shared the same name.

8   In the spring of 1917, a group of soldiers from northern Vietnam (Faurel calls them "Tonkinese") supposedly fired on a crowd of antiwar demonstrators and soldiers' wives at Saint-Ouen. They were under orders to suppress the rebellion.

9   Madame and Monsieur Prudhomme were two late-nineteenth-century cartoon characters, created by Henri Monnier to satirize the Parisian bourgeoisie.

10   Bouclo and Pécuporte/Boucri and Pécupure. With these names Cripure plays on his name and the title of Flaubert's satirical unfinished novel *Bouvard and Pécuchet*. Flaubert's novel was originally titled *Les deux cloportes* (the two woodlice).

11   Punchinello's secrets are false secrets meant to be spread. Punchinello, a clever hunchback, makes up a lie about a nobleman of the court and tells it to others on the condition that they will swear to secrecy. This vow of silence ensures that everyone repeats the gossip.

12   The Sedantag was a German holiday marking September 2, 1870, the day Napoleon III and 83,000 French troops were taken prisoner after the battle of Sedan.

13   A reference to a passage from Dostoevsky's *The Brothers Karamazov*. "And if the suffering of children goes to make up the sum of suffering needed to buy truth, then I assert beforehand that the whole of truth is not worth such a price. I do not, finally, want the mother to embrace the tormentor who let his dogs tear her son to pieces! ... Besides, they have put too high a price on harmony; we can't afford to pay so much for admission. And therefore I hasten to return my ticket. And it is my duty, if only as an honest man, to return it as far ahead of time as possible. Which is what I am doing. It's not that I don't accept God, Alyosha, I just most respectfully return him the ticket" (translation by Richard Pevear and

Larissa Volokhonsky, 2002). Guilloux cites the 1888 French translation by Ely Halpérine-Kaminsky and Charles Morice: "Je rends mon billet."

14 In *Madame Bovary*, Flaubert's tax collector, Binet, is so busy working on his carving of a table leg, hollowing out circles within circles, that he can't hear Emma asking for an extension on her taxes.

15 The man in the square is singing *La chanson de Lorette*. The anonymous song appeared after the bloody battles surrounding Notre-Dame-de-Lorette, in Artois, and it circulated during the 1917 mutinies. Other battles were added as the war progressed. The lyrics were finally published by ex-artillery captain and militant socialist Paul Vaillant-Couturier in 1919.

16 The riot which occurs on the preceding pages is modeled on a real demonstration that took place at the Saint-Brieuc train station on July 10, 1917. In the actual event, a few "Permissionaires" (men on leave) protested being sent back to the front.

17 An allusion to the words the famous French military commander Henri de la Tour d'Auvergne, Vicomte de Turenne (1611–75) reportedly said to himself when he was heading into battle. The whole quote reads: "You tremble, carcass? You would tremble a lot more if you knew where I am taking you." Nietzsche used this quote for an epigraph in *The Gay Science*. Cripure refers to Nietzsche throughout the book, exhibiting an admiration for the German philosopher that would have been dangerous in the nationalist climate of the lycée.

18 The soldiers who have been "officially reported missing" presented something of a mystery, since the Marchandeaus have been notified that their son is about to be executed. Through Alice Kaplan, I was able to get a response from French military historian General André Bach. According to the documentation of the "fusilés" (the executed mutineers), the family would not have been notified of their son's execution either before or after it happened. Both the family and the local authorities in charge of notifying them received the standard notice, which did not state how the soldier had died. In fact, widows only learned of their husbands' executions when they failed to receive the standard pensions that were given starting in February 1915 to widows and orphans of men killed in combat, under "honorable" circumstances.

19 Here, the Prudhomme alluded to is Sully Prudhomme (1839–1907), the writer of sentimental poems and essays on philosophy.

20 A famous song about Breton sailors by Théodore Botrel (1868–1925). Botrel was a Breton who spoke Gallo, but the majority of his songs are in French.

TITLES IN SERIES

For a complete list of titles, visit www.nyrb.com or write to:
Catalog Requests, NYRB, 435 Hudson Street, New York, NY 10014

J.R. ACKERLEY Hindoo Holiday*
J.R. ACKERLEY My Dog Tulip*
J.R. ACKERLEY My Father and Myself*
J.R. ACKERLEY We Think the World of You*
HENRY ADAMS The Jeffersonian Transformation
RENATA ADLER Pitch Dark*
RENATA ADLER Speedboat*
AESCHYLUS Prometheus Bound; translated by Joel Agee*
LEOPOLDO ALAS His Only Son *with* Doña Berta*
CÉLESTE ALBARET Monsieur Proust
DANTE ALIGHIERI The Inferno
KINGSLEY AMIS The Alteration*
KINGSLEY AMIS Dear Illusion: Collected Stories*
KINGSLEY AMIS Ending Up*
KINGSLEY AMIS Girl, 20*
KINGSLEY AMIS The Green Man*
KINGSLEY AMIS Lucky Jim*
KINGSLEY AMIS The Old Devils*
KINGSLEY AMIS One Fat Englishman*
KINGSLEY AMIS Take a Girl Like You*
ROBERTO ARLT The Seven Madmen*
U.R. ANANTHAMURTHY Samskara: A Rite for a Dead Man*
WILLIAM ATTAWAY Blood on the Forge
W.H. AUDEN (EDITOR) The Living Thoughts of Kierkegaard
W.H. AUDEN W.H. Auden's Book of Light Verse
ERICH AUERBACH Dante: Poet of the Secular World
EVE BABITZ Eve's Hollywood*
EVE BABITZ Slow Days, Fast Company: The World, the Flesh, and L.A.*
DOROTHY BAKER Cassandra at the Wedding*
DOROTHY BAKER Young Man with a Horn*
J.A. BAKER The Peregrine
S. JOSEPHINE BAKER Fighting for Life*
HONORÉ DE BALZAC The Human Comedy: Selected Stories*
HONORÉ DE BALZAC The Unknown Masterpiece *and* Gambara*
VICKI BAUM Grand Hotel*
SYBILLE BEDFORD A Favorite of the Gods *and* A Compass Error*
SYBILLE BEDFORD A Legacy*
SYBILLE BEDFORD A Visit to Don Otavio: A Mexican Journey*
MAX BEERBOHM The Prince of Minor Writers: The Selected Essays of Max Beerbohm*
MAX BEERBOHM Seven Men
STEPHEN BENATAR Wish Her Safe at Home*
FRANS G. BENGTSSON The Long Ships*
ALEXANDER BERKMAN Prison Memoirs of an Anarchist
GEORGES BERNANOS Mouchette
MIRON BIAŁOSZEWSKI A Memoir of the Warsaw Uprising*
ADOLFO BIOY CASARES Asleep in the Sun
ADOLFO BIOY CASARES The Invention of Morel

* *Also available as an electronic book.*